J L Mumford is a veteran wargamer and fantasy Games Master, known as "Slim" within the environs of the hobby. His aim in writing this novel is to encourage others in the use of figurines in role-playing games. His rules claim to create *realistic* fantasy! His players in *Exiled!* were a group of five people of different generations, all with a young-in-heart enthusiasm for medieval fantasy:

Arthur's knights, Robin Hood, the Lord of the Rings,
Fantasy fables and figures are our favourite things.

Amanda, Heather, Lorna, Brian and Ewan made the decisions, made the moves and threw the dice that progressed the adventures and kept their figure characters alive. Without their kind participation and feedback, there would have been no story!

For my friend Morag Allen
a fellow Ink Stain

John Mumford

Exiled!

Volume One

The Adventures of Morgana

by J L Mumford

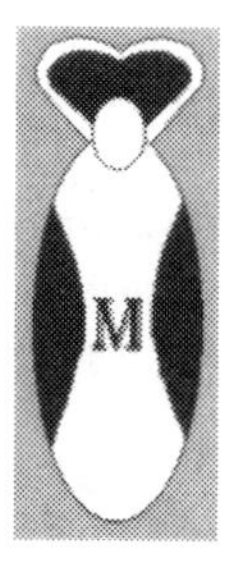

morvalearth.co.uk

First published in 2002 by morvalearth.co.uk
49 King Street, Bathgate
West Lothian, EH48 1AZ

www.morvalearth.co.uk

Distributed by Gazelle Book Services Limited
Falcon House, Queen Square
Lancaster, England LA1 1RN

British Library Cataloguing in Publication Data
A catalogue record for this book is available from the British Library

ISBN 0-9541178-0-8

Typeset by Amolibros, Watchet, Somerset
This book production has been managed by Amolibros
Printed and bound by T J International Ltd, Padstow, Cornwall

Contents

Simple Abridged Morval Earth Fantasy Rules

Dice used are D10s, numbered 0 > 9 plus the odd D6 1 > 6.

Morval Earth Fantasy Rules aim for realism and are more lethal for players' characters than most other sets of rules. Beginners can get by with figures for the quest characters and around twenty general figures for the opposition, friends and neutrals. Flat, map-like scenery can be easily drawn on cardboard or purchased as "dungeon tiles". Characters & types each have a 5"x 3" card made out listing their varying attributes. Naturally quest characters tend to be better than average. Weaknesses, languages known and other abilities are listed (such as the ability to swim, lock-picking, plant identifying, tracking, substance identifying, etc.). A *move* covers the time taken to try a spell, fire a missile or ask a long question, but for melee is divided into two *rounds*.

Movement: Figures move a basic 6" for men & 5" for women on Good cross-country. An inch is added if on a paved surface or deducted if on Bad cross-country. These rates are doubled if the figure runs but a fatigue point is expended. Wearing heavy armour deducts an inch and also diminishes Fatigue stamina. Bcc, quadrupeds half moves.

Moving Cautiously deducts 2". Moving furtively is normally half-rate but not possible in heavy armour.

Fatigue: Figures have a Fatigue basic stamina rating of 6/12 for men and 5/10 for women. A point (Ft Pt) is expended for each move fighting, running or carrying out other strenuous activities. When all the first total is consumed, the character is tired, -1" to moves -1 to spells & missile hits and -2 in melee. When the second total is consumed, the character collapses, & can only speak. One point regained per move resting.

Melees: Figures have a basic Melee Rating (MR) 0 for civilian men, knights +2 and -2 for women plus a weapon modification and any modifications for circumstances. In a one to one melee, a D10 (0 > 9dice) is thrown for each figure and the lower score subtracted from the higher, which has inflicted a blow. To this difference is added any weapon strike bonus and the result read against the losers' wounded/crippled/dead (W/C/D) values. If the loser has a shield, however, he can dice to parry, basic D10 7+ he does & deducts 4 from the strike total. If the scores are equal each dice, 0 weapon broken, 1 or 2 weapon dropped -2 next round. If two fight one the two mean their scores (rounding up) and add 3. If three fight one, mean of the scores add 5. If four fight one, mean of the scores add 6. ***Dodging*** adds 3 but cannot hurt the opponent.

Melee Weapons Modifiers: (St = strike value) Bare hands -2 St -3 stun 5, Knife -1 St -1, Dagger -1 St 0, Sword 0 St 0, Club -1 St -1 Stun 5. Staff -2 St -1 +1 1st Round, Stun 5, Spear -1 St 0 1st Round +2, Mace -1 St +2, Axe -1 St +2 Breach -2, Two Handed Axe -2 St +4 breach -1, Two Handed Sword -2, St +4, Halberd -2 St +3 1st round +2, Teeth -1 St -1, Claws -1 St -1, Morning Star -2 St +3 shield parries -2. ***Stunning*** If the aim is to stun rather than kill, for each point worse than Wound rate a D10 moves stunned.

Other Melee Modifiers: Foot charge +1, Mounted charge +2, Full surprise +4, Half surprise +2, Superior height +1, Wounded -2, Tired -2, Demoralised -2, Dazed -4, Blinded -5, On ladder -2, dropped weapon -2.

Breaching: Each move D10 + Basic MR + Weapons Breach Strike - Obstacles Breach Strength (BS)
Result -1- failed, 0 weaken breach strength by 1, 1+ Breached.
Weapons: 2H Axe -1, Axe -2, Mace -3, Crowbar -1, Spade -3, pickaxe -2, Jemmy -2, Sledgehammer -1.

BS Strengths: Door 6, Strong Door 8, Gate 10, Portcullis 12, Inner wall 8, Outer Wall 12, Tile roof 6, etc.

Bolt Saws These are used for sawing through door bolts. D6 +1 per move = 8 success, 7- failed

Missile Weapons: D10 Hit chances at various ranges with strike value. D10 + St V compared with W/C/D values. Again shield bearers have a chance of a parry, basic 7+ shield strength 4.
Sling 4" 5+, 8" 6+, 12" 7+, 16" 8+ St -4

Self Bow 5" 5+, 10" 6+, 15" 7+, 20" 8+ St -4
Long Bow 6" 5+, 12" 6+, 18" 7+, 24" 8+ St -3 One Fatigue Point used per two shots
Latch Crossbow 5" 5+, 10" 6+, 15" 7+, 20" 8+ St -4 Fired alternate moves +1 to hit if rested
Heavy Crossbow 6" 5+, 12" 6+, 18" 7+, 24" 8+ St -3 Fired every third moves, +1 to hit if rested
Dart 5" 5+ St -3
Javelin 4" 5+ St -2
Ordinary knife 4" 6+ St -4
Throwing knife 5" 5+ St -3
Dagger 3" 6+ St -3
Chakram 5" 6+ St -5
Handstones 3" 5+ St -5
Dropped from heights -1 per 4" hit chance but +1 to strike per 2" vertical.

Terror Resistance: Characters may have to Dice (D10) for Natural or Magic Terrors adding their TR or Spell Resisting values. Basic TRs Horses -2, Nidderlings -1, Followers 0, Independents +1, Officers +2, Leaders +3. Magicians add their level to Spell resistance. Adventurers normally add 1 to 3 on experience. Monsters and wild animals are given Terror Infliction Values, tested once when within 6" of a figure. Results 0+ Unaffected. -1 Demoralised -2 melee & Missile hits. -2 Terrified can only dodge, steed's quarter moves. -3 Paralysed, stand helpless a move. -4 Prostrate falls to ground, steeds stampede. -5- Faint, steeds stampede. If Fainted D10 each move 8+ to improve to Dazed (-4 in melee) next move to Demoralised. Stampeded steeds flee at double move rate until they are tired.

Morale: Morale is diced for D10 when Leader is lost, 25%, 50% or 75% of a party is lost or an allied party is routed or wiped out within 6". The one throw is applied though the party will usually have differing Natural TR values and hence possible differing reactions. Modifiers, lost Leader -1, lost 25% -2, lost 50% -4, lost 75% -7, Tired -1, Demoralised -2, Terrified -4, previously routed -2, defeated enemy +2. Results 4+ Unaffected, 3 stand two moves demoralised, 2 retreat two moves demoralised, 1 routed two moves at double rate then ralliable on 5+, 0 routed three moves then ralliable on 7+, -2+ routed without hope for the day, -3- surrender unless allowed to flee without a chance of rallying.

Charm Influencing CI (A Charmers skill +1 > 4) CI - D10 +F Victim op sex -2, Reasonable request -2, unreasonable request +2, Guarded +2, = 3+ refuses, 0+ dithers try again -1- agrees (or D6 moves wasted if just trying to distract victim.)

Terror Coercion TC (A Thug skill +1 > 4) TC- D10 +F Victim Nidderling -3, Woman -2, Follower 0, Independent +1, Officer +3, accompanied +1 = 1+ resists, 0 dithers, try again, -2+ Coerced in sight of Coercer, -3- coerced fully.

Fire Rules: Fire implements have a Fire Strike (FS) Held candle -3, Torch -1, Tinderbox -4, Fire arrow -3, Projected candle -6, Torch -3, Fire arrow -4, Fire pot -1. D10 +FS +Factor s: Wet -3, easy burn +1, hard burn -2, Full armour -1, Unclothed +1 = 1+superficial burn/scorched 2+ wound burn/charred, 4+ cripple burn/ on fire, 6+ dead/spreading fire

Obstacles Steep slopes -1", Fords -1" per 2"s, Deep fords or Marshes -1" per 1" & D6 (+1 if roped) = 3+ OK 2- submerged.

Submerged dicing D6 +F Marsh -1, Plate or Heavy -2, Medium -1, Shield -1, Roped +2, Demoralised -1, Unclothed +1, Laden -1, floundering -1= 1- drowned, 2 floundering, 3 Recover losing hand held items, 4 Recover OK in same place, 5 Recover forward 1", 6 Recover forward 2".

Climbing and jumping over Obstacles. Figures can climb & jump according to **Ob**stacle Classification.
Ob = (2 x Move rate + F) x 0.1 gives length distance & x 0.05 height cleared without a problem. Ran (costs 1 Fat Pt) +3, No shield or pack +1, Lightly clad +1, Hero +1, Ranger etc +1, Female -1, Long Gown -1, Laden -1, Has shield & pack -1, Heavy laden -2, Medium -1, Heavy -2, Plate -3, Has Rider -4 When easy clearance exceeded dice as below. For High Obstacles: Ob + D10 - Ht in 0.05s = 0+ OK, -1 -2", -2 -4", -3 Fail*, -4 Fail* -1 next try, -5- Give up! * fall off steed if riding, Hit strike of -4 For wide Obstacles: Ob + D10 - width in 0.1s = 0+ OK, -1 -1", -2 -2", -3 -4", -4- fall in!

Falls D10 + Hit strike against faller. Rocky ground -3, Normal -4, soft -5, spikes -2, +1 per each extra inch.

Trap Spotting Diced when within 2" D6 +F + Personal Bonuses, Moving Cautiously +1, Searching +2 (2" moves), not first -1, Plate or Heavy -2, Medium or encumbered light -1, Mounted -1, LC loosely Concealed +1, Normally Concealed 0, Well concealed -1 = 5+ Spotted

Sleeping & Poisoning Drugs The stronger they are the more likely to be noticed Strengths DS 1 > 4. To attempt to drug D6 - DS+F = Factors: on Guard -2, strange offer -1, usual drink +1, influenced +2 = 2- Refuse, 3 Reject at -2 to DS, 4 reject at -1 to DS., 5+ Full effect Victim dices Each move D10 -DS (antidote +5, vomit -2)= 8+ Revert a phase, 4+ no change, 3- drop a Ph

Poison: Phase 0 normal, Ph 1 nausea, Ph 2 dazed, Ph 3 helpless delirious, Ph 4 coma, Ph 5 DEAD!

Soporific: Phase 0 Normal, Ph 1 nausea, Ph 2 dazed, Ph 3 sleep, Ph 4 coma DS xD10 moves. Then reverse, Ph 3 to Ph 2 to Ph1 to Ph 0.

Nausea = -2 to melee, -1" move,

Dazed -4 to melee -3 to move.

Magic: Magic artefacts may *usually* be used without penalty by non-magicians. *Magicians* generate one Magic Power Unit (MPU) per move per level, holding them up to a maximum of four times their level.

Magicians can only cast the spells they have learnt and for which they have currently enough MPU.

Normal casting they need D10 3+ less any Spell resistance involved. Super spells add +3 to the dice but cost double the MPU. Most spells are cast from 2" to 6" but some can have the range extended with extra MPU. Some spells with a natural chance of reversion (2- on D10) which can be averted with a Hold spell.

Magic in Morval Earth is less powerful than in other systems and there are few Magicians above 4th level.

Air Blasts extinguishes torches, -2 to hits by missiles, Hand items dropped on 4-. Creatures in blast D10 + Cubits size (men 4) 5- blown over (-4 next round of melee) Range 6" by 1" 4MPU.

Blinding Flash Cast an inch in front of the magician, he & allies need to shut their eyes! 3" diameter 2MPU D10 - 2 = 1+ Blinding Flash -4 in melee for two rounds Undead Terror Infliction 3

Breaching Bolt Conjures a breaching blow against a door etc. Counts as D10 +3 used as Magic Bolt.
Range 2" 7MPU. D10 -2 = 1+hits = D10 +4 - Breaching Strength = 1+ breached 0 weakened 1, -1- fail.

Charm Person To persuade person to do a reasonable favour. If it fails, victim becomes hostile. Range 2" 3MPU. D10 -2-SR = 1+ succeeds, 0- fails.

Cling Deducts 2 from climbing or riding fall chances. Duration until 1- thrown on D10 each move Range 2" 4MPU D10 -2 -SR = 1+ succeeds, 0 fails. Hold spell 1MPU per move negates duration chance.

Control Palantyte Used to contact an ochyo, mirror or other palantyte spying device. No super or Hold spells. Range 2" 3MPU D10 -2 - 1 per 100 myles distance, = 1+ succeeds. D10 each move 2- loses contact.

Counter Spell To counter a spell the MPU used plus the margin of success times 1.25 must be equalled. (D10 -2 +MPU x 1.25 = Counter Target) If the margin of success is not known, use a D6. Range 2" D10 + nMPU -2 = to equal to counter the spell.

Detect Magic To detect presence of magic in person or object. Includes magic trail left by magicians. Range 3" 2MPU. D10 -2 = 1+ reveals magic or not. One attempt only.

Disarm To force to drop hand held items -2 to next round of melee. Range 3" One hand 6MPU Two hands 9MPU D10 -2 -SR = 1+ succeed.

Double Crop To make a small field or specific group of plants grow faster and larger. Range 6" 6MPU. D10 -2 = 1+ succeed in D6+4 days time.

Earth tremor To create an earth tremor affecting an area, D10 -2+F inches. Terror strike 3 within 12" Range 6" 12MPU. Rock Factors, Metamorphic +1, Igneous 0, Sedimentary -1, Buildings in zone D10 - F = inches collapse, Huts 4, Houses/Walls 3, Mansions/ Temples/Castle walls 2, Towers 1. Strike of -4 against those in the open and 0 against those in collapsing buildings.

Ease Pain To reduce melee deductions by 1. Touch 2MPU. D10 -2 -SR = n x3 hours duration.

Evaporate Liquid This evaporates a water based liquid down to its solid constituents. Range 3" 1 MPU per bottle volume, D10-2 = 1+ succeeds.

Fire Missile A small ball of fire projected at a victim or object Range 12" 4MPU. D10 -2 = 1+ struck target. D10 -3 +Factor s: Wet -3, easy burn +1, hard burn -2, Full armour -1, Unclothed +1 = 1+superficial burn/scorched 2+ wound burn/ charred, 4+ cripple burn/ on fire, 6+ dead/spreading fire.

Fit of the Giggles Range 2", 2MPU D10 -2-SR +F =Rounds giggling -3 in melee, -2" moves cannot fire. Factors: Female +1, age 19- +1, Relaxed +1, solemn 0, tense -2, hostile -4, fighting -6.

Forget & Reversal Range 3" 6MPU. D10 -2 -SR = n x 5 hours duration. Reversal needs only 1+ to revert.

Guilt Blush To detect a liar. Range 3" 3MPU D10 - 2-SR =1+ to blush. For 6MPU, force a blush!

Ignite Range 3", 3+ for attempt. Has fire strike of -2 3MPU.

Inflict Revulsion Give the victim a revulsion for items or creatures, amounting to a Terror Infliction of 5. Range 6" 6MPU. D10-2 -SR = plusses give the number of days affected.

Inflict Vertigo Gives the victim a vertigo attack with -3 to melee & missile hit chances & -2 to spell casting Range 2" 3MPU. D10 -2 -SR = moves affected. Moves D10 -5 inches only each move, minuses = 0 & Fall

Levitate Allows the subject to move, hovering in the air at D10 -2 inches. Rising 1" costs 1", dropping 2" adds 1" to distance travelled. Caster himself 6MPU. For an other within 12", 10MPU.

Magic Bolt Conjures a stunning blow against a victim. Range 6" 4MPU. D10 -2 = 1+ hits = D10 – wound rate = D10s moves stunned If 5 diff = dead.

Magic Illumination Makes an item light up 4" diameter circle. 1MPU D10 each move, 0, goes out.

Mouthwash Makes the victim foam at the mouth with a bitter taste, -1 in melee. Range 3" 1MPU. D10 -2 -SR = moves affected.

Reshape Flesh Used to alter face or to close wounds, improves melee deductions by1. Touch Range, 3MPU D10 -2- SR = n x 5 hours duration.

Smoke Screen Creates a ball of smoke 3" diameter which lasts 4 moves in still air, 2 in Light wind 3" per Move & 1 in moderate wind 6". Range 3" 3MPU. Hold spell 1MPU.

Stranger Sensing To detect hidden living beings within Magic Arc. Magician senses size & rough number. Range 9" to 6" wide Marc. 3MPU. D10 -2 = 1+ succeeds, 0- fails. One attempt per location.

Strike Dumb & Reversal Range 3" 6MPU. D10 -2 -SR = n x 5 hours duration. Reversal needs only 1+ to revert. Does not work on naturally dumb subjects.

Stun Gas Creates a 2" diameter cloud of Gas, duration 4 moves still air, 2 Light wind & 1 moderate wind. Range 3" 6MPU, each creature in zone D10 = 6+ unaffected, 5 Demoralised, 4 Dazed, 3 Stunned D6 moves, 2 Stunned 2xD6 moves, 1 Stunned 4xD6 moves, 0 Stunned 7xD6 moves.

Telepathy Used with a subject controlled by the magician. Range 30" 8MPU. D10 -2 = 1+ to succeed.

Wood Crumble This weakens a piece half inch square piece of wood. Range Touch, 12MPU. D10-2 = half the number of breach points deducted per move until it crumbles to dust.

Morval Earth Coins & Measures (1 man = 4 cubit size)

10 copper pfenni = 1 silver florin, 10 florins = 1 gilden pezzo (gold piece, plural pezzi)
50 drops = 1 phial, 2 phials = 1 draught, 4 draughts = 1 bottle, 20 bottles = 1keg, 2 kegs = 1 barrel
10 pinches = 1 spoon, 10 spoons = 1 bag, 10 bags = 1 sack. 4 kets = 1 het (1 table inch)
Merchants' Price Lists for basic items (Selling price/buying price in Florins) One move each deal.
Basic knife 60/45, Throwing knife 80/60, Dagger 120/90, Axe 100/75, 2 Handed Axe 180/135, Sword 300/225, 2 Handed Sword 400/300, Spear 60/45, Long Bow 60/45, LB Arrow 20/15, Self Bow 48/36, SB arrow 16/12, Latch Crossbow 80/60, Quarrel 16/12, Spade or Pick 100/75, Shield 120, Medium Armour 400/300, Heavy Armour 800/600, Plate Armour 1200/900, Bolt Saw 60/45, Tinderbox 80/60, Candle 4/3, Torch 8/6, Oil Lantern 100/75, Draught Oil 4/3, Bandage 8/6, Wound Dressing 16/12, 6 hets Rope, 60/45, Grapnel 100/75, 6 hets Cord, Phial 4/3, Glass Bottle 8/6, Leather bottle 12/9, Canvas Bag 4/3, 2 cubit Sack 12/9, Haversack 80/60, Pack 120/90.

Haggling Rules Use the above prices as a starting point and use two rounds to start haggling. Haggling Abilities (HA) Merchant +2, Expert (Housewife)+1, Adventurer 0, Inexperienced (Soldier)-1, Knight (Dummy) -2. D6 + Own

HA- Others HA = 5+ add or subtract 10% & can haggle on. 3+ No deal but can haggle on. 2- Must accept price offered.

Refreshments Draughts: Ale 4, Wine 6, Mead 6, Spirits 8, Milk 6, Fruit juice 4.
Stable Horse 5 per day.
Meals: Snack 2, Breakfast 4, Lunch 4, Dinner 8.
Bedding Common straw 4, Own room 15, Shared 10.
Days' Hire Rates Unskilled Man 20, Unskilled Woman 16, Skilled Man 24, Skilled Woman 20, Soldier 28, Sergeant 36, Hobilar 36, Mounted Sergeant or Squire 44, Mounted knight 60. Ox 3, Pack Ass 5, Packhorse 7, Hack or cart horse 7, Rouncey 8, Destrier 14 10 cubit carrying Canoe 30, 35c Canoe 100, 24c Punt 50, 14c rowing boat 60, 36c rowing boat 100, 14c cobble 80, 34c smack 120, 60c Scow 200, 200c Cog 400, 160c Lymphad 400.

Character Card Abbreviations (Cards 5" x 3")

Lea = Leader
Off = Officer
Ind = Independent
Fol = Follower
Mo = Move rate
Fa = Fatigue endurance
TR = Terror Resistance
SR = Spell Resistance
D-n = Death margin
C-n = Crippled (cannot fight)
W-n = Wounded margin (-2 in melee)
Ob = Obstacle easy jump dist.
Me = Basic + Weapon Melee abilities (mounted +2)

Align = alignment
TC = Terror Coercion Ability
CI = Charm Influence Ability

Specimen Cards

Sir Hardasbras, Thentian knight Plate Off, Mo 5", Fa 5/10, TR +3, SR +1, D-7, C-6, W -5, Ob 0.7 Me +2 -1 = +1 axe strike +2, breach -2, Align ***N***
Shield Parry Melee 7+, Missile 7+ strength 4, TC2
Speaks: Simnith, Edin. Reads: Tengthin
Weakness cruelty, Torments prisoners D10 -4 moves.
Wide Will, Perigordan Arbalister. Medium
Fol, Mo 6", Fa 6/12, TR 0, SR 0, D-5, C -4, W-3, Ob 1.3
Me 0 +0 = 0 sword strike 0, Align ***N***
Crossbow & 8 quarrels, 5" 5+, 10" 6+, 15" 7+, 20" 8+ strike -4+1 if weapon rested. Has tinderbox
Speaks: Edin.
Weakness Alcohol, -3 to temptation Needs D10 8+ to stop.
Madame Miste, Alpenais Sorceress. Light, long Gown
Ind, Mo 5", Fa 5/10, TR +1, SR +3, D-4, C-3, W-2, Ob 0.8 Me -2 -2 = -4 Staff strike -1, stun 5. Align ***L***
CI 3, 2nd level Magic, 2MPU per move, maximum 8
Blinding Flash, Control Palantyte, Detect Magic,
Smoke Screen, Strike Dumb & Reversal, Wood Crumble
Speaks Simnith, Quenith, Reads: Tengthin, Lerumint.
Tiger 10 cubit size, Wild Beast Terror Infliction 5
Mo 9", Fa 7/14, TR 4 SR -1, D-5, C-4, W-3, Ob 1.9
Me +6 -1 = +5 strike -1,
Scent Tracker +3, Neuserk 8" (Distance at which it will attack)

These rules are published by J L Mumford of ***morvalearth.co.uk.***
27th July 2001

Other titles in the series

Horg!

Lady Morgana, having accomplished the dangerous mission set by her powerful Uncle Quixano, can now justly call herself a true "Lady Errant". Whilst fulfilling her youthful dreams, she has to admit that living in constant terror and acute discomfort, is a bit wearing. She grieves for the loss of Sergeant Hrolf who taught her to fence and she has the others of her menie to care for. Still within the hostile State of Narchad, she now hopes to find her mother, abducted twenty-three years ago. Don Incio, one of her knights, also seeks a dark vengeance here, on his traitor brother, presuming he can trace him. However neither of these perilous tasks will cost Morgana and her party, as much suffering, as when Peron Quixano sends them all to the Chaotic State of Horg!

This novel was created from a role playing game, using 25mm figurines and scenery. Consequently the dice ensured that the storyline, often varied from that desired by the author and his players.

Horg ISBN 0-9541178-1-6

Other titles in the series

The Return!

Dame Morgana's fortunes are at a low ebb. Having been sent as a diplomatic official to Delvon, the land of the little dimini people, she is now in prison. She and her menie are accused of acts of brigandage in a neighbouring State. Princess Maudette, whom Morgana freed in the best traditions of knight errantry, says she can obtain her freedom, if she will help her regain her lost State of Bara. In Bara lie most of Morgana's own forfeited estates. Meanwhile Morgana's Uncle, Peron Quixano, also says he will obtain her freedom–if she will carry out another perilous mission for him, in Chaotic Elysia! This mission will also bring her within reach, of the Wizard who murdered her father! In the return to her homeland of Bara, "Two Unicorns Morgana" faces up to all of these challenges.

This novel was created from a role playing game, using 25mm figurines and scenery. Consequently the dice ensured that the storyline, often varied from that desired by the author and his players.

The Return 0-9541178-2-4

Notes on the Creation of the Adventures and Acknowledgements

The Adventures of Morgana comprise three volumes, being the embellished account of a Role-Playing Game, (RPG) created in forty-two evening instalments. Role-Playing Games, using figurines and appropriate scale scenery, are an offshoot of the Wargaming hobby, which started to appear in the late 1960s. As Games Master (GM) I created the background and main storyline but my players made the decisions, moved the figures and diced for the results. Our Fantasy group formed around 1995 playing *Adventure Quest* and various board games at the house of Bill & Heather Ray. When we had exhausted the *Adventure Quest* modules, Heather made up her own saga, which we called *Heather Quest.* I did a spell as GM with Slim Quest 1, using my Morval Earth background and rules. Taking it in turns, Brian Stirling ran *Brian Quest* and Ewen Clarke ran *Ewen Quest* using the Advanced Dungeons and Dragons' background and rules. With Heather doing another stint, the *Adventures of Morgana* were fitted in as Slim Quest's 2, 3 and 4.

My background sub-continent of Morval Earth owes a lot to J R R Tolkien's *Lord of the Rings*, Tony Bath's *Setting up a Wargame's Campaign* and the *Dungeons and Dragons* (D&D) culture. It was originally created with my *Fantasy Rules* (1st edition 1979) to provide a background for fantasy skirmish actions. The inspiration of D&D led to the rules becoming more and more role-play orientated. A great incentive was the large numbers of suitable figures, produced by: Miniature Figurines, Minot, Garrison, Grenadier, Lamming, Pendragon, Asgard, Ral Partha, Citadel, Irregular Miniatures, RAFM, Mithril Miniatures, Tin Soldier, Hinchliffe, Games Workshop, Wargames Foundry, Gripping Beast and others. Some figures of other periods were converted into "something useful", usually "innocent civilians". My collection built up to over four thousand figures. The core of Morval Earth was the Kingdom of Thentis, with the surrounding states of Perigord, Bara, Stetia, Limura, Alpen and Porcia. These were taken from "Son of Hyboria", a postal campaign I took part in as the King of Thentis. Created by Douglas Harold, I was given a twelfth-century Feudal State. In this many prominent family trees were created, each with their own coat of arms. These I kept, though the map was completely different. The original maps were hand-drawn but I eventually transferred them to the Campaign Cartographer software.

Over the years we played many "one-off" scenarios in Morval Earth, including Public Participation versions, at War Games Conventions. These actions each contributed to its 'history' and some are touched upon in the *Adventures of Morgana*. Not, however, Slim Quest 1, which chronologically happens three years afterwards. The key action, played before I had even thought of running a quest, was the assassination of King Reginald and Queen Bettrys.

Attempting for more realism, my rules are more dangerous for player characters than most other sets. In my one-off scenarios, the players had many costly losses and occasional disastrous defeats. When I started Slim Quest 1, I was fearful that it could come to an abrupt ending. In fact, it lasted thirteen episodes, ending naturally in a final battle. With the *Adventures of Morgana*, I soon realised giving it that name was a rash thing to do. Morgana's death would have instantly cut it short and this was a very real possibility the whole time. She had ten close shaves and several of her companions had their luck run out, along the way.

The germination of the saga began when my daughter, Zenobia, gave me the Games Workshop figure of "Morgana le Fay" mounted on a unicorn. Brandishing a sword in one hand and a chalice in the other, it immediately set my mind racing to provide an appropriate background. Since I knew I would need a dismounted figure as well, this led to the purchase of a second figure and some conversion work. Hence also the existence of the second unicorn. Without the players, there would have been no story and in fact many sub-plots were inspired by their responses. Thanks then to Heather Ray, Amanda Jeffries, Lorna Clipstone, Brian Stirling, and Ewen Clark. These played the principal characters during *Exiled!* I must also thank my tolerant and supportive wife Elizabeth, usually known by her code name of Betty. She has for many years endured not so much absence of body, as absence of my mind, far away in Morval Earth or other wargames' worlds.

A GM has to try and fit in with the aspirations of his or her players. I thought Amanda Jeffries would like the Morgana character and she ran her very well. Brian Stirling preferred "ranger" type characters so he was given Bergand. Lorna Clipstone *always* played Dwarves, hence Minut son of Moltin. Due to the lethality of the rules (no wimpish hit points system in my rules!), players ran two or three characters as a norm in my games. Credit is due to the players who developed the characters, for without them there would have been no story.

The adventure venues were laid out on Heather's wargames' table for all the early episodes. These covered an area of about three feet by three feet. The illustrations by Gordon Redrup were drawn from photographs recreating the actions, using the actual figures, buildings, and other items used at the time. From the start I had in mind the three main strands of the saga, though I did not really believe I would complete them all. My task was to have enough adventures prepared to last three and a half to four hours each evening. For this I had to make plans of the two or three areas to be used, with lists and dicing chances for the various things to be encountered. Because we met only once a fortnight and some players would miss episodes, I wrote reports of each action. Further, to be fair to the players, I wrote accounts of the activities of the enemies of the characters, before they were likely to encounter them. This produced the material from which the novels were derived.

When the players are making the decisions, the GM has far less control than a normal author does. Sometimes their idea of what a character would do differed from mine but one has to adapt and to be honest as to what happened on the table. The truth is that the Games Master can never be sure what will ensue on the night or how long it will take. If his problems and adversaries are easily vanquished, it is not too much of a problem, though if it happens too often, the players will lose interest. On the other hand, a night where the dice run heavily for the opposition, or the players take a suicidal decision, can end the quest prematurely. D&D-type players are used to getting treasure and enhanced abilities from their adventures. In this saga I did give *very* occasional improvements to abilities but I supplied objectives other than treasure. This did not mean that money was not a consideration, as the story shows. What I have minimised was the sometimes lengthy bargaining, whenever anything was purchased. My players (all true Scots) were very keen hagglers and beat me (an easy-going Englishman) far lower than I should have allowed, many times.

Amanda, playing Morgana, started off splendidly at the priory, with her act of the spoilt young lady. The party never did discover that Pazan and the prioress had powerful magic spells. When Morgana fought with Sir Phanuel, she had her first big chance of getting killed but the dice went in her favour. Meeting her guardian outside the city was a severe shock to the party players. Sir Richard's combat with Sir Mordant Bec and Harold's with the dun unicorn were other actions where luck ran for the party. As it also was lucky for crossing the River Arwyn, in the gale. Perhaps that was Lorna's finest hour. I had a complicated dicing system for the crossing, with chances of running aground or having people swept overboard in the gale. Lorna threw such consistently good dice that it became obvious that the gale must have abated.

One problem in role-playing is when there is a chance of the questers finding something hidden or triggering some sort of alarm. If normal dice are used, the players know whether they have thrown high or low and may react accordingly, even if they do not know what the throw was for. This is especially relevant when they are searching for something in particular. If they have thrown high and found nothing, they know there is no point in continuing. I solved this with "Mystic Dice". These were two six-sided dice painted with symbols instead of numbers. The combinations of two thrown symbols I would read off one of several tables. Though 1 to 36 was possible I found 1 to 6 enough for my needs. The players could check their throw scores at the end of the evening. One dice (Elemental Essence) had the four elements, earth, water, air and fire plus male and female. The other (Ethereal Phase) had the symbols copied from an enchanted wellhead model, which I had bought from some forgotten maker.

The players started to get nervous whenever I said, "Throw the mystic dice!" though it could trigger beneficial happenings as well as bad. Of course if something bad happened, they would blame the dice-thrower! I put in building the temporary bridge at Carrels, because on that night I knew I had only the three female players. They overcame the engineering challenge perfectly well. At Lozana, it was just chance that led to Ines being killed by Jinisti instead of Morgana. Her fight against the powerful demon Testronitz was another event where good dice won her through a dangerous situation. As GM I was really pushing my luck. Of course I had no idea the saga would result in a book at that stage.

At the temple of Khali, the dice turned against Heather, controlling Sergeant Hrolf, so he was killed. Ewen, running Don Incio, was also frustrated in that game at not achieving anything. He was at that stage wanting to kill everything that moved. He developed an ambition for his Don to have more kills than Lady Morgana, a competition that continued for the rest of the saga. For their benefit I kept a tally of kills for all the characters plus a points total from the Lawic point of view.

The SAVEWAY famine relief network was inspired by a well-known supermarket chain. Amanda was working part-time at one of their branches and the stripes on their overalls were used for their lozenge device.[1] We had a real instant feminine reaction from Morgana when she met Countess Bronwyn whose gown was shimmering, "Shimmer!"

The Zhentrim episode was put in to give Ewen Clark a hint. His verbose comments on the current D&D products of that time were holding up the game. In Slim Quest 1 the players had raided the Makgh village of St Bandade, the source of the holey water. I thought that they might realise there would be a supply of this vital healing aid in Flora Makbuta's hospital. They did not and I was not prepared to prompt them. The action at the Sektarar's tower was a disorganised mess from the players. If Don Incio had not managed, after three attempts, to get a foothold on the top, they would have been forced to flee. As it was, they were lucky to get away without pursuit. When the arrow struck Morgana, Amanda was rightly worried, as an 8 or 9 on the decimal strike dice (0-9) would have meant her death. Fortunately it was only a 3. Since the attack on the tower was supposed to be a feint I expected them to flee once the alarm gong sounded but they were determined to get what loot they could. Lady Pandora's party-saving speech was my brainwave between episodes. Otherwise they would have been overwhelmed.

At the end of *Exiled!*, Morgana hopes to rescue her mother and the Princess Maudette. Don Incio hopes to get revenge against his wife and brother. However, it is not these objectives that lead the party to near disaster in *Horg*, Volume II of the *Adventures of Morgana.*

1 Following heraldic tradition, fighting ladies of coat armour bear lozenge-shaped shields in Morval Earth.

Players' Character Information in *Exiled!*

Lady Morgana Lefey

You are a good-looking, dark brunette with brown eyes. Your waist is not as slender as fashion dictates and you are a trifle more muscular than most damsels are. You are wearing a new purple shimmering gown, with a vast matching heart-shaped hennin. The hatmaker was led to believe this was for Lady Mavys, so it is more suited to the mature wife of a Knight Banneret. Lady Mavys never knew of its existence. You also wear, hung open, a Thalian silk cloak, lined with coney fur. This is also of purple, covered with embroidered fleurs-de-lis of gold thread. You are girt with the sword Taglier and the magic mirror Argent and carry the Vinkalik chalice. Your spare clothes include a plain yellow gown with a dark green hennin.

Sir Richard Nogent

Your ancestors were Edini commoners from across the Sundering Sea. They married into the local Barii. Your Grandfather Raoul chose the "*vert a club or sangued*" coat of arms from the spiked club his father used. This aided his endeavours to buy enough land to become a knight. Your father was a poor knight in the Royal Seneschal of Bara's service. He saved enough to build a small manor on the estate near Suie. This you inherited twelve years ago. Before then you were dependent on your pay in the Royal service. Your wife Colombine died five years ago. You have two daughters, Giselle, twenty-two, married to Sir Bertrand Avoirdupois of Wardour in Thentis and Blanche, twenty, married to Lodric the Master Clothier at Charles. The latter is the only one in the family with any money. Most of your life you have been plodding up and down the River Arwyn's borders. Your heavy armour is old-fashioned and your steed Melonda only a rouncey. But she is sure enough in the marshes. People laugh at the extra length of your lance, but it has proved its worth fishing objects and people out of the river. You always dreamed of having more exciting (and possibly rewarding?) adventures. Now Lady Morgana, to whom you are devoted, appears to be giving you the opportunity.

Sergeant Hrolf

You are of trusty Barii stock. Your family has farmed along the north bank of the Arwyn since time began. With three brothers (and two sisters) to share the family plot, you had to look elsewhere for a living. You joined a company of the Royal Foot Guards in which your uncle Jlaton was a sergeant. Eventually you came under Sir Daffyd's command, patrolling and fighting on the Narchadian border of Stetia. In 683 when you were twenty-three, Sir Daffyd promoted you to sergeant and took you into his own employ. After Morgana's mother Berenezia was carried off, he re-enforced the manor. In later years the numbers dropped until now there is only you, Jack, and Gurth, who is over fifty (and away visiting his nephew). You married Margery when she became cook at the manor in 694. (She was not so fat then.) You have two children, Hlidric and Megan, who are following in their parents' footsteps. You are proud of the way you taught Arthur and Morgana to fence and very angry at the treacherous murder of Arthur. You are very ready to follow Morgana to the ends of Morval Earth, if she wants to go there.

Bergand, Mounted Arbalister

Your family really starts with your grandmother whose own family disowned her when she was made pregnant by an Ombardi chapman (travelling trinket seller). Her daughter, your mother, married a deaf mute, Berg of unknown origins, who became a serf on the Lefey estates. Bored with the hard work involved in farming the land, you volunteered to become a soldier nine years ago, joining Sir Richard Nogent's River Patrol. Five years ago Berg and your mother died of a fever. You married Jeta, the girl from the hut next door. Cham, her brother agreed to work your land strips for any profit he could get out of them. Though the estate and the Church benefited the most, he was doing well out of the deal. Jeta, reliant upon your pay, was not so happy. She was even less happy when she caught you in a compromising position with Mistress Mabel, the boatman's wife and has been shrewish ever since. Your explanation that you were trying to obtain information on the king's business carried little water although it was true–in part! One of the tasks of the River Patrol is to stop smuggling and Mistress Mabel's husband Jassyn is a notorious smuggler. During the moral reforms of King David III, or more accurately of his Queen Flacilla, a very heavy import toll was put on the perfume Chanelsanq. This Oblivian perfume, sometimes called Aphrodisia's magnet, was supposed to attract men like flies. "I was just questioning Mistress Mabel because she smelled of this perfume!" Since King Eudes' army returned, Jeta has been even worse. The lads that returned to the village came back laden with loot, whilst all you have ever got on the river patrol is rheumatism. You are of course devoted to the Lady Morgana but hope she will help you to a little treasure along the way.

Cherry, Lady Morgana's Servant

You are an attractive, mature young woman. As recounted, you were of a peasant family, living near Firmaz. Life was pleasant enough until the Narchadian raid killed your husband and baby son and carried you off. You eventually became the slave of the warrior Paedlok living near Wassugh. There, from the other women, you learnt a higher standard of cooking, using herbs, vegetables and meats from the great forest. The warriors were lazy and drunk most of the time, so the women had to go out to trap and collect the food. You were able to pick up quite a lot of woodcraft. The men were always quarrelling over something. One day at Wassugh, they were playing a game kicking a deer's stomach stuffed with leaves up and down the street. There was a big argument as to whether the stomach had gone over the end line or not, which ended in bloodshed. You took the opportunity to escape into the depths of the forest. It took you several days to get to the River Arwyn through the forest, feeding yourself as you went–then three more, cutting free a broken piece of trunk and levering it to the riverside without being detected. Your problems after floating across have been described. Your life with Morgana has been a great improvement and you are ready to follow her to the ends of the earth. Especially to avenge her Brother Arthur's death!

Minut son of Moltin, Dwarf Locksmith

You are one of a long line of important Kazid Varadh dwarves who have lived in Varadh since time began. You were apprenticed into the family locksmith's business, though in fact they made all sorts of weight- and spring-operated machinery, as required. Unfortunately you have a sense of humour and a temptation to play practical jokes. Starting with gluing your teacher's goblet to the table when you were six, life has been a string of laughs. Alas, such humour is little appreciated in Varadh. You tried to curb the amount of trouble you were getting into by writing a history of all known dwarf jokes but you are still only on page fourteen. Your forte has been the timed prank and it was one such that led to you being exiled from home. The Lord Hakhul was just getting up to make a speech at the 1,700th anniversary, when the water-operated peal of bells started and rang for ten minutes. Only your influential great uncle saved you from a worse fate. As it is, you are banished from Varadh for a hundred years. You tried to set up business as a locksmith in the city of Borolon, but the guild, jealous of your renowned dwarfish skills, would not let you in. However, by going round the manors you have got enough business to get by and buy (by & by, get it!) a little workshop at Pincelle. You enjoy the humour you find amongst mankind and have started another book concerning it. Now the Lady Morgana, to whom you feel strangely attracted, has asked for your assistance. You hope it will lead to more amusing experiences. You are dwarf enough to appreciate the gold necklace she gave you, made by the men of Dabbra you doubt not.

Lady Abigail Clove (Morgana's Aunt)

You are a middle-aged brunette, accustomed to running your own affairs in practical ways. You habitually wear a black widow's gown of Thalian silk. You normally follow the Stetian fashion of having your hair uncovered but when travelling you wear a sky-blue wimple. Your ancestors were always leaders of the Stetii. Many of them have magic powers and you have inherited some of them. You were found to be able enough to use the Cobret. However, when you married your beloved Sir Damerus, you moved to Bara, where magic was frowned upon. So you used your talent only to assist your botanical experiments. After four years your husband was killed by the Narchadians, who carried off your sister Berenezia (Morgana's mother). Sir Daffyd made you Chatelaine of the St Visseille hunting preserve. There you created a large herb garden, which has been the focus of your life ever since. Whenever you encounter writings on herb lore, you store them into the memory of the Cobret. Following your own experiments, you had written the particulars in your journals and then stored them in the Cobret too. Now the journals are burnt but you have got the Cobret back. You are appalled by the murder of Arthur and determined to use your magic in any way you can to assist Morgana.

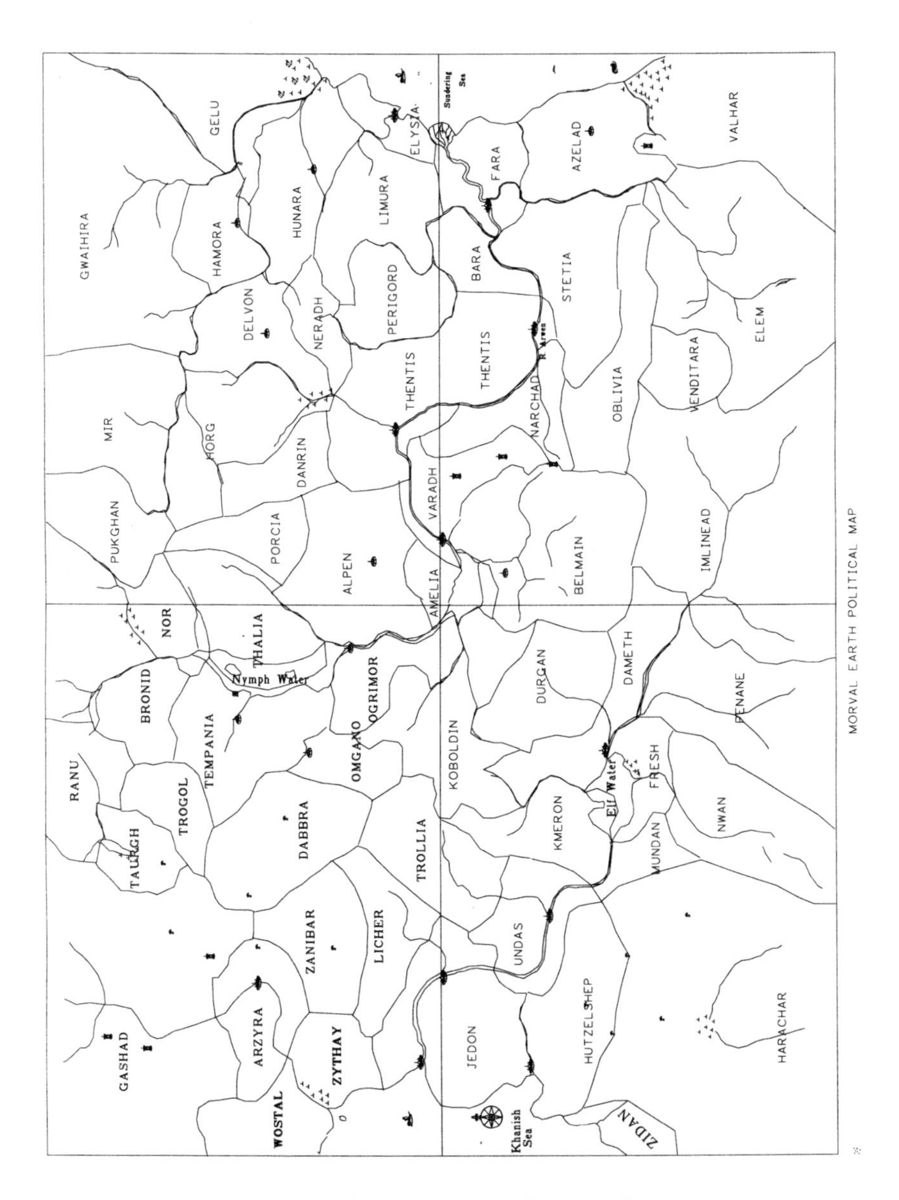

Map One, Morval Earth

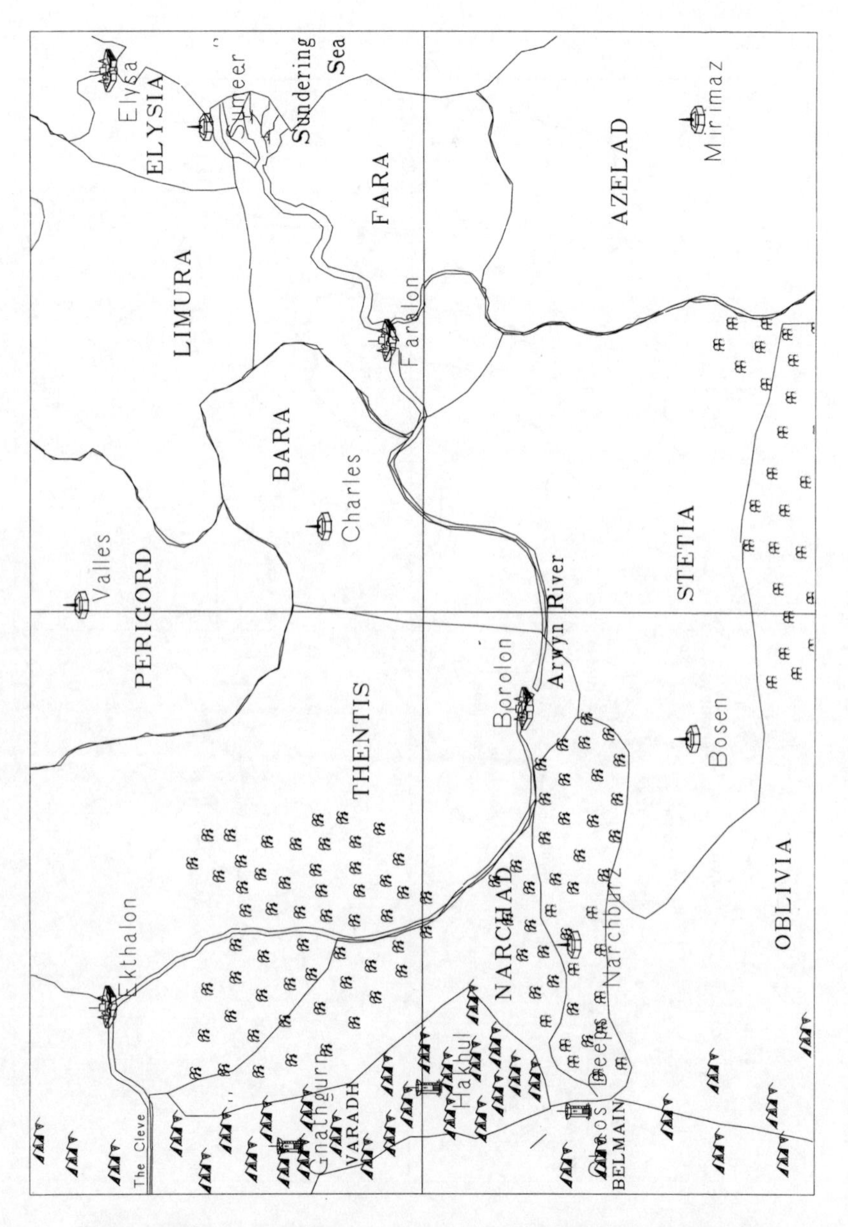

Map Two, Eastern Region of Morval Earth

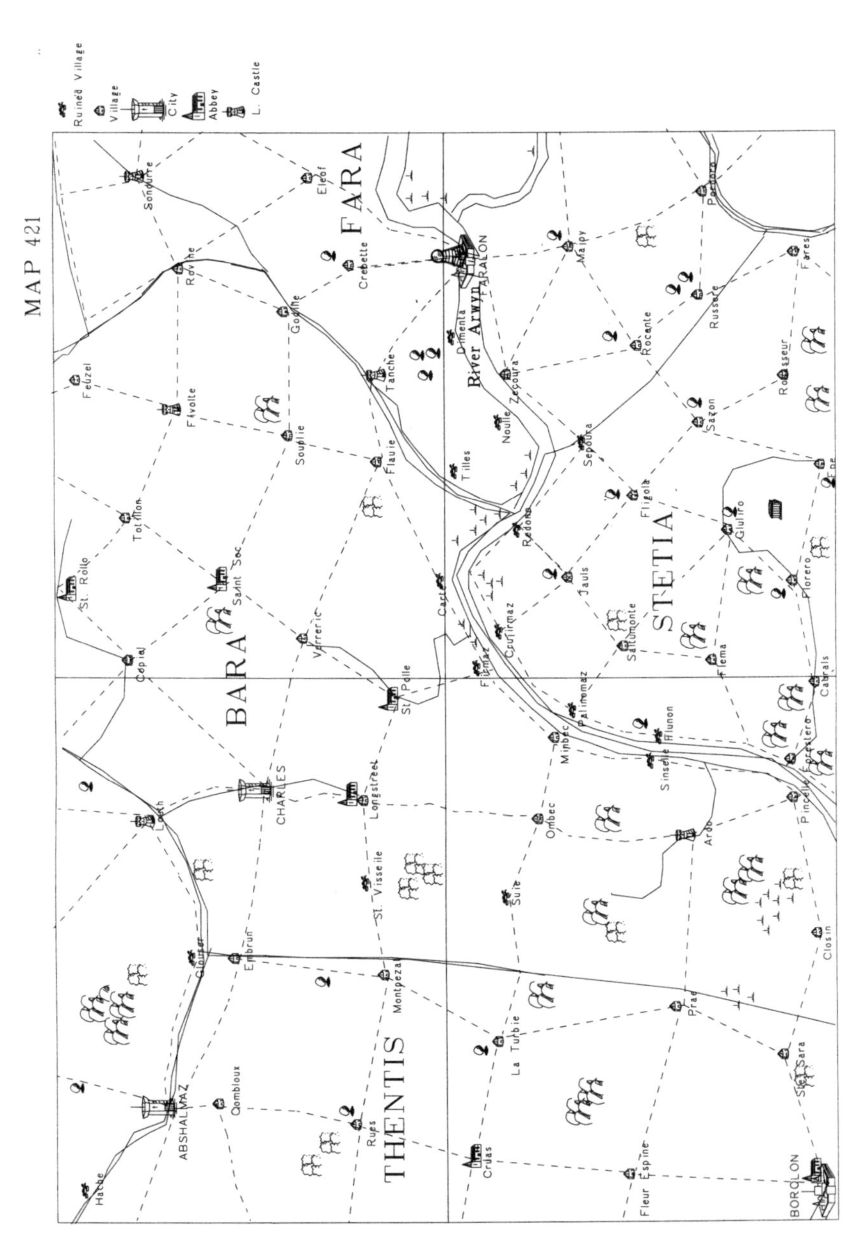

Map Three, Bara

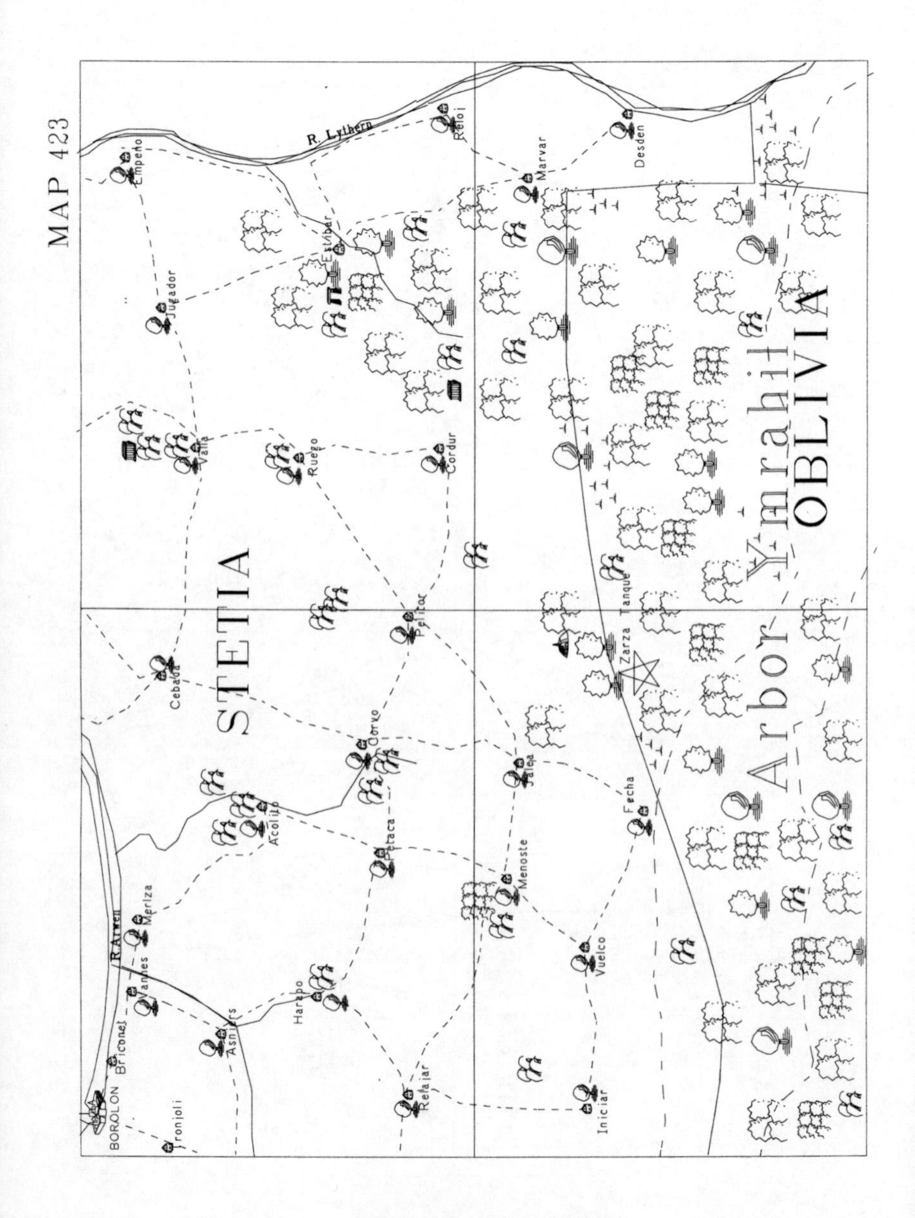

Map Four, Stetia

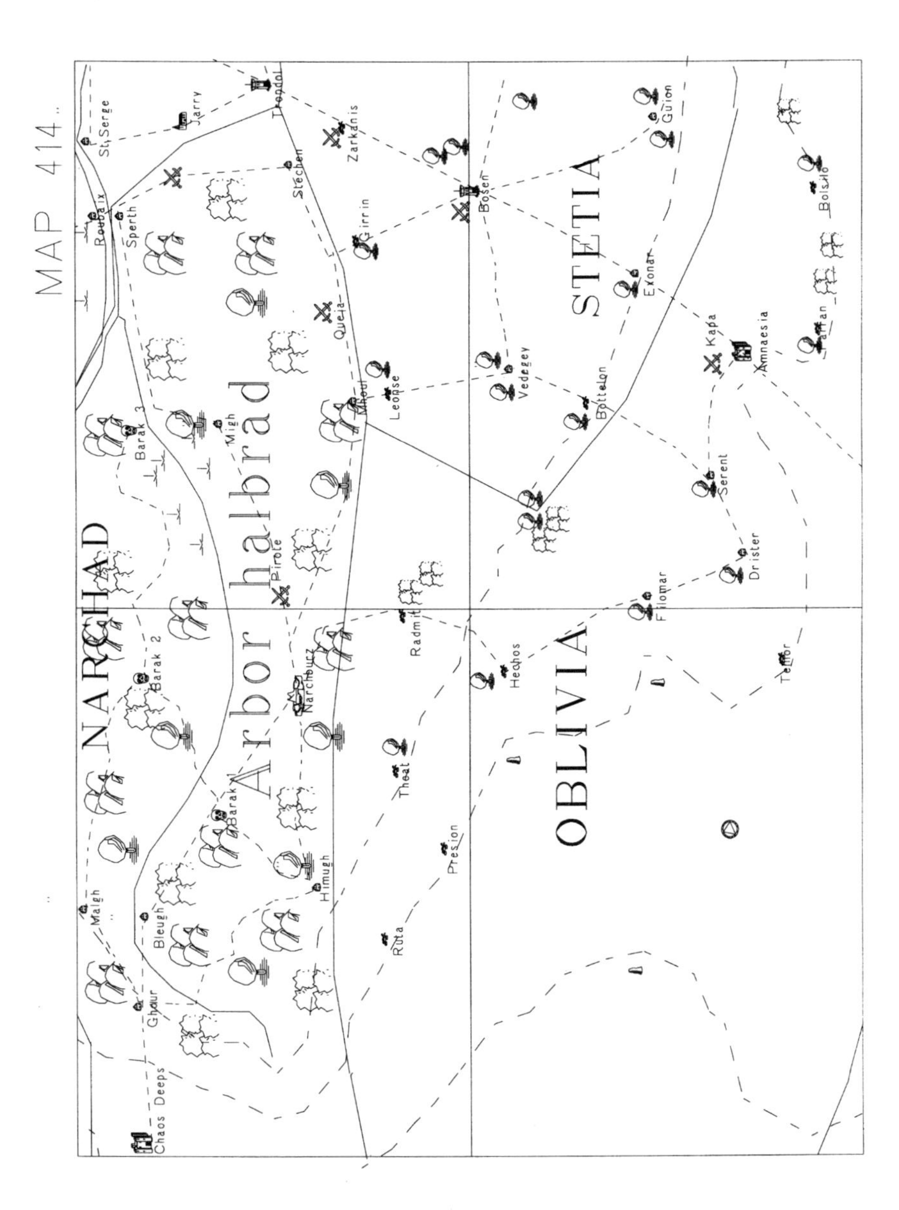

Map Five, Southern Narchad

Prologue

Morgana pulled her fur-lined cloak tighter, she felt cold. Not that it was really cold for this time of year. All her life she had dreamed of riding off, to have adventures, just like those of her heroes, the "Doughty Knights of Renown". Well now she was truly forced to do it. Some desperate and dangerous adventures lay ahead, inconceivable a moon ago. In her daydreams of course, she would start off on the morning of a sunny summer's day. Now here she was, riding through the mud, in the early dark of a Second Moon evening. Her world had been overturned, her life was threatened and unless she intervened, her Aunt Abigail would be burnt! Good kindly Abigail, who lived for her herb garden, and had never been a threat to anyone, to be burnt as a witch! Could they rescue her in time? The Order of St Judas would not be in any great hurry. They had no reason to fear any rescue attempt, as yet. Ahead of her rode Sir Richard Nogent and his crossbowman Bergand. They had patrolled the Arwyn

River for many years. They knew this Bara countryside as well as anyone could, they would not get them lost. No, her fear of failure centred on the nun beside her, Sister Inegal. She knew the whereabouts of the secret prison but would she lead them there? What if she was leading them into a trap? Morgana grimly resolved that if so, the nun would die first.

Adventures were a lot more messy than she had thought. Having often read books and heard bards' tales of "bloody affrays", the shocking events of yesterday had given that term a disquieting new meaning. She shook her head, she was a Lefey, think on the positive side. Had she not organised a successful ambush? Had she not proved her prowess by killing a knight in single combat? Now she led a band of loyal followers to fight for justice, what more could she want? None of the "Doughty Knights of Renown" had had all her advantages–some spells, her father's magic sword, her ever-flowing chalice and the finest steed ever known.

She rode side-saddle on Harold, her blue unicorn's broad back. It was as well old Queen Flacilla had made side saddles the norm for Foixian Ladies. Riding Harold astride, as in the old days, would have presented serious problems, he was just so big. The chalice hung upside down the other side from her, dripping Odki. An ever-flowing chalice presented damp difficulties, when one was on the move. Odki was a fierce pine spirit from the far north. The chalice was slow to produce it here, far from the pine forests. When they stopped to eat, she would command it to produce sweet white wine again. Odki was the rarest drink she could think of. The odd splash would not leave much of a trail. She had to think of such problems, because her six loyal followers would not. Since their loyalty was due to the

Vinkalik, the chalice's magic potion, they accepted her judgements entirely. Unfortunately commanding the magic potion was a slow and uncertain business or she would have tried it on Sister Inegal.

Taglier, the magic sword, hung from her pommel. She would have to get used to wearing its belt and scabbard, illegal or not. Though she had fenced for years in secret, women were not allowed to carry swords. Well now she was going to change a lot of things. Or die in the attempt, which was just as likely. Positive, positive, she reminded herself. On her head she was wearing her new double heart-shaped hennin of purple silk to match her gown.

"You're not wearing that, milady!" the potion-free Margery had exclaimed back at the manor. "Lady Mavys will have apoplexy!"

Indeed her stepmother might be upset and tell her she was too young for anything so imposing, but she was far away up at Valles. An independent Lady Adventuress must surely dress as she wished. The hennin caught what little breeze there was, it was so large. More pins, or perhaps a weight, would be needed for stronger winds.

She was now truly a lady errant. Funny, she had never heard that term before. The troubadours sang of knights-errant but not of ladies-errant. The damsels that sometimes accompanied knights were rated as their not very respectable appendages. Lady Mavys was right in one thing, *Eru* had created a man's world! Lady Mavys had also said that it was a Lady's duty to control and civilise the men in her life. This meant taking as much advantage as possible of the current code of chivalry, in order to aid her designs. This idea had led Morgana to drop the idea of wearing any armour. There had been chain-mail hauberks that she could have worn but she had left them behind. Dressed as a lady, arrows would be aimed at her armoured companions rather than herself. If she wore armour, she was proclaiming herself a warrior. Dressed as a lady, she could be an unpleasant surprise for her enemies. Besides, as she knew from her brother Arthur's experiences, armour was heavy, cold in winter and difficult to look after. Unless treated with dirty oil or grease, it rusted. It would certainly ruin any gown she wore under it.

She heard a laugh from behind her. Minut the Dwarf was joking with Sergeant Hrolf. A most unusual dwarf! The troubadours said that dwarves never laughed. The grim one was her maid Cherry, riding behind her and not appreciating the joke! Cherry was riding Hilda, her other unicorn, to give Dobbin, her normal mount, a rest. Cherry was a young widow with a lot of practical skills. She could cook and wash clothes. And she could haggle with merchants. Morgana had saved her from a very unpleasant future, so her loyalty was undoubted anyway. She would be a great asset in the trials ahead.

So would all her menie she thought, optimism taking over. Sergeant Hrolf was an old soldier, who had taught her and Arthur to fence. Steward of their Manor at Closin, he was married to Margery the cook. Minut, son of Moltin, was a locksmith dwarf from Varadh. Like most dwarves he wore chainmail and he was armed with a large sledgehammer. They all of them knew that it was her family duty to rescue Aunt Abigail and to avenge Arthur's murder. Well, come what may, she would try her best.

Background to the Adventures

Until these adventures began, Morgana Lefey was generally believed to be a well-brought-up damsel of gentle birth. Handsome rather than pretty, with hazel eyes and dark brown hair, her stepmother kept her dressed in the height of fashion. True she was more well built and her waist less slender than the current mode required but she was rated attractive, even without her sizeable dowry. At the court events in Valles, she had always behaved with the appropriate modesty and civility. Little the courtiers knew of the battles her stepmother, Lady Mavys, had to fight to get her appropriately dressed and to keep her from expressing publicly the boredom she often felt. When young, her nurse Christine had regaled her with stories of ancient strife with goblins, monsters and wizards. These tales had fired her imagination, especially when they were confirmed by lays she heard sung by troubadours.

Then she read and re-read many times *Ye deeds of twelve doughty Knights of Renown*–a book from her father's extensive library of nine. She would have liked to have been a knight of renown. It was rotten luck being born a girl. In the Kingdom of Foix, girls were supposed to look pretty and do as they were told. Her father was a knight banneret who had long served the kingdom. He did scouting and intelligence work against the chaotic enemies of Foix. She had asked if she could help him when she got older, several times, but he had just laughed. Ladies did not get involved in such matters, he said. It would be her young brother Arthur, who would get all such fun–plus the family estate as well! Alas, she felt he was too easy-going and, fond as she was of him, stupid! She always beat him at chess and also in most of their secret bouts of sword fencing. He, of course, did not have her motivation for fighting the Chaotics. It was her Grandmother Benedicta, her Uncle Damerus, who had been killed, and her real mother, Lady Berenezia, who had been carried off. Officially the Lady Berenezia was now dead but Morgana thought it possible she was still alive.

Being too young at the time, she could not remember what her mother looked like, but her Aunt Abigail had shown her a view of her in her magic orb. She had long shiny black hair, which, in the Stetian fashion of those times, she wore with one tress down on her left shoulder. Everyone told her that girls did not fight, yet she dreamed she could still "aim at the moon" and change that. One of the "Knights of Renown" had had a sister, Dismalda, who slew one evil villain. Unfortunately she had committed suicide shortly after, which rather spoilt the story. Then she knew there were fighting women in the pagan lands. Belmain had many and there were also the Amazon tribes of Thalia and

Durgan. She had actually seen the Thalian Ambassadress Phaedra at court. She now wore Foixian-style plate armour, rather than the indecently scanty dress of her homeland. Thalia, though in the north, was warmed by igneous heat, which kept its rivers and forests warm. A Lawic land, surrounded by enemies, it supplied most of the silk used in Foix, hence its importance. Morgana's secret hope was that her husband, whichever knight he proved to be, would take her on a mission to avenge the loss of her mother. She had been told often enough that it was the duty of the eldest daughter to marry, to strengthen her family's political connections. She also knew her father was kindly enough to let her have some say in the matter. After all, he held enough lands and was held in enough esteem by King Reginald and his court not to be too ambitious. She believed that in his intelligence work, he was the equal of the "Knights of Renown".

The Lefey family was of the original (big and stupid) Barii people. The founder of their fortune had been Gram Lefey, born around 590ATN[1]. Fighting as a sergeant in the Foixian army, he had had the good fortune to capture a magic sword. This sword, "Taglier", had originally been forged especially for Prince Shazendir Birin of Azelad by the elves at Valhoth. Unfortunately, the rather headstrong Shazendir was killed in a suicidal attack on some Hamorans. A succession of Hamoran officers then carried the sword until Gram killed the last one in an ambush. Already a capable fighter, with this sword he found himself easily

1 ATN stands for After Talarth Narnienor. It was typical of the gloomy elves that they should number the years after a catastrophic Lawic defeat. This had led the loss of central Morval Earth and the formation of the matriarchal Thalian Amazon tribes because their menfolk had been killed in the battle.

cutting swathes through the enemy. For his exploits, King Rutebeuf himself knighted Gram in 615ATN.

Two years later, he obtained the treasure with which to buy the beginnings of the family estate. This was gained in the sack of Sumeer City. Most of it came in a chest belonging to the wizard Denostr. He had owned the luxurious Chateau Mirabelle in the city but had been killed in the assault. Entering the chateau with some soldiers, Sir Gram encountered a Limurian woman, Benedicta. She had been enslaved by Denostr two years earlier. She led Gram up to the strong-room on the third floor and they had forced the door. Inside was a pile of record books, several bags containing money and jewellery (each with a name ticket on it) and a strong chest. One of his men tried to force this open with a crowbar but died in a vivid blue flash. The rest lost interest but Sir Gram reserved the chest for himself. Later, on the advice of a sage, he gained entry into the chest by cutting only at the wooden parts. Inside was a veritable fortune in treasure, a magician's grimoire and also three pieces of palantyteware. These were a portable circular mirror and two orbs, one the size of a Baratrean turnip and the other of a gilden pezzo piece. Sir Gram sold the grimoire to the sage but kept the palantyte pieces. Benedicta fancied the mirror and it seemed a pity to break up the set.

In 622ATN Sir Gram married Benedicta and they bought an estate at Closin in Bara. Their son Alwyn was born in 624. In time he also became a knight. When King Villibert introduced the Register of Arms in 635ATN, they picked the Lefey family device from a cloak of Benedicta's: a purple cloak covered with gold Limuran lilies (*Purpure, Fleury de Lys Or*).

Sir Gram died in a hunting accident in 644. Sir Alwyn

fought in the wars against the Chaotics of Narchad, mainly on the borders of Oblivia and Stetia. After the victory of Zarkanis (650ATN) he was elevated to the rank of knight banneret. Amongst other treasure he gained from the Narchadians was a large magic chalice, the Vinkalik. Not being endowed with magic abilities, he was unable to use it.

In 651 Sir Alwyn married the Stetian Lady Jeningal Senelar. Their son and heir, Daffyd, was born in 652. Sir Alwyn lent the Vinkalik to Jeningal's brother Eusebe, as he had the magic power to use it. As a knight banneret of the Royal Province of Bara, Sir Alwyn bought property in its capital, Charles and a hunting estate at St Visseille. Sir Alwyn and Lady Jeningal had several more children, Phanuel 652, Lothrop 654, Rebecca 657 and Congal in 659. Phanuel and Congal became knights of the watch in Charles, in the service of Basylt Devisage the Royal Seneschal. Lothrop became a cleric of *Eru,* rising to the post of Dean of Charles Cathedral. Rebecca married Sir Achard Hartsel, a Frankish family knight, from the Duchy of Lonnen. Sir Alwyn KB died of a fever in 680ATN. Daffyd had also become a knight, fighting on the Narchadian border. In time he also achieved the rank of knight banneret, as a lieutenant in the Royal Guard. Unlike most of the Royal Guard, who closely attended the king, he was sent on detached service to the most dangerous borders of the realm and its allies.

In 679 he married Lady Berenezia Rasguno, a Stetian, distantly related to his mother Jeningal. A younger sister of Berenezia's, Abigail Rasguno, married one of Sir Daffyd's knights, Sir Damerus Clove at the same time. Lady Abigail had some magical powers and after instruction from the Grand Pheador, could use the turnip-sized palantyte orb, the Cobret as it was known. Originally the Cobret had been a gift from the Elves of Elem Vale to Prince Khazoldir of Azelad. It would alter its temperature to order, and so could be used as a hand-warmer or to cool a bucket of fruit juice. Not capable of transmitting sound, it could exhibit pre-recorded views of events at a word of command. It had a large stock of elfish dance performances for which Lady Abigail had a partiality. The witch Mirziam (who was nasty) had added many unpleasant scenes, most of which the Grand Pheador removed at Lady Abigail's request. Mirziam had tuned the Cobret into her other palantyteware pieces, which she used for spying.

Meanwhile, when Sir Daffyd was away on duty his mother, Lady Jeningal, ruled with a rod of iron at the Closin Manor. The other brothers thus tended to stay at the Mansion in Charles. Lady Berenezia bore Sir Daffyd a daughter, Morgana, in 681. In 683, Narchadians raided Closin. Lady Jeningal, Sir Damerus Clove and twenty others were killed. Lady Berenezia and five other damsels were carried off. The village was burnt but the manor house with Morgana and the family treasures held out. As a result of earlier actions, which had proved the treachery of the Narchadians, offering ransom was forbidden. The Foixian law was that if prisoners were not rescued within a day of capture by Chaotics they were assumed to be dead. After a year they were legally declared dead, forfeiting all their property. Thus in 685 Sir Daffyd married again, this time to Lady Mavys Decret, of a Perigordan family. She bore him a son and heir, Arthur, in 686.

In later years, Sir Daffyd told Morgana that he had married so soon again, especially with the intention of providing her with a mother. She felt that the desire to have a male heir had played a greater part but kept quiet about it. Under the law of male primogeniture, at his birth her stepbrother Arthur became heir to the main family estates. When old enough to understand, she had accepted that this was the normal pattern of things in Foix. Rather more disappointed at the birth of Arthur was his Uncle Sir Phanuel. With Sir Daffyd always involved in dangerous missions, he had had some hopes of succeeding to the estates himself. Though technically Morgana's husband would have held the estates, in fact the number of orphaned young heiresses who actually succeeded in marrying anyone but the Church was small. Sir Phanuel and the other two brothers always carped on about Daffyd being born with a silver spoon in his mouth. They had had to earn their livings by hard work, or so they claimed.

Lady Mavys was always obsessed with the festivities and fashions of the Foixian Court at Valles. She regarded Closin as a rustic backwater in which she had little interest. She found Morgana and Arthur rather a bore to look after, so she left them with servants and relatives whenever possible. This meant they stayed at Closin for most of their younger years. Morgana's Nurse Christine married a miller and her stepmother replaced her with a governess, Ishbel. The Manor at Closin was built of pale greenish-grey limestone, two storeys high. It was surrounded by high stone walls, broken only by a stout gate facing the road. Though not officially fortified, when the gate was barred and the windows were shuttered close raiders had a big job on their hands. Morgana and Arthur were happy enough there. The willow-edged clay fields sloped very gently down to the great River Arwyn, four myles[2] away. It was a very fertile arable area, using a three-year system. Corn was rotated

2 A myle was six arrow flights' long, its actual length differed from province to province.

with root crop and fallow years. The road past the manor was slightly raised by the stone ballast used to surface it. Even so, in wet weather it became very muddy. The landscape for myles around was flat, large arable fields, dotted with small copses of trees and farms. Closin village, a myle to the East was a mixture of brick and wooden huts surrounding the small church. They were all roofed with thatch, made from the excellent reeds, grown along the riverbank. Despite the raid of years ago it was reckoned wealthy, having ten teams of oxen and two windmills. Christine, Morgana's old storyteller, lived in one mill; that is until Morgana was twelve, when Christine died with her baby in childbirth–alas a common fate of women in those days.

Morgana and Arthur often visited their Aunt Abigail at St Visseille. Sir Daffyd had made Abigail chatelaine of this hunting estate after the death of her husband. His brothers had resented this, even though St Visseille was too far from Charles to be convenient for their use. At Closin, when Arthur was five, Sir Daffyd set Sergeant Hrolf to instruct him in sword-fighting and other knightly pursuits. Sergeant Hrolf was often left in command of the manor as steward. Morgana had wanted to learn sword-fighting too! After a fierce campaign against her governess Ishbel, she finally triumphed. Ishbel said Morgana could fence, provided she always remained dressed, as a young lady should. Thus for many years she became her brother's fencing partner early each morning. Because of the age difference, she always won in the early years. Hrolf and Ishbel decided that there was no point in mentioning this practice to Lady Mavys, as such doings might seem strange to her Perigordan eyes.

The children were both taught to ride by Sir Richard Nogent. He was a knight of Sir Daffyd's, often in command of the mounted troop that patrolled the River Arwyn. Unlike in most of the kingdom of Foix, horse-riding was not common in Bara. Even their knights preferred to fight on foot with the infantry. When her horse stampeded once, Morgana shouted, "Cling on!" to herself and realised she was now locked rigidly to the horse until it quietened down. She tried this on other occasions and found it of assistance, especially when jumping obstacles.

Sometimes Morgana was sent to visit her Stetian grandparents, Stenger and Bice Rasguno. They lived at Relajar in Stetia, around fifty myles as the goose flies from Closin. Stenger told her that her mother owned land near Relajar, which he was overseeing. Her mother was probably dead but there was no way of knowing. If she were dead, this land would come to Morgana and any other daughters. Berenezia had left a Stetian Will to this effect on her marriage. She had known that, in Foix and especially in Bara, women could only benefit from land through their fathers or husbands. She hoped to leave a possible escape route to more liberal Stetia for any future daughters. Stenger told her that the land was badly overgrown and the house dilapidated. Around a dozen people worked the land, when it could have supported a hundred.

This was Stetia's great problem, rich land but too few people. For long years they had been afraid of being swamped by the faster breeding Edini races from over the sea. Then again they needed the might of the Edini to keep the Chaotics at bay. Stenger felt their future might rely on the influence of people like Morgana. Being half-Stetii and half-Barii, her blood was wholly of the original inhabitants but her rank meant she could have influence in the immigrant Edini-dominated Kingdom of Foix.The magician, the Grand Pheador, also lived near Relajar in semi-retirement. When Morgana mentioned her clinging ability, he discovered that she had a small amount of magic power (*Magh Pozum*) within her. As a safety measure for these dangerous times, he taught her *Anima Inquisitio*, a spell for indicating hidden beings. On a later visit she brought what she called the "Mirziam" mirror (Mirziam was written on it in runes), and the small palantyte orb. Pheador taught her the spells that would help her use them. With the mirror she could see the view visible to the small orb that Pheador said was called an ochyo. They then discovered they could also tune into Aunt Abigail's Cobret. They found they could communicate by writing messages and holding them in front of the palantyte objects. The mirror's name was Argent and the ochyo's was Gules. Her brother Arthur was very impressed with this. He had been away visiting his mother's family in Perigord, which he found deadly boring. He thought it would be a splendid trick if they could use the Gules ochyo to spy on their uncles at Charles. He succeeded in putting it unnoticed into the decorative wall-carving of the dining hall at the Charles Mansion. In the event, watching their uncles and associates eat soon became boring too, as nothing could be heard of their conversation. But there the ochyo stayed.

From Ishbel and Father Gervase, Morgana was taught the tenets of the Church of *Eru*, or *Arragh* as he was called in the West. *Eru* had long been accepted as the overall deity by most of the peoples of Morval Earth but they tended to worship the *Maghi*, the many minor deities who took an active interest in the activities of the people. The *Maghi* were split between the Chaotics, the Lawics and the Neutrals. The Chaotics followed *Hagoth* who had a creed of "Might is Right", saying the Lawics must be destroyed. The Lawics followed Valarian who had a creed of "Do as you would be done to", saying the Chaotics must be destroyed. The Neutral *Maghi*, had originally belonged to the other creeds but had followed the example of *Baphomet*, *Magho* of magic, who felt his interests were better served by not being involved in the perpetual war between Chaos and Law. These *Maghi* were responsible for the phenomenon of magic, in all its various forms, in Morval Earth. The worshipping of *Eru* had come with the Edini immigrant races from over the Sundering Sea. *Maghi* had not been active where they had come from and they had very little magic. Though their numbers and skill at arms helped them colonise large parts of Morval Earth, they despised and feared the magic of their opponents. By Morgana's day, the Church of *Eru* had a monopoly position in the Kingdom of Foix. Its head, the Monseigneur, had proclaimed that magic should only be practised by members of its Church, other practitioners of magic being declared guilty of witchcraft, in varying degrees. Since members of the Church were barred from marriage, this meant the number of people inheriting magic abilities ever dwindled in Foix. Like all monopolistic Churches, it had had internal disputes and schisms in the past. Theological arguments as to how much *Eru* affected day-to-day life were still continuing. A century ago the Bishopess Barbara of Goujon had written the *Madre Vera* casting doubts on certain Church teachings and claiming that *Eru* was female! She was eventually poisoned and her followers suppressed as heretics. Women were thenceforth banned from full priesthood and the militant order formed by the Monseigneur Judas became a potent force in Foix.

One of the duties of female gentlefolk, according to the Church, was giving aid to the sick and unfortunate in their estate area. Thus Ishbel would take Morgana to give food and other small gifts to the indigent in Closin and its surrounds. One such was Squinty Peg, an old washerwoman who lived at the far end of the village. She had bad rheumatism, making walking and working difficult. She had an acid tongue and the local urchins called her a witch. These urchins, when there was no seasonal work to keep them occupied, would hang around annoying passers-by in the village. From their insults Morgana discovered Lady Mavys was known as "Leafy" and herself as "Leaflette". Ishbel always told her that the ladylike thing to do was to ignore any unpleasant comments or jeering. Morgana found this hard to stomach, especially as they had no trouble whenever a man accompanied them. Even if it was only her brother Arthur! Visits to Squinty Peg were becoming a sore trial. One day they went and were jeered at by four older youths standing behind a pond.

Young Leaflette and her snooty bitch
Sneaking to see bad Squinty the witch
Collecting potions to make her fair
Or evil charms deceitful and rare
Those who have a brimming purse
Need never fear old Squinty's curse

Morgana had had enough and when she left Squinty Peg's she borrowed a stout stick used for stirring the washing in the tub. She held it hidden in the folds of her skirt, away from Ishbel and the youths who repeated their ditty as they walked past. Reaching the haven of the first house past the pond, Ishbel said, "Really, these boys are getting out of control. Poor Peg has much to bear from them. I think we will have to bring a man with us next time."

She turned to look at Morgana but she was not there.

She had doubled round the back of the house to surprise her tormentors. The first had his back to her and she felled him with satisfyingly heavy blows just above his ear.

"You didn't oughta done that, Missie!" said the next youth, brandishing a cudgel and coming towards her. She thrust her stick like a sword at his chest and he was knocked backward, desperately trying to regain his balance. This gave her time to smash the cudgel out of his hand and then beat him on the head. He fell down shielding himself with his hands. The two others behind him, who had been coming up in support, had second thoughts. Morgana ran towards them and they fled.

"Morgana! Come back here! For *Eru's* sake leave such chastisements to your father!" shouted Ishbel.

Morgana stopped, she knew the boys could outrun her anyway. Her first victim still lay insensible but she was tempted to strike another blow at the second one, who was now sitting up. Reading her intention, he held up his hands: "Pax, Lady."

"Peg is not a witch, she is just a poor old woman!"

"Anything you say, Lady Morgana."

"Pax then." She took the stick back to Squinty Peg's and rejoined Ishbel. Ishbel gave her a lengthy scold for behaviour both unladylike and foolhardy. But the urchins never taunted her again!

Father Gervase, the village priest was more sympathetic about her action. "It is well seen the blood of the Lefeys flows in your veins. I fancy *Eru* made you an instrument of his power in correcting those lads."

He often read extracts to Morgana and Arthur from the *Tome of Eru*, the Church's authorised book of guidance and information. Hearing the Church's policy on magic, they kept very quiet about the enchanted family heirlooms and

Morgana's powers. She asked the priest why, when most of their allies fighting the Chaotics used magic, the Church was objecting to it.

"The Church believes that only its own members have the moral wisdom to use it properly."

"But my father says the Sages of Faralon and the Wizards of Stetia have often contributed much to aid our cause."

"But these are from pagan lands, as yet unresponsive to the *Eru's* message. Our King allies with them as a matter of expediency. In time we hope they will come to our way of thinking."

"What if their great wizards come into Foix on business? Are they then accused of witchcraft?"

"No, provided they keep our laws and do not try to corrupt our people with their ways. They tend not to spend long here anyway. There is a debate in the Church at present, deciding on whether to accept some of the Lawic *Maghi*, as Saints."

"Which ones?" asked Arthur. His knowledge of the *Maghi* was limited to the evil ones in Christine's goblin stories.

"*Doucer* of just rewards, *Prudella* of marriage and *Tennorito* of duty."

"If some, why not all?" asked Morgana.

Father Gervase laughed. "The objective is to use temples of these *Maghi* to spread the word of *Eru* in lands like Stetia and Fara. The other *Maghi* are not amenable to the Church's doctrines."

Morgana forbore to question further, for she knew Gervase was a good man. However, she also knew her Stetian relatives had strongly different views on the importance of the *Maghi*, and the magic they controlled.

The Vinkalik and the shimmering gowns

In 697ATN when Morgana was sixteen, she again went to Relajar, for her Grandfather Stenger's funeral. Her Uncle, Quixano Rasguno, was elected Hidalgo of Relajar in his place. Knowing of her magic talent, he sent her to try and use the Vinkalik chalice. This had remained unused for years since the death of Eusebe. It had been put in the care of the Great Pheador but he had not dared to use it. He knew its history, which he imparted to Morgana. It, along with a quantity of lesser chalices, had been created by Alikaar, a devotee of *Bakkup*, the *Magho* of Intoxicating Pleasures, with Paschil an elf silversmith from Belmain. Alikaar lived in Chaotic Koboldin, at a time when Belmain was still a Lawic Elf Kingdom. Paschil was a slave who had been captured in a raid. Alikaar made the chalice for his favourite apprentice, Lilhaar. Lilhaar had little magic talent, so apart from its other attributes, the

Vinkalik was also a talisman, bestowing additional magic powers when held. Later Lilhaar was killed and the chalice fell into the hands of the Belmainian elfess, Morazia, Countess of Osiwile. The chalice accepted her as its new master and she added some refinements to its attributes. The wise say she was cursed to do so by *Bakkup.* At that time, as ever, there was friction between the dwarves of Varadh and the elves of Belmain (and elves everywhere else). A Nuncio of *Valarian* had the good intention of trying to improve these matters. He suggested that a Youth Festival be arranged between an equal number of elves and dwarves, with none to be over the age of 100 years, in order to ensure friendship for the future. The Kings of Belmain and Varadh grudgingly agreed to this, restricting the numbers to fifty each and putting Countess Morazia in charge. She had all the participants drink out of the ever-flowing Vinkalik. The result was that the elves and dwarves fell madly in love with one another and demanded to be married! After around fifteen years of dispute, they were allowed to do so, on condition that they be exiled to a wild part of Oblivia. This happening was of great shame to both dwarves and elves, who would prefer to forget all about it. And, forget the existence of the *Dwelf* descendants of the festival-goers! The Elf King confiscated the Vinkalik from Countess Morazia and had her dispossessed of her magic powers. Later when Belmain fell to the Chaotics, Morazia led some renegade elves who had accepted Chaotic rule. She is still, to this day, Countess of Osiwile in Belmain. The Vinkalik was taken by the Chaotics when Belmain fell. It changed hands several times before Sir Alwyn captured it in Narchad. Eusebe had used it sparingly, in cases of need only. The Grand Pheador warned Morgana that, if she tried to use the chalice's powers as a talisman and it rejected her, there could be nasty or even fatal consequences. It was known to accept neutral magicians, as with Countess Morazia. As a talisman, it enabled the use of a few spells up to the third level, provided it was held at the time of use and added one MPU (*Magh Pozum Ulse* or Magic Power Units) to the caster's talent per two hundred heartbeats. Its main attribute was that it constantly refilled itself, drawing constituents from the atmosphere. The liquid could be changed on the word of Command (*Mando*) though quality and actual success was variable. Also additions of natural or even magic potions could be inserted into the current beverage in the chalice. These were dependent upon the level and skill of the Vinkalik's master. Being headstrong and imbued with the confidence of youth, Morgana decided to demand the chalice accept her. Assisted by the Grand Pheador, she did gain acceptance and found her magic powers augmented, as long as she held the chalice.

Sir Daffyd took steps to provide her with a dowry, ready in trust for when she married. The main part was an estate called The Green Mill fields, with two ox teams, twenty-three villeins and eight free tenants, plus the mill itself. Also in the dowry was ownership of a street in Charles called Cabbage Lane. She started to take a proprietary interest in the Green Mill Fields, which were only five myles from Closin. She got to know the people there, her people. Cabbage Lane, however, was in a seedy part of the city and she was not allowed to go near it. Her Uncle Phanuel had the stewardship of it and was supposed to forward the rents to Closin every year. He received payment for the stewardship but everyone suspected he was withholding some of the rent money for himself. However, Sir Daffyd was very easy-going about monetary affairs, to the despair of his mother whilst she was still alive. The Closin Manor's affairs were rather neglected. Lady Mavys could have taken much more interest but she was always away at the Valles Court. She owned a small mansion in the city and her dowry estate was only a day's ride away. With Sir Daffyd usually away on duty and Arthur still a minor, Father Gervase, the village priest, kept the estate accounts. The rents for Morgana's dowry went into a separate chest, with "Lady Morgana Lefey's Dowry" inscribed on its brass plaque. This had occasioned argument with her stepmother. She maintained (correctly) that the "Morgana" was not needed as she was the eldest (and only) daughter. Morgana felt it was more personal to have her own name on it. After all there had been other Lady Lefeys, her Aunt Rebecca in Lonnen for one. Morgana kept on good terms with Father Gervase. He taught her something of keeping accounts and caring for the estate's people. He was a bit conservative in his thought, so she kept quiet about her fencing and of course anything connected with magic. The magic items had always been kept secret in Foix.

Later Morgana and her father visited the Lefey Mansion at Charles. Her father had a few weeks' leave from his missions and felt duty-bound to visit his relations. Unfortunately he fell out with his brothers–first a big argument with Lothrop, at that time a canon of *Eru*, who did not believe Foix should be allied to any races not devoted to *Eru*. Then he caught Sir Phanuel and Squire Congal taking a bribe to let a merchant go free of a breach of the peace charge. Sir Daffyd was scandalised and said such happenings were a dishonour to the family. Phanuel told him not to be so archaic, the merchant was innocent anyway! He had been in the wrong place at the wrong time. Morgana never really liked Sir Phanuel. The servants had told her that he had been forced to marry Ava, the daughter of a Master Armourer, on the orders of Queen Flacilla. This had been in 680 and both mother and baby had died in childbirth three months later. He always treated Morgana as just another mouth to feed. Canon Lothrop was a cold calculating man, who watched more than he spoke. Squire Congal dressed smartly and was always ready to try and impress others with his own wit and cleverness. You can pick your friends but not your family, thought Morgana.

Then at the market, Morgana caught a woman stealing a scoop of salt from a stall. She used her cling spell to hold onto her. A soldier of the watch then took hold of the thiefess until Squire Congal arrived. He said he would take her and the salt for "due process of law". The salt-seller objected to his salt being taken away from his stall. A stout woman said that "due process of law" would best be seen in daylight. Women were safer a week in the pillory than in the squire's office! Congal said hanging or imprisonment, at the very least, was likely to be the criminal's fate. Furthermore, if Madam did not move on, he would arrest her as an accomplice. Morgana by now was regretting she had caught the woman. Fortunately at that moment Sir Daffyd arrived. Listening to the entreaties of his daughter, he paid the salt-seller to drop the charge. Then they brought the woman back to the mansion for questioning. Her name was Cherry and she had been a peasant living near Firmaz. Four years ago she had been carried off in a Narchadian raid in which her husband and baby son had been killed. She had become the slave of a warrior, Paedlok, living in the Arbor Deowyn near Wassugh. Some weeks ago there had been a big fight between two factions there. She had fled into the forest and escaped. Whilst there, she had learnt a bit about the edible plants of the area from the other women, as well as how to trap small animals and birds so she could feed herself. She managed to paddle across the great River Arwyn on a log. When, after more adventures she reached her old home, she found it occupied. Her husband's brother had sold it and the crop strips to a couple with five children. As they quickly explained, she had no claim, as she was officially dead! She decided to go to Charles to plead for restitution from the Royal Seneschal of Bara there. However, the Podesta (magistrate) who heard her case said nothing could be done. If she wanted an occupation, the streetwalkers' guild could enrol her or else the Church was always needing assistants for the Leper Hospital. Revolted, she had decided to try for a job as a cook but needed wares to prove her skill. Hence the theft of the salt, her money being long exhausted.

Morgana felt very sorry for her, especially as her own mother had been carried off to Narchad. She asked that Cherry be taken on as a maidservant. She could be useful helping in the kitchens and she herself was now of an age when she should have a maidservant. She would guarantee her good behaviour and loyalty. (In this she had in mind the Vinkalik's Devotion Elixir, of which her parents were still unaware.) Sir Daffyd agreed, though his brothers were plainly against the idea. Back at Closin, Cherry soon proved her worth as a cook and maidservant. Better, she told Morgana that she thought her mother might still be alive in Narchad. A Stetian woman called Berenezia had been in the train of the mighty General Branamog, when he had visited Wassugh two years ago. Morgana secretly experimented with the Vinkalik to produce the Devotion Elixir in some good wine. After ten days, she was satisfied that the elixir was ready. At the time there was a dwarf locksmith putting new improved locks on the doors of the fortified manor. It seemed a good idea to ensure that the dwarf be made loyal to her, in order to help maintain the future security of the manor. Her plan was to give the elixir to Cherry, the dwarf and her governess Ishbel. Ishbel was getting to be a bit of a problem. She had long regretted allowing the fencing practice and was forever nagging about how a young lady should behave. However, when Morgana went down to the dwarf (Minut son of Moltin), he was joking with Sergeant Hrolf, Sir Richard Nogent and Bergand, a crossbowman of his who had just ridden in. They immediately demanded a drink too and she could not think of any excuse to stop them.

"Aha, one of those conjurers ever-flowing cups, I see," said Sir Richard, impressed. "That will be from your Stetian relatives no doubt. They do not make anything useful like that here in Bara."

From their later attitude, asking permission to do things and eventually to return to their duties, it was obvious that the elixir had worked–on all, that is, except her governess, Ishbel. She now seemed to have acquired an acute dislike of Morgana. Three days later she left, going to seek another post in Valles. Later, when Lady Mavys got word that Ishbel had left, she ordered Morgana to go to stay with her grandmother's Senelar relatives.

One of Sir Daffyd's officers in the Royal Guard was Sir Peter Volent and he suggested that his son, Squire Peregrine, might be a suitable groom for Morgana. Accordingly, some months later, Lady Mavys and Morgana undertook a ceremonial visit to Lady Rolinda and her son Peregrine at Decame in Perigord. Morgana had already received two pages of poetry praising her dignity, gentleness and beauty! She would have appreciated it more had it born some resemblance to her actual character and appearance. Squire Peregrine was a slender fair-haired youth who would obviously have preferred to be a troubadour or an artist. Many of the castle internal walls were adorned with landscape scenes, painted by the lad when he should have been training to be a knight. However, he had a very showy suit of armour and made the mistake of trying to impress Morgana with his fencing skills by using them against two of his retainers. Morgana watched this with an expert eye and soon realised the retainers were only managing to lose with difficulty. She started to criticise and tell Peregrine how he should fence. Peregrine, now rather hot in his armour and a bit nettled, said the fatal words, "This is a man's skill, I doubt your brother would allow such carpings at his practice!"

Morgana thereupon snatched one of the wooden swords from one of the retainers and assumed the on-guard position. "My brother *really* knows how to fence! If you want to know how, I will show you how he does it."

"It is not the part of a gentleman to cross swords with a lady," said Peregrine haughtily. However, several sharp blows that left his helmet ringing enraged him enough to change his mind. Lady Mavys, who had been deep in conversation with Peregrine's mother, only now realised what was going on. Her aghast entreaties went unheeded. Morgana speedily achieved six hits on the squire and broke his sword, before she drew away.

"You knew I could not strike a woman," said the outclassed Peregrine, whereupon the retainers and a host of other servants who "just happened to be in the area" burst out laughing.

"Sir, fencing the way you do, you would not hit *anyone* in a serious fight."

"Morgana! How dare you! Come away at once!" shrieked her stepmother.

Poor Peregrine retired humiliated and Morgana got a fine row for her behaving like a hoyden. This was the first inkling Lady Mavys had that Morgana could use a sword. "A useful skill for soldiers no doubt but none whatsoever for a lady!" she said. "No wonder your embroidery work is so poor if that has been how you have been wasting your time."

They left for Valles the next day! Squire Peregrine was sent to polish up his military training with the citadel guard at Signy. There he wrote books of poetry about his hopeless passion for the beautiful and unattainable constable's wife. (She thought him an utter bore but was too polite to tell him so. Her husband thought it a splendid joke and kept all his friends up, on the latest instalments.)

To avoid awkward questions about the proposed match, Morgana was sent to stay with her mother's brother, the Hidalgo Quixano. He had ambitions to become a Peron and was now living at the Stetian Fortress Court of Bosen, where he was secretly involved with the Stetian Foreign Affairs Chapter. He felt Morgana could well be useful to him in the future, for assisting Stetian affairs of state. He instructed her on the current political situation, as seen through Stetian eyes. With Prince Reginald, the then heir to the Foixian Throne, married to the Stetian Lady Bettrys, relations with Foix were improving immensely. The main Chaotic armies were retreating from distant Hunara and the Narchadians were quiet, having quarrelled with their Belmainian ally. Don Quixano's wife Hesqueza, like Lady Mavys, was more concerned with court entertainments and fashions. Morgana had hoped to learn more magic from the Grand Pheador but he had died after a long illness.

Cortivan the Nizandor of Oblivia, had settled the despised Dwelfs at a place they called Amnaesia. He ensured they received ample food supplies to keep them quiet. However, they resented the way they were patronised by the other Oblivians and even more by the attitudes of the Elves and Dwarves. They wanted to achieve some feat that would make their race known and respected throughout Morval Earth. Their numbers were very small, so this was going to be difficult. However, their leader, Count Ruffin, thought he had a solution. The Elves of the vast area called Elvenor were cut off from those in Valinor by the Erde Khazed Mountains. There was some contact maintained by magical means and by the flying peoples of Venditara but trade and military assistance were impractical.

Count Ruffin suggested they tunnel through the mountains to the Elf Kingdom of Imlinead. Some thought this much too ambitious, as the distance was over a hundred myles! However, the Nizander was enthusiastic and offered them every assistance in his power. It was certainly a project that would keep them busy and away from the eyes of the world. He emphasised that the project should be kept secret and it became known as the Hidden Way. In fact it kept the Dwelfs busy for 143 years. They used the excavated stone to make Amnaesia into a mighty fortress city.

Early on in the tunnelling, they struck a vein of Schmerite rock. Produced by *Maghi* interference in the geological processes of forming Morval Earth, it had a property which produced a shimmering light. This light tended to go out after being exposed to the air for a time but could be recalled by a word of command. Then it would stay glowing as long as the variable ambient magic in the Morval Earth air allowed it to. The Dwelfs realised that here was an easy means of illuminating the tunnel. Earlier, they were expecting to use a variety of luminous fungus but this was smelly and did not give as much light. The word of command was standardised to the Simnith (New Originali as opposed to Quenith, Ancient Originali) "*Shimmer*!" and the rock was chipped into pieces of a suitable size.

After some years, an Ombardi trader called at Amnaesia. He normally bought the spices, drugs and perfumes for which Oblivia was famous but always had an eye for any other marketable goods. On the off-chance he bought some mule-loads of the discarded fine chippings of Schmerite. These he sold to the Wizard Gingillo at Exonar in Stetia. Gingillo had weak powers and was more of a conjuror than a serious magician. He thought he saw possibilities of making money with this magic substance. After a series of experiments, he discovered that by heating the rock in a certain liquid (almost certainly vinegar), it would turn into a soluble sludge that could be added to cloth dyes. Cloth so dyed would produce the same shimmering light as the rock, only for a considerably shorter time. Aiming high, Gingillo dyed some bales of the finest Oblivian silk, which he sold to a leading Bosen dressmaker. The resultant gowns immediately became the height of fashion for formal events. Every lady *had* to have one and the demand was so great that other dressmakers had to be enrolled.

Keeping his source secret, Gingillo imported more of the Schmerite chippings, intent on making his fortune. Used on silk, the Schmerite caused liquids to run straight off the material, in other words making it rain proof. The gowns kept selling and after two years a shimmering gown became the national dress for Stetian Ladies. The command "*Shimmer*" was used so often, it became an automatic minor expletive for those wearing the gowns. The shimmering was then found to have another facet. Two ladies and their gentlemen escorts went for a picnic beside a stream. After lunch, the two men went fishing upstream, whilst the ladies did some embroidery.

"*Shimmer*, those are aughed!"

"*Shimmer*! So they are!"

Four aughed or dark goblins, rushed to attack them but it became obvious the shimmering gowns were distracting them. Though only armed with a piece of driftwood and an eating knife, the ladies killed one aughed, stunned another and drove the two others away. After this, there was some talk of Stetian Officers having their armour covered in the shimmering silk. Unfortunately for Gingillo's hopes of an even larger fortune, the first man to wear shimmering clothes was a noted Pansy. None of the other men wanted to look anything like *him*!

In Bosen, Morgana bought a pink gown and several ells of the shimmering silks to make others for herself and her stepmother. She had heard that Princess Bettrys had spread the fashion to Valles, the royal capital of Foix. Around this time Squire Congal was knighted by Basylt Devisage, then the Royal Seneschal of Bara.

The Court at Valles and the year of change, 702ATN

After a reign of fifty years, King David III of Foix died of a fever. Lady Mavys ordered Morgana and Arthur to come to attend the coronation of Prince Reginald with her. As usual Sir Daffyd was away on duty on the Narchad border. The two Lefey ladies were at the forefront of Valles fashion. Much envied by the many great ladies, whose useless husbands and fathers had not been able to get the shimmering silk in time. Morgana stayed at Valles for a year and met Queen Bettrys and her fifteen-year-old daughter Princess Maudette. She still practised her fencing exercises whenever possible–usually whilst her stepmother was still in bed!

One of Lady Mavys' closest friends was Lady Jocette Tancreton, who suggested that her son, Sir Reginald, could be a match for Morgana. Sir Reginald *was* an able sword-fighter and had had noted successes at jousting tournaments. Morgana found his polite coolness to her an irresistible challenge. Their mothers threw them together for around two months and had lawyers drawing up the dowry settlements. Alas it was not to be. Sir Reginald retired to his castle with the true love of his life, Lady Myrtle Suivant. Lady Myrtle's husband, Sir Hildric, took a large force to besiege the castle. Morgana thought her heart was broken! Should she cast herself from the city battlements, or retire to a convent? Perhaps if Lady Myrtle died young, he might return to her? No, it was too obvious, she had just been used as a smokescreen to distract attention from his meetings with Myrtle. It was so humiliating. Now she was wanting Sir Hildric to chop Sir Reginald into small pieces! And Lady Myrtle as well! Alack, after six weeks, with winter coming and scant finances, Sir Hildric had to abandon the siege. His errant wife sent him a poem.

Once I was awed by a Lord who snored
Even in accord with a Lord who snored
Was to him my guardian's wedded reward
Though he knew not that the Lord snored
Alas for speaking he was not too forward
I soon became bored with the Lord who snored
But then I found a better man, one I adored
Farewell, farewell, to the Lord who snored!

He then applied to the Monseigneur Gerald, head of the Church of *Eru*, for a divorce. After five months of argument and a lot of money, this was refused!

Meanwhile Morgana was hurt and not a little embarrassed. Sir Daffyd joined them for a while and decided to buy her two rare blue unicorns to cheer her up. Another of Lady Mavys' friend's son had married a Lady Palida from Tyron on the edge of the Arbor Deowyn forest. She had met and tamed a pair of the blue unicorns found in that area a few years ago. When her marriage was arranged to be held in the royal capital, she thought it would be a splendid publicity coup if she and her groom could ride from the service on these exotic beasts. Morgana met her and visited the beasts several times. Their names were Harold and Hilda. What the Lady Palida had not bargained for was that unicorns would not allow men to ride them (as a result of a whim of *Polymorphia*, *Magha* of Monsters, but it's a long story!). At the first attempted rehearsal, her unfortunate groom was thrown, breaking an arm and a leg. Palida tried to whip Harold in her anger, but he knocked her over. The trust between them was gone and she never tried to ride them again. They remained in the stables day after day looking miserable, where Morgana and other damsels sometimes visited them. Palida put them up for sale but ladies with the courage and ability to ride such large beasts were few. When Sir Daffyd bought them, the price had dropped to almost reasonable. In the event they did take Morgana's mind off her romantic troubles, as she rode them slowly back to Closin. In their way, they were far more intelligent than horses and she came to realise that when they snorted in a certain way it meant NO! Also there was no changing their minds. Lady Palida had trained Harold to hunt deer for her. Unlike horses, blue unicorns were not wholly herbivores. She would dismount, point at the prey and whisper, “Deer,” and the unicorn would charge and transfix it on its horn. During the journey, Sir Daffyd told Morgana that he had confirmed that her mother was indeed held by the Narchadian, Lord Branamog. He was very sorry but there was nothing they could do about it. He thought it better not to mention it to Lady Mavys or Page Arthur. He was most impressed by Morgana’s fencing ability and laughed when he heard of the Peregrine episode. Nevertheless he said it would be best to keep such activity secret for fear of being labelled eccentric. It seemed to be keeping her figure trim so she had as well keep it up.

Sir Daffyd disappeared off on his missions again and Arthur did a tour of duty with Sir Peter Nogent and the river patrol. He was now promoted from Page to Squire and felt very important. Morgana took the unicorns to show off to her Aunt Abigail at St Visseille. Abigail spent most of her time in a large herb garden she managed there. She carried out experiments, cross-pollinating plants, and recording the results in ledgers. With this and the Cobret orb’s entertainments, she lived in a dream world of her own. She had strong magical powers but she had studied little concerning their potential. Morgana eventually talked Abigail into riding Hilda on a promise that they would not go faster than a walk. Morgana tried Palida’s hunting trick with Harold and bagged a rabbit! Arthur joined them and was green with envy with regard to the great unicorns. Eventually she had to stable them at Closin and return to her stepmother at Valles. When she arrived there, the news had just broken that Prince Eudes[3] had won his great victory

3 Prince Eudes was the son of Prince Moro, brother of King Reginald.

at Lungstrete. The Chaotic armies of the Northwest had been shattered. The war would soon be over for a while. Lady Mavys brightened up. With the veterans of the war returning, she could surely find a husband to get Morgana off her hands. If only her own husband would get a job at court and stop gallivanting off to wild foreign places! She was even ready to accept a Stetian husband for her stepdaughter. After all she was half Stetian. (She did not know Don Quixano had already "discouraged" three potential swains of Morgana's. *He* wanted her to marry an influential Foixian, as a source of information and influence.) Much as she cared for her, Lady Mavys felt Morgana was best taken in small doses. She had too much energy and asked too many searching questions. Worst, she did not seem terribly interested in the matters of fashion and scandal that obsessed Lady Mavys and her friends. She knew Morgana was still doing her silly fencing exercises, when she got the chance. She just did not seem interested in ladylike pursuits like embroidery and playing the harp.

The Royal family went to Naigre Manor for a holiday. Many other courtiers also returned to their estates for a break. In Valles, preparations began for the great victory feasts, which would be held when Prince Eudes returned with the Foixian army. Then they heard the incredible news. King Reginald and Queen Bettrys had been murdered, at Naigre Manor! Princess Maudette, daughter of Queen Bettrys and her first husband, Don Estival Lurte, had been taken into Church care, "to be treated for certain ailments of the soul". On top of that, the Bishop of Chantilly, Herbert Longuard, had disappeared. A score of servants of the court and one of the murderers had also been killed. Chancellor of Foix, Stefan Complan, declared martial law and went to Naigre "to make safe the Royal Regalia". After a few days, the Monseigneur Gerald had a proclamation read out in the streets, saying:

> The Order of St Judas has made an arrest of the witch Maudette of Stetia. Unfortunately her witchcraft involved summoning evil elements, who have taken advantage of her ailments of the soul, with the consequent heavy loss of lives, including our beloved King. The Church believes the witch Maudette responsible and will try her as soon as a Court can be assembled.
>
> Eru preserve us all

Prince Moro at Ekthalon received information that the chancellor had been embezzling the kingdom's taxes and was probably implicated in the murders. He ordered Redibert, Duke of Rathen to arrest him. Redibert gathered others to his side and took the citadel by surprise. Both Redibert and Stefan and also the latter's wife Liligild were killed in the fighting. Lady Mavys kept Morgana indoors with the shutters up whilst all this was happening. Bertrans FitzBorne, the Fortress Inspector Royal, assumed control in Valles. He declared himself "Grand Duke Regent of Foix", holding the kingdom in trust for Princess Maudette who was only sixteen.

At the Church Court, the Bishop of Chantilly, supported by a Lady Pattipan, testified that Maudette was indeed guilty of black witchcraft. Her mother, the late Queen, had been consulting with him about the matter, that very week. Maudette's spells had induced innocent bystanders to attack savagely the Church's officers at great cost to themselves. Sir Obedience, a Knight of the Order of St Judas, testified that it had been as the holy Bishop said and that his witch-finding orb had glowed its brightest ever when he held it next to Maudette. She was sentenced to be burnt the next day. Strangely this was not done publicly and for some years there was a rumour that she was still held in Church custody. The Grand Duke declared the day she was due to be burnt a public holiday of celebration. The bells rang and the Church had oxen roasted in the streets with free portions for all, washed down with Church ale. As a result of this the Stetian ambassador and other leading Stetians left for home. Nine days later, Stetia declared war on Foix, demanding the immediate release of Princess Maudette. They were sent a casket of ashes!

Suddenly it was felt unwise to wear shimmering gowns or to own anything smacking of witchcraft in Valles. It was most unfashionable to be connected with anything Stetian for a while. Basylt Devisage, Royal Seneschal of Bara wrote to the Monseigneur, claiming the throne of Foix by right of his wife Disildt, sister of the late King. Prince Moro also wrote to the Monseigneur, saying that burnt or not, Princess Maudette had not been heiress to the throne. As only *brother* to Reginald, he was the rightful heir and was summoning the "Grand Duke Regent" to Ekthalon to explain himself.

Instead, Bertrans gathered an army of supporters and retired to his fortress at Hetchy. Sir Daffyd and his men left the Narchad border and reported to Prince Moro at Ekthalon. The remaining courtiers and the City Council of Valles felt that despite these disputes, they were duty-bound to give Prince Eudes and his returning army the celebrations they deserved. Preparations went ahead, led by Sir Siegfried, Master of Revels. There was to be a troop of maidens of gentle birth, throwing flowers around Prince Eudes, to be led by one holding a wreath of laurels to place on his brow. Lady Mavys was very angry to discover that at twenty-one years, Morgana was declared too old to be included. Morgana was less concerned as it indicated her mature status. It gave her the justification to start wearing head-dresses, though her stepmother would only allow the simplest as yet. Morgana had realised that status amongst the ladies of the court was measurable by the size of their hennins. Moreover, her own dull dark brown hair was a disappointment to her. She had always preferred the glossy black, native to Stetia. She did not miss anything anyway.

The head of the troop of maidens would originally have been Princess Maudette and competition was hot to replace her. Sir Siegfried, in his wisdom, selected a far from respectable person called Imagela as wreath-placer. Imagela[4] had been accompanying the victorious army. The maidens of gentle birth all resigned in protest! Unfortunately there were droves of far more beautiful maidens, eager to replace them. This was unkindly referred to by one city alderman as the "rout of the horse-faces". Meanwhile Morgana was a little uneasy. Having met Princess Maudette and having her own "secret witchcrafts" she felt insecure. Father Gervase wrote that Basylt Devisage had requisitioned large amounts of food supplies from the estate at Closin, ostensibly to stock the fortresses for the war with Stetia. Arthur was again with the forces watching the river. Everyone knew that really the Stetians were in no condition to make a serious attack on Bara. Such food stocks were really for the expected war with Moro and Bertrans. At Valles, the arrival of Prince

4 After causing several scandals, Lady Imagela would be sent to accompany Sir Hans Neuman and a party of other undesirables, on a suicidal quest to find a palantyr in the Chaotic lands to the west.

Eudes' army caused a change of mood. The soldiers had lived long in distant lands and were now a law unto themselves. The clergy and lawmen glowered and there were many bloody incidents. The Monseigneur Gerald was constrained to make a proclamation that "all good peoples should realise that the Church, the city and the army were all on the same side!" The agents of the witch-hunting Order of St Judas were constrained to moderate their activities for a while. As soon as the victory celebrations were over, Morgana returned to Closin to keep out of the public eye. Father Gervase had also been impressed by the unicorns. He came to the manor whenever Arthur was present if possible. "I had read that Saint Fabiola had a blue unicorn but I never expected to really see one. *Eru* forgive me for my lack of faith, I doubted that part of the tale."

"Who was St Fabiola?" asked Morgana, interested in any other owner of unicorns.

"She was a lady who lived alone in the Arbor Deowyn and founded the Order of Anchoresses."

"What are Anchoresses? Female anchors?" inquired Squire Arthur. His experience on the river patrol meant he knew what an anchor was.

"Anchoresses are female anchorites, holy persons who live alone."

Arthur's interest evaporated.

"The Church prefers such women to go into convents but St Fabiola made the case for allowing solitary women to tend shrines. Some have been sent to the pagan lands to preach *Eru's* message. The Saint and her unicorn died long ago."

Early next year, Moro had himself crowned "King of Thentis" at Ekthalon! The majority of the Foixian Lords backed him. Only Bertrans and Basylt held against him.

However, he did not wish to fight his sister Disildt in Bara and he wanted to escape the close scrutiny of the Monseigneur in Perigord. So Moro allowed these two provinces to go their own way. In Ekthalon and Borolon, he had two of the wealthiest cities in Morval Earth and expected Valles to become a provincial backwater. The Monseigneur Gerald died of a stroke on hearing that the Archbishop of Ekthalon had crowned Moro! By the end of the year, Herbert Longuard, the Bishop of Chantilly, was elected in his place. He negotiated a peace settlement with the Stetians. Queen Bettrys had been a devotee of the *Magho Doucer* and as part of a deal, a church to St Doucer was built in memorial to her at Naigre, which thereafter adopted that name. Apart from some small raids, more to do with personal feuds, there had been no fighting. The Lefey family were now ruled by Basylt Devisage, *Grand Duke* of Bara, though Lady Mavys preferred to remain a national of Perigord. Sir Daffyd, meanwhile, was employed by King Moro, as a mercenary. Moro posted him to the small forces left watching the Limuran Elysian border, where he resumed his intelligence-gathering role.

Morgana visited both Aunt Abigail and her Senelar relatives in Stetia and then returned to Closin once again. Despite Uncle Phanuel's short change, her dowry chest now held well over 2,000 gilden pezzi. The harvest had been good and despite Basylt's depredations the people at Closin were prospering and happy.

In 704 the citadel well at Ekthalon became polluted and King Moro, Queen Ernestine and many of the Court died. Prince Eudes was crowned King of Thentis. Not being a Thentian subject, Morgana did not attend the coronation. Instead she visited her Uncle Quixano, again at Bosen. He was expecting to be elected to a first year as a Peron soon and again discussed the political situation with her. He told her that if she was willing, he expected to be able to employ her magical talents, for the good of Stetia. Morgana said she would consider any proposal at the time, as long as it did not mean acting against her own people. She was feeling unsettled. There did not seem to be any more suitors for her hand at present. She helped her brother and Father Gervase to run the estate and this gave her some interest. She still fenced with Arthur and he was winning more often now. Eventually she knew he would marry and his wife would take precedence over her at Closin. She hoped that Quixano's offer, when it came, would provide her with something interesting and challenging to do. She often thought of her own mother and wondered if there could be any way of rescuing her. Narchad was in turmoil at present, because one of its Lords had kidnapped Queen Gimawl, one of King Grocus of Belmain's six surviving consorts. She had been eventually returned but relations between the two Chaotic states were severely strained.

Exciting Times

In the second moon of 706ATN, Litwe the messenger brought a letter from her Uncle Peron Quixano:

Dearest Niece,

I have need of your assistance. We know of your mirror Argent, which belonged to the witch Mirziam. We know of the Cobret, owned by Abigail and of the ochyo Gules, which has been in the Lefey Mansion at Charles. We know all this and this is a state Secret, because we have Mirziam's master mirror Or. We know the whereabouts of most of her other ochyos but do not possess any of them. We have a most urgent need of at least one. We are offering to pay 1,000 gilden pezzi each for them.

Your devoted Uncle, Quixano Rasguno

She discussed this with Arthur. They had not been to the Charles Mansion since the Cherry incident. It could be tricky to recover the ochyo. Dangerous too, if Deacon Lothrop caught wind of such witchcraft. The uncles were definitely hostile and had not yet paid the rents due to the estate (or Morgana's for Cabbage Lane). Morgana wished her father would return. He knew all about the palantyte pieces and would be sympathetic. In fact thinking about it, Morgana wondered if her uncles might know anything about them? Arthur speculated about where the other ochyos might be. He rather fancied some knight errantry, searching for them. The letter did not say but perhaps some would be easier to get than their own. Fancy that small marble being worth 1,000 gilden pezzi! Perhaps they could hire a thief. They had heard tales of thieves' guilds in the cities. They asked Cherry but she knew nothing of such things, she had been an honest thief! They told Litwe that they were rather favourable but awaited advice from Sir Daffyd.

Then the blow fell! They had still not decided what to do, when Sir Peter Volent (Father of the poetic Peregrine) arrived at the manor. Their father, Sir Daffyd was dead! For some time he had been trying to make contacts and improve relations with the citizens of Sumeer, one of the two main cities in Elysia. This had been done mainly with messages passed on by travelling merchants. The Faraese, were still, with good reason, hostile to the Elysians but in

Limura the natives had largely abandoned the border area. The Lawic Alliance forces were hoping to win the Elysians away from their Chaotic ambitions. They were now very much cut off from the other Chaotic states. Eventually a letter was received from a Sumeer Consigliore with the name Kralja, who wanted to speak with Sir Daffyd. The meeting was to take place at a neutral spot in the countryside, on a one-to-one basis. Sir Daffyd was on guard about it being a potential trap and Sir Peter had a troop that comprised a score of horsemen, ready to intervene. Sir Daffyd went forward alone to meet the figure advancing from the Sumeeran force. When they were close enough to speak, the Sumeeran dropped flat on the ground. Three springald darts were fired at Sir Daffyd! One missed, one struck him in the shoulder but the other pierced his heart. Sir Peter and his men charged and killed five of the enemy, before they escaped. One was the figure who had met Sir Daffyd but it was not the Consigliore Kralja. A bag of money was found on the body.

Sir Peter believed that as a result of his activities in Narchad (Sir Daffyd had done a lot of damage to the Narchadians) the Chaotic High Command had put a price on his head. There was a pot of poison beside the springalds so he thought their darts had been poisoned. With a shot in the heart it had made no difference, except that it emphasised that *someone* wanted Sir Daffyd dead. Sir Peter had delivered Sir Daffyd's Knight Banneret seal to the Grand Duke, Basylt Devisage at Charles. He had also sent his sergeant to inform Sir Phanuel of his brother's death. He brought a sack with Sir Daffyd's armour and some other personal effects in it. Into Arthur's hands he put Sir Daffyd's family signet ring and the magic sword Taglier. He then left them to their grief.

Some time later Father Gervase arrived. He had been told the news by Sergeant Hrolf. After offering his commiserations, he brought up the point that was worrying him. "You, Squire Arthur, are not yet of age. You are the clear heir to your father's estate but you cannot inherit it yet. Therefore you and Morgana will be wards of whomever the Grand Duke appoints as your guardian. Theoretically it could be your mother but since she is at Valles and is not a Baratrean subject, that is most unlikely. It could very well be your Uncle Phanuel or one of Basylt's favourites. Such are likely to want to make a personal profit, whilst they have the properties in trust. I would counsel you to get the books in order. A copy of the treasures held at the moment would be advisable to help any claims against the guardian. Also as you will know, when you do inherit, you will have to pay a hefty Heriot tax. Another thing to consider is Morgana's possible marriage. As a Knight Banneret, Sir Daffyd could give consent to your marriage. Now, however, even with the consent of your unknown guardian, you will need the Grand Duke's approval. It will be to him that the Merchet bride tax will be paid."

"Very well let us see what we can do now," replied Arthur. They found Morgana's dowry chest and inventory correct but still awaiting the Cabbage Lane rents. They opened the great chest and found that its written inventory was sorely out of date. The coin total was short but there were several pieces of jewellery and ornate objects, which were not listed. Sir Daffyd had usually brought some such back, when he returned from his adventures. Living at Valles as she did, Lady Mavys had seen very few of them. There was also a bundle of legal documents relating to the terms of ownership of the various parts of the estate. Father Gervase suggested that these be sent somewhere safe, perhaps to Lady Mavys, as such papers in the hands of others could be conveniently lost. When the good Father had gone, Morgana and Arthur discussed his advice. They decided to cook the books. The old inventory would stand, with the missing money accounted for, with an amount forwarded to Sir Daffyd on paper. (He had probably taken it anyway.) Morgana would copy out his inventory as a check against any guardian's depredations. The surplus treasures they would hide elsewhere. Morgana's magic chalice and mirror were hidden under the floorboards under her bed but there would not be enough space for all these other pieces. A suspicious guardian might find this hiding place anyway. Arthur suggested burying them all in a chest in the middle of the nearest wood. Morgana said that unless he was thinking of sacrificing his clothes chest, they had none to spare. A barrel would perhaps do? For the moment they put the treasures including Morgana's items into a keg of dried peas down in the food cellar. They decided to take the title deeds to Aunt Abigail. Perhaps she had a hiding place or could hide them with her magic powers. If this was not possible, they might organise taking them to Perigord. Aunt Abigail would need to know about Sir Daffyd's death and the consequences. Her position as Chatelaine of the St Visseille hunting preserve *should not* be affected? Squire Arthur would go there with a retired soldier servant, Jack, and Cherry. Cherry wished to collect a quantity of herbs and spices grown by Lady Abigail. She also wished to learn the recipe for Lady Abigail's cinnamon biscuits, of which Arthur was very fond. Morgana would stay behind to complete the copy inventories and check on sundry other estate matters that had been neglected. She considered contacting the Stetian Or mirror. She wanted to tell Uncle Quixano about these developments and that she wished to try and recover the ochyo for him. In the end she decided against. She did not know who was operating the Or mirror. It had shaken her to find her own operations had been spied upon. Who knew what other magicians were on the watch? She would first consult with Aunt Abigail, when, one hoped, their futures were clearer.

The day after Arthur left, she had a practice with the magic sword Taglier. Arthur had put it on its mount above the fireplace where Sir Daffyd left it when he was home. Arthur was fond of his own sword. Normally, when alone, she practised with a heavy exercise sword, striking at an ash tree trunk in the corner of the yard. Taglier felt lighter than even the wooden practice swords and was beautifully balanced. She knew it sharpened itself, drawing on the ambient magic in the air to do so when necessary. After a few blows she stopped. The ash tree trunk, tough veteran of years of sword practice, was being cut to matchwood. The sword seemed to adjust its edge and weight to the point of impact. What a sword! Arthur was so lucky to inherit it.

Next morning, a wagon with two men and with another on horseback, was seen approaching the manor. They drove into the courtyard and the plate clad rider dismounted. Morgana advanced to greet him with her practised hostess smile.

"You are the damsel Morgana Lefey?" He had long black flowing hair and a devil-may-care expression.

"Yes, sir," she answered.

"Where are your brother, Squire Arthur, and your mother, Lady Mavys?"

"Squire Arthur is gone to St Visseille to visit my aunt. My stepmother, Lady Mavys is residing at her mansion in Valles, sir."

"No matter. I am Sir Helric Blaggart, Banneret. I am hereby appointed by His Grace the Grand Duke to take over guardianship of you, your brother and this estate. Take us to your treasury."

(The "treasury" was in fact Sir Daffyd's bedchamber.) He demanded the keys to the two chests and had a quick look in both. Then he re-locked them and pouched the keys. "I am taking these into safe custody. Call servants to help us get them onto the wagon. I would stay here but His Grace has put me in charge of the St Simon's Hopeday Feast, at Charles. I shall return as soon as convenient. Get us some lunch and then send for your brother to return here. By the way, this is Sir Flamen Swyn and my man Sergeant Dublit. You can trust them as you would myself."

Not very much, thought Morgana. She realised the warnings of Father Gervase were proving fully justified. She wrote a note for Arthur and another for Father Gervase. She sent young Hlidric, the son of Hrolf and Margery to the priest, to tell him the news and to dispatch the note to Arthur when convenient. Gervase would probably give it to some pack merchant travelling north.

That afternoon she watched the cart carrying her family's wealth creak slowly into the distance. Sir Helric had not admitted it but presumably it was going to his castle at Arlo. At Basylt Devisage's instigation, he had married Lady Rosalie Bracouer three years ago. Her father had died suddenly some months later and he took over in his wife's name. He was known as a ruthless collector of taxes for the Grand Duke and was much feared by the merchant guilds.

The next evening Cherry rode in alone. Both she and her horse Dobbin looked utterly exhausted. Her face showed that she brought terrible news. "Arthur is dead! Your uncles have killed Arthur! Lady Abigail is taken for a witch! They will come here for you too!" Morgana slowly got the full tale out of her. The morning of the day before, a nun had called to purchase some herbs from Lady Abigail. In the afternoon, the three uncles Sir Phanuel, Sir Congal and Dean Lothrop arrived. With them were three nuns, including the one who had called in the morning and some soldier familiars of the Order of St Judas. Dean Lothrop had called out, "Abigail Rasguno, you are accused of blackest witchcraft and we have come to arrest you."

Lady Abigail had just stood there dithering with her hand-warming ball in her hands but Arthur jumped up to stand between her and the uncles. He did not even draw his sword but a crossbowman of St Judas shot him in the chest. Sir Congal rushed forward and cut off his head!

Cherry had run upstairs to get her knives. From there she heard Dean Lothrop say, "Any more wishing to defend a witch?" Then there was a clashing of swords and more shouting as Jack intervened. Realising there was little she could do, Cherry had climbed out of a window and ran to the stable. She rode off unpursued, for the brothers may not have realised she was there. She rode cross-country past the forest. She tried to carry on in the dark but the stars were covered by cloud and she got lost. Next morning she hit a stream, which she found was the Arl, flowing towards Arlo. Afraid of being stopped at the bridge there, she backtracked upstream until she could ford it. She believed that the arrest was all part of a plot designed to kill Arthur. The brothers knew he would try and defend Lady Abigail. As Cherry pointed out, now only Morgana herself stood between Sir Phanuel and the whole estate! She was sure they would be coming to Closin, with some plot to deal with her!

Morgana was shocked and distraught with this further terrible loss but she realised it was a time for hard thinking. Cherry had come by horse but not by the quickest route. Whomsoever the uncles sent would probably come on foot. As permanent town-dwellers they did not keep their own horses and members of the Order of St Judas were sometimes known as the horseless knights. They would not all come, as they would know there was little to oppose them. Or would there be? She considered getting Father Gervase to rouse the peasants to defend the manor. However, opposing the Church of *Eru* and defending a witch were not likely to appeal to either the priest or the villagers. As well as Jack, there were two other servants away, visiting their relatives. At the manor were only Sergeant Hrolf, his wife Margery the cook and their two children, Hlidric, nine and Megan, eleven. To fight Lothrop's Church allies, she needed people she could really depend on–people devoted to me by the magic of the chalice perhaps?

But it would not be just a case of defending the manor. More forces would come and they would be overwhelmed. She could try to escape to her stepmother but what would be the point? It was unlikely Lady Mavys could do anything useful. Also Valles was the capital of the Church of *Eru,* the lions' den! She could run to Stetia but that would be just giving in. She could run to her guardian but he might just demand a cut from Sir Phanuel, before handing her over. None of them knew of her magic powers but in Church hands they could find them out. They did know of her shimmering gowns and could use that as an excuse to arrest her. The manor was lost, her dowry was lost but she was not going to give in without a fight. Her pain increased as she missed having Arthur to discuss these problems. Lady Abigail! She must save Aunt Abigail or she would be burnt and the Cobret lost. The Church would seize the Cobret, perhaps Lothrop was even now trying to use it. Or someone was forcing Abigail to show him how to! She must assemble those bound to her, to form a party to rescue Aunt Abigail–also if possible to get revenge on her uncles. Sir Richard Nogent, with his long experience could be a great help, as could the others. Even the dwarf Minut. She had heard that he now had a workshop at Pincelle. A lock or two might have to be dealt with before she was finished. She wrote out two notes in readiness. Then she went to sleep; she now had a plan of action.

In the morning she arose early. She told Sergeant Hrolf and Cherry of her plans. Hrolf was to ride off to find Sir Richard Nogent and his man Bergand, to deliver a note calling them to her. They were expected to be somewhere along the River Arwyn's patrol circuit. Cherry, her own horse still blown, was to take Hilda the unicorn to Pincelle to collect the dwarf. She was to give him a heavy gold necklace, as earnest payment for his services, just in case the spell had worn off. Dwarves were notoriously resistant to magic. Then she herself helped Margery and Megan prepare travelling rations for them all, biscuit and salt meats in the main. Hlidric was set to keep watch in the afternoon, though she was not expecting the enemy that day. She hoped her messengers would find their quarry quickly enough. She was to be disappointed! An hour or so before dusk Hlidric gave warning! A sinister-looking party was approaching on foot–five figures, of which two were nuns. Morgana set up her contingency plan and opened the gate into the courtyard in readiness. She stood at the door of the house, facing the gate with the chalice in her hands, as if to welcome the visitors but with the sword Taglier propped up behind her. A few minutes later her guests came through the gate. Sir Congal led them and, besides the two nuns, were a sergeant and a crossbowman of St Judas. The crossbow was set loaded!

"Ah, my interfering niece herself. In the name of the Church of *Eru*, I command you to give yourself into its care. This for a questioning, concerning certain allegations of witchcraft made against you. I have also come to collect the sword Taglier, which will be mine henceforth."

"You murderers!" she shouted. "If you want the sword, try and get it!" She picked it up from behind her. "Though I have trust in *Eru,* I have none in your Church!"

"Do not dare to question the Church, blasphemous woman!" snarled one of the nuns, who carried a short knotted whip at her belt.

"*Shimmer*," said Morgana and her gown obeyed.

"Witchcraft!" shrieked the second nun.

"Loose," ordered Sir Congal to the crossbowman. Morgana skipped to her left and the quarrel sped past her and stuck in the door.

"Take her," ordered Sir Congal and the sergeant and the nun with the whip rushed forward. Behind them the second nun was pulling out a pair of handcuffs from a bag and the crossbowman was reloading.

"Deer!" shouted Morgana, pointing at him. Unnoticed, in the stable shadow, against the wall, Hlidric had been holding Harold. Now he loosed him and the great unicorn began to charge. The two rushing towards Morgana heard the clatter, turned and slipped and fell on the buttered cobbles under their feet. Sir Congal stood transfixed but it was the half-loaded crossbowman who was truly transfixed by Harold's great horn. The second nun fled out of the gate. Morgana skipped forward and thrust at the sergeant, as he tried to get to his feet. The blade went through his mail as if it were cloth. The nun crawled away as quickly as possible. "Stable!" shouted Morgana and Harold trotted off with the crossbowman still impaled on his horn. She did not want Sir Congal to injure him. Sir Congal Lefey was a rogue but not a coward.

"Impressive! But now we shall fight for the sword." He circled round the edge of the butter and advanced along the left front of the house. Two small boulders hurtled towards him from upstairs windows but the aim was poor. He halted and drew back out of range. The nun with the whip started to circle round the right front of the house. There was a twang from the stables and she was trying to pull a quarrel out from her side. Hlidric had only a small crossbow and barely knew how to use it, but at that range he could hardly miss.

Sir Congal looked about him cautiously; the sergeant was lying down, still moaning. Morgana advanced towards Sir Congal, in the on-guard position. He waited for her to be well clear of the stone-throwers. He was confident; he thought he was a good fencer and though faced with a magic sword, to do its damage it had to hit him. He was, after all, wearing plate armour, whilst she...she only had this ridiculous shimmering dress that was hard on the eyes to look at. Morgana knew the dangers. If they were evenly matched, she would tire before him. But he knew nothing of her years of practice. He would try for a quick kill, so she acted as if she was new to the game, waiting for him to strike, with the chalice held out like a shield. He lunged forward and she chopped into his sword arm. He swore and tried to lift his blade but the wound slowed his arm.

Morgana thrust her point through his face and found it went through so far she dropped it! She jumped back, alarmed, but he was finished. Taglier had pierced his brain. She retrieved her weapon and turned round. Margery was battering the wounded nun with a door bar. By the time Morgana got to her, the nun was dead. So was the sergeant. Margery had stuck a kitchen knife into his neck to finish him off. They went to the stable and found the nibbled body of the crossbowman, lying there in a pool of blood.

Morgana mounted Harold and rode out. She was determined not to let the other nun raise the alarm. The nun was running up the road towards Pincelle but took to the fields, when she saw Morgana coming. The great unicorn soon closed the distance and she stopped and turned. There was nowhere to hide in the large expanse of ploughed fields.

"*Eru* will protect me," she cried, clutching a silver cross that was pinned to her breast.

Morgana dismounted, fearing a spell that would upset her steed. She advanced on the nun, sword in hand.

"Be gone foul witch! *Eru's* curse be upon you!" the nun shouted but doubt was in her voice. "You know it is against the law for a woman to carry a blade longer than twelve inches!"

At this Morgana felt a twinge of pity. She had been determined, in the heat of battle, to kill this last hostile witness but this would be more like murder.

"Give me the handcuffs and turn round," she ordered.

"Mercy," cried the nun, falling to her knees, afraid Morgana would cut off her head. Morgana stuck her sword in the soil and grabbed the handcuffs from the nun's bag. She felt a tingle of pain and saw that they glittered. They were coated with ground aquetate, the magic-resisting rock.

Worth a hundred ordinary pairs of handcuffs, the Church had been taking things seriously. Despite the pain, she locked them on the trembling woman's wrists. Then she led her back to the manor, with the unicorn following. Morgana's mind raced. Perhaps this nun could tell them where Lady Abigail was held.

In the courtyard the tidy-minded Margery had laid out the four bodies in a row. Morgana noticed the other nun also had a silver cross on her chest. They were of the split-ended design like that of the Knights of St Judas. "You are not Lucrecian nuns then?" she asked the prisoner (the Lucrecian nuns wore similar black habits).

She was looking aghast at the bodies of her colleagues. "We were but some of us have been formed into a new order, especially to assist the Order of Saint Judas."

"What is this order called? I had no knowledge of this."

"A name has not been established. The Sisters of St Judas was proposed but the knights are against this. There is now talk of calling us Chiarites after our founding Abbess Chiara who took the witch Maudette."

"I met Princess Maudette some years ago," said Morgana, her mind whirring. "She seemed such a quiet pleasant girl then. I wonder how she is now?"

"Oh not much different but you never can trust a witch…" the nun broke off. She realised she had given away the secret that Princess Maudette was still alive! Morgana saw her jaw tighten with a determination to give no more information. So she led her to a storeroom and bolted her in. It was now dark and neither of the messengers had returned. Morgana and the servants had a hasty meal and went to bed early. Morgana cried herself to sleep, the reaction to the fighting and the aching loss of Arthur sinking in.

In the morning she told Margery to give the nun some breakfast. Soon there was a clatter and screaming! Margery had thrown the breakfast at the nun and was beating her with the water jug. "This pig helped to kill our Arthur!" panted Margery when Morgana pulled her off.

"I had no part in it," sobbed the nun. "I had the handcuffs for the witch but I did not expect any fighting. The men said the Squire Arthur started to fight for the…for the…the lady Abigail."

"If we are to keep you alive, we must know where you are holding Lady Abigail? If we know, we have some chance of rescuing her and we will need you to show us the way. If we do not know, then we had as well kill you and flee to Stetia across the river. You do know I have Stetian relations?"

The nun just stared at her white-faced.

"I will swear on mine honour as a lady of the Lefey family that, if you lead us true to where Abigail is held, you will be set free."

The nun thought a moment, then said, "She was taken to our priory in the wilds beyond St Polle. The Order of St Judas has it well guarded, so I doubt if even your spells will win you through."

Morgana was surprised, half-expecting that she would have been taken to Charles but she said, "Nevertheless you shall take us there!"

She found out later that the nun's name was Sister Inegal. Later that morning her party members all arrived, Sir Richard Nogent, Sergeant Hrolf, Arbalister Bergand, and Minut son of Moltin and Cherry. They were all rather taken aback by the row of bodies in the courtyard. "We will decide what to do with them at a council of war, after lunch," decreed Morgana and everyone accepted this without comment.

Where the players had to decide what to do and the adventure started

After lunch, they decided to use oil and other flammable materials to burn the bodies in the courtyard. Searching them first, they found eighty-four gilden pezzi, weapons and the nun's silver badge. On Sir Congal was a bunch of keys and his silver necklace and medallion of authority, as a Charles City Officer of the Watch. The armour they buried in the vegetable garden. They decided that the most urgent objective was to rescue Aunt Abigail and her Palantyte Cobret. After that, Morgana wished to take revenge on her remaining uncles and recover the ochyo at Charles. From the items available, they decided to take twelve quarrels, twelve hets of strong rope, three hets of cord, six bandages, one satchel, one spade, one tinderbox, one oil lantern, one leather bottle of oil and three empty two cubit sacks. The rations included one large box of Margery's biscuits, three large pieces of ham, two cheeses, a sack of sultanas, a sack of prunes, a sack of wheaten flour, a condiment casket of salt, pepper, fennel, sage, mace, coriander, cumin and saffron.

Apart from Lady Mavys' set of jewellery, they decided to take the rest of the treasure from the keg of dried peas. It included: a jewelled silver vanity mirror, brush and comb; Morgana's own jewelled silver vanity mirror, brush and comb, a gold chain and a silver chatelaine (both of which she would wear) Morgana's silver and ruby bracelet with the Senelar device in pearls, a large emerald engagement ring given by Reginald Tancreton to Morgana; a large gold fleur-de-lis brooch, a walrus ivory brooch with diamonds, a small hardwood knee desk with scrolls, quills, ink and a blank parchment journal, and a large clay tablet engraved with runes. Sir Daffyd had told her that if it were broken it would make an enormous bang, scaring everyone nearby.

It was the eighteenth of the Second Moon. The party decided to start off at dusk (around the seventeenth hour) going towards Pincelle. Arriving there, after a two-hour ride, they found the palisade gates shut for the night. They then took a track regularly used by Sir Richard and the river patrols that skirted the village. Unknown to them, Old Mistress Habsore saw them, recognising Sir Richard, Morgana and her unicorns and Minut the dwarf. Once past the village, they rested the horses a while before proceeding. The plan was to follow the river road to Firmaz. Sir Richard hoped to reach an area of thickets beside the river, which he knew lay beyond Minbec. For the Second Moon, the weather was not too cold and there was little wind. However, it started to drizzle a little. Travelling at a leisurely pace to conserve the horses, they arrived short of Sincelle around midnight. Sincelle was burnt years ago by the Narchadians but was now being resettled by a few survivors and their relatives. The party decided to follow the road through the village, risking being spotted, rather than slogging through the waterlogged fields in a detour.

Again at Minbec they followed the road skirting the village but in the small hours of the morning little was stirring. As they neared Sir Richard's thickets, they spotted a thin plume of smoke rising from amongst them. Beyond they could make out the mast and furled sail of a vessel. Hrolf and Bergand crept forward and found three figures sleeping around a small fire. They woke them at sword point, demanding their identity. The sleepers pretended to be innocent fishermen but when Hrolf offered to buy some fish from them, they admitted they had none. It became obvious that they were smugglers and indeed Bergand recognised his neighbour Jassyn, when two men emerged from on board the vessel. Sir Richard told them to be gone and thank their lucky stars he was off duty. This they did and the party moved into the thickets to hide. Morgana made sure that the unicorns were concealed from the river as well as from the road. With there being no leaves on the bushes this was not easy. Then they settled down to sleep around the smuggler's fire.

They had a large meal in the late afternoon and set off again at dusk. After an hour they approached Firmaz, another village sacked by the Narchadians. As with Sincelle, they went through the village to save time. In fact the two unicorns, the dwarf and Sir Richard were all spotted and became a topic of conversation for days afterwards. Later, they passed the wooden bridge over the Ver stream between Firmaz and the Simonite Abbey of St Polle. Two myles further on, a track led off to the right, beside a small birch hurdle coppice. Sister Inegal told them that the track would lead to the Stregafume Priory and demanded that she be set free as promised. Morgana replied, "We cannot see it yet. You must come further until we are sure of it."

As they talked beside the birches, footsteps were heard crunching down the track towards them! Hrolf and Bergand dismounted and crept to the corner of the coppice. Four figures, with two at least carrying shields, were approaching along the track. The two greeted them and asked if this was the way to St Polle. One of the soldiers replied, "Carry along the main road. As it happens we are going that way ourselves. We are escorting this gentleman back to Charles."

"And what is down this track?"

"None of your business. This is all Church property."

At this moment, Sister Inegal, suspecting the talkers were soldiers of St Judas, screamed for help. "Aaaagh. Help me! Save me from this witch and her demons!" Morgana drew the sword Taglier and tried to silence her with the flat of the blade. However, magic swords are balanced always to strike with the edge and she felt it turn in her hand. At the same time the nun started her horse so the blow missed altogether. Morgana and Cherry chased back down the road after her, to try and silence her. She dodged out of the way, again and again. She was obviously a skilled rider. When Morgana did manage to strike her, again trying to stun, the blow clove her from shoulder to hip, silencing her for ever! With Cherry's help she hid the gory body in the coppice. Then they brushed mud over the bloodstains on the road. Meanwhile, realising the game was up, Hrolf and Bergand attacked and killed the speaker sergeant and a crossbowman. When the remaining soldier was wounded, he and a merchant surrendered. The merchant said he was Master Chilric, a Master parchment maker. He had just given evidence against a witch, a Miss Vanova at the priory. He only wanted to return home to Charles. Hrolf and Bergand tied up him and the soldier. Then they hid them and the two bodies in the coppice.

As the whole party started down the track they felt the light wind behind them freshen and it began to rain. The track followed a gently meandering brook with gentle grassy slopes on either side. It was very dark but, stumbling along the track someway, they saw a glimmer of light up on the hill to the left. As the party drew closer, it showed as smoke illuminated by an unseen fire below. Minut went up to investigate. The fire was in a circular enclosure of stone, a sheepfold. Inside was the monk Brother Kalow, on duty as a shepherd. He showed Minut the door into the fold and allowed him to warm himself by the fire. Minut pretended he was a traveller looking for employment and asked the Brother about the area. "The area belongs to our Abbey of St Polle. I am having to shelter in this sheepfold, instead of the old shepherd's cottage, because that is now part of the Priory. That has been built by Order of St Judas and is a little further on down the track. They *might* give you shelter."

As soon as he felt it polite, Minut thanked him and left. The others had moved on quietly and sighted a tall crenellated wall with a slender watchtower on its left. Going closer, they spotted a gate in the middle of the wall. Morgana thought of a plan of action and they all dismounted. They led the steeds out of sight and left them under the care of Cherry. Going up to the gate, Minut banged on it. A head appeared at the top of the watchtower. "Who goes there and what is your business?"

"We seek shelter for the night here, wherever it is," called up Morgana.

"Well, go somewhere else. We do not take visitors."

"I am not coming to visit this place, I am asking for shelter for the night! These fool servants of mine have got me lost, wet cold and miserable!"

"St Polle is only five myles away. They have visitors' accommodation at the inn and the monastery."

"Five myles! I am soaking, I shall have died of exposure by the time these imbeciles find it. Do you know who I am? I am Lady Constance de Haut, send your constable to me!"

"I will call milord the Justicar, madam."

They stood waiting in the rain for what seemed a very long time. Then a hooded man appeared on the tower. "I am Pazan, Justicar of the Order of St Judas. I have jurisdiction over this establishment whilst I am present. No one enters without my authority. I think you should go to St Polle."

"Sir I am in dire need and am sure my servants are foolish enough to let me die. I do not think I can walk another step. I will pay fifty gilden pezzi for us to stay the night even if it be only in a stable."

"Very well, madam, for this money, paid in advance, we will shelter you for the night. Open the gate!"

The Order of St Judas was always short of money and this seemed a very good bargain. Pazan showed the men into a barrack room, which had eight bunks. Morgana he led to his own chamber. He led his three off-duty soldiers from the barrack room into the chapel nearby. In the Justicar's room was a bed, table and large locked chest. Shutting the door, Morgana called on the Vinkalik chalice to produce its "Sudden Sleeping" drugged wine. Hoping the spell had worked, she gave the chalice to Bergand, to take up to the crossbowman in the watchtower. Up there he chatted on a soldier-to-soldier basis, until the guard fell asleep. Bergand tied him up and, donning his helmet, took his place. Meanwhile Minut the dwarf went out from the barrack room for a smoke. He could see flames flickering, in the courtyard beyond the chapel. At the chapel door, he met a sentry who told him smoking was forbidden!

"No smoking on Church of *Eru* premises!"

Minut emptied his pipe out. "Alas one of the only consolations I have. I am a bodyguard for the Lady but she is driving me demented. Nothing ever pleases her."

Hrolf and Sir Richard Nogent tried to slip past into the next courtyard but were spotted and the Justicar came out.

"We need some firewood for our young lady's chamber. We can surely take some of these?" said Sir Richard.

Hrolf grabbed some logs from a readymade pyre. Beyond it, they saw the charring remains of a witch burning on the next pyre. The Justicar Pazan told them, "Without special permission, you are not permitted in that courtyard! You may take those logs. Louis, it is about midnight, go and relieve Bertrand in the tower. I will take over guarding the Chapel."

Sir Richard kept talking to Pazan until the sentry entered the foot of the tower. Then he drew his sword and killed the Justicar with a single blow. The corpse fell back in through the chapel door, alerting the two soldiers resting there. Sir Richard and Hrolf rushed in to attack them. Lady Morgana, waiting at the barrack door, ordered her gown to shimmer and then ran to assist them. She was not needed, as the two soldiers were by then dead. The sentry, ascending the tower steps in the dark, was killed by a quarrel from Bergand at the top. Sir Richard and Hrolf surreptitiously went into the forbidden courtyard to investigate the next building. Morgana wished to follow but her gown was

Stregafume: Minut, Sir Richard and Hrolf investigate the forbidden courtyard. For one woman at least, their rescue attempt was too late!

shimmering like a beacon! Whilst waiting for it to cease of its own volition, she had a look around the chapel. On the altar were two wooden candlesticks and a large volume of court records.

Hrolf found the door of the next building unyielding.

"What are you doing down there?" demanded a woman from above.

"There has been a disturbance here and we have been sent to check everything."

"Who are you? I don't recognise you! Or your shifty friend! No one has told *me* of any extra breakfasts tomorrow. Go away!"

They moved on to the next building, which was again locked. However, Minut had found a bunch of keys on Pazan's body (plus Morgana's fifty gilden pezzi) and after a trial, found one to fit the lock. Inside was an unlit lantern on the floor and a stair leading upwards. Lighting the lantern they went up, finding a long corridor with four doors on the right and an alcove at the far end. The doors were all bolted on the outside.

Opening the first, an old woman greeted them. "I knew *Lord Hagoth* would send you to help old Edie, if I asked him nicely. Mighty is the great *Magho Hagoth!*" She held her handcuffed hands out to them but they told her to wait a while. In the next cell was a glamorous, raven-haired woman, wearing a revealing blue silk gown.

"Well, hello, you handsome men. Rescue me and I am yours. I am Mistress Vanova unjustly called a witch by that dog Chilric. They want to burn me! Please save me!"

"Wait a moment, please." In the third cell they found a red-haired woman, still asleep. In the fourth cell they found, at last, Lady Abigail, minus the Cobret. It had been taken from her, with sundry herbs and bottles of medicines she had made, to be used as evidence against her. They had been questioning and whipping her gardener Raymond, to try and testify against her. Minut started to unlock all the handcuffs with his bunch of keys. In the alcove they found only a table, a chair and a heap of women's clothes. Her gown now normal, Morgana checked the stable on the right side of the forbidden courtyard, but it was empty apart from some hay. Then she returned to check with Bergand up on the watchtower and ordered him to fetch Cherry and the steeds. Cherry, who had been standing worrying in the cold and rain for over two hours, was not very polite to poor Bergand. Hrolf and Sir Richard went on to the last building, which again was locked. Returning they found the gardener, Raymond, tied up in the undercroft of the cells.

When Minut was free, he unlocked the last building's door. Inside was a chamber with a cupboard, a stair leading upwards and a door into another ground-floor room. Hrolf sneaked into this, to find a woman sleeping on a pallet. Putting his sword at her throat, he woke her up, telling her to stay silent. Unfortunately she screamed in a panic, so he was startled into killing her.

Sir Richard rushed upstairs to find three nuns, rising from their pallets, roused by the scream. They pleaded for mercy and he tied them up. He noticed there were also three empty pallets in the dormitory. Two for the nuns that came to Closin but where was the third? Minut found none of his keys fitted the chest in the dead woman's room. Remembering that there was still the cook's building to take, he went back.

"Go away or I'll call the Justicar!" shouted the angry voice from above.

"The Justicar is dead! There is no one left to help you.

You had better surrender." He began to batter the door with his great hammer but was hit by a chair thrown from above. Fortunately his helmet cushioned the blow and he was able to continue. As he pounded on, he heard feet clumping down a ladder, clatter about and then go back up again. At that moment the door gave way and he rushed in and up the ladder. There were two women at the top, with a collection of kitchen implements and other likely missiles. But their nerves gave way and they surrendered. He tied them up and Morgana sent him to try the chest in the Justicar's office. Finding its key, he found sixty-three gilden pezzi, writing materials and a half-filled notebook. Then he went to pick the lock of the dead woman's chest. Inside was a diary inscribed *Mania Sub Prioress of Stregafume, a Tome of Eru* and a just-started copy of the same. Also there were quills, ink and sand, and a bag with thirteen gilden pezzi, five golden rings, seven other rings and nine pairs of earrings. Deeper into the chest were six brooches, eight bracelets and four eating knives. Apart from a table and chair there was also a trapdoor with an acrostic keyboard and some loose letters. Obviously a code combination was needed to open the trap. Morgana sat down to try to figure this out. Held back by a misspelling she eventually solved the puzzle and opened the trapdoor. In the cellar below were shelves laden with goods: the Cobret, four of Abigail's wasp smoke pots, seventeen small bags of herbs, three skulls, six bags of bones and hair, seven wax dolls with pins in them, three bottles labelled poison, a bottle labelled St Bandade water and twenty-two other bottles of mysterious liquids. There was also a silver spoon with the rune 𝔚 on it, an illustrated book with all the Chaotic *Maghi* in it, a grimoire of spells by Prudella, a *Madre Vera* book (by the heretic St Barbara) and four bottles of wine. Lady Abigail took her Cobret and the grimoire and discovered that she had a chance of learning one of its spells each full moon. For the rest they took one bottle of poison, the St Bandade water, the *Madre Vera* and the silver spoon. Looking at the diary, Morgana discovered that the nuns Mania and Faith came from St Tugen, Hope and Inegal from St Retaud and Gravity and Charity came from Suffers. Did this mean Princess Maudette had been held at St Retaud? By this time, in the small hours of the night, she and all the rest were exhausted and they went to sleep.

On to Charles

Sometime just after dawn a somnolent Morgana was shaken awake by the red-headed woman, Louise Berde. “There is a monk at the gate demanding his breakfast! What shall we do?”

Morgana ordered Cherry to tell him that, due to a large influx of people last night, he would have to do without breakfast. The monk expostulated, “The priory is duty-bound to provide me with breakfast! It is part of the contract with the Abbey of St Polle. It was made when the Order of St Judas wanted to use the shepherd’s house and area as a priory! You have no right to refuse me!”

“Let him in,” said Morgana. Then the two of them fought to overpower and tie him up. He put up quite a struggle and help was too slow in coming from their male companions! They were only just waking up. Minut recognised the monk as Brother Kalow who had shared his fire with him. The rain had ceased and it was now a bright frosty morning. Cherry was put in charge of making breakfast for everyone, including the prisoners. Hrolf and Bergand were sent to fetch the two captives left overnight in the birch coppice. It was discovered that the witch Edie, had been tormenting the three nuns, Faith, Hope and Charity. Their faces were now covered with red lumps, they had been struck dumb and been given a revulsion for men. Morgana let them stay that way. She did not feel she owed them any favours. After breakfast the five dead bodies on the premises were burnt on the unused pyre. Then the priory was generally tidied up. (*A woman leads this quest party*!) The steeds were all transferred to the forbidden courtyard and the nine prisoners put in the cells.

Raymond, Lady Abigail's gardener, said he wanted to return to his former home, at Vuelco in Stetia. "They don't rightly seem to appreciate herb lore in these parts anymore, m'lady." He was willing to escort the other accused witches to Morgana's relations at Relajar–if given sufficient money! After a certain amount of haggling for expenses and the pay he was still owed, he was given eighty gilden pezzi. Louise Berde and Miss Vanova agreed to go with him, once Morgana gave them a letter of introduction for her relatives. Old Edie said she had plans of her own. Morgana invited her to help herself to the remaining contents of the nun's cellar. This she did very thoroughly and departed alone. Whilst this was happening Morgana asked Louise Berde how she came to be locked up.

"I lived with my parents, glove makers on the market square in Charles. They recently died of the spotted fever and I was left alone, trying to run the business. One day the Order of St Judas came to search the house. They found a wax doll with pins in it, some bones and a banned book, none of which I had ever seen before. I believe my aunt must have planted them. If I am disinherited my Uncle

Grade will get the house, which is in a prime selling location. I will go with the gardener to serve you as best I may. I thank you for rescuing me."

She, Mistress Vanova and Raymond left soon after.

The main party knew their next step would be to go to Charles. To recover the ochyo and get revenge on the two uncles. But they needed to decide when and how to do it? Charles' city gates were open only from dawn to dusk, but a raid on the Lefey Mansion had best be done after dark. Therefore they decided to arrive in the daytime and stay somewhere until ready to mount a night raid. Then they could either return to the lodging, or try to escape over the walls, depending on how much uproar they caused. They could hardly take the unicorns into the city and even the horses might be recognised. It would also cost a lot of money to stable them. Despite the money found in the priory, coins were in short supply. Sergeant Hrolf said he knew of an old comrade, Negg, who lived with his family at a coppice they owned, south of the city. They sold brooms and hurdles in summer and firewood in winter. He was sure they would look after the steeds for a small fee and not betray them later. Negg had served under Sir Daffyd, years ago. Sir Richard said that, at a pinch, his daughter Blanche and her husband Lodric could put up some of them in the city. But he was loath to put them in danger, especially as they lived very close to the Lefey Mansion. Minut said he knew of a "No questions asked" place they might like to stay in. It was at Filo the Pawnbrokers, in Cabbage Lane. Cabbage Lane was in the thieves' quarter, where the watch preferred not to go. Minut had been hired by Filo four months ago to put strong locks on his cellar doors. Filo liked to put up people from foreign parts because he collected information. Sometimes he even paid for it but he never betrayed his guests, no matter what they were up to. He claimed it was just good business sense. This is not to say some of his guests did not come to a sticky end. A dangerous area is Cabbage Lane! Morgana finally decided they would travel to Negg's coppice by night, circling round St Polle and Longstreet. If they went via Verreric, they would have been on the wrong side of the river. If it stayed bright and frosty, the ground would be firm for travelling cross-country that evening.

Around noon, a knight with three hobilars, (mounted spearmen) trotted up to the priory, demanding entrance. Challenged by Bergand, he declared he was Sir Herbert Decre from Decame in Perigord. He had come to visit his sister Mania, the sub-prioress. He had a present for her, as it was her birthday on the morrow. Bergand hastily consulted with Morgana. She went up the tower. "Sister Mania is away. She has gone to the Abbey of St Polle, to help tend spotted fever victims there. Unfortunately we now have cases here! We regret we are unable to provide the hospitality that should be your due." Disappointed, he replied that he would go on to St Polle, in search of his sister.

At Charles, Sir Phanuel had control of the South Gate quarter, with Sir Congal as one of his officers. His brother, Dean Lothrop managed the cathedral in the West Gate quarter. The marketplace was shared by the quarter guards, each taking a week's duty at a time there. Sir Congal had set out for Closin on the 16th and Sir Phanuel had rather optimistically expected him back by the 20th to help cover the market. Dean Lothrop did not have so much trust in Congal. He was afraid that he would loot far more than the sword from Closin Manor. He would have gone with him but there were important affairs to deal with at the cathedral first. When by noon of the 21st Sir Congal still had not returned, he set out himself, telling his bishop that he needed to confer with Father Gervase. He suspected Congal of delaying due to one of his amorous adventures but was mainly concerned to find out in what condition the estate was. He had no faith in Congal's judgement on such matters.

Lothrop and his two servants stayed at the vicar's house in Ombec that night. On the 22nd, they walked to Arlo and stayed at Sir Helric Blaggart's castle. Sir Helric was away at Charles but his chamberlain, Sir Hildebrand, offered him hospitality. He told the dean that Sir Helric was now the guardian of his nephew Arthur and his niece Morgana. This was a sore blow! Lothrop felt that, as family, he and Sir Phanuel had a better right to the guardianship. He did know Sir Helric was a favourite of the Grand Duke and that there would be little use in complaining. He feared Sir Helric would plunder the estate far more thoroughly than Congal ever could! Thinking about this, Lothrop told the chamberlain that, because of an unfortunate accident, Squire Arthur Lefey was now dead. This would surely mean that the estate would come to his brother, Sir Phanuel, as the next male heir? If Sir Helric had already collected the deeds, perhaps he would hand them over to him, for safe-keeping, under the circumstances. Sir Hildebrand said Sir Helric had brought back two chests from Closin but it was more than his life was worth to hand them over without authority. But surely it would be the husband of the Lady

Morgana who would inherit the estate anyway? Lothrop was torn between going back to Charles to tell Phanuel to get his claim for the estate presented to the Grand Duke as soon as possible or of carrying on to Closin. In the end he decided to carry on. He wanted to check on Sir Helric's depredations and to be sure that Morgana was securely held. Her husband would be the Church if she were not burnt! Usually very careful with his money, he hired mounts in Arlo for his party. He wanted to reach Closin by the evening of the 23rd of the second Moon.

It did remain clear and frosty so the ground was firm. Morgana's party travelled cross-country to Negg's coppice and found his hut without any problem. For seven gilden pezzi, Negg agreed to hide and feed the mounts for two nights. Then they split into two groups, to enter the city in mid morning. Charles, the capital of Bara, was a medium-sized walled city, separated from a large citadel by the River Char. Its buildings were a mixture of half-timber and plastered wattle and daub. At its centre was a large market square, on the west side of which was the cathedral. The citadel had a very large turreted keep surrounded by towers and a curtain wall. The only gate faced the bridge connecting the citadel to the city.

Morgana was wearing her yellow gown, trying to remain unrecognised. In her initial group she took, Lady Abigail, Cherry and Minut the dwarf. They joined a steady trickle of people entering the city. The sentries at the gate asked their business. Minut replied, "I have a locksmithing business in Cabbage Lane but first I will escort these three ladies to relatives of theirs within the city." Having first checked that they were not carrying any saleable items, upon which tolls were due, they were allowed to pass. They proceeded up South Street, where the clothiers lived and worked. Then they doubled back along the alley beside the wall that separated the thieves' quarter from the rest of the city. This wall ended close to the city's external crenellated wall. There they met an apple-seller and bought ten apples at a florin apiece. Fruit was expensive by the Second Moon. Passing a seedy tavern, The Shaking Bones, infamous for its gambling, Minut led them to the pawnbrokers. Three brass roundels hung outside denoting the presence of an Ombardi agent. The Ombardi were a trading people, originating from Omgano in central Morval Earth. Many had fled from the chaotic conquests to scatter all over the east. There were large concentrations of them at the mouth of the Arwyn, in Fara and Elysia. A suspicious servant at the door called down Filo Prestato, the pawnbroker himself. Minut reminded him of his recent work and told him he and the three ladies needed accommodation, and also that they might be joined by three men later.

"For you I can give you full board at eight gilden pezzi for the four of you. Per night, paid in advance of course! If these men come, we think again."

"Don't you think that's a little high?"

"But I am making no profit as it is! These are reduced prices for an old friend."

"Just pay him," said Morgana. "You also buy and sell jewellery and other valuable items I believe?"

"We have a long honourable tradition of doing so."

Morgana brought out the engagement ring given her by Reginald Tancreton. "What will you pay for this?"

Filo held it up to the light. “Hmm, made in Perigord. Not a popular style here. I can at best offer you nineteen gilden pezzi.”

“That is not very much for such a fine piece!” Morgana complained.

“This is a ‘No questions asked’ establishment. Prices are naturally lower than you might get in a market square shop. Cedrics for instance.”

Morgana knew Cedrics, where she would certainly be recognised. No sense in going there!

“Very well, nineteen it is.”

“Milady, that ring is worth at least thirty,” hissed Cherry.

“I am sure Maestro Filo is offering me an honest price in present market conditions.” She handed over the ring. Filo grinned at this backhanded compliment and counted out the money. Morgana was glad to get rid of Reginald’s ring and the bitter memories that went with it. Cherry shook her head at such profligacy, she was sure she could have haggled another four Pezzi out of the skinflint.

Sir Richard with Sergeant Hrolf and Bergand had little trouble at the gate. The soldiers were suitably obsequious to the knight, although they did not know him. He first called on his daughter Blanche and her family in Lefey Street. He rather upset her, first by trying to refuse her wine and biscuits and then hinting, “There might be trouble around here soon.” He was then unable to explain what sort of trouble he meant. It was not a very satisfactory meeting. The worried stares of Blanche’s husband and their housekeeper followed them out. They wandered round to the wall entrance to Cabbage Lane. Feeling short of money, Sir Richard refused to buy the apple seller’s wares. As a consequence he was loudly abused as a “High and mighty miser!” by that shrill-voiced harridan.

“I think we had better be on our guard,” muttered Hrolf. “I think that belle dame has alerted every rogue in the quarter.”

Resisting the temptations of the tavern, they quickly arrived at the pawnbrokers. The suspicious servant denied them entry until they said they belonged to the dwarf’s party. Since Minut was still upstairs, Filo charged three gilden pezzi per person for the remaining three, in advance! Asked about current news, Sir Richard said he had heard that a priory belonging to the Order of St Judas had been raided. Filo admitted he did not know this. He said the Order had been active arresting witches in the city. Such happenings were very unsettling for business. Now that the party was complete, Morgana decreed they stay indoors, out of trouble until nightfall.

Morgana decided Lady Abigail and Cherry were to remain at the pawnbrokers. Filo had told them there was a curfew, sounded by the cathedral bells each night, four hours after dusk. Thus the remaining five left with an hour to go. Outside the Shaking Bones Tavern they were accosted by drunks but, given a coin with which to treat themselves, they went back inside. At the wall end, a one-legged beggar had replaced the apple-seller. He was given a tip even before they noticed his large guard dog! Through the gap an evil smell drove them back a pace or two. The night-soil-men’s cart was parked there, against the city wall! They walked up South Street, encountering few passers-by. Proceeding cautiously close round about the Lefey Mansion, they saw the arrow slits either side of the front door were dark. Around the back, however, there were both lights to be seen and voices to be heard on the ground floor. Minut tried the back door but it was bolted. The voices inside stopped suddenly, so Morgana miaowed like a cat and the talkers started again. Then Minut spotted the watch coming from the far end of Lefey Street, so they boldly walked past them. Then they doubled back up the alley behind. The ground floor light had gone out but Morgana knocked on the door. "Who is it?"

"My servant and I are lost in the city. We have been looking for my Cousin Louise Berde's house. I am worried about being caught out after curfew."

Indeed at that moment the cathedral bells began to ring. "I think you had best go to the sentries at the South gatehouse."

"But we are lost. I do not know where we are, never mind how to find the gatehouse."

"Well I will see what Sergeant Norman says."

Some conversation ensued but eventually the door was opened. Morgana and Bergand burst in, killing the sergeant. The cook woman dodged Morgana's sword but she had no weapon to hand. She retired to the support of two maids against the wall as the others arrived. Bergand tried to stun one of the maids but, striking too hard, landed a mortal blow. The remaining two women surrendered but steps were now heard descending the newel stair, outside the kitchen. Hrolf met a soldier coming down for the first clash of arms.

"Pull back a bit so I can help!" ordered Morgana. "Fight him on the level floor."

"They're playing it clever!" shouted the soldier "Wilf, bring down your crossbow, so you can fire from the stair, over me." However, the speaker and another billman were killed and Wilf and another man fled back upstairs. When Morgana trapped them in the dining hall, they too surrendered. They, like the kitchen staff, were bound and gagged, though there had been enough shouting and screaming to waken the dead anyway.

On the second floor Sir Richard encountered Corinne the housekeeper who fled back into her room. The three other small chambers on this floor were empty. They were guest chambers that had been used by Morgana and Arthur, when they came to stay long ago. Minut was left to make sure the housekeeper did not come out again. On the third floor they met Sir Phanuel, hastily dressed but carrying his heavy sword.

"You murderer of my brother! I challenge you to fight and may *Eru* grant me the winner!" cried Morgana.

Surprised, he stared at her for a moment. "I accept, on condition that, when you lose, your followers leave at once." He realised this was a golden opportunity to gain inheritance of the estate.

"Agreed. Perhaps we had best go to the hall where there is more space."

They descended and pushed the table and benches to one side. Like Sir Congal before him, he knew nothing of Morgana's years of practice. In those days she and Hrolf had assumed that she might have to fight if the Narchadians raided again. For this, they had evolved a fencing tactic based on the expectation that any opponent would think a woman would be a complete novice. Such novices normally took a wild downward swipe at their opponent. The accepted counter was beat the sword aside, knocking the novice off balance so that he could be dispatched easily. Morgana advanced, her sword held high and flourished it, feinting, at Sir Phanuel's head. On cue, he made the side-sweep blow, expecting to knock the blade from her hand but she stayed her hand until his point was past and ran him through the heart. Within a few seconds he was dead and the fight was over! What Arthur had called the Flailing Female stratagem had worked! She was glad it ended so quickly. There seemed to have been a complete staff changeover since she had stayed here last but those killed had been Lefey retainers and it hurt her that she had had to fight them–all except Sergeant Norman, who she knew for a hard-headed follower of Sir Phanuel. They were duty-bound to protect the brothers and really she had had no choice but to attack. Looking around the hall brought back memories of times past, when she had shared it with Arthur and her father. And Lothrop, where was he? He was as guilty as Phanuel!

They checked the third floor but there was no one else. In Sir Phanuel's room was a calendar and his badges and seal as Captain of the Quarter. In his chest was a book of accounts, a roll of deeds, including that for the mansion and 1,271 gilden pezzi. In Sir Congal's room, Minut picked the lock of his chest. In it were some cheap jewellery, four brooches, three bracelets, two sets of earrings and forty-three gilden pezzi. The room used by Sir Daffyd in times past was empty. Dean Lothrop's, however, also had a chest for Minut to open. In it were *his* book of accounts and twenty-three gilden pezzi. Then Morgana noticed an acrostic square on the windowsill, of the same kind as that on the trapdoor at the Priory. With the loose letters put correctly in place, a trapdoor opened in the ceiling and a rope ladder dropped down. It was dark up there and they were afraid the dean might be waiting to ambush them. They procured a lamp and Hrolf began nervously to ascend the ladder. The attic was empty!–Except for a chest well banded with iron. Its lock was beyond even Minut's skill so he had to smash it open with his hammer. In the process the contents suffered some damage. A bottle of some unknown liquid was shattered and two out of four mistletoe skewers were also beyond use. Recovered from the wreckage was a stout leather bag holding 931 gilden pezzi. They then descended to question Corinne the housekeeper. Morgana told her that she had killed Sir Phanuel in fair fight, because he was involved with the murder of her brother Arthur. She asked where Dean Lothrop was? Corinne replied that the dean had left that midday. He was off to look for Sir Congal at Closin. Morgana offered the housekeeper 100 gilden pezzi to "tidy up" the problems left by the raid. She also suggested that if she collected the rents from Cabbage Lane she could keep thirty per cent of the money. Corinne readily accepted. She expected things would be changed when the dean returned but 100 gilden pezzi, unseen by witnesses, was a welcome gift. They then found and extracted the ochyo from the carvings above the fireplace in the dining hall.

Back at the pawnbrokers in Cabbage Lane, Lady Abigail and Cherry were sitting worrying. Though it was past the curfew hour, there were rather noisy "goings-on" in the lane below. The candle burnt out and they were left in darkness. They wondered just how trustworthy Filo and his shifty-looking accomplices were. Cherry made sure her throwing knives were ready to hand. They heard the cathedral bell toll midnight. Just after the last strike they felt a cold chill and there in the room stood a tall form! It was holding a candle with a very weak orange flame in one hand and a glittering dagger in the other. It stood still and they mastered their fears to stare at it.

Speaking good Simnith it said, "I am Lady Buija, now of the otherworld. Once I was lady-in-waiting to Princess

Maudette. After she was taken prisoner at Naigre, I was murdered by Pazan, the Justicar and his men, at Valles. I had stayed there with some of the court, when the royal family went to Naigre Manor on holiday. I had had no news of the assassinations there, when Pazan and his familiars strode into our quarters. They killed all of us Stetians. However, members of my family wear magic pendants of *Nemeke, Magha* of just retribution and I called her name as I was struck down. This took me to the otherworld flaches for I do not know how long. In time I discovered the means to return to this world though I cannot endure the sun. I determined to track down Pazan but I had enormous difficulties finding him. I am as yet unskilled at finding my way around the planes.

"After some moons I discovered Princess Maudette was yet alive. She was held at a great Abbey place and well guarded. I sensed a great dangerous magic there and left the place, as Pazan did not seem to be present. I searched in many places for him with no result. Then in the city of Charles, I saw a sergeant familiar of the Order of St Judas, who had aided Pazan. He was arresting a Stetian woman for witchcraft. I followed them to the priory called Stregafume. There I found Pazan but was wondering how to deal with him. Just killing him in his sleep did not seem adequate enough punishment.

"I spied on the place for two nights. I stole this magic dagger from a secret chamber below the nuns' quarters. They were afraid to touch it but I recognised the N symbol for *Nemeke* on it. I heard them condemn the Stetian woman, Vanova. I saw them bring you and your servant in. When they actually burned a woman in white, I thought I had to strike soon–to try to stop the burning. Killing people is not anything I have been involved with before, so I was nervous. I planned to strike in the small hours of the morning but it was that night your rescuers with the blue unicorns arrived. They achieved so much that I would have desired. Nevertheless as a fellow Stetian I feel I must ask you to try and arrange the rescue of my Lady, Princess Maudette. I feel so sorry for her kept alone in prison. I am sure that if it suits them, the Church will burn her too. The Juanta of Stetia would be duty-bound to shelter the Princess if she were taken there."

Abigail replied, "I will put this to our leader Lady Morgana. It will be for her to decide and she is occupied with many problems. Would you be able to help us at all?"

"I will when I can. I am confined to the dark and unsure of my way but I will return." She faded from their sight. Lady Abigail and Cherry lay back on their pallets. The streets outside were quiet at last but it was a long time before they fell asleep.

Morgana and Sir Richard decided that it would be unnecessarily risky to break the curfew by sneaking back to the pawnbrokers. They investigated means of disposing of the bodies. There was no garden outside for burial. Minut upset the cook by demanding she bring up a drink from the cellar and then going down himself. The floor was stone-flagged and besides there would be little room for five bodies. And where would they put the earth? In the end they resolved to burn them one at a time in the great fireplace in the dining room. They put Sir Phanuel on first, but, despite adding oil to build up a goodly blaze, the corpse was barely consumed by dawn. The larger bones remained.

Worse, the smell of burning flesh was really nauseating. Thus the bodies of Sergeant Norman, Brouta the Maid, and Wat and Dint the billmen remained on the floor of the dining room when they left. Morgana wracked her brains but could not remember "Ye Twelve Doughty Knights of Renown" having had any problems with corpses. It looked as though they had left them to rot in the wild. This could not have been the case in castles or villages. Perhaps there had been squads of servants, following, ready to deal with such problems. Well a Lady Errant must learn to cope as well as they must have done!

They hurried out as soon as the dawn bells had rung. Very few people were stirring out of doors yet but they met the night-soil cart beginning its malodorous round. The gate guards gave Sir Richard a weary salute as they passed by. The gap in the wall was unguarded but as they went through they noticed a body lying in the alley behind the pawnbrokers. Filo's men let them in and he was curious.

"What news in the city?"

"Well first, did you know there is a body lying behind your shop?" Filo sent two men to investigate and dispose of the problem, probably by sneaking the corpse away and to the back of someone else's property.

Meanwhile after a quick consultation with the others, Morgana decided to tell the truth. "I have killed Sir Phanuel Lefey in fair fight, because he murdered my brother. Some of his servants are also dead. We will be leaving soon."

"Indeed you will! This is strange news. Sir Phanuel collects all the rents in Cabbage Lane! He was a Captain of the Watch, there will be a great hue and cry!"

"We have arranged for Corinne the housekeeper to collect the rents, which come to my dowry."

Filo regained his impassive look. "I would counsel

departing within the hour before word gets abroad."

They split back into the two groups they had been in when they entered the town. Sir Richard, Hrolf and Bergand left first. They had no trouble with the gate guards and sped down the road. When they reached the area where they needed to branch across the fields they stopped and hid in some bushes. There they waited for the others. Meanwhile these had just started from Filo's establishment. Morgana readily bought some more apples at the gap. At the gate the sergeant stopped them. "Who are you and why are you leaving the city?"

He had just had a woman and Wilf the crossbowman report that a Lady Morgana, with four male accomplices, had murdered his Commander of the Quarter, Sir Phanuel. The dwarf was spinning a yarn about being a locksmith and generously escorting the ladies to visit relatives. Three women and only the black widow one looked like a lady!

"Our officer Sir Phanuel has been murdered and we are looking for a Lady Morgana," he said, staring hard at Lady Abigail.

"But this has nothing to do with us," said Minut. "We really must be on our way."

"I am sure that if you see the Podesta he will issue a pass to leave the city."

"But really, surely you could issue such a pass here and now. Would 100 gilden pezzi cover the cost?"

"Well, I suppose that might be in order, Madam...if you just give me the money and go, it would save us the formality of writing out the pass." (Especially as I cannot write and do not think for a minute you have anything to do with the murder, he thought.)

Morgana gave him the money and they hurried under the tower. The last they heard was the crossbowman above calling out, "Where's mine?" as he rushed down to get a share of the bribe. Fortunately none of them saw the sword Morgana carried behind her back.

They sped on to rejoin the others at the bushes. Together they crossed the fields towards Negg's coppice. The day was cloudy but dry. The ground was firm but a little slippery in places. Breasting a rise near the coppice, they found a group of men working near the edge of it. Even nearer were two men in plate armour watching their approach. Hard by them were four spearmen watching the workers. There were eight of these, cutting saplings and making them in to hurdles. Hovering to one side was Negg, looking worried. As they came closer one of the men in armour seemed horribly familiar to Morgana.

"Good morrow to you, my fair ward. This is indeed an unexpected pleasure!"

It was Sir Helric Blaggart, her guardian!

"What brings you so far from Closin? And where is your brother?"

"We are escorting this lady to her sick relative. But Arthur my brother is dead. My Uncle Sir Phanuel murdered him whilst Squire Arthur was trying to protect a lady."

"What? This seems a most unlikely tale. You say that the respected Captain of a Quarter, Sir Phanuel has murdered a ward, theoretically under my protection! We had best return to the citadel to investigate this. Sir Miles, you take charge here and keep them at it."

Meanwhile Minut had gone down to Negg. Negg told him that the steeds were safe hidden by his sons, deep within the trees. "But I'm worried about my trees. The knight there says I'll be well paid and gave me this slip of paper. He says that the Grand Duke's treasurer will give me twenty gilden pezzi for it in the Citadel but I don't trust him. I cannot read so I don't know what it actually says."

Minut read the slip, which said that the bearer should be paid one Pezzi each year, for twenty years!

Morgana was desperately saying how important it was to escort the lady widow to her sick relative. She would return as soon as possible. Sir Helric was saying that this matter sounded most unlikely and needed immediate investigation. Sir Richard eventually won him round by saying he gave his knightly word that, indeed, Sir Phanuel was responsible for the death of Squire Arthur Lefey. He would swear that in court if necessary. Reluctantly Sir Helric let them go and returned to the city by himself. Morgana wanted to get to the steeds so they could flee as fast as possible but Minut came back with Negg, claiming he was being swindled. Restraining Minut from attacking Sir Miles she agreed to pay ten gilden pezzi to Negg in advance to help keep the peace and aid the St Simon's Day festivities. (And most of all to get away from the pursuit she was sure would follow soon!) She hurried the party through the coppice and, with a quick thank-you to Negg and his family, they rode off. They first headed south-south-west over the fields to avoid being seen but then cut back onto the south road after a couple of myles.

Hostile reactions

Meanwhile Sir Herbert Decre had gone to the Abbey of St Polle in search of his sister, the Sub Prioress Mania. The Abbey knew nothing of any plague but they were putting up a sister from Stregafume Priory in the guest chambers. She had been buying food supplies and was away at the moment visiting a nearby farm. Sir Herbert awaited her return. She was Sister Jeanette, the refrectress of the priory. She too knew nothing of any plague, either at St Polle or the priory. According to her, the sub prioress had had no plans to leave her post in the near future. Jeanette asked who had told the knight this tale?

"It was by the crossbowman on guard duty, conferring with a woman below. No names were given."

They both worried about this peculiar circumstance. However, it was now dark and they decided to return to the priory the following morning. Sir Herbert worried most of the night. If Mania had gone all-reclusive, surely she would have sent word. Last time he had visited her, three years ago, she had been glad to see him. Later she had written that she had been promoted to witch-punishing duties in a new order of nuns. He felt that getting involved with witchcraft was a dangerous occupation. He was very ready to fight enemies with cold steel but witchcraft was a dirty business. However, Mania had magic powers of her own (white magic of course) so she could fight the enemies of *Eru* in her own way.

Sir Herbert, with his men and the refrectress, rode out early to the priory. There was no guard on the tower! The gate just pushed open and the place appeared to be deserted. Sister Jeanette said this was the men's part of the priory but she looked into the chapel. It was empty but there were two swords and dark stains on the floor. In the second courtyard, a large pyre still smoked and seemed to have the remains of more than one body on it. Sir Herbert entered the barracks, finding it empty apart from the bunks and some soldiers equipment. In the Justicar's office the chest lay open and empty. He heard a shriek: the refrectress had discovered the kitchen door had been smashed open. A pile of dirty bowls and cutlery stood on the table! Then they heard shouting from the prison block and discovered the survivors of the raid. Soon unbolted from their cells, Sir Herbert was upset to discover that his sister was not amongst them. The cook told him that Mania had been murdered and burnt in a pyre with the Justicar and three soldiers.

"We were overcome by witchcraft! A hag riding on a giant blue horse with a spike on its head flew in a troop of demons! One of them smashed in the kitchen door and then locked us in the cells. They have eaten all the food and left all the washing up! And they have left the nuns speechless and disfigured by red lumps."

Brother Kalow corroborated the story, though he did say the breakfast provided had been better than that normally supplied. He was worried about how his sheep had fared in his absence and hurried off. Master Chilric, the parchment-maker, also wanted to flee the premises, as soon as he was allowed. The two surviving familiars agreed that they must have been defeated by witchcraft. The purpose must have been to free the witches already captured, who were now gone. They said that some of the attackers had human appearance and there was a knight with a green shield with a yellow club on it. They reported that their sergeant and another of their comrades lay dead in the coppice at the end of the track. Sir Herbert ordered them to find them and bury them with the help of Brother Kalow.

He then asked the nuns to show him where his sister had died. In her chamber the pallet was still stained with blood but the bedclothes had been burnt on the fire. Her keys lay on the floor. Her chest lay open except for two *Tomes of Eru.* One was a copy that had only just been started. Sir Herbert took that as a memento as it contained his sister's writing and he could use it as a journal in his hunt to avenge her.

Surely someone could identify a knight with *arms vert a club or?* Blue horses were so rare he had never seen one. They would have left no tracks on the roads–especially if they could fly anyway. No, he would go to Charles and see if the coat of arms could be identified, keeping an eye open for any blue horses. The refrectress told him Sister Faith, one of the survivors, was writing a letter for the Bishop of Charles. This was to tell him what had happened and to ask him to pass the news on to Abbess Chiara, the head of her order, and to the Order of St Judas. She asked if he could take it there and gave him a set of the aquetate handcuffs, left behind by the raiders. Finding some very tolerable wine in his sister's cellar, he had a pleasant lunch. He thus headed back to St Polle in the late afternoon of the twenty-first day of the second Moon. Early next day he and his men took the north road via Verreric, arriving at Charles an hour before the gates shut.

Dean Lothrop rode into Closin Manor in the late afternoon. He discovered none of the family was present. There were only the manservant Gurth, the maid Bettine, the cook Margery and her two children Megan and Hlidric. Margery told him that Sir Congal and his party had taken Lady Morgana, Sergeant Hrolf and Cherry all away. This had been on the 18th and nobody had called since. They had taken all the steeds with them. She cooked a fine dinner for the dean and his party whilst he was ferreting around the manor and its outbuildings. She confirmed that Sir Helric had taken two treasure chests from the manor earlier. Lothrop was worried. Where could his harebrained brother Congal have gone? Presumably to wherever the Order of St Judas had taken Morgana. He knew it was a locality near St Polle but no more. Or perhaps he had carried off the maid Cherry somewhere. He now recalled there had been some brush between Congal and Cherry some years ago. Just like Congal to take advantage when he could! Anyway the estate looked a little neglected but nothing a little good management could not put right. Congal and Sir Helric appeared to have taken all the valuables between them. He called on Father Gervase at the village. He revealed that the estate was actually in a worse state than he had thought. He had heard from Margery the cook that Sir Congal had taken Lady Morgana away but knew nothing else. On the morning of the 24th, Lothrop rode back to Pincelle.

He stopped to enquire if Sir Congal had been seen. At first no one in the village knew anything. Certainly Sir Congal had not called there in daylight hours. Eventually he checked with the night watchmen. One of them, Heult, said he had seen a mounted party, including Morgana and her two unicorns, ride past the hour after dark on the 18th. With the river patrol riding past the village so often he had not thought it anything important.

"No," said Dean Lothrop not bothering to tip him. "It was nothing important." He led his party back up towards Arlo. A few myles from the town, a knight with four mounted hobilars thundered past, heading south. He thought he recognised the knight as one from the Grand Duke's menie. At Arlo he handed back the hired mounts. Unused to riding, he had become painfully saddlesore. Walking would be fast enough for the return to Charles. Meanwhile he again tested the hospitality of Sir Hildebrand at the castle. On the morning of the 25th he headed north, reaching the Bois de Proscrit around the eleventh hour.

Back at Charles, after Morgana's departure from the mansion, Corinne the housekeeper debated with the other servants as to what they should do. They all thought the raid should be reported. Sir Phanuel and the sergeant would be soon missed. Though there was no knowing when Sir Congal and the dean would return, when they did they would be asking a lot of awkward questions. Corinne went with Wilf to the South Gate. There they spoke to Sergeant Brunne. "The Lefey mansion has been raided! Sir Phanuel has been killed with Sergeant Norm and three others. What should we do?"

It took a little while for all this to sink into the sergeant's head. However, he had the sense to question a little more. Wilf told him that it was the Lady Morgana who had killed Sir Phanuel in fair fight but she and her four men had used dirty tricks to get into the building. The sergeant decided to send his regular soldier, Guibert, with Corrine and Wilf to tell their story to the duty knight at the citadel. He meanwhile would keep a watch for this Lady Morgana and her four thugs. He was glad he had not already allowed such a party to pass. He also sent John the weaver, one of the town watchmen, to alert the West and North Gates.

At the Citadel, the duty knight was Sir Desmond Fraicheur. He had been awake on duty all night and was looking forward to breakfast and a lazy day resting. True it had been a quiet, almost uneventful night but one always felt a little detached from reality after a night without sleep. Troubles would come soon enough with the St Simon's Day feast. But now here was that soldier Guibert, bringing some sort of trouble. He had with him a woman and a crossbowman who he recognised as being one of Sir Phanuel's. He invited them in courteously, to hear their story. This caused him to send out reinforcements to all the gates and patrols to search the city! He than reported the matter to Basylt Devisage, the Grand Duke himself. His Grace, a gaunt dark-haired man with piercing dark eyes, was shocked and uneasy, pacing the room. If a Knight

Banneret could be murdered in his own home, so could others. He knew that he himself was not the most popular of rulers. "Surely not actually murdered?" said Sir Desmond. "The crossbowman said it was a fair fight. If it was some internal family quarrel, surely the law need not be involved?"

"What about the three soldiers, in the service of the city under Sir Phanuel? They were not family and neither was the maid. No, the law must be invoked, even if the matter can be settled by wergild. It is indeed rather unusual that the damsel used a sword. Usually the fair sex use poison or a dagger in the night to solve domestic disputes. Women are banned from using swords or any blade longer than three hands under the law. In truth that is really a church ruling that King David ratified, so I do not take it too seriously. What wealth has this Lady Morgana? Wait, it comes to my mind now, that this lady is the brother of Squire Arthur Lefey. They are under the guardianship of Sir Helric Blaggart. The woman Corrine said the fight was about Sir Phanuel having killed Arthur? If Arthur is indeed dead, the estate stays in wardship until Morgana marries. An interesting tale indeed. It could even be true! Where is Sir Helric?"

"He has taken a party to make hurdles, ready for the festivities, your grace. They were to go at dawn-break."

"Very well, I will question him on his wardship of the young Arthur, when he returns. Meanwhile, as you have already roused the city, send also couriers to all the towns and villages, to proclaim that Lady Morgana Lefey is wanted for unlawful killing." Sir Desmond hurried off to summon some clerks. It would be a very late breakfast for him!

Meanwhile Sir Helric Blaggart had returned to the South Gate, only to hear the news of Sir Phanuel's death. This was a severe shock to him. He sent a message, hotfoot to Sir Miles, to have all his men including the workmen search for and arrest Morgana. He wished he had asked her more precisely for the location of this sick relative of her lady friend. Surely it was somewhere near the coppice, or why go there, so far from the road? What was the truth of the matter? Morgana had said her brother Arthur had been killed by Sir Phanuel and now Sir Phanuel was reported dead? He strode towards the citadel. The report was that Morgana had killed him but surely it would have been the knight with her. The knight Sir Richard Nogent! He had heard of him as a knight of minor importance, who rode with the river patrol. What did it matter? His own problem was that he himself was supposed to be guardian of Arthur and Morgana and was now at severe risk of losing the Grand Duke's favour! Whilst he had been a very loyal servant of Basylt's and knew a good few of his less reputable secrets, this made falling foul of him likely to be fatal. His devil-may-care attitude almost deserted him, as he was ushered into the Grand Ducal presence.

In the late morning, Morgana's party reached the village of Longstreet, with its large Simonite Abbey. They bribed a peasant to allow them to shelter their steeds in an orchard. He was impressed by the unicorns but had heard about them before. "A young lady passed by here with some such as they, some moons ago. It were the talk of the village for days but I did not see them then. That were half a moon before the flying creature came. It were seen only by night. A dragon some called it."

Morgana was more concerned with finding Dean Lothrop. She sent Sir Richard, Hrolf and Bergand to make enquiries in the village. The people they met did not remember any dean passing through but with so many travellers this was not significant. At the village inn, the owner, Jasper, said that as a matter of policy, he did not comment on the identity of guests. He had a room upstairs, available for the gentry and plenty of *clean* straw for the common room. When pressed he said that anyone connected with the cathedral would surely stay at the Abbey. He paid his rent to the abbey but they put up most of the better-paying travellers, snatching the bread from his mouth! After drinking some of the innkeeper's ale, which Bergand thought was watered, they headed for the abbey. The abbey porter was most reluctant to let them in. "This is a place of peace, not war. What have soldiers like yourselves to do here?"

The three were seriously considering a night break-in but a monk, attracted by the commotion, said that no dean was accommodated there at present. They returned to the orchard with the news. The others had had a light lunch and the party rode back down through the village on the way south.

The clouds thickened and the light wind grew chill as they rode, myle after myle, down the long grey road. As they rode, they debated the best means of finding Dean Lothrop. He would be travelling by day and staying under cover at night. He would undoubtedly be returning at some stage. Sir Richard suggested they take shelter in the Bois de Proscrit and wait to ambush him there. This lay seven myles beyond Ombec. The short Second Moon daylight faded to darkness as they came to the crest of a low hill. There ahead of them was the village of Ombec, lit by the flames of a burning hut. Morgana decided that they should all ride to give any assistance they could. It crossed her mind that this could be the work of the "dragon" mentioned by the orchard man. In the village the people were thronged about the flames but what water they could draw from their well was insufficient to make any headway against the blaze. Indeed pieces of burning thatch were being blown away and threatening to set fire to other huts. The villagers had long poles and rakes to drag the burning thatch off but then it was difficult to extinguish even these. The party started to give such assistance as they could. A villager told them that Carl, the hut owner, had managed to escape but his wife and three children had perished in the flames. Careless banking of the hut's fire they thought had been the cause. Watching the burning fragments showering around Morgana said, "If only *Eru* would send rain!" with a meaningful glance at Lady Abigail. "I will pray for rain!" This was little noticed until, as a result of a spell by Lady Abigail, it did commence to rain. The burning fragments ceased and the fires began to produce more smoke than flames. "A miracle! A miracle!" cried the villagers, looking at Morgana with considerably increased respect. Noticing the unicorns, some even remembered who she was, from times past. They wanted to feast the party and shelter them for the night but Morgana said they were in a hurry. As indeed they were. There was no knowing how far behind any pursuit was but staying in the village could be fatal. Followed by the blessings of the villagers, they rode onwards through the darkness.

The Grand Duke glared as Sir Helric entered the audience chamber. "I hear strange tales about the two wards I entrusted to your care. Would you trouble to explain the position?"

"Your Grace, I know little definite myself. I have secured the treasure and documents of the late Sir Daffyd's estate in my castle of Arlo. The son, Squire Arthur, I believe to be at their hunting lodge, at St Visseille, though I have not yet seen him. The daughter I believed to be yet at the Manor of Closin until I met her this very morning. I was early out getting hurdles made for the St Simon's Hopeday Feast, when she appeared. She was walking over the fields with a knight, a lady and some servants. She claimed to be escorting the lady to visit some sick relative and, indeed, claimed that this matter was desperate. She also claimed that Sir Phanuel had killed her brother, Squire Lefey and the knight, Sir Richard Nogent gave his word that this was the case. They were to return to resolve this matter but I have sent Sir Miles and some men to find her and bring her here."

"When I give one of my trusted knights the profitable guardianship of minors in my realm, I expect them to ensure the safety of those minors, just as much as of any treasure involved. I am most displeased about this. I suggest you ascertain that the Squire Arthur is as dead as Sir Phanuel undoubtedly is. When the damsel Morgana is taken, I will hold her in the citadel, here under my protection! Should she not forfeit the right, through criminal acts, her husband will hold the Lefey estate and I shall decide who he will be! Go!"

"Yes, your Grace, it shall be as your Grace desires," said Sir Helric as he backed out.

Sir Desmond eventually managed a hasty breakfast, after

he had dispatched messengers with proclamations throughout the Grand Duchy. He had an uncomfortable nap until waking up in the late afternoon. Remembering the problems of the morning he went through to the Duty Chamber to find out the latest news. The duty knight, Sir Geoffrey Nombre, told him that Sir Miles had reported that Lady Morgana and Sir Richard Nogent had ridden southwards. His Grace had dispatched Sir Mordant Bec and five hobilars to track them in the expectation that they were fleeing to Closin, or the Stetian border. Sir Helric was in a foul temper and had sent Sir Flamen Swyn on foot with some men to St Visseille to find out the truth about Squire Arthur. Sir Desmond had no great liking for Sir Helric and rather relished his being out of favour with the Grand Duke. The Grand Duke was no paladin himself but Sir Desmond had always felt that Sir Helric was just a brigand in the armour of a knight. As he was musing thus, there was a hail from the gate and an old friend of his, Sir Herbert Decre, rode in. Sir Herbert had served alongside him in Prince Eude's army, four or five years ago. In those days it was the Royal Foixian army and they were all together. Now he was from Bara and Sir Herbert was a foreigner from Perigord! "Hey you old rapscallion, is your armour squeaking yet?"

"In truth a little, but well met my old comrade. However, I have affairs of moment to attend to for the nonce. There has been devil's work at the Priory of Stregafume and my sister has been murdered in her bed. I need to discover the bearer of arms *vert a club or spiked sangue*. He and a witch, with demons and two giant blue horses, raided the priory and killed my sister Mania. I have sworn to be avenged on this green knight. Who could tell me his name?"

Sir Desmond and Sir Geoffrey were shocked by these tidings but the latter said, "*Vert a club or* is Sir Richard Nogent. There is an order just out for his arrest for unlawful killings here in Charles. We know naught of witches but he has with him an unknown lady, dressed in black and the damsel Morgana Lefey."

"Where does he live? Where has he gone? I must be after him!"

"Hold, not so hasty, Perigordan. These sound like Baratrean matters to me. You must report more fully to his Grace the Grand Duke. Also, since church property was raided, I suppose Bishop Innocent should be told too."

"Yes," replied Sir Herbert. "There have been strange happenings indeed and perhaps there should be long debates before action is decided."

"Your talk of witchcraft makes this black-clad lady sound most sinister. May *Eru* protect us all. It will soon be dark; rest here, my friend, and resume your chase tomorrow. In fact if his Grace permits I would like to accompany you. I saw but three men with you and Sir Richard's party numbers at least six."

Whilst Sir Geoffrey went to arrange for interviews with the Grand Duke and the Bishop of Charles, Sir Desmond had the gratifying task of telling Sir Helric about these other warlike acts of his ward. To his amusement, Sir Helric blanched white. "Dagon take her and all the Lefeys! What have I done to deserve this?...I have much work to do for the St Simon's Hopeday Feast. Alas, I need to go into the city."

He hurried away, out of the citadel. Sir Desmond guessed he would stay away some time, for days if possible. His Grace was going to be even angrier.

Indeed Grand Duke Basylt was both angry and worried.

When he had heard Sir Herbert Decre out, he summoned a council to debate the matter.

Bishop Innocent of Charles was also shocked to hear of the deaths of Pazan, the Justicar of St Judas and the Sub Prioress Mania. He was appalled to know that the witches had been freed, to do who-knows-what evil deeds against his congregations. Normally reliant on his dean, Lothrop, when there were difficult matters to be dealt with, he made a conscious effort to act on this one himself. He surprised the other members of the council with his vehemence. These demonic raiders who had desecrated church property and persons must be destroyed by any means possible! He would draft out a Church Ordinance demanding the bodies of the guilty ones, dead or alive! Also present at the council, as was her right, was her Grace, Grand Duchess Disildt, by whose right her husband ruled Bara. She rarely spoke at council but prompted by one of her ladies-in-waiting, she declared an interest. The lady-in-waiting was Genevieve Fraicheur, sister of Sir Desmond. The Fraicheur family was at a low ebb, due to the Narchadians laying waste their small estate near Sincelle.

Their manor was a smoke-blackened ruin and the land a sparsely populated hunting wilderness. Some of it lay in the outlaw-infested Bois De Proscrit. At twenty-nine, Lady Genevieve was left firmly on the shelf; her intended groom, selected by her father when she was nine, died long ago in the wars in Hunara. She had the Roman nose of her family and while it made her brother look distinguished it was not at all in the established mode of female beauty. Disildt, who turned few heads herself, had taken her on partly because of her plainness and partly because of her patient efficiency. When younger she had been accustomed to do much hunting on the family preserves and found little scope for her energy in Charles. She had a hound, Dulcie which served as an excuse to take many walks around the citadel bailey. Now she viewed the arrival of Sir Herbert with his mission as an opportunity for herself. Waiting on the Grand Duchess was a comfortable, secure post but she hankered after a little adventure or at least a travelling holiday.

Disildt spoke. "In this regrettable affair are concerned two ladies of this Grand Duchy. As first lady in this realm, I am concerned that all the proprieties should be observed, whether or not those accused have brought disgrace upon us. To represent us I propose that Lady Genevieve Fraicheur, escorted by her brother Sir Desmond, accompany Sir Herbert. I suggest she take the woman Corinne as her lady's maid, since she can identify the accused. I believe the church should also play a part in this. Presumably the Order of St Judas can provide some forces to assist?"

"Alas," said the bishop, "I fear that with Pazan and many of his men dead or otherwise occupied, the Order is in disarray. I shall write to the Grand Master at Ekthalon, asking for more support but this will not aid us now. We are fighting witchcraft and need a priest with the powers of *Eru* to assist those facing it. I have such a one but he is away on business with my dean. One other is here that could suffice. I suggest you send Psalmodier, the Grand Ducal Chaplain with the quest."

And so it was thus ordered. The party was given authority, by signet ring and writ, to order all officials, church and lay to assist them. Their quest to seek and take, alive or dead, the persons listed in the Bishop's Ordinance. The party, all mounted, comprised: Sir Herbert and his three hobilars, Sir Desmond Fraicheur and his sister Genevieve, Chaplain Psalmodier and Mistress Corinne.

Genevieve took her pointing hound Dulcie with her and her small hunting arbalist. The hound was a first-class tracker and could come in useful.

Remembering Sir Mordant Bec had already headed down the south road towards Arlo, Pincelle and Closin, Sir Herbert decided to visit Suie first. He knew Sir Richard Nogent's manor lay nearby. If that drew a blank, he thought it would be cunning to cross the border into Thentis, before turning south again. That way he could approach Closin from the west.

Sir Mordant, meanwhile, had camped overnight in the wilds between Longstreet and Ombec. He had stopped to make enquiries in Longstreet at the inn and the abbey. Neither had seen Lady Morgana or her unicorns. There had been some inquisitive strangers looking for a priest, said the innkeeper; a dean said the abbey porter. This meant nothing to Sir Mordant, so he pushed on until it was dark. He was afraid of passing his prey in the night. In the morning he came to Ombec and there he did hear news of Morgana and her party. Apparently they were fire-fighting heroes to the villagers. Sir Mordant kept his counsel as to why he was seeking them. By the village well, trodden into the mud, he found a tattered copy of the Grand Duke's Proclamation. If there was anyone in the village who could read, they had not read it yet! He replaced it with a new one, of which he carried several copies. One of his men had fallen sick so he paid a peasant to care for him. Around the eleventh hour, he found he was approaching the notorious Bois de Proscrit. An ancient haunt of outlaws it had many times been cut back from the road. There was a gibbet complete with body dangling, so he nailed a copy of the proclamation to it.

Proclamation

The Lady Morgana Lefey is hereby ordered to present herself for trial with her menie, for the unlawful killing of four servants of the late Captain of Charles, Sir Phanuel Lefey. The said Lady is also accused of using a bladed weapon in excess of three hands in length. The trial to be held at the Citadel, Charles, on the first day of the third Moon 706ATN. If she fails to attend, she and her menie shall be declared Outlaw.

By Order
Basylt Devisage
Grand Duke of Bara

Some time after noon, he reached Arlo. Stopping in the town he split his men up, so they should get any news they could of the fugitives. He assumed that the castle would have received one of the proclamations by the earlier messengers. When his men reassembled, they had all drawn a blank. Over a belated lunch in an inn named the Golden Pile, Sir Mordant decided what to do next. The Lady Morgana's party had left Ombec last night, riding south, yet they had not been seen at Arlo. Of course the gates would have been shut anyway but the river made bypassing almost impossible close to the town. They would have known that and possibly have cut across country to the Arwyn Road Bridge, to the east. Or they could have hidden in the Bois de Proscrit? But why should they do that except for just a rest? Sir Mordant thought Morgana would head for the Pincelle ferry. He had been told she had relatives in Stetia and that seemed her obvious destination. It was possible he could catch them yet, at Pincelle. Impetuously he ordered his men to horse again. If he forced the pace, they could get to Pincelle before the gates shut at dusk. A few myles down the road, his party thundered past three clerics, walking the other way. Sir Mordant recognised the Dean of Charles Cathedral. As he rode on, he remembered that this dean was the brother of the now deceased Sir Phanuel. Just as well he had kept going. It would have taken half an hour at least to tell the tale. The dean would discover the news of his family bereavement soon enough. He looked anxiously at where the sun should be, behind the clouds. Still a good few myles to go. Would they make it?

Behind him followed the bishop's messenger, Luce, with his hound Trix. Riding messages could be a dangerous occupation, even in these civilised times of peace. Luce used Trix to search out the way ahead when he feared a possible ambush. He arrived at Arlo, two hours after Sir Mordant. There, as was his custom, he stopped at the Sheep's Head Inn for a meal and to rest his horse. For Arlo he had two ordinances to deliver, one for the town square and one for the castle. Usually he tipped Ned, the inn's boy to deal with these but Ned was away on an errand. Gille the landlord asked Luce what the latest ordinance said, not being able to read himself. Luce spelled it out.

Church Ordinance

Wanted, dead or alive, the miscreants: Sir Richard Nogent, Lady Abigail Clove, Lady Morgana Lefey, a number of demons in their control, including one of dwarf stature. For murders most foul, witchcraft, theft and sacrilege. Also the escaped fugitives: Miss Edie a witch, Miss Vanova a witch and Miss Louise Berde under suspicion of witchcraft.

Decreed by

Innocent, Bishop of Charles

Gille and Babette, the maid, were most shocked. Lady Morgana had stayed in the inn for a night, when she brought her unicorns down from Valles. Lady Morgana had let Babette stroke them and had given her a large tip. Surely there was some strange mistake or plot, thought Babette. She could not believe Lady Morgana would be involved in murders and witchcraft and such, she did not know about the others named. She offered to take Ned's place and deliver the ordinances herself.

Gille said, "Yes, one nailed up on the stage in the square and the other delivered to the castle. But do not think it will get you out of washing the dishes! They still be there when you get back!"

Babette went out but she did not go to the square stage or the castle. Instead she visited her friend Louise, the maid of the Hegeux family household. There they cut the parchments into thin strips, for use as ribbons or garters. Meanwhile Luce left to ride south. Just after leaving the gate he passed Dean Lothrop and his two companions. He did not stop. The dean had made a fuss when once he brought his dog into the cathedral. There was little love between them. He carried on, to sleep in an abandoned peasant's hut he had used before, a little way off from the road. He would visit Pincelle and Closin on the morrow, the 24th.

The Bois de Proscrit

In his state chambers at Bosen, Peron Quixano Rasguno felt restless. This was normal: whenever things were quiet he would look round for some other scheme to set in motion. He had been elected Peron because his energy and ability were recognised by his more relaxed peers. His messenger, Litwe, had returned more than a week ago, saying Morgana would try to recover the ochyo from Charles. The news from Narchad was good. The Narchadians had spent a long winter feasting and quarrelling amongst themselves. There was a possibility of civil war which Quixano was hoping to foment. Because of tit-for-tat border raids, food was running short and parts of their country faced starvation. However, the Chaotic High Command was as ever sending a trickle of goblin and other reinforcements to them. Eventually, leaders would come, demanding more forceful action on the borders. This is why he wanted the ochyo to smuggle into position, at their headquarters, whilst the Narch was in recess. He now had a wizard able to use the Or palantyte mirror, a man called Begus. His powers were small but that was an advantage in that he was prepared to watch the mirror for long hours for pay. He had been trying to contact Morgana's Argent mirror but it had always been in darkness. Nothing had been heard from her and he really wanted that ochyo. Perhaps her uncles had caught her and Arthur trying to recover it with unknown consequences? He felt he had to do something. The overloud twanging of a mandolin irritated his ears. He was not very musical at the best of times but that Minstrel Tonaldo's songs annoyed him to distraction. Morgana might appreciate him more. His music might be dreadful but he was a resourceful and able paid agent of the Juanta. His mother had been the daughter of an Ombardi agent but no one knew who his father was. The Juanta suspected that he passed on information to the Ombardi business network but were not too worried about that. His brash debonair approach sometimes obtained information quicker than cautious undercover spying. He was also of course wholly expendable. Who else could he send? The rather fractious and grim knight, Don Incio Fulminar, was available. He would do; he had actually met Morgana once, though whether she would remember him was doubtful. He would send the pair of them to assist her in obtaining the ochyo and possibly putting it into place. They could also tell her to look into her mirror each dawn so messages could be passed. Begus had a blackboard and chalk for writing these communications. He would give Don Incio 500 gilden pezzi as earnest money. They could buy the ochyo if necessary.

"Guard! Fetch me Don Incio and that caterwauling minstrel!"

Don Incio Fulminar

You are a Stetian knight from a Hidalgo family. The Fulminars have long owned the castle village and estates at Girrin. Close to the Narchad border, the castle and village were burnt eight years ago. A few of your peasants still try to live on the estate but it is always a question as to whether they or the Narchadians will reap the harvest. The castle had survived many raids previously but your brother Sucio was bribed to let the enemy in. He ran off with your wife Lealtad. You and your father tracked after them but were ambushed. Your father and most of his men were killed. Your mother Muerta committed suicide as a result. You then took up service with the Juanta's forces, hoping for a chance to obtain revenge against Sucio, Lealtad and the Narchadians ever since. However, after a life of disappointments, you have grown accustomed to expecting the worst of everything. Now you are to act as lapdog to Peron Quixano's favourite niece. Worse you have been lumbered with tone-deaf Tonaldo as escort!

Tonaldo the Minstrel

You are certainly the finest mandolin-playing minstrel in Stetia. You were taught from a young age by Fidel the elf. He, however, never really fully appreciated your talents. He was paid to teach you by your benefactors. You believe your benefactors were a highborn hidalgo family who preferred that their name remain unknown. Probably your mother was a disgraced daughter of the family. To judge by your appearance, ruddy-cheeked and red-haired, your father was not a Stetian. It matters not, as you have been successfully making your way in the world through your own efforts. Being handsome, charming, an expert swordsman and above all a superlative minstrel, the world is at your feet. The Juanta of Stetia is paying you to carry messages and collect information, giving you the opportunity to display to foreign parts your musical genius. You have so far visited Thentis, Perigord, Bara, Fara and Azelad (alas, the Azeladians have very peculiar views about music). You are now going to assist this Lady Morgana with the grumpy Don Incio. What a charmingly romantic prospect!

As Morgana's party rode south down the road, the rain ceased. Sir Richard Nogent and Hrolf led the way, with Bergand guarding the rear. Ahead of them lay a clump of bushes to the left of the road and Hrolf sensed there was something lurking there. At his signal they halted. Before he could investigate, a great flying creature swooped down to attack them, from the rear! Jack the pack mule immediately stampeded off to the right. Cherry had been leading it with a piece of rope and the jerk pulled her from her mount onto the muddy road. Bergand loosed hasty quarrel at the creature, but it went well wide. Sergeant Hrolf had the wit to dismount quickly as his mount stampeded to the left, followed by Lady Abigail's unicorn Hilda. Abigail also managed to drop off onto her feet without discomfort. From the bushes ahead, three deer stampeded into the darkness, Hrolf's ambush revealed. The flying creature, a night wyrm, swooped back to attack the pack mule. The desperate beast managed to evade its first strike, as Sir Richard charged up to its rescue. The wyrm was forced to turn to face the knight, who spitted it with his long lance. In death its body turned out to be smaller than they had thought at first. A non-fire-breathing member of the dragon species, it was the first that Morgana had seen in the flesh.

The party then took half an hour to recover the panicked steeds. Cherry scraped as much mud as she could off her formerly yellow dress.

They approached the Bois de Proscrit forest a little short of midnight. A gallows stood beside the road with a figure dancing beneath it! At its feet crouched a cat. As they came near the figure turned towards them and shouted, "Awa awa, ye'll break the spell! Leave me! Leave me to call ma brother doun. Leave us in peace!"

"I can cut him down from my horse but he's well dead and smelling!"

"Nae nae, it's his spirit I need. He stole oor mother's money. My money, the money she left to me! He has buried it in the forest and I need his spirit to find it. Awa from us, or I'll curse ye with an imp. I hae the powers, I warn ye. Aye, folks keep well awa frae me. They say I'm a wee bit mad but I'm no mad. No mad at all. It's just that I see things as they really are."

"And how are things now?" asked Sir Richard as they backed away.

"Things will be just fine once I get ma mother's treasure. Then I'll be able to assume my true greatness and you, with all the world, will listen to what I have to say. And Michael, ma brother Michael, I'll make him wish he'd never died! Or lived! Aye, [mutter mutter], and yon horseman

"Awa awa, ye'll break the spell! Leave me! Leave me to call ma brother doun. Leave us in peace!"

feller, he's wishing he had never startled Mark about his business, [mutter mutter]."

"What horseman?"

"Him lying yonder. Go, get on your way. I doubt but the spell is ruined!"

The party skirted past him and his cat, leaving him muttering and cursing. Moving in close to the black edge of the trees they heard rustlings and saw movements at several points. Hrolf dismounted and crept towards some bushes. Immediately two wolves leapt out to attack him. Nine others followed in support. Bergand dropped one with a bolt as Hrolf killed another. Sir Richard spitted the largest he could see, the leader and his pack fled. They found a dead horse with two crossbow quarrels sticking in it, which the wolves had been eating as their dinner. Nearby was the body of a man, also a little gnawed. Everything of value had been stolen from him except for three sheets of parchment, which they took. Groping into the wood, they stumbled into an obvious camping site clearing. There was an outcrop of rock guarding one side and the long dead ashes of a fire in the middle. They tethered the steeds and lit the fire and then set watches to sleep out the rest of the night. This was the first time Morgana had slept out in the open but she was so tired she fell asleep immediately.

She awoke in the middle of the night, cold and feeling a twig digging into her hip. For one used to sleeping in a feather bed, the ground was very hard. On one side of her lay Cherry and the three men, all snoring. By the other side of the fire sat Minut on a log with his back to her, staring into the trees. She turned over and found Aunt Abigail lying beside her looking at her.

"Morgana, I have not had a chance to thank you for saving my life. Years ago when my husband was killed I first thought my life was finished. Your father gave me St Visseille to care for and I learnt to be happy there. Then those people came and Arthur gave his life trying to save me. I thought I was dead and gone. Those people tried to pretend I had done all sorts of ridiculous things–most of it sheer nonsense about black witchcraft, which I am sure the Chaotics themselves would laugh to scorn. They were going to burn me the next day. With Arthur and Sir Daffyd dead and all the brothers helping those people, I thought I had no hope left. Then when you and your friends came I could hardly believe it. I will serve you from now on in any way you wish. I have the Magh Pozum though my spells are limited as yet."

"Thank you, dearest Aunt. I will be most glad of your company and assistance. Once we have dealt with Lothrop we have the ochyo to deliver to Quixano. Then I think he has some other task in mind for me."

"Quixano, eh? My brother was always hatching complicated schemes and getting someone else to do the difficult bits. Probably when he hears we are on the run, he will just let you settle at Relajar. Or Lozana! That is an old property owned by your mother near Relajar."

"Well, if Quixano has nothing for me to do, there is always your ghost woman's princess to rescue."

"Morgana, much as I sympathise with anyone in the clutches of the Order of St Judas I do not want you to get yourself killed in a suicide mission."

"Well, we will see. We had better get to sleep so as to be fit in the morning."

At dawn they breakfasted and set Sir Richard and Minut to watch the road for the dean. Since they had not met him, they believed him still to be in the south. Lady Abigail was sure he had been the brains behind the plot to kill

Arthur and it must have been his doing to involve the Order of St Judas in her capture. Morgana looked at the three parchments found the night before. They were identical proclamations.

Proclamation

The Lady Morgana Lefey, is hereby ordered to present herself for trial with her menie, for the unlawful killing of four servants of the late Captain of Charles, Sir Phanuel Lefey. The said Lady is also accused of using a bladed weapon in excess of three hands in length. The trial to be held at the Citadel, Charles, on the first day of the third Moon 706ATN. If she fails to attend, she and her menie shall be declared Outlaw.

By Order
Basylt Devisage
Grand Duke of Bara

So she was now a fugitive from the grand duke's justice as well as that of the Church. She realised it would be suicidal to return for the trial. Bergand noticed a very faint path leading deeper into the forest at the back of the campsite. Hrolf, Lady Abigail and Bergand set off down it in single file. A few paces in, there was a hideous groaning sound from nearby. Nothing else happening, they proceeded cautiously. Hrolf found a well-hidden treadle-trap triggering mechanism on the path. He told the other two to stand back and took a heavy piece of dead wood from nearby. He threw this onto the treadle. It bounced off and nothing happened. He retrieved it cautiously and tried again. This time they heard a click and two arrows sped straight down the track towards them. Hrolf and Lady Abigail managed to jump to the side but Bergand was too slow. One arrow glanced off his helmet but the other stuck in his left elbow. They took him back to the camp as it was bleeding profusely. First Lady Abigail drenched the dressing with the St Bandade water, which was known to speed healing, and then bandaged it tightly. Sir Daffyd had always kept some wound dressings at the manor, though the infection-countering herbs may have lost their merit.

"I do not think we need to risk ourselves anymore that way," said Hrolf.

"No, it is absolutely certain Dean Lothrop will not be in the forest," replied Lady Abigail.

"Alas, I will not be able to use my crossbow for a while, but my sword arm is good," sighed Bergand.

Around the eleventh hour, a knight with four mounted men at arms trotted down the road from the north. They stopped at the gallows and nailed a piece of parchment to it, before carrying on southwards. When they were out of sight, Sir Richard rode across to look at the parchment. It was another copy of the proclamation, which he tore down. Half an hour later a lone figure came up from the south. Sir Richard rode out to challenge him, thinking he might be the Lothrop. However, he said he was Panka the healer. He carried a great bundle of parchment slips, which were the recipes for medicines, and said to cure all known diseases. Sir Richard said he was more interested in treating wounds. Panka said he had some slips with herbal recipes, for making healing salves for those too. Many of the herb ingredients would be found in this very forest beside them, said Panka. After some protracted bargaining, Sir Richard was pleased to buy five salve recipes for only ten gilden pezzi. The writing was in dwarf runes but Sir Richard knew Minut would be able to translate it. Proudly he showed the others his purchases when Morgana and Cherry took over on the road.

Minut could indeed read them. "Green mistletoe! The nearest of that is 600 myles away. Red ivy! There is some of that but it's only to be picked under the full moon! Bishop's ragwort, never heard of that. Purple toadstools! They grow only in the tunnels of Varadh, from whence I have been exiled." He burst out laughing: "I think you have been swindled."

Lady Abigail said, "Bishop's ragwort is a flower developed from common ragwort. There is some in the bishop's garden at Charles. It is used for dyeing vestments purple. There may well be merit in these remedies but the time needed to collect and produce them is ridiculous. I fancy that the holey[5] water from St Bandade will be far more effective anyway. Under normal circumstances I would expect Bergand's wound to heal in a fortnight to three weeks. We will see how long it takes, treated with the magic water. Luckily it is his left arm, so he can still wield a sword, if not his crossbow."

Some time after noon, a rider with a dog following him arrived. He too stuck a parchment to the gallows and rode on. Morgana found it was the Bishop's Ordinance.

---

5 Holey water, from Arteisia's healing spring at St Bandade, was so called because of its bubbles or holes!

Church Ordinance

Wanted, dead or alive, the miscreants: Sir Richard Nogent, Lady Abigail Clove, Lady Morgana Lefey, a number of demons in their control, including one of dwarf stature. For murders most foul, witchcraft, theft and sacrilege. Also the escaped fugitives: Miss Edie a witch, Miss Vanova a witch and Miss Louise Berde under suspicion of witchcraft.

Decreed by
Innocent, Bishop of Charles

Morgana took it down and put it in her saddlebag as a memento. She felt frightened but a little proud as well, to have become famous or rather infamous in this way. They will be singing songs about me next, she thought. Eventually Lady Abigail and Hrolf took over the watch. Morgana and Sir Richard decided they would have another attempt at searching the forest path. As with the previous party, they had advanced only a short distance when there was the hideous groaning sound.

"An alarm trap," commented Sir Richard. Carrying on, they found the sprung treadle that had loosed the arrows that hit Bergand. Further on, on the left side, they found a boggy patch. Sir Richard tested it with his sword, which found no bottom. The track then veered sharply left, going between dense bushes. There they spotted a less well-concealed pit-trap with spikes at the bottom. This was a dangerous route for strangers! Further on, Morgana sensed someone watching them from the right. Sir Richard led on and soon felt the ground give beneath him a little–another treadle but it had already been sprung. Then Morgana saw a face showing through the leaves ahead. "There are men about us. This is too dangerous for just two of us. We will go back now and leave the forest dwellers in peace." They went back, blazing the bushes nearest the traps they had found to mark their position.

At dusk they saw Mad Mark return to the gallows, to make another attempt at his spell. They left him to it. Morgana did not expect Dean Lothrop to travel after dark, so they all returned to the camp. Knowing they had been spotted by the forest denizens, they watched in shifts of two, through the night.

In the early hours of the 24th it began to rain and dawn broke to a wet miserable day. Visibility was down to twelve hets (a het is a unit of measurement, the height of a tall man) much of the time. At breakfast Cherry told them that the food supplies were running low. If they tightened their belts they could last perhaps another two days. No game had been seen in the forest, perhaps the wolves had frightened it away. These must have returned to finish the rider, horse and their own pack mates, as there was little but bones left out there now. Sir Richard suggested they look for berries and nuts. Lady Abigail reminded him of the children's nursery rhyme: "Here we go gathering nuts in May. May is the Azelad word for the fifth moon, when there are no nuts, as they ripen in the eighth moon at the earliest."

"There might be some still from last year."

"Not likely but there will be edible roots we may dig."

"Yes," said Cherry, "I know of some and also some bush leaves which they used to eat in Narchad."

She and Lady Abigail plunged off into the thick of the trees.

Mad Mark's spell must have failed again, for the body still hung on the gallows. On the road no one came until the tenth hour, when a party of three appeared–a tax collector and his escort of two soldiers. This being Woeday, there were few travellers but with the rain so heavy it was difficult to be sure the road was empty. They stuck it out nevertheless. Towards dusk Lady Abigail and Cherry returned, soaked to the skin, but carrying large bundles of assorted roots. Well cleaned and boiled, they tasted rather peculiar. In fact, had it not been for the liberal seasoning added, they would have been plain nasty. Nevertheless they were much needed food, which would eke out the rations for another two days. In the camp Bergand had spotted a face peering round a tree at him. Their presence must be keeping the local outlaws worried. They kept a good watch at the camp, to deter any attack.

That midnight Lady Buija suddenly re-appeared before Lady Abigail. "You have gone the wrong way! Princess Maudette is to the north." Just then a raindrop almost extinguished her candle's flame, with a hiss. "I will come again!" she said quickly and disappeared before poor Abigail could make any response.

By dawn the rain had ceased but it was overcast and chill. Being a midweek day, there were more travellers on the road. Around the ninth hour a sizeable group of peasants appeared led by a cleric. Sir Richard rode out to investigate, on a pretext of asking for food. The cleric replied, "*Eru* be with you, I am Friar Temoin. Alas, we have little food ourselves; we hope to obtain some at Ombec. We are pilgrims travelling to Valles to celebrate the St Simon's Hopeday feast."

"I have money to pay for any food you may have."

Immediately he was offered an array of pathetic fragments, a crust of bread, a small carrot, an apple core and a rind of cheese. Even Abigail's roots looked more appetising. "I thank you kindly for your offers but I was looking for heavier fare. Your need looks to be greater than mine." He threw them a handful of silver florins, which they accepted with many thanks.

An hour later three more figures came, also from the south. Sir Richard rode out again with his tale of needing food. He could see they were churchmen but did not recognise any of them. "Who are you?" he asked. The closest one replied, bridling, "I am Sexton Ragout and we have no food to spare! *Eru* favours the provident."

They strode on and Sir Richard let them go. He was in trouble enough with the Church already. Hardly had these gone when a string of mules with three merchants and four soldiers appeared. These he left alone but continued the watch until he was relieved.

Sir Herbert Decre and his party rode all day. They went via Longstreet and some myles down the road towards Ombec. Then they cut across country, avoiding that village. Unfortunately, with the night being cloudy, they missed their way. It was a long time after dark when they sighted the village of Suie. This would be shut up for the night and none of the party knew where Sir Richard Nogent's home was, relative to the village. Thus they camped for the night in the open. They were glad of their two tents, as it rained heavily in the small hours. Next day they rode into the village. A funeral was taking place–Guilleam Tim and his wife Jeaneton, burnt in their hut on the night of Startday 22nd: a strange affair because Jeaneton had always been so careful about everything. They had been so happy, now that their troublesome neighbour, the witch Edie, had been taken away. No one in the village admitted to having seen Sir Richard recently. The way they spoke revealed that he was popular in the area. Neither the Proclamation nor the Bishop's Ordinance was present on the village green's notice tree. Sir Herbert suspected they had been posted but then removed. Reluctant directions were extracted as to the whereabouts of the Nogent Manor (in sight of the village as it happened).

They split into two groups to approach from two sides, trying to stop anyone escaping. Cautiously they crept into position, keeping an eye on both the manor and the village. No movement was seen. Then Lady Genevieve sounded her hunting horn and both groups charged up to the manor. It was in rather a shabby state. The woodwork was in need of repair and the tapestries and hangings inside were faded and moth-eaten. Even the rushes on the floor were ancient and dusty. The only people present were the Steward Rent with his wife and son. They were taken greatly by surprise. They had not seen Sir Richard for three weeks. They had been told that there were some ridiculous accusations against him but they did not believe them. They knew that Sir Richard had made enemies, through his successes against the smugglers, and believed these accusations were all part of a plot by them. Sir Herbert had come with the intention of burning the manor down but now felt that perhaps he should not be so hasty. They had a substantial lunch instead. The weather was turning wet and miserable outside. Sir Richard had had some Stetian wine in his cellar but it was poor quality. Sir Desmond used the Grand Duke's writ to requisition some extra food supplies. The cheese and smoked ham were excellent. At the meal they discussed again their mission. Realising that the two knights were getting rather too comfortably settled, Lady Genevieve said they must be on their way. The villagers would now warn Sir Richard away, if ever he came near the manor again whilst their party was still there. She insisted that they should stick to their original plan. Dolefully the two knights agreed and they rode over the border into Thentis in the afternoon.

There was no hindrance at the border stone, not a soul to be seen through the drizzle. With Thentis and Bara having been so recently parts of the same realm, with the same customs, there had seemed little point in setting up border posts. In the village of La Turbie, they put up at the inn, the Toufou Arms. Whilst there they were visited by Sir Jean Toufou whose family owned the village and much of the land around it. His nephew, the head of the family, was standard-bearer to the Duke of Wardour. Sir Jean said he was duty-bound to check the intentions of so powerful a party entering this duchy of Wardour. Sir Desmond showed him the Proclamation and the Ordinance and told them of their mission.

"Well of course we frown on murder and witchcraft and such but the Grand Duke has no authority here. Neither does your bishop. We come under…under…forget the fellow's name, his grace the Archbishop of Borolon. Of course, eventually the Church may spread the net. Probably using those nosy zealots of the Order of St Judas but until then I am afraid my hands are tied. Good luck in your endeavours but meanwhile let us hear what other news you have."

He sent for some wine from his manor cellar and joined

them for dinner. He was a pleasant, entertaining fellow, especially for the ladies. They spent a merry evening discussing the latest happenings in Thentis and Bara.

Sir Mordant Bec and his men did manage to reach Pincelle before the gates shut on the evening of the 23rd. There they stayed for the night. They discovered Dean Lothrop had also been asking questions about Morgana Lefey there. She had last been seen there Midweek Day, the 18th. Then her two unicorns had been recognised amongst a group of other riders' mounts. The villagers were sure that Lady Morgana would be found innocent when the trial was held. The Lefey family was held in high esteem in Pincelle. The villagers were shocked and horrified at dawn, when Luce the bishop's messenger brought his Ordinance.

Even Sir Mordant was surprised and began asking questions about Sir Richard Nogent and Lady Abigail Clove. He knew himself of Sir Richard's years of service with the river patrol. He rated him far more worthy than, for instance, Sir Phanuel or Sir Congal. He surmised that Sir Richard, an old friend of Morgana's, had rescued her from the Order of St Judas. Then presumably she had talked him into aiding Lady Abigail as well. He knew just how such an affair might have got out of hand and that the churchmen were likely to exaggerate things. However, he had to comply with his orders as best he could. It seemed to him that since Lothrop had not found Morgana at Closin and she had not been seen in Arlo or Pincelle, two possibilities remained: first, that she had fled to Stetia via Minbec or Sinselle, or second, she was lurking in the Bois de Proscrit. As he was deliberating, the river patrol, under Sir George Bellin, arrived. Sir Mordant ordered him to stay at Pincelle for three days, just in case the fugitives did come that way. Luce had still to take an Ordinance to Closin so Sir Mordant gave him a copy of the Proclamation to go with it. He was to keep his eyes open and report back to the river patrol on his return. Running the fugitives down was not going to be easy now. If they had crossed the Arwyn into Stetia he was too late. If they were in the Bois de Proscrit, an army would be needed to drive them out. However, knowing Sir Richard was a man of honour, he decided to give him the option of a trial by battle. He wrote out a challenge and led his men back up the road to the north.

On the afternoon of the 25th, Morgana saw the knight with the four hobilars come back. They dismounted and began to erect a tent, somewhat upwind of the gallows. The knight himself rode over to the forest edge carrying a stave. He stopped and shouted, "I challenge Sir Richard Nogent! I challenge Sir Richard Nogent to combat!" Then he hammered the stave into the ground with the pommel of his sword and rode back to his men. The party were concerned that this force had been set to block the road, just where they had hoped to catch Dean Lothrop. They sent Minut to check the stave and, as expected, there was a parchment attached to it. This he brought back and Lady Abigail read it out loud.

To Sir Richard Nogent,

I am Sir Mordant Bec, Servant of His Grace Basylt Devisage, Grand Duke of Bara. I have intelligence that you are hidden in this forest. You have served this realm long and well. I regret this quarrel that has arisen between you and the laws of His Grace. Your disagreements with the Church are not my affair. On behalf of His Grace I make you a fair offer. I challenge you to single combat a L'outrance, my sword against your famous long lance. If I fall, my men will return to Charles to report my failure to bring you to justice. If you fall, I shall take your head and return to Charles, reporting that your followers had escaped safely to Stetia. If you do not respond to these generous terms, I shall wait here until His Grace sends sufficient forces to kill every person hiding in the Bois de Proscrit without exception.

Mordant Bec, Knight

They considered this offer at length and Sir Richard declared he would take up the challenge. He forced his horse Melonda through the undergrowth, so as to emerge not too close to the campsite. Then he rode up to the soldier on guard on the road. "I am Sir Richard Nogent and I accept the challenge issued by Sir Mordant Bec, on the terms offered."

Sir Mordant emerged from the tent and mounted his horse. "The terms as written?"

"Yes."

They then rode to positions opposite one another some ten hets apart, parallel to the road. Then they charged one another. Sir Mordant had thought that Sir Richard was past his best and that his long lance was mainly used for fishing things out of the river. He thought he could deflect it easily but, as the night wyrm and the great wolf had found, it was deadly. Catching the base of his helmet it almost decapitated him and the joust was over.

Sir Richard rode over to the hobilars. "I salute the bravery of your master. He was a good servant of Bara. Take his body to be buried with honour."

The soldiers growled and shook their spears at him but did not try to attack him. He returned to the forest whilst they collected Sir Mordant's body and dismantled the tent. As they did so, a cowled figure came up the road from the south. It stopped and spoke to the hobilars, accompanying them when they departed. Morgana suspected this might be Dean Lothrop but she felt fighting the soldiers would be a breach of the terms of the joust. She sent Cherry to investigate.

Cherry rode up to them: "Beware of outlaws around here, sirs."

"Ha! It is the outlaws that should beware of us. Come hither, pretty damsel. We will protect you!"

"Nay, I have companions nearby and must return to them but thank you for your offer." She took a good look at the cowled figure but he did not look like the dean.

Flight to Stetia

As Cherry was reporting back to the others, two more riders came up the road from the south. Neither looked like a cleric, so Morgana said they would ignore them. But in fact they headed off the road directly towards them. Hastily Sir Richard and Sergeant Hrolf rode out to parley. "Who are you that come to this forest?"

"We are Stetians seeking to aid the Lady Morgana Lefey. To whom do we speak?"

"I asked your names first and you have not given them."

"I am Don Incio Fulminar and this is my attendant Tonaldo."

"Tonaldo the *Minstrel* at your service," added Tonaldo.

Politely Sir Richard said, "Would you care to partake of some herb tea we have at our camp?"

"Nay we have our mission. We must find the Lady Morgana, for we have messages from her uncle the Peron Quixano Rasguno. We understand the lady is in some trouble with the Baratrean authorities."

"I am Sir Richard Nogent and am a friend of Lady Morgana. Morgana! These are friends from Stetia."

Morgana herself came out and invited them to the campsite. It was approaching dusk, so they prepared the evening meal. Fortunately the two Stetians had food with them so they were not so dependent on the unpalatable roots. Of course with the Vinkalik, there was no shortage of sweet white wine. Don Incio said he had seen the Proclamation and the Ordinance about her posted at Pincelle. He told them that Peron Quixano was desperate for them to obtain the ochyo and that he had been given money to buy it if necessary.

"We already have it."

"That is good news. Peron Quixano wishes you to have the Argent mirror ready, to receive messages at dawn each day. There is now a wizard on duty at the Or mirror who will try to contact you. He has tried several times already but been answered only by darkness. The Peron wants us to smuggle the ochyo into the Narch Hall at Narchburz. The Narch sit at a table carved with a map, the easier to plan their campaigns. If the ochyo is placed to view it, we can see where they are pointing. The Narch is still in winter recess. We have agents in Narchad who can assist us, especially if we can receive orders from Peron Quixano."

"We may as well go to do that, sir. Sir Mordant's men will soon bring more troops here after us. What do think?"

The party all agreed with her. Don Incio had a good map and they decided to try and cross the Arwyn at Sincelle. Sir Richard knew Sincelle had no palisade and was still half-ruined from a former Chaotic raid. Then Tonaldo played some of his music for their entertainment. Most of them found it pleasant enough and Cherry sat totally enchanted. However, Don Incio muttered, "Not to my taste," and stalked off out into the darkness.

Minut, on watch an hour or so before dawn, heard some loud rustling in the bushes nearby. He quietly roused Sir Richard and Hrolf in time to see a great black bear crash into the clearing. Minut and the knight engaged it at once but it was a formidable opponent. Hrolf joined in, and it turned and lumbered back into the forest. The commotion had woken everyone else, so they decided to make breakfast and get ready for an early start. Just before daybreak, when Morgana was thinking of trying her mirror, a scruffy damsel appeared. She came from the forest track, holding up her hands to show she was unarmed.

"I come as messenger from Faroch the Foul, lord of this forest. Faroch is annoyed because you are attracting trouble here. He wants you to go away."

"We are just about to go," declared Morgana.

"Also as this is Faroch's forest, he expects you to pay him for staying here. Three nights you have stayed, which will be fifteen gilden pezzi if you please."

"What! Pay for staying in the greenwood! We are outlaws too, you know. We will pay nothing! We are going now, goodbye. Our compliments to Faroch on the good camp site."

They filed out into the open and mounted up. As they left they saw a ragged band shaking their fists at them from the forest edge. Riding south, clear of the shelter of the woodlands, they met the strong cold blast of an easterly wind. As Morgana stopped to try her mirror it started to rain. Sheltering under her cloak she called, "Or," and a face appeared, holding an inscribed piece of wood,

"Prove Identity."

Morgana showed her signet ring. The wood was turned over:

"I am Begus, wizard for Peron Quixano."

He then disappeared. After a few minutes Morgana gave up and remounted and they rode on into what was now a storm. This at least meant that they met no one, as they rode across country to Sincelle. At the village, a face or two appeared at door or window at the noise of their passing, only to be withdrawn immediately. On a post near the quay they saw their Proclamation and Ordinance, pinned one above the other! Tearing them down, they rode onto the quay. In the water alongside were a rowing boat, a sailing smack and a cog. Cogs were the much-sailed merchant vessels used on the broad River Arwyn. Able to carry as much cargo as any merchant vessel, they lacked the fore and stern castles of the more showy and warlike lymphads. They had a steering oar instead of a rudder and a small cabin was provided under the poop deck. One could possibly have transported half the party or all if they were to abandon the steeds! Morgana dismounted and went to the cog called the *Lettys*.

"How much to transport my party across the river, my good sir?"

"More than you could afford. You are the witch Morgana Lefey, I recognise your blue horses. My men are gone, there is a gale blowing and it would cost my soul to serve you."

"Then go! We will sail the ship ourselves!"

"Not with my ship, you'll not!"

He and Morgana drew their swords. The captain fenced well and Sir Richard hurried to give help. But Morgana ran her opponent through the chest before he could arrive.

Sincelle: despite the gale, with Sir Richard's skill as a mariner, they made it, losing only the contents of Cherry's stomach.

Lady Abigail bandaged him and tying him hand and foot they set him ashore. Cherry looked out at the white-crested waves, a full het high, and the lashing rain. She could not even see the far bank. "Lady Abigail, you have an evaporate liquid spell. Could you not use it to help us across?"

Abigail's jaw dropped and words failed. Minut laughed. "With all the *Maghi* casting together, it might work for an instant![6] It reminds me of the tale of the old dwarf hero, Oddun. He drank the Deepwater Lake dry but a shark fin caught in his throat. It made him sick, so the whole lake was filled again. Ho ho ho."

Sir Richard had learnt the skills of sailing long ago and fancied he could sail the cog over the stormy waters. With eleven steeds it was obvious they would need two trips. They began craning the animals aboard one by one, putting some in the hold first. Some of the villagers had gathered to watch nearby and began to mutter amongst themselves. A priest of *Eru* was in their midst, egging them on. With five steeds in the hold and Harold on deck, they prepared the first sailing. Sir Richard steered whilst Morgana, Abigail and Cherry tried to control the sail at his direction. With the gale against them, they were forced to tack. They could have run downstream and taken potluck on the problems of running ashore but Sir Richard preferred to go to the quay at Flunon. The gale made the crossing frightening, with the cog heaving up and down in every direction on the muddy waves. Nevertheless, under Sir Richard's guidance, they made it, losing only the contents of Cherry's stomach. They then began the laborious task of winching the steeds ashore.

Back at Sincelle, the growing mob of glowering villagers

---

6 The Arwyn was over fifty hets wide and up to ten hets deep at this point.

was beginning to look dangerous. Tonaldo began to play his mandolin to try and soothe them, calming some. Hrolf then rode to the end of the quay and threw a handful of Pezzi in their direction. The priest with them shouted that it was only elf gold and would turn to leaves. Some, those most appreciative of Tornaldo's music, said they would take their chance and rushed to scrabble for it. Others stayed with the priest, shouting abuse. While the defectors hurried home with their coins, the rest began to throw stones at Hrolf, hitting his horse. He charged down among them and a desperate mêlée ensued. The rest of the party rushed to assist him and Don Incio killed the priest. At that, the remaining villagers fled. Six, plus the priest, remained on the ground. They saw no one else but had a nerve-wracking wait until the cog re-appeared. Again, it was a slow muscle-straining job, loading the remaining steeds. By the time they put off, the wind had abated and even veered a little in their favour. The crossing was not as testing but again there was the labour of disembarking the steeds. They were exhausted and darkness was only an hour away. They stayed in Flunon's one and only rather seedy inn. The fare was basic but considerably tastier than Lady Abigail's roots. Cherry, though pale from her seasickness, managed to eat a few mouthfuls. Everyone went to bed early. At least, now they were in the safety of Stetia, they did not need to keep watch!

Whilst passing by the Bois de Proscrit, Dean Lothrop and his two companions saw a knight riding towards them from the forest.

"Greetings, fair sirs. Would you by any chance have some food to sell?"

"No, sir. Do we look like merchants?"

"I suppose not–it is just my comrades and I have run very short. What is your name?"

"I am Sexton Ragout and we have no food to spare! *Eru* favours the provident."

They strode on, leaving the knight looking after them in a puzzled fashion. When they were well clear, Canon Umble said, "I thought that knight meant to attack us. The forest there is dreaded for its outlaws."

"Nonsense, why should he? If I a remember aright that is Sir Richard Nogent, a knight concerned with patrolling our borders."

"Well, your reverence, I felt as if he were inspecting us," said the Sexton.

"Perhaps he is looking for some outlaws on the road?"

"Perhaps indeed!" responded Dean Lothrop. He had other matters on his mind and strode on so fast the other two were hard put to keep up. How could they protect the Lefey estates from the grasping hands of Sir Helric Blaggart? After the success of the plot to dispose of Squire Arthur, he did not want the benefits to be plundered by such a known villain. Where was Morgana and what had happened to Congal?

They reached Ombec by the thirteenth hour. The weather was chill but dry. "I think we should carry on and camp out if necessary," the dean was saying to his unenthusiastic companions when his eye fell on a parchment at the village well. It was headed by the four crosses of *Eru,* common to the documents of his bishop. He went across to read it and had to sit down with the shock. Sir Richard, Lady Abigail and Morgana were all wanted dead or alive! And that had been Sir Richard back there on the road! He must have rescued Morgana from Sir Congal! Then also Lady Abigail, from the Order of St Judas! Abigail would tell them how Arthur met his death! Sir Richard may well have been looking for himself! His own life could be in danger. On the well was also a Grand Duke's Proclamation. Another shock! The *late* Sir Phanuel! And the deaths of four of the servants! This was grim news indeed. But no mention of Congal! If Morgana was free, he was likely to be dead or sore wounded at best.

He curtly read the two parchments to his companions and then they lunched at the Brush Tavern nearby. He needed to regain his strength. With the hue and cry raised, the "miscreants" could either hide in the Bois de Proscrit or flee out of Bara. Both Abigail and Morgana had relatives in Stetia. Relatives who would shelter and support them, like as not. The Church of *Eru* carried almost no weight there. Sir Richard would know how to spirit them over the river if anyone would. From there Morgana could remain a threat to him. Dozy Lady Abigail was not likely to be a threat to anyone and Sir Richard, once his distressed damsels were safe, was not likely to want to feud. This romantic nonsense about knights being duty-bound to protect women annoyed him. If he became bishop he would ban every saga or lay encouraging such foolishness. Women were responsible for half the evils of Morval Earth. Morgana would try to get him killed. From the writ it appeared she had killed Sir Phanuel herself but she would more likely get some other agent to deal with himself. He must strike first! Assuming the authorities did not catch her first, she would eventually go to her relatives at Relajar. In fact, her mother had had a manor near there, which Morgana would probably use as a new home. He needed someone there, ready waiting for her and here in this very village of Ombec was just the person, Jinisti! Three years ago, there had been several women murdered in Charles and Jinisti had been arrested as the prime suspect. He was a known misogynist. At the time, the "hearthmaid" of one of the cathedral canons was threatening to cause a scandal. It appeared she had powerful relations, so Lothrop paid Sir Congal to release Jinisti, on condition he disposed of the problem hearthmaid. This done, Jinisti was found a cottar's assart near Ombec to make a new living. Lothrop suspected Sir Congal had hired him for similar work. Congal was always in woman trouble. Jinisti would be the very man to kill Morgana. He would be glad do it, for just as small fee, when he knew it was to aid the Church. Leaving his assistants at the tavern, the dean headed for Jinisti's assart.

As instructed, the chambermaid woke a reluctant Morgana before dawn. The gale had died away but there was a chill wind with occasional showers. Why had these mirror exchanges to be made at dawn, her least favourite time of day? Begus appeared and again asked for proof of identity. This established, Morgana wrote on the back of a Proclamation:

"I have Gules safe."

Begus disappeared for a couple of minutes. Then:

"Peron suggests start mission via Thentis."

followed by

"Save having to cross Arwyn."

Morgana wrote:

"Have crossed Arwyn, will carry on."

Begus held up a piece of wood with

"Understood, farewell!"

on it and disappeared. Nevertheless, Morgana decided she would visit her cousins at Relajar on the way. She would be able to tell them what had happened to Arthur, Abigail and herself much better than in the short messages via the mirror. Her cousins might help them with equipment and supplies. Thinking of supplies, she realised they must be still several days' march from Relajar and more would be needed. She would send Cherry and Hrolf out to buy some in the village after breakfast. The bill for the inn was twenty gilden pezzi, but now they had the money brought by Don Incio, this was not a significant problem. The Don himself might be, thought Morgana; she had heard him asking Sir Richard what *his* plans were, as if he was in charge of the party!

Cherry and Hrolf found food stocks were low at this time of year. The more so, as Narchadian raids had reduced the population over the years. After two hours of searching and haggling, they returned with a shoulder of salt beef, a bag of prunes and two sacks of corncobs, for eight gilden pezzi. The corncobs had the merit of being suitable, like oats, for both people and steeds. "We will buy more food at the next village."

The next village was Forestero. On the way there Sir Richard's horse cast a shoe so they had to remain at a walk. At Forestero there was a blacksmith who they got to check all the steeds' hooves. Cherry and Hrolf went shopping again and returned with just a further three bags of corncobs. Morgana, fearing a future diet of roots and corncobs, decided they should stay at the local inn that night. This was more upmarket than that at Flunon and cost them twenty-five gilden pezzi. At dinner, Don Incio said, "It is convenient the direct route to Narchad passes through Relajar. There we can leave the ladies with their relatives whilst the rest of us carry on to fulfil the Peron's mission."

"But it is the mission he has entrusted to me!" replied Morgana. "If I am not with the party Begus can pass no instructions via my mirror."

"I go where Morgana goes," added Lady Abigail.

The Don's face lengthened but he remained silent.

They were wakened early next morning by shrill neighing from outside. Morgana immediately realised Harold was the culprit, and hurried as fast as she could to the stables. On the way she heard a similar but deeper neighing. A challenge from another unicorn! Harold had kicked his way out, doing damage that later added six gilden pezzi to the bill. Hilda had followed him to meet the strange unicorn. Morgana arrived in a nearby field in time to see the two stallion unicorns. They were neighing at one another, whilst Hilda stood watching. The stranger was dun-coloured, with a purple mane, but otherwise a match for Harold. Seeing

Morgana coming, Harold forced the issue by charging at his opponent. In an instant he had transfixed him in the chest so he sank to the ground dying. Morgana called to Harold but he ran off, back to the stables giving victory neighs as he went. Morgana went back with Hilda. She did not feel like breakfast. First had been the worry of the danger to Harold and then beholding the tragic sight of the dun unicorn dying had upset her deeply. She asked Hrolf, Minut and Bergand to bury the poor creature. Lady Abigail told them that unicorn horn was a very valuable commodity and that the dead one's should be saved. Morgana felt revolted by the thought but Hrolf agreed to cut off and clean the horn for Lady Abigail. Whilst the men were away, the innkeeper told them that the bridge at Carrels had been swept away in the storm. The way south was blocked. "Surely they will rebuild it soon? It is a long way to go to bypass it."

"Who knows? Manyana it may be re-built."

It was dry but windy when they left and they reached Carrels around the tenth hour. The bridge had indeed been swept away and the river was still running high. Nobody seemed to be doing anything about it. From Don Incio's map it looked as though it would take them at least two days to circle round back onto their road. They met a woman at the edge of the village.

"Why is no one repairing the bridge?" asked Morgana.

"I do not know, senora. Such a question would best be put to our Hidalgo[7]. I will take you to his house."

After a while, waiting at his house door, the Hidalgo appeared, complete with the sash of his office. "Senores,

---

7 The Hidalgo is the local leader of a village or area. Although subject to election he is almost always the senior local knight or landowner.

it will take many days to remake the bridge. It is a two-day trip to the stone quarry for a start! Here it is not the time of year for bridge building. The labrieghi are doing other things. Though I suppose I could, in an emergency, ask them to re-arrange their calendar, they might not, for fear of the crocodiles. When it is stormy, the crocodiles shelter up here. We do not harm them, as it is bad luck to kill a crocodile. We believe both Saurus and Snagass protect them, as it is not decided whether they are dinosaurs or reptiles. Their flesh is not good to eat anyway."

"Why not build a wooden bridge?" asked Morgana. "That wood there has plenty of trees."

"It is not the tradition. The bridge has always been of stone. The repair stipulations only mention stone."

"I think we had best get started on the long journey round," said Don Incio, himself a Stetian and used to frequent delays.

"No, I think we should build a wooden bridge. I am sure the Hidalgo will let us hire some of his villagers to help. We are well armed and have no fear of crocodiles." Seeing the Don glowering at her, she added, "Perhaps we should put it to the vote? I propose we build a bridge for the village, which will also enable us to proceed. Hands up all those who agree."

Five hands shot up, followed an instant later by Lady Abigail's.

"Well I hope it does not take us longer than it would to travel the distance," growled Don Incio. He was offended by Morgana's going against his advice. When Peron Quixano had given him the mission he had expected that she would naturally defer to his suggestions as an experienced knight. At first he expected decisions to be taken between himself and Sir Richard. In fact, Sir Richard always did what Morgana told him! He knew Morgana had some magic powers but even so, in Stetia as in Bara, Thentis and Perigord, women were expected to defer to men's superior wisdom. He had been both startled and impressed when she had run through the cog's captain with her sword. His gloomy face became even glummer. Peron Quixano had entrusted him with the mission and this bossy woman was the Peron's niece. He would have to buckle down to it.

The Hidalgo allowed them to hire four peasants with an ox cart for the day. Now they had to decide how to build the bridge. Morgana remembered that the bridges over the deep ditches around Closin comprised of two large baulks of timber with planks nailed on top of them. "But we have no nails," said Don Incio. "The bridges in the Narchad forests had the walk-on bits tied with leather thongs," said Cherry. "They just used small tree trunks with the bark still on them. Not like the finished planks in Bara."

"We do not have any leather thongs," demurred Don Incio.

"We could use rope instead."

"It will take a lot, perhaps more than we have."

"We will buy some. We are likely to need our own later. Lady Abigail and Cherry, go, please, and buy some. The rest of us had better start felling small trees in the wood."

They set to but found tree-felling hard work. Including the peasants, they formed three felling teams. Bergand was given the easier task of trimming the branches off because of his wounded left arm. Searching for two thicker trunks to carry the main weight, Hrolf encountered a giant blue flightless bird.

"Help me! There is a giant bird here!"

Another one appeared but the noise of the party rushing

to assist Hrolf, frightened them and they fled further into the wood. The peasants called them diatrimae. Only the Hidalgo was allowed to hunt them. They used the oxcart to transport the lighter timber to the bridge site and their own horses to drag the two larger trunks. To position these to span the river meant standing them on end and lowering them over. In the strong gusty wind, this was far more difficult than Morgana had expected but they managed it using their own ropes. Abigail and Cherry were nowhere to be seen. The crocodiles in the reeds started to take an interest, to the terror of their peasants. Don Incio and Hrolf chased them away; this was a job much more suited to the Don's taste. Morgana realised that when the timbers were put on the logs there was quite a step up from the road, so ramps would be needed at each end. Fortunately the village had piles of stones ready for road-mending, so she sent the peasants to bring a couple of cartloads. Whilst this was in progress Lady Abigail and Cherry returned with twenty-four hets of rope. They had had to go back to Forestero to buy it. Morgana set up two teams, tying the timbers to the supports and in an hour they were all tied in position. The cart was backed across in order to tip the stones for the further ramp and the bridge was complete. The Hidalgo who had been watching from a safe distance thanked them on behalf of his village and said they could stay in some of the houses for the night, *free*!

With the excitement of the unicorn fight, Morgana had missed contact with Begus at Forestero. She fully intended to try next morning, Startday the first of the Third Moon. However, their Stetian villager hosts were late risers and tired by her physical exertions she overslept. It was raining again and the strong gusty wind continued. It was behind them, helping them on their way to Cebada the next village.

Carrels: Don Incio and Hrolf found chasing crocodiles more to their taste than the hard work involved in rebuilding the bridge.

There, disappointed by a badly cooked lunch at the inn, they decided to try the next long leg to Corvo. Now the wind blew more from the side and the rain grew heavier. They were soon soaked and miserable. Cherry started to snuffle and sneeze. Perhaps weakened by her seasickness she had caught a cold. They did not reach the inn at Corvo until an hour after dusk.

Morgana's own finances were now running low so she asked Don Incio if they could draw on the 500 gilden pezzi designated for buying the ochyo. "I would need authority from Peron Quixano first."

The next morning she had an inn servant wake her before dawn so that she could contact Begus. He had no news and she wrote,

"Lack money. Can we use 500 GP?"

Begus responded with

"I will check. See you tomorrow."

She hoped she could manage another dawn rising. The weather was still grim but they carried on, lunching at Petaca. "If we had travelled west from the Bois de Proscrit we would have been on the Narchad border by now," commented the gloomy Don Incio. Five minutes later he sneezed. By the time they reached Harapo not only he but Lady Abigail and Morgana herself had Cherry's streaming cold. Sir Richard insisted they book the inn for two nights at least and ordered the sufferers to bed. He worried about the problems of sickness in bad weather in the wild. In Stetia they could stop and stay at an inn but in Narchad and elsewhere there would be no shelter. He also suspected that, at the behest of her uncle, Morgana was likely to drag them all to a good many outlandish places. Next day, the 3rd, he bought two pavilion tents in the village for forty-five gilden pezzi. This was expensive but, being made of silk and thus light to carry, he thought them well worth it. He suspected that they had been stolen from over the border in Thentis but he would not make any enquiries. The spare rouncey would carry them.

Morgana had overslept and missed communication with Begus. She was too ill to care and stayed in bed all day, as did Don Incio, Lady Abigail and Cherry. Bergand practised firing his crossbow and found his left arm almost healed. A tribute to the holey St Bandade water and Lady Abigail's nursing skills.

On the 4th Morgana contacted Begus. He showed her two separate messages:

> **"Archbishop of Borolon has Ordinance for your arrest, Dead or Alive!"**

and

> **"You can use 500 gilden pezzi for mission."**

At the last, she called Don Incio to witness it. He was not too keen to get involved with such witchcraft. "I will take your word for it that that was a message from Peron Quixano," he said. The colds were all improved and they would move on after lunch. Morgana's relative's estate lay only seventeen myles away. The fittest members of the party practised erecting and striking the pavilions. One was striped purple and yellow, the other green and yellow. By chance they had the tinctures of both the Lefey and the Nogent families!

They reached the Murada[8] Rasguno at Relajar, Peron Quixano's principal mansion, around the seventeenth hour. Since he and his wife were at the Stetian capital Bosen, it was their daughters Donna Sancia and Donna Ines who welcomed them. Both had the fashionably pale faces and glossy black hair common to Stetian ladies. Sancia, the elder, was plumper and more serious but they were both fine looking damsels. Sancia explained that her oldest brother Don Carlos was away serving in the Guarda del Junta at Bosen. Her other brother Don Jerome was "around the estate somewhere or other". Donna Ines winced. Morgana gathered Don Jerome was out of favour with his sisters. Servants tended to all the steeds and the party were given rooms and bathing facilities whilst a large dinner was cooked.

At the meal Morgana had to give a full account of all their trials and tribulations. The two ladies' eyes grew rounder and rounder.

Sancia explained, "Raymond the gardener arrived with Louise Berde and the woman Vanova two days ago." From the way she spoke she did not think much of "the woman Vanova". "Raymond and Louise Berde are helping in the garden at present but probably you will want them on your mother's old estate of Lozana. Jerome has been showing the woman Vanova our property since yesterday morning! I am afraid we have bad news about Lozana. As you know, with few people to work there, the orchards have become overgrown and the old house dilapidated. The arable fields are left waste. Last year my father rented the house to Vejiga

8 Stetian name for a large manor house

the hechicero [sorcerer] to set up his laboratory there. Vejiga was an apprentice of your old friend the Grand Pheador at one time. He lived at Lozana with an apprentice of his own for a while. One night, during the eleventh month, there was a bang so loud we heard it two myles away! When Paez the gamekeeper went to investigate there was a large hole in the mansion. Several pieces of the apprentice lay a dozen hets from the building but of Vejiga there was no trace. Paez had just picked up a scorched grimoire when he heard an unearthly cackling sound nearby. An enormous grey face breathing smoke materialised above him, so he thought it time to report back to us. Lately there has been a giant serpent seen in the grounds. Recently, I told Paez that it was his responsibility to deal with this snake, so he has bought a Gashad Blaster. This is a chaotic device that roars flame like a dragon. It was captured from the Narchadians. He hopes at least to drive the serpent away with it, if he can get it to work. Perhaps you would care to assist him tomorrow? I have estate business to attend to myself but Jerome should collect Paez and show you the way?"

"I would like very much to take over my mother's old property. It would give us somewhere to come back too after Quixano's mission is done."

"Good, here is Vejiga's grimoire, in case it is still of any use." She produced a linen bag with a very burnt book and a lot of dirty ashes in it. Lady Abigail sifted through it and found a few pages in the middle intact enough to be readable. In them were the complete instructions for casting two spells. It was of the chaotic, Kharsh language, written in runes. Fortunately she had studied that language a little. "Ye enchantment whereby a wizard of the power may send ye undead to nothingness." And "Ye means whereby a wizard of power may release ye stresses of ye earthly rocks to cause a small earthquake."

Abigail spent the rest of the evening copying these out.

"Will you be able to do these spells?" asked Donna Ines, watching her.

"Not straight away. My Kharsh is not perfect anyway but it would be blasphemy to use their words of command. However, if I can call for the good intentioned *Maghi* to send me the wisdom I may well construct a Lawic enchantment that activates the same forces."

Ines looked blank.

"Do not worry about it, I shall experiment when I have some spare time and doubt not I shall succeed in the end."

Morgana added, "Certainly these spells could be very useful for us in our missions, do what you can."

The Murada Lozana

Sir Herbert Decre and his party set out early from La Turbie on the 25th of the Second Moon. He was fully resolved to cover the long thirty-five myles to Saint Sara in the day. Unfortunately the chill wind blowing over the shelter-less fields brought down both him and his hobilar Drex with bad colds. Genevieve insisted that they stop at the inn in Prae, after all. The 26th was the day of the gale but they battled on to Saint Sara. By now Chaplain Psalmodier and Hobilar Odo were also ill, so they stayed put. Sir Desmond and Grant, the third hobilar, took it in turns to watch the eastward road. There was little traffic on the road to Closin at this time of year. Weakened as they were they were glad not to sight their prey. Not until the first of the third Moon was Psalmodier, the last of the Genevieve's patients, fully recovered. On that day Sir Desmond and Drex made a furtive reconnaissance of the manor at Closin. It seemed quiet and the stables were empty. Now they were fully operational again; they even kept watch at night but no one appeared. On the 3rd Sir Desmond made another visit to Closin and discovered Sir Flamen Swyn had taken possession on the orders of the Grand Duke. He said that *unofficially* he was to suggest that they follow the fugitives over the Arwyn into Stetia. Morgana had Rasguno relatives there at Relajar and Senelar relatives at Jugador. A search of the map showed Relajar to be the closest of these, so Sir Desmond decided to go there first. Whilst he was away, a messenger arrived at Saint Sara from the Archbishop of Borolon. He brought an ordinance concerning their miscreants, similar to that of Bishop Innocent's. Next day they travelled the twelve myles to Borolon and visited the archbishop. He knew nothing of the whereabouts of Sir Richard Nogent's party but he gave them some food supplies and 100 gilden pezzi to aid them. He told them that there were a few *Eru* worshippers in Stetia under his protection but none around Relajar or Jugador. He suggested they contact Sir Huibert of the Order of St Judas at the fortress of Trondol. He could counsel them on the best way to proceed in Stetia.

That night they dined in the archbishop's hall and conversed with clerics and knights at his table. None of the party had been in these parts before, so they enquired about the current situation. They were told that in Matham, south of the Arwyn, the young baron commanded strong forces that kept the Chaotics at bay. Units from both King Eudes and the Order of St Judas reinforced his own knights. Though quiet at present, the Narchadians had always found it easier to raid Stetia and Oblivia. Some young and zealous members of the Order of St Judas were pressing for conquering the part of Narchad, south of the Dire River. Older knights, who knew what an ambusher's delight the Arbor Halbrad was, were happy to let sleeping dogs lie for a while. A canon said that a great opportunity had been missed two years ago. Then the kidnapping of Queen Gimawl had caused a breach between Narchad and Belmain, its main ally and source of supplies. At that time an invasion might have pushed the Chaotics back to Chaos Deeps for good. Unfortunately, King Moro of Thentis had just died and his successor Eudes was busy establishing the unity of his kingdom. There had been some at that time who had suggested the Barony of Matham and the Duchy of Wardour could as well join the Grand Duke of Bara as stay in Thentis. To Sir Desmond this was idle talk wholly relevant to his mission. He wanted to know what manner of soldiers the Stetians were but got little answer.

The next day they rode all the way to Trondol to ask Sir Huibert's advice. He was sympathetic to their cause but could not assist them materially. Soldiers of the Order were banned from entering Stetia without express permission at King Eude's behest. Since Relajar was so close, he suggested that they travel overnight and attack at dawn. So that is what they did.

In the morning, Don Jerome had still not appeared. "Neither has that woman Vanova!" snarled Sancia. "Ines has gone to collect Paez for you. They will meet you at the park gate. You know the way to the property?"

"Yes. I visited it years ago when I stayed here," Morgana told her. Her party mounted up and rode off after breakfast. Proceeding down the road they heard a shout from beyond some bushes further on. A stampeding horse careered towards them and then veered to their left. Only Morgana reacted quick enough to chase after it and it jumped over a nearby stream to escape. The stream was broad and Morgana tried to adjust Harold's stride for the jump but they hit the mud on the far bank and got stuck. By the time they got clear, the runaway was far distant. With Donna Ines and Paez waiting for them, Morgana felt she had no more time to waste. She jumped Harold back over the stream with no trouble. The horse's owner had now appeared on foot. He was dismayed to find they had chased his steed over the water and scowled at Morgana. "There is a ford only a myle back, sir." she told him and he plodded away muttering.

They reached the Lozana park gate between the ninth and tenth hours. Donna Ines and Paez were waiting for them with the ornate brass and wood Gashad Blaster. They could see the path beyond the gate was through heavily overgrown woodland. "We will all go in on foot," decided Morgana.

They left the steeds hitched to the fence, with Cherry and Tonaldo to watch after them. Paez unlocked the rusty gate and it opened with a squeal. They started up the gloomy weed-covered path. "A good job it is broad daylight," said Donna Ines.

A little way in, a second track led off to the left and they could see a ruined cottage at the end of it. They decided to split into two. Sir Richard, Don Incio, Lady Abigail, Donna Ines and Minut headed for the cottage whilst Morgana, Paez, Hrolf and Bergand carried on up the main track. Sir Richard's party heard some rustling in bushes beside the track. He and Minut investigated these, whilst the other three continued on abreast. They saw some wooden box structures in front of the ruin. "Beehives, I think," said Lady Abigail. At that moment a dark figure leapt out of the doorway of the ruin. He threw a knife at Donna Ines, shouting "Morgana Lefey!" as he did so. They saw the knife veer to his left but this was the way Ines flinched so it caught her full in the chest. She fell with blood streaming from her wound. The assailant turned to flee as Don Incio rushed towards him but Lady Abigail felled him with a magic bolt. Then she bent to assist Ines but she was dead. Sir Richard and Minut who had flushed out only rabbits from their bushes rejoined them. They tied the unconscious murderer to a nearby tree trunk. On him were a dagger and twenty-three gilden pezzi. Minut pulled out the throwing knife that had killed Donna Ines. It was inscribed with Kharsh runes:

"Hal his name and I strike hame!"

Minut translated: "A real assassin's magic weapon!" Lady Abigail confirmed that the boxes were hives. A few bees were out even this early in the year. Inside the ruin were only a brushwood couch and half a loaf of black rye bread. Sir Richard said they had better go to assist Morgana. They headed into the trees so as to circle round to approach the mansion from the flank.

The others meanwhile had encountered a simply gigantic serpent–dull green with black stripes and a bright red tongue which was darting forward! Paez collapsed to the ground in fright and Hrolf stood rooted to the spot. Bergand, at the rear, loosed a hasty bolt, which went wide and stepped back to reload. Morgana shouted, "*Shimmer*!" and charged forward, sword in hand. As she thrust at the colossus, it vanished! She halted, incredulous for a moment. Then she realised it must have been a magic illusion. She called the others forward though Bergand was still reloading his crossbow. A little way round the corner and the mansion came into full view. It was a white, two-storied building, roofed with red tiles where they were still in position. The top left floor had suffered some explosion that had blown out wall and roof. Tiles and rubble still lay scattered over the paved forecourt. This had a low well in front of the porticoed front door. What immediately occupied their attention, however, was a loud deep hum, emanating from a ruined building, to the left of the mansion? Morgana crept towards it but four giant black chickens, four times the normal size, came out from a coop at the side of the mansion clucking loudly. She did not want to harm them but the rooster flew up at her. She tried to swat it away with the flat of her sword but Taglier turned to take its head off. A hen came at her and despite her efforts perished in another flurry of feathers. The next one she kicked over with her foot and it and the remaining survivor fled squawking.

Meanwhile Hrolf went to the door of the ruin, whilst Bergand sneaked round to the open back. He saw a colossal wasp, almost the size of a man, peering at Hrolf and loosed his crossbow at it and again missed. "A giant wasp, Hrolf!" he shouted. The wasp tried to attack Hrolf through the doorway but it was impeded by having to curl its tail sting through the aperture. The sergeant hewed it in two. The sting was around fifteen bets long (fifteen hundredths of a het) so he cut it off carefully. Doubtless it carried a potent poison and could be used as a weapon. Many people frowned on poisoned weapons but Hrolf was a realist. They could be facing less scrupulous foes, against whom they would need their maximum efforts.

Morgana and Paez went to investigate the mansion's open front door. A few hets from it Morgana suddenly felt so frightened, she could go no further. What horror lay ahead? Paez gave a groan and fled!

Sir Richard's party meanwhile had cautiously filtered through the woodlands without difficulty. They came to the edge of what had been formal gardens at one time. The flowerbeds were a jungle and the lawns, hay fields. In the centre was a large stone urn. To their right they saw the mansion and they spotted some enormous black hens rushing round behind it. Advancing, they saw two doors and four windows along the ground floor, at the back of the mansion. At the first window Sir Richard peered in, seeing a kitchen range covered in dust. He and Don Incio went in the first unbolted door and found the kitchen empty. There was a cupboard, which the Don opened. The cupboard was bare.

Morgana got hold of herself. "What sort of a Lefey are you to be trembling at nothing?" she muttered and ran for the open doorway. Hrolf gave the wasp's sting to Bergand and sped after her. They found themselves in a hallway, with a staircase leading upwards. There were open doors on both sides and a trapdoor under the stair. Morgana went up the stair, encountering the foulest of smells on the way. At the top landing she faced a door reinforced with heavy iron bars. There were also open doorways to both the left and the right. The right one had a black demon pointing a scarlet-shafted trident at her! As she went towards him, he uttered a terrifying maniacal laugh but she attacked him fiercely. He managed to keep parrying her blows with his trident. Hrolf came up behind her but there was no room for him to give any help. Confident Morgana could hold her own, he checked out the left-hand room. It contained a mildewed bed and a chest that had been forced open. There were some clothes lying around that he guessed had belonged to the hechicero Vejiga. Morgana was beginning to tire and she knew demons had infinite energy. Desperately she struck such a blow that her opponent fell to the floor. Glaring, he started to shout a spell at her but she thrust home through where his heart should be, if he had one. He went limp and his red eyes clouded over. Sir Richard and Don Incio joined them and they searched the ruined room beyond. On the floor was painted a pentacle of Baphomet, Magho of Magic Power. Beside a large blackened hole in the floor were a table and two chairs. On the table were two beakers, a rusty knife and part of a pack of playing cards.

"These are Stetian cards but not the full set," said Don Incio.

"Someone quarrelled over their game?" suggested Sir Richard.

They searched downstairs, finding a neglected dining room. Since her gown was still glowing, Morgana descended into the cellar–two sacks of mildewed barley, a barrel of flour, now green with fungus and an empty wine barrel. This left only the strong room on the landing to be searched. None of her keys would fit and Minut could not pick the lock. So Lady Abigail cast a woodrot spell on a patch of the timber. When a quarter of an hour later this had taken effect, Minut made a hole. Peering through this, all they could see was a white garment hanging on the opposite wall. Minut took his great hammer and battered the door until it gave in. The garment was seen to be a wedding dress in a style of many years ago. The only other item in the room was a large locked chest. This Minut was able to pick open at the first attempt. Inside it were a copy of the deeds of the Lozana estate, a bundle of letters tied with a green ribbon, a copy of Lady Berenezia's will, a promissory note for 300 gilden pezzi cashable at Valles, a wooden articulated doll in an old-fashioned frock and a small silver bird shape. This last Morgana found was a whistle that made bird-like noises. She decided to take it as it could be used for signalling. The letters were addressed to Morgana's mother and were dated before she married Sir Daffyd. The will read:

The last Will and testament of Lady Berenezia Lefey, nee Rasguno.
Whereas I Berenezia Lefey, being in sound mind, do hereby bequeath
Mine estate of Lozana and all goods, chattels and servants appertaining to it, to be shared between my daughter Morgana Lefey and any future Daughters borne to me.

Signed this 12/05/682 ATN
Berenezia Lefey
Witnessed
Quixano Rasguno Hildalgo of Relajar
Pheador Great Wizard
Patrizia Selenar Donna

Morgana wondered if her mother had had any more daughters? As it was, she needed to take over Lozana, as otherwise she was now homeless. She set Minut to fashion a key to re-lock the chest. She wanted the strong room made as secure as possible again. Paez was sent to collect Cherry, Tonaldo and all the steeds. They would be tethered in the grounds. Morgana asked Lady Abigail if she could destroy the Pentacle. Abigail said she would try. In fact she found her unicorn horn easily peeled the paint from the floor. Then she thrust this into the black demon's body and the horrid creature crumbled into a heap of grey dust. "Master Paez, could you find a sack to shovel this dust into? I have heard that demons' dust will kill plants within the hour. If this is so, it will make a most useful weed killer. Looking at that garden, weed-killer we will need in abundance." Morgana set the red trident over the fireplace in the dining room as a trophy. Its tines were of a black steel-like metal that burnt to the touch. Engraved into it in runes was

Testronitz,

probably the demon's name. Bergand fashioned a simple wooden handle and sheath for the wasp's sting, which he gave to Lady Abigail. Cherry meanwhile plucked and prepared the two dead fowls ready for cooking.

Sir Richard broke the news that Donna Ines had been killed, so Morgana and the two knights went back to question the assassin. He was still bound to the tree by the cottage. Threatened with a slow painful death by Don Incio, he confessed his name was Jinisti and that he had been paid to kill Morgana Lefey. Dean Lothrop had offered him fifty gilden pezzi plus expenses to do the deed. He had told him Morgana was a damsel who customarily wore a purple gown and who would eventually visit her estate of Lozana. He had laid in wait for her for only two days. He was annoyed but not repentant for having killed the wrong damsel. He hated all women. When questioned about the great snake and the demon, he said he was glad that he knew nothing about them. He had assumed there were servants living in the mansion, so he had kept away from it. Don Incio was all for killing him immediately but Sir Richard thought they should hand him over to the Stetian authorities. Morgana agreed since this area was under her uncle's authority. Morgana set Jinisti to clear all the rubble out of the well, watched by Sergeant Hrolf and herself. As the job neared completion, she saw him examine and pocket an item that glinted under the water. When he came out she confiscated it. It was a gold ring, inscribed with the pentacle symbol of Baphomet, plus some Quenith letters. Lady Abigail said it was a magical talisman ring. It must have belonged to the late Vejiga. To obtain its powers, one would have to swear allegiance to the neutral Magho Baphomet and hope the ring would accept one as its master. Rejection could result in madness or death, so such an attempt was not to be taken lightly. She would not try it and neither would Morgana. Morgana decided she would keep it because it would have a considerable monetary value for existing magicians, depending on its level. Don Incio and Paez transported the body of Donna Ines, back to the Murada Rasguno. The Don felt it was his duty to tell her sister Donna Sancia as he had been present when she was killed.

They had a gloomy dinner, in the still dirty Lozana dining room. The death of Ines had blighted their triumph in recovering the property. To take her mind off it, Lady Abigail returned to the grimoire and the complexities of the earthquake spell. When she thought she had them mastered she went outside to experiment. At the far side of the forecourt was the heap of rubble now tidied off from it. Cautiously she pointed at it and spoke the words of power. The stones erupted and sprayed out in a fan shape across the grass beyond. Success! She was on the right track and could increase the Magh Pozum (Magic Power) next time. She would need to learn a bit more about rocks. Apparently the effects varied with the type of rock. Minut should be able to help her. A dwarf from the caverns of Varadh should be an expert.

She was going up the stairs when she felt a familiar chill and Lady Buija appeared in the dim orange light from her candle.

"At last I have found you again! But what is this you have that repels me? You have something now that is of danger to us of the otherworld? I feel it."

"Oh? Perhaps it is this unicorn horn? I will put it aside so you can speak."

"I have been searching for the Princess Maudette. She has been moved from the Abbey she was in before. That Abbey is called Saint Relaud and lies in Northeast Perigord. I will search on until I find her new location. You will help to save her? I cannot rescue her by myself."

"We have some other missions at present but you can be sure Lady Morgana and I will not forget. When we are free we will assist you, if you can find where the princess is held."

"Thank you. I will return when I know." She faded away.

Lady Morgana was on the third watch covering the hours before dawn. This was so as to be ready for her mirror contact with Begus. His message read:

Go to giant tree stump, South of Zarkanis for guidance

Morgana responded:

She did not feel up to passing on that Quixano's daughter Ines was dead by these cryptic means. Sancia would have to write to him. She felt guilty that it was her that the assassin had been after. Indeed, if she had gone up that side path, she would now be dead. Not a pleasant thought. "Wake up! Time to get up," she shouted.

Cherry clumped past, heading for the kitchen.

"Morgana! Morgana!" A man was running up the path towards them. "Morgana! To arms!"

She recognised him as the elusive Don Jerome. "I am here," she said from the ruined room.

"There is a troop after you, led by a knight from the north!" he panted breathlessly. "They attacked the Murada Rasguno and have taken Sancia and the servants prisoner. There are a priest, two women and several soldiers in the troop, all with horses. The boy Garcia escaped and came to tell me in the house where I was staying. He will come to tell us if they come this way. What will you do?"

"Get ready for a fight, everyone! We will fight here. It seems as good a place to make a stand as anywhere. Paez, Minut, Bergand! Get the steeds and put them at the back of the house in case we have to escape. Do you stand with us, Don Jerome?"

"Indeed I will. I like not those that have invaded my home. Your enemies are my enemies' fair cousin."

On the first floor Don Jerome manned the first window with his bow, Lady Abigail the second, and Bergand the third. Paez sheltered where the fourth window used to be in the ruined room. Morgana and Don Incio stood inside the front door and Sir Richard and Sergeant Hrolf guarded the two at the back. Minut and Cherry waited in the dining room. The prisoner Jinisti was still securely bound down in the cellar. Hardly had they taken their posts, when those upstairs saw a small boy racing up the path. It was Garcia. "They are coming! Don Jerome, they are coming!" he gasped.

They let him through into the dining room. Just in time. A troop of eight riders was clopping up the path, riding two by two onto the forecourt where they halted. "I come to arrest Sir Richard Nogent for his crimes!" shouted one of two knights in the lead.

Lady Abigail chanted, "*Ventus Impetus*!" which created a blast of wind that blew him off his horse. Don Jerome, Bergand and Paez all fired. The bows had little effect but the Gashad Blaster gave a mighty roar. It gouted flames that enveloped one of the knights. Horse and rider collapsed, burnt black! Four of the horses stampeded away, carrying the priest, the two women and a hobilar. At the back of the mansion, the Blaster's roar stampeded four of their own steeds, including the unicorn Harold! One of the remaining hobilars was having a job stopping his mount from running but the other dismounted and joined the blown-over knight in advancing on the door. This knight Morgana recognised as the one who had come to the Stregafume Priory at such an inopportune time. The burnt knight got up from his dead horse and limped round to the back of the mansion. Don Jerome loosed an arrow that stuck in the shield of the still mounted hobilar. The hostile knight smashed Don Incio's target to matchwood with his mace. They fought on until the Don prevailed. Those upstairs saw the stampeders reappear at the edge of the trees, their horses now under control. Morgana and Don Incio engaged the two hobilars. Morgana cut hers down as Don Incio lopped the head off his. The mounted enemies decided they had

had enough and rode off. At the rear of the mansion, Hrolf had fought with the burnt knight and stabbed him in the lung, so he had to surrender. Good, thought Hrolf, there should be some sizeable ransom money for me in good course.

They brought the wounded inside for treatment. These were the burnt, Sir Desmond Fraicheur and the hobilar Drex. Sir Desmond's left leg was burnt from ankle to thigh, he had a punctured left lung and a black eye. Drex also had a punctured lung where Morgana had run him through. Abigail decided not to use the holey water, as they had so little but did what she could with the herbal antiseptic dressings. Some of the others went to find the stampeded steeds. They also collected the dead knight's destrier and the two hobilars' rounceys. Cherry searched the bodies. On Sir Herbert, she found a gold ring, a pair of gold spurs, sixty-four gilden pezzi and a just-started *Tome of Eru* that he had been using as a diary. The dead hobilar, Odo, had seventeen gilden pezzi in his pouch. Morgana thanked Don Jerome for his assistance and told him the sad news that his sister was dead. When he heard that the murderer was still held in the cellar, he said that he would organise a trial for him that very afternoon. He sent the boy Garcia to collect the lawyer and went back to the Murada Rasguno to inform Donna Sancia. In fact he met Donna Sancia, Vanova, Louise Berde, Raymond and some other servants coming towards Lozana.

With them was a lady from the raiding party and a small dog. She, Genevieve Fraicheur, had returned to untie them. She had been worried about the fate of her brother Sir Desmond. She was very relieved to find he was still alive, though saddened by the death of Sir Herbert. She told them the rest of her group was returning to Trondol under

Chaplain Psalmodier. She did not think they would ever be back. She told Sergeant Hrolf that he would have to wait many years before the Fraicheur estate produced enough money for a knight's ransom–unless, perhaps, the Grand Duke valued his services enough. They debated about this, the standard ransom for a knight was 2,000 gilden pezzi. However, they knew Basylt Devisage was a vindictive skinflint and it was not worth the risk sending anyone back to Charles. They then buried Sir Herbert, Odo and the dead horse among the trees. Morgana wondered if Sir Herbert had any brothers and Lady Genevieve said at least two.

Donna Sancia was very upset still over the loss of her sister and was eager for the trial. For this, they assembled at the scene of the crime, after lunch.

"I am Don Jerome Rasguno. In the absence of my father Peron Quixano and my older brother Don Carlos, I assume the responsibilities of Hildalgo of Relajar. I declare this court open. Let Senor Bocardo record our proceedings. We are here to try the Baratrean freeman Jinisti for the foul murder of Donna Ines Rasguno, yesterday in this place. Let the first witness speak."

"I am Don Incio Fulminar of Girrin. I was accompanying Donna Ines and Lady Abigail as we approached the building and hives before you. The accused rushed towards us from within the building. Shouting, 'Morgana Lefey,' he threw the knife that struck Donna Ines in the heart. I believe he mistook Ines for Lady Morgana."

"Has the prisoner any questions for the witness?"

"No but I question the court's authority! As a freeman in the employ of the Church of *Eru*, I claim 'benefit of clergy'. I should be tried at the court of the Bishop of Charles, not here."

"Here in Stetia, there is no benefit of clergy. This crime was committed on Stetian land against a Stetian subject. Your objection is overruled! Call the second witness."

"I am Lady Abigail Clove, nee Rasguno, originally from Stetia but more recently living at St Visseille in Bara. I was accompanying Donna Ines and Don Incio here and it occurred exactly as he says."

"Jinisti of Bara, I find you guilty of the murder of Ines Rasguno as charged. Have you anything to say before I pronounce sentence?"

"I have no faith in this court, How fair can it be, to be judged by the victim's brother? I did the deed in the belief that she was the witch Morgana, another damsel in a purple gown. My regret is that I failed in my mission. But rest assured that there are others who will complete the task. The Church of *Eru* will triumph in the end. If your sister was not a witch, she was assisting one! May all such perish in *Eru's* name!"

"Jinisti, I sentence you to be hanged until dawn tomorrow on the hanging tree of Relajar. Then your body is to be cut down and burnt on ivy branches, the ashes to be scattered on the village dung heap. This trial is now concluded."

For Lady Genevieve the mission had not been as exciting as she had hoped. Not very nice weather and too much waiting around in Saint Sara. But she supposed most knights' quests were really like that. The minstrels left out all the uncomfortable or boring bits. Dulcie, her pointing hound, was enjoying it very much, disappearing off to investigate strange scents and chase rabbits. Genevieve had liked Sir Jean Toufou but the knights at Borolon and Trondol had been a disappointment. Mostly they were members of the Order of St Judas, whose manners were not always as they should be. Since members of the Order were supposed to be celibate, they were no use at all for a single lady with dreams of a manor of her own. Her acting woman-in-waiting was no help. As was too often the custom in bachelor establishments, the housekeeper had been selected for her looks rather than her abilities–looks that completely outshone those of poor Genevieve! It was painfully obvious that all the men in the party, apart from her brother, appreciated Corinne's rather *blowsy* and *vulgar* appearance.

Sir Herbert she liked, but he was so obsessed with the mission to avenge his sister! His one aim in life was to find and kill Sir Richard Nogent, whom he deemed responsible. However, it did not put him off his enjoyment of good food and wine. Used to dining well, where there were hosts of servants, she suspected that catering for such a man in a humble manor could be fraught with problems.

And now here they were, riding through the dark to Relajar, in imminent danger of bringing the adventure to an end. It was cold but there was little cloud. This meant they could see the stars and the waxing quarter moon. This made it easier not to get lost, an important consideration when travelling through strange territory without a guide. She had heard that there were devices called lodestones, which always indicated north no matter how dark it was. Unfortunately they did not have one. With Chaplain Psalmodier present, anyone using such a device would probably be burnt at the stake–unless he used it himself, of course. He claimed to have *Eru*-given powers but Genevieve never saw him use them. He was a pompous little man who kept worrying about his responsibilities back in Charles. He was much of the opinion that their mission should be carried out by the Order of St Judas rather than themselves.

They sighted the Murada Mansion near the village of Relajar well before dawn. Scouting around it, they saw an ornate porticoed front entrance, with iron grills over the windows. Outbuildings within a walled yard protected the rear. Sir Herbert sent the hobilar Grant to do a close reconnaissance. Lady Genevieve had been shocked to discover Grant had once been a burglar in Valles. Her brother Desmond said such skills could be useful but she thought all such criminals should be hanged as the law decreed.

Grant scaled the yard wall and checked all the doors and windows. He unbarred the yard gate as he returned to report to Sir Herbert: "All the doors and windows are secure. Best wait till someone comes out before we strike, sir."

"Right. Sir Desmond, do you take Odo and Drex with axes ready to force the front door. The rest of us will go in through the back. Genevieve will sound her horn when it is time to strike."

Genevieve tied Dulcie to a tree well away from the house. She readied her crossbow and horn. Then with the others she crept as close as they dared and waited. And waited and waited, it seemed! The sky lightened a little in the east. Was there anyone in there? Perhaps they were all prepared with weapons at the ready! When dawn came, surely they would soon be seen. Then there was a rattle of bolts! A young maid came out of the back door and trudged over to the well to draw some water. Sir Herbert charged forward without giving the signal and Grant followed him. The maid dropped the bucket down the well and stood open-mouthed as Sir Herbert pushed the gate open, dismounted and raced in through the back door. Genevieve blew her horn and then cantered into the yard behind the other two. "Shut the gate, Corinne, to keep the horses in. You, inside!" She motioned with her crossbow to the young maid.

They assembled all the occupants they could find in a sizeable hall. These comprised three children, four women, including the maid and four men. One man was badly wounded and another was stunned. Her brother brought down a struggling, continually shrieking lady in a long lacy nightgown. Genevieve, like all the Edini knightly classes, had learnt to speak correct Simnith from *Cyng's Primer* but this lady was using words she was sure were not in that book! With that accent she could not be Lady Morgana and she was too young to be Lady Abigail. With disapproval she noticed Sir Desmond was holding onto the lady far longer than he needed too. Chaplain Psalmodier must have had the same thought as he went across and gagged her and then tied her hands. Reluctantly Sir Desmond let her go and Genevieve could see that his left eye was red and puffing up. The lady had punched him!

To Sir Herbert's angry disappointment, it was obvious that Sir Richard's party was not there. The oldest manservant, with a look at his mistress, said that he did not know of any Sir Richard Nogent. Chaplain Psalmodier scowled: "We will soon find out! Bring me that girl, she will know!" Grant seized the young maid and they dragged her screeching out into the corridor. "Silence, you pagan! This is your chance to earn a little of *Eru's* ever-merciful grace. Tell us where the Baratreans with the blue unicorns have gone. Speak!"

"I don't know anything. I am just a servant!"

"You lie! Tell me what you know or *Eru* will give me the power to give you a hundred years of torment! You shall be chained in a place of eternal darkness, lit only by the glimmerings of the fire burning under your feet. Speak! Speak or die!"

"Your lordship, sir, they went to Lozana yesterday. Lozana is but two myles to the east of here. Please spare me, that is all I know."

Psalmodier went back into the hall. "They are at Lozana, two myles to the east. Let us go there." They tied up all the occupants hand and foot. Genevieve collected Dulcie and they rode off again.

The sun was not long up when they sighted the gate at the edge of the park.

"Should we not reconnoitre first?" asked Sir Desmond.

"No. With haste, we will catch them unprepared," replied Sir Herbert.

The ornate gate was wide open and they sped up the path, bending low to avoid the low branches. En route Dulcie spotted rabbit holes and disappeared. Genevieve left her without a check. She was better out of the way at present. Corrine and herself brought up the rear. Her crossbow was in her left hand, her right was holding the reins. They came to a sudden stop and the mansion was just in front of them. It had been a handsome building at one time but the top left floor was ruined and open to the sky. Black stains indicated that there had been a fire there.

"I come to arrest Sir Richard Nogent for his crimes!" called out Sir Herbert. He would have said more but at that moment a sudden gust of wind from nowhere blew him off his horse. Two arrows flew at them, plus a great gout of flame that enveloped her brother and his horse. A roar like a clap of thunder smote them and her horse bolted. It turned so fast she was almost thrown, but she managed to hang on and keep her head down as it careered through the trees. A skilled horsewoman, she soon managed to get the normally mild-mannered palfrey back under control. She met Corinne and Grant who had had similar problems and they rode back towards the house. She looked for her brother but he was gone, though his horse's body still lay there, black and smoking. Sir Herbert was fighting someone in black armour at the mansion door with Odo hovering behind him. Drex was dismounting nearby. An arrow hit Odo's shield and at the same moment Sir Herbert collapsed to the ground, a pool of blood forming under him. The black armoured knight sprang forward to fight Odo and from behind him came a lady in a shimmering purple gown with large hennin to match. This lady bore a shining sword, with which she attacked and defeated Drex who fell. Chaplain Psalmodier rejoined Lady Genevieve and the other two, a twig with two leaves on it stuck to his habit. He had had a ride through the wood as well. At that moment, the black knight cut Odo's head from his shoulders and Corinne gave a scream.

"Nothing we can do now, lady," said Grant, turning his horse.

The chaplain took a quick look at the scene. All that remained of the other half of their force were three horses scattering at the sight of the two enemies at the door.

"Witchcraft!" He and Corinne turned and rode away, so Genevieve followed them. She wondered what had happened to her brother. She was sure his body was not in front of the house. It was no use trying to find out now. She would just get an arrow in her.

They rode a long way out into the open before they stopped to confer. "I must report this unfortunate reverse back to the bishop," said the chaplain, sweat streaming down his face.

"I must report Sir Herbert's death to his family," said Grant.

"That was definitely not Sir Richard fighting at the door," said Corinne. "Lady Morgana was wearing a yellow dress at Charles so I am not sure if that was her either. Perhaps we have attacked the wrong people?"

"They attacked *us* unprovoked and used black witchcraft to defeat us!" said Psalmodier "We had best head back to Trondol before we are pursued. We have not now the strength to make a fight."

"But I must find out about my brother!" exclaimed the distraught Genevieve. "We are not even sure Sir Herbert is dead."

"Well I am going now," said the chaplain, spurring off as he did so. Grant and Corrine followed him. Lady Genevieve stayed put, thinking quickly. She soon decided it was her duty to establish her brother's fate. She headed back to Relajar.

At the Murada she untied the lady in the lacy nightgown first and then started to release the others. The lady, Donna Sancia asked, "What has happened? Why are you releasing us?"

"Your people at Lozana have defeated us. I am here to try and discover what has happened to my brother. Those that are left in my party have gone back over the border. We need to take bandages, medicines and shovels to Lozana because they will be much needed there."

Going to Narchad

A polk (platoon) of exhausted Schwaz aughed, black goblins from Gashad, straggled down the stony road. Behind them, on the skyline, glowered the mighty fortress of Chaos Deeps, guarding the cleft between the towering mountains either side. The polk had been expecting a meal and a rest there but had been sent on their way. Lord Madhgrund had said that they were badly needed at the battlefronts of Kaosium and certainly everyone had hurried them on their way. It was now forty-two days since they had left Bolgburz, on the completion of their training. Lord Madhgrund had told them that the Tarkgh lands of Thentis and Stetia lay waiting for them to reclaim for Kaosium. Rich lands, full of food, wine and soft slaves, where the living was easy. They had been looking forward to arriving but the way had been long and hard. Back in the Gashad Fatherland, under *Hagoth*'s eye they had never realised the earth was so large. In Ranu, Tempania, Ogrimor, Amelia and Belmain, they had been told to hurry further down the road. These countries of the greater Kaosium were supposed to feed and assist reinforcements for the fighting fronts. Alas, they took on these duties reluctantly, or not at all. Seven of their number had fallen on the way. Sickness, accidents and a hostile puma had taken them. Were they not so half-starved, they would have been fit. The four-day climb to Chaos Deeps had really tested them. At times only the thought of a rest at the fortress had kept them going. The fame of the wealth, the power and the luxury of the Chaos Deeps inmates had spread even to distant Gashad.

With what eagerness they had hurried the last few hundred hets. The gate tower was closed, however. A man from above had said, "Another aughed gang! Just keep going! We will signal so that you're met at the Halbad County border."

The aughed stared up, unbelieving. "Right, get moving! His Lordship gets nervous of riffraff skulking around the walls."

Riffraff! The casual insult hurt. *Hagoth*'s chosen warriors were what Lord Madhgrund had called them! Well, they were warriors and they would soon show how tough they were against the Tarkghs. It was that just now they were disheartened, exhausted and very, very hungry. They hobbled down the rough way, towards a standing boundary marker. They had seen a lot of boundary markers recently. They were normally just large stones stood on end. This one looked different. It had large spikes sticking out of its sides. As they got closer, they had just noticed it was made of wood when a large ogre appeared from behind it. "I'm Ordrer Fynigh of the Narchadian Army. Whose youse?"

The leading aughed stood to attention. "Hetaug Ignathik,

in command of the 1,473rd Polk of Schwaz Aughed." He held out a baked clay tablet inscribed with runes.

The ogre spat on it. "Dagon! They are scraping the bottom of the barrel these days. The Tarkgh knights will be really shaking in their armour if they ever sees youse! Laughing like! Never mind, a few moons digging roots and latrines will toughen youse up a trifle."

Ignathik bridled. "Lord Madhgrund has sent us here to fight the Tarkghs for the greater glory of all-powerful *Hagoth*! We expect to be treated as warriors!"

"Youse free your minds of all that glory-hunting guff or I'll call my own big boys. Lord Madhgrund is a-far-away. If youse want to eat, youse join the Narchadian Army and do as youse told. Otherwise, get back over the border!"

Ignathik and his aughed muttered amongst themselves. Truly they knew there was nothing for them back in Belmain and the "want to eat" phrase gnawed at their stomachs. They surged forward. "We'll eat!" they said hopefully.

"Good. Well it'll be root soup flavoured with garlic. Food stocks are low. We burned some of the Tarkghs' crops, so they burned some of ours. Now everyone hungry. Yep, war is hell. And don't youse let Madhgrund let youse think the Tarkghs are soft. Round here their iron armour is so heavy, youse aughed can't lift it. Theyse ride fire-breathing horses the size of dragons. Maybe theyse are dragons! Ah came from Ogrimor, with a polk of eighty, eleven long summers ago. Now there's only me left. Right, now youse appreciate this soup. With the first mouthful youse are enlisted in the 16th Swarm, Barak One, the Narchadian Army. Right now, we under Dame Arisha Save the Commissary General."

The aughed jaws dropped. Females had a very lowly status back in the breeding colonies of Gashad. Noticing this, the ogre Ordrer said, "Youse got to start thinking new if youse want to live. Dame Arisha, she's killed almost as many aughed as Tarkghs. "With a sword, not the soup!" he laughed, seeing some staring horrified at their bowls. "She Commissary General 'cause she can count, and not drunk all the time, like the rest. She keeps us fed whilst the others fight one another."

Morgana's stepmother, Lady Mavys, had heard of the death of Sir Daffyd, on the 14th of the Second Moon. She was staying in her mansion in the former capital city of Valles. She felt sad but not broken-hearted at the loss of her husband. She had gained much prestige by marrying the hero Knight Banneret. She had done her duty and produced a son to carry on the family name. But in fact they had had differing interests. He had never entered society, or taken any notice of the fashions and court gossip she found so absorbing. He was always away fighting on some distant frontier or other. People who did that too often had a tendency to get killed. In fact it had surprised her that he had lasted so long. Ah well, alas, she was a widow now. Widows were allowed more freedom than ordinary dutiful wives. She thought black would become her very well. She spent the next three days in her mansion, receiving only drapers and gown-makers. She also wrote letters to Arthur and Morgana, informing them that their father was dead and that they were to come and stay with her. She would see that they were suitably attired in mourning black when they arrived. She knew the best tailors in the city. She had been chaperoning the two daughters of Sir Teodor Nachet to court functions for some time. His late wife Lucotte was the sister of Sir Gregor Tanault who was married to her own sister Pearl. Lucotte had died ten years ago but he still remained unattached. He appreciated her help in keeping him and his daughters up with fashionable society in Valles. Most of the powerful lords had gone to Ekthalon but with the courts of the Monseigneur and the Grand Duke of Perigord present, Valles was still more fashionable. Now she would be able to play the brave hero's widow part to her friends in society. She had received no communications from Arthur or Morgana for many weeks. Letters were slow to arrive, even when they did write, so this did not bother her. Then on the 26th of the Second Moon a letter from Father Gervase arrived.

Milady Mavys,

I trust *Eru* has kept you well, for I send you dire tidings. As you may know, we have received the sad news of your husband Sir Daffyd's death at Sumeer. Alas I have to report to you that your only son Squire Arthur is also dead. The story I have been told is that Lady Abigail of St Visseille fell under suspicion for witchcraft. When members of the Church arrived to take her to trial, your son interceded in a fit of misplaced loyalty and unfortunately died from a quarrel wound. This was at St Visseille. Sir Congal and members of the Church have also come to Closin and taken Lady Morgana into custody. Because of this foolish fashion of wearing magickly shimmering dresses I think. His Grace the Grand Duke had already put Arthur and Morgana under the protection of Sir Helric Blaggart. He has removed all the family treasures from your manor here. Alas that these dark days should have befallen the Lefey family. I shall ask your people here to pray for you and Lady Morgana in your affliction.

Your ever Faithful servant
Gervase Vicar of Closin

This was indeed a sore blow. Lady Mavys could well bear the loss of her husband but she had really loved her one and only son, Arthur. She had dreamed of arranging a very splendid match for him when he was older. She had expected to have him enrolled in the Grand Duke of

Perigord's Guard. She wept for many hours. As for Morgana, what was the wretched girl doing wearing a shimmering gown amongst the bumpkins down there? She really needed to be watched all the time. Doubtless she had upset some traditionalist who was making a fuss to put her down. She was such a hoyden, it was no wonder people took offence. All that sword-fencing nonsense for instance. Well if she had to become a nun, she would raise a few eyebrows in the Church. Very likely this was a trick of the Church's to wring money out of the family estates. What was Sir Congal's part in all this, she wondered? Lothrop was the churchman of the family. Whose side were they on? Why had no one else told her before now? It would be too late now to attend her beloved Arthur's funeral but she supposed she must make an effort to assist Morgana somehow. It was a duty she owed Sir Daffyd. She needed to stay at least another two days as she had agreed to escort Teodor's daughters to the Melville's ball. That would give her an opportunity to ask his advice on how to deal with the Church over Morgana's problem. Meanwhile she must make sure that Lady Deirdre, the younger of the two daughters, kept her hair in the simple fashion appropriate to her status. Millicent, the eldest would be entitled to wear it *a la crespine.* Alas, few people appreciated just what problems there were getting damsels to wear suitably demure apparel to court functions. She remembered Morgana's constant battle to wear ever more extravagant head-dresses. Get yourself a husband first, then you can wear whatever hennin you fancy, she had told her. To be fair, Millicent and Deirdre Nachet were far easier to handle than the strong-willed Morgana had been.

On the afternoon of Restday the 28th she arrayed herself in her new black silk gown, ready for the Melvilles' Ball.

Sir Teodor and his daughters would come to collect her with his lady's wagon. This was provided with seats and was painted in his heraldic colours. It was a much more dignified mode of travelling to a ball than riding or walking.

She heard a knock at the front door and stood up ready to leave as she heard Belfred her steward draw the bolts back. She made a stately descent down the stairs, smiling graciously but there were only two ill-dressed varlets at the door.

"These persons wish to speak with you, milady," said Belfred. I have already told them that you have other matters to attend to at present."

Lady Mavys was tempted to tell them to be gone but curiosity got the better of her. Such persons normally came to the back door on matters regarding supplying food or doing repairs to the building. "Speak on, who are you and what do you need to say to me?"

One of the varlets, wearing a turbaned hood of mismatched colours, answered, "I am Javier, clerk of the Order of St Judas and this is my assistant Hartwig. We understand that you are the mother of the witch Morgana Lefey. She has murdered members of our Order and damaged Church property. We are here to take inventory of this property, the which we will claim in restitution for her misdeeds."

Poor Lady Mavys felt faint and had to sit down. "Wh...what strange tidings are these? This is mine own home, not Morgana's! *Eru* preserve me, I have ever been a dutiful daughter of the Church."

Javier produced a wooden tablet covered with wax and a stylus. "Bear witness, Hartwig. One black silk gown and matching hennin. A necklace, chatelaine, two bracelets and three rings of heavy gold."

"Aye I see them, Master Javier. She has new black kid shoon also." Javier scratched industriously at his tablet. "Now this hallway. Two medium-sized tapestries of indifferent quality, depicting countryside and animals."

At that moment Mavys spotted Sir Teodor ride up beside his cart through the arrow slit. She ran to re-open the front door. "Sir Teodor! Sir Teodor! Thank goodness you have come. These dreadful men are trying to rob the clothes from my back. Please rescue me. They say Morgana has upset them and now I must give them my house and clothes and *everything*!"

The knight swung down from his horse in a trice and drew his sword. "Who are you, sirrah, and how dare you upset this lady?"

"Milord we are servants of *Eru* in the Order of St Judas. We are merely carrying out our holy duty. This lady's daughter has been accused of witchcraft and killing members of the Church. I have here a copy of an Ordinance issued by the Bishop of Charles. Our Archbishop of Valles is now writing one for this diocese."

Sir Teodor took the creased document and read:

Church Ordinance

Wanted, dead or alive, the miscreants: Sir Richard Nogent, Lady Abigail Clove, Lady Morgana Lefey, a number of demons in their control, including one of dwarf stature. For murders most foul, witchcraft, theft and sacrilege. Also the escaped fugitives: Miss Edie a witch, Miss Vanova

a witch and Miss Louise Berde under suspicion of witchcraft.
Decreed by
Innocent, Bishop of Charles

He read it a second time. “It seems rather unspecific. Lady Morgana is mentioned as third among many, and how the various crimes are shared out is not mentioned. Who has been murdered? How is it known that the demons were under their control and not the other way around? Surely it would be for a trial to decide these matters?”

Javier looked hangdog at all these awkward questions. “Our intelligence is that our Justicar Pazan, the Sub Prioress Mania, and five familiars of our order have been killed at the priory of Stregafume.”

“And who gave you orders to harass this lady before a trial has been held?”

Javier looked even more uneasy. “Our preceptor is away at Signy so I have acted on his behalf. You must realise, Sir Knight, that it is vital to be beforehand in these matters. Persons in similar circumstances have been known to hide their treasures away, pretending they do not exist. Some even flee the country, taking their valuables with them.”

“Out you rogue! You are nothing but a thief! You doubt the honour of a noble lady, the widow of one of our most heroic Knights Banneret. I know your Preceptor Borgainaille and will speak to him of your effrontery when he returns. First you are operating on an Ordinance that has no force here in Perigord. Then know you that Lady Mavys is *not* the mother of the accused Lady Morgana. Accused, not condemned! Her mother died long ago. Also know that Lady Mavys will not lack protection whilst I am around.

I find it most unlikely that a well brought-up damsel like Morgana could be guilty of any of the crimes mentioned. Get your foul-smelling bodies away from here!"

The two immediately scurried away, as fast as they could. "I knew you shoulda waited!" they heard Hartwig mutter to his leader. Lady Mavys sped forward, ready to give Sir Teodor a more effusive thanks than perhaps a newly widowed lady should. However, the sight of Millicent and Deirdre staring out of the wagon, open-mouthed, brought to her a sense of proper decorum. She thanked Sir Teodor graciously and allowed him to kiss her hand. Assuming her most impassive expression, she ascended into the wagon. The two damsels were obviously bursting with questions but lacked the courage to ask them.

"Now let me have a look at you two. Do you not think that bracelet is not a little ostentatious for a young lady, Deirdre?"

After the trial, when Jinisti had been taken away, they returned to the mansion to plan for the future. Donna Sancia agreed that Sir Desmond and Drex the hobilar should be taken to the Murada where it would be easier to care for their wounds. She would allow Lady Genevieve to assist in their treatment. The matter of Sir Desmond's ransom would be left in abeyance for now. Morgana said that she wanted the Lozana Mansion and estate brought back into service. She intended that in time she, Lady Abigail and perhaps her mother could retire there when their adventures were over. She asked Raymond to start putting the gardens into order and to create a herb garden for Lady Abigail.

She set Vanova as housekeeper, to be assisted by Louise Berde in righting the mansion. Don Jerome said he would ensure they got all the assistance they needed from the Murada estate workers. The damage to the building would need to be repaired. The three captured horses could be used to carry materials. They would need to build a new stable. "I will be glad if you can take charge of these matters for me. Your father wants us to proceed on a secret mission as fast as we can," said Morgana.

"Certainly, you need have no worries," replied Don Jerome confidently.

Early next morning Morgana tried to contact Begus but the mirror remained cloudy. The party set off again after breakfast. Since they had been staying at inns most of the time, they still had enough rations for about four days. It was a dry but cloudy day with a strong wind from the east. The road was potholed and neglected. They met no other travellers.

"Fear of 'Mighty Morgana Chicken Slayer' has frightened the people away," suggested Minut. But it was more likely that the Narchadian raids had depopulated this area. Ruins were more common than habitations on either side. Clumps of narcissi and violets indicated that spring was arriving. Then they came to large blackened areas where crops had been set on fire. Green shoots were now beginning to show up through the ashes. Her gardener's soul affronted at the damage, Lady Abigail cast her *Duplex Messis* (Double Crop) spell on field after field as she rode past. It would aid the harvest later in the year.

As they crested a low hill they caught a glimpse of the snow-topped Erdh Varadh Mountains, perhaps a hundred myles away. Morgana turned to look at Minut. The dwarf had not been his somewhat gratingly cheerful self recently.

He looked sad, he knew he was going towards his forbidden homeland.

In the late morning, they reached sight of the better-paved Bosen to Trondol road. A knight with four blue-clad hobilars was riding northwards. Drawing back from the crest, they sent Tonaldo the Troubadour to find out who they were. He was told to get out of the way by the knight since he was taking important dispatches to Ekthalon. Tonaldo circled back to the party and they followed the knight's party at a very discreet distance. Two myles further up the road they saw, silhouetted on a hill-crest ahead, a large tree stump. Could this be the giant tree stump mentioned by Begus? Bergand and Minut were sent ahead to inspect it. They found a rolled slip of parchment stuck in a crack high up the trunk. Since it was written in the Tengthin alphabet which neither could read, they brought it back.

"Light a fire beside the wall on the crest."

They could see a small stretch of crumbling drystone wall up near the stump. There they found a heap of dry kindling wood, heaped ready. Looking around, they could see over the wall, to the west, the Arbor Halbrad. Lady Abigail told them that the true elvish name was Arbour Hallabraid–the treeland of Hallabraid but the Chaotic interlopers had mispronounced it, as was their wont. Doubtless there would be watchers around its eaves if not closer. To the north they could see a ruined village, which Don Incio told them was Zarkanis. His own home at Girrin was but a two-hour ride away but he felt no urge to visit it. "It will probably be even more of a gloomy ruin than when I last saw it. The winter and the Chaotics will have seen to that."

"Light the fire," ordered Morgana. "The wall will hide its flames from the forest. We had best stand clear, for it must be a signal for someone." Indeed, two hours later they saw a figure riding towards them. Morgana was entranced to see he was half-horse and half-man. Her governess had taught her that there were such creatures living in Oblivia but she had not really believed her.

"I am Akkates." He spoke with a very deep accented voice. "You are, I can see, Don Incio with the lady with the unicorns. I have been ordered to lead you to Don Cuerpo and his men. They are to help you with your mission. They have a hideout in the village yonder."

"I know Don Cuerpo," commented Don Incio as they set off, back onto the road.

As they entered the long ruined settlement Akkates suddenly stopped. "Something is wrong. We should have been challenged by now. Be on your guard!" As the rest of them halted too, six armed men rushed out to block the way ahead.

"Let us charge them?" said Sir Richard.

"No, let me try some magic first," replied Lady Abigail, moving ahead as Akkates and Bergand loosed their bows. Their enemies included a wizard in their second rank and he cast a spell that stampeded Sir Richard's Rouncey, Melonda. She dumped him off, a few hets up the street but he landed safely. Lady Abigail's spell blew the wizard and two other men off their feet. Morgana charged forward and cut the wizard in two, whilst he was scrabbling for his skull-topped wand. The remaining enemies tried to run but the companions rode down and killed them all. Morgana searched the two halves of the wizard. On him were a bag of sawdust, 143 gilden pezzi and a piece of parchment with a series of numbers on it:

Zarkanis, the ruined village: six Narchadians led by a wizard blocked the street ahead!

24. 35. 22. 22. 31/30. 32. 31. 29. 26. 37. 25/31. 35/30. 26. 24. 25//21. 38. 36.28//38. 31. 37. 26. 29/
(2)/25. 32. 38. 35.36/29. 18. 37. 22. 35/33. /40.32.35.21/33. 26. 31.22/ -/30. 18. 35.37.26.31//17+

The money, a very large sum to be carried, was stowed in several pockets in the now hideously ruined gown, a gown of good quality black satin, with a green belt secured by a skull-shaped bone buckle. Obviously he had been a person of rank. His head was shaved and his ears somewhat pointed; his ornate boots had rags tied round them, as did those of his followers. Their clothes were dark-coloured and they had black smears on their faces. They had only broad, short curved swords for weapons. There was little on them but small amounts of money and three cloves of garlic.

"Garlic drains the energy from Risen Dead creatures," quoted Lady Abigail, "but I cannot stomach the stuff."

"I'll take it," said Bergand. "It gives good flavouring to stews."

Minut picked up the wizard's wand. "This has been used as a club. The skull has been reinforced with bronze but done poorly. See, the bone is cracked. Ah, the foot is a signet." He pressed it into some soft mud at the edge of the road. The impression left showed a skull surrounded by runes. "Lindeskel," Minut read out.

"Lindeskel Mark of Stechen that will be!" exclaimed Don Incio. "I am glad he is dead. I believe he was involved in the attack on my castle. His death may well stir up the Narchadians."

Morgana then showed Abigail the wizard's sawdust. She

sniffed at it and ran it through her fingers. "Perindaeus wood. Such will scorch a dragon's skin or that of other fireproof beasts. Perhaps even demons."

Akkates then checked the second ruin on the right-hand side of the road. In it were the bodies of Don Cuerpo and two of his men. They had been surprised and robbed by the Narchadians.

"Alas, he will not give you any assistance. My guess is that he was to help you over the border into Narchad. If so, I am afraid you will now have to attempt it alone. I myself have never tried it and anyway I must go to report this sad loss."

"Yes, you must do that but what think you of this parchment with the numbers on it?" asked Morgana, producing it.

"I understand it not because I cannot read. Such is a game for the halls of men," responded the centaur.

"Let me see it," demanded Don Incio. "I think this may well be a coded message sent to Don Cuerpo which the wizard had taken. Perhaps we can unravel it?"

Morgana, Lady Abigail and the two knights sat down and puzzled over the numbers. Tonaldo went back to recover Melonda and the others made a thorough search of the other ruins. There was nothing there. Zarkanis had been ruined and empty a very long time. From the hillock beside it, they could see the trees of the vast Arbor Halbrad, stretching for myles to the west. Closer to the village were the burial mounds of those slain in the great battle of Zarkanis years ago. They hid the Narchadian bodies all together in a ruin.

After a long while, Morgana exclaimed, "I have it! The number at the end is that added to the alphabet to give the letters numbers."

Spelling it out produced:

Green Monolith nr Migh. Dusk until two hours later. P. Word. Pine - Martin.

They found Migh on the map. It was thirty-five myles away in the depths of the forest. “What do you know about getting into the forest, Akkates?” asked Sir Richard.

“It is a bad place for mounted people. Narrow winding paths with low branches. The Narchadians keep them that way to keep our knights out. Along the eves they grow dense bramble thickets, penetrable only via paths bristling with traps. They also have sentries and patrols, night and day. Undead creatures guard by night and live ones by day. It is a fearsome place. You will have to pick your time to suit you. There has been relative peace throughout the winter but that does not mean they are sleeping.”

“I expect we shall die trying to get into the trees, but try it we must,” mourned Don Incio. “It was hard enough last time I was there.”

Lady Abigail offered, “We have the unicorn’s horn and the garlic to counter the undead, we may find it easier to go in by night. If we go by day, they will see us as soon as we leave the village.”

“Yes I agree,” said Morgana. “We will have dinner first and then head down to the forest, after sunset. Don Akkates, thank you for your help. You can stay to share our dinner, or go to give your report if you wish.”

“I think I will head back. My comrades will have food more to my taste than yours will. We will call back tomorrow to deal with the bodies.” He rode off southwards.

Into the Arbor Halbrad

Once the sun had set, they filed down towards the forest on foot. The moderate wind blew from behind them and there was a certain amount of light from the waxing moon. Passing the battle burial mounds, they noticed that they were pitted in places, as if someone had dug into them in the past. As they had found elsewhere, they were trudging through the ashes of burnt crops. As they neared the forest edge, they could see huge marker posts, with giant thorns sticking out of them. Bergand whispered that there must be paths beside them, or why put them there? He was in the lead, with Minut, Sir Richard and Morgana as the advance guard. Then a little way back came the eleven steeds, led by Lady Abigail, Cherry and Tonaldo. Don Incio and Sergeant Hrolf guarded the rear. They made a very long column. At that moment, a harsh trumpet-blast rang out from the forest ahead. They had been spotted! A whispered conversation ensued as they advanced–to decide whether they should try a path, or try to hack through the bramble thickets. Morgana decided that hacking through would be too slow and tiring. As well try a path, before the enemy could concentrate a force. They headed for a marker. They were still five hets away when Sir Richard gave a stifled curse. He had stepped on a caltrop! Bergand and Minut discovered these spiked obstacles scattered all around them. Slowly they cleared a safe path by the shielded light of Minut's oil lamp. Sir Richard found it very painful to walk so they helped him onto his horse. Apart from the creaking of boughs and the sighing of the wind, the forest stayed black and silent.

Scouting cautiously, Bergand discovered a pit trap near a marker but it was possible to edge round it to the left. An undead skeleton leapt from behind the marker and thrust at Bergand with a spear but he was ready and smashed its skull. It fell, a pile of disconnected bones. Further on was another pit trap. It was only a het wide so they all jumped it once it was revealed. Careful and experienced with woodland traps as he was, Bergand missed the next one. There was a whoosh and a heavy branch swung out from the side striking his helmet with a clang. He was knocked away into the undergrowth and lay there groaning faintly.

The others passed him back to be strapped to his horse and Minut took over the scouting role. His dwarf eyes had good vision in the gloom and he soon spotted some boxes of rocks, suspended in the tree above them. He traced ropes downwards that led to the treadle mechanism in the path. Hidden beside the treadle was a lever, which locked the treadle solid and safe. The Narchadians would set and unset their traps to suit their own needs. He set it and prodded cautiously forward round an S bend. Ahead was a long straight and six hets on was yet another treadle. The rope led back to two bent bows in the trees behind. "Perhaps we could get the arrows," he suggested to Morgana.

"No, it would waste time. Remember the alarm was raised. Just disable it."

Minut cut the rope and crawled on. Ahead the path joined a broader track at right angles. He had just discovered a much larger pit trap, when a rider arrived at the far end. "Disable the trap!" hissed Morgana.

Obediently he prodded out with the haft of his hammer until he found the lever that locked the lid of the pit. As he turned it he felt his helmet jerk and tingle. The rider had cast a spell at him! They could see it was another skeleton, wearing a hooded cloak and riding a pale horse. Morgana held up the Vinkalik and intoned *Ibi Nebula*. A ball of mist enveloped their opponent and they heard him back away.

From the stamping of hooves, and some harsh muttering, it sounded as though there were more riders on the track ahead. Morgana re-organised her force. Sir Richard whispered that he could fight very well on horseback, and Hrolf also mounted and worked his way to the front. With the path so narrow this was not an easy process. Though the dense forest gave shelter from the wind, Morgana's magic mist drifted away after a few minutes. Now there were five skeleton riders peering at her from the track. The cloaked one gave an order in Kharsh and a rider wielding a scythe rode up the path towards her. Dodging under the scythe swing, she cut it in two and it fell into another heap of loose bones. Its skeleton mount just stood inert until she pushed it into the bushes.

There was another Kharsh order and the enemy riders drew back, two either side of the junction. Morgana realised that they would be charged as they emerged from the path.

Ibi Nebula, she formed another ball of mist at the junction. Now the enemy could not see them as they crept out onto the track. When ready, they charged out of the mist and caught the riders standing. To the right Sir Richard engaged the enemy leader, whilst Morgana, still on foot, felled another on a skeleton horse. She then turned to help Sir Richard whose opponent was putting up a good fight. To the left, Hrolf and Minut found their opponents, both armed with long lances doing the same. Both had their armour dented before they triumphed, destroying both opponents just as Morgana finished the leader. Suddenly everything was quiet. By lantern light they searched the piles of bones. They found only weapons and the ragged cloak of the leader. The weapons had black steel blades with the skull symbol and runes of *Heghate, Magha* of the Undead.

"These probably are *Nehruth* enchanted, bestowing the curse of undeath on those wounded by them," said Lady Abigail. Hrolf threw them as far as he could into the undergrowth. Abigail struck the bones of each skeleton, including the two horse ones, with her unicorn's horn and they crumbled to dust. The three live horses, they added to their long train of mounts. Morgana authorised Cherry to treat Sir Richard's foot and Bergand's head with phials of the St Bandade Holey water. Only three more remained.

Following the track to the left they soon came on another narrow path leading deeper into the forest. Minut led, followed by Hrolf and Morgana. They had barely started when there was a loud groaning sound. They stopped and it stopped, only to restart as they moved on. An alarm treadle! Immediately a file of spearmen ran towards them. Minut crushed the first, shield and man with his great hammer. Slipping past him, Hrolf cut down the next with his axe. Morgana, her gown shimmering, killed the third in turn and the fifth, sixth and seventh spearmen wailed and ran. The fourth, however, was of sterner stuff but soon died a violent death. Morgana chased down the track, turning right at the next fork. The Narchadians were outrunning her so she cast the first spell that came into her head at the nearest, *"Armae Mutatio!"* Revulsion of weapons! The man fainted, though whether from the sight of her shining magic sword or his own spear there was no way of telling. Morgana left him and rejoined her party.

Don Incio was stabbing the spearman whom Hrolf had felled. "Just putting him out of his misery. He could never survive a wound like that," he said, sensing Morgana's disgust.

Just short of the Y-junction they found the guard hut the Narchadians had come from. It was now empty apart from some bedding. The bodies yielded only a few coins. Since the enemy had taken the right fork, they took the left. It was now the twenty-first hour but they wanted to get clear from any possible pursuit. "We must be through the trap zone now. Let us move faster," ordered Lady Morgana.

"You lead the way, madam," responded Don Incio.

The undergrowth was not as dense now and could be penetrated if necessary. The path meandered on for myles, joined every now and then by another. Sometimes they thought they heard people or creatures nearby. Several times there were the calls of wild beasts in the distance. At one spot something large rushed away from them in panic. Looking down one side path, Morgana spotted the glimmer of a fire but she led them on. There were a few small clearings but now the sky had clouded over. Neither the moon nor the stars were visible. With the many twists and turns of the path they were no longer certain of their direction.

"It would be funny if we found ourselves back where we came in," laughed Minut.

"With the alarm raised, it would not be very funny at all!" snapped Morgana. She knew very well who would be blamed if they had circled back.

"We must have covered fifteen myles into the forest and I for one cannot go another step," said Lady Abigail.

Morgana was exhausted herself. She had been on the go since dawn and had fought in three dangerous skirmishes. "We will look for somewhere to rest for the rest of the night," she said.

Vechad, the Spokesman of Stechen, lay worrying as his wife snored beside him. Would the food last out till the spring greens were ready? Should he organise another hunt? With the famine, game was getting scarce. If they killed all the animals now, the larder would be empty in the future. Would the seeds they had planted in the burnt fields come to crop? Shoots were showing through but it was too early to see if they belonged to crops or weeds. If they did come up, would they stay unburnt? That was a foolish move of Count Duffric's to burn all those Stetian crops. It was just bravado on his part, trying to show his loyalty to the Chaotic cause. The old Count, Panric, would not have done it. He would have had more sense or the countess would have had more sense for him. The Stetians were bound to retaliate and where easier than the fields closest to the forest? In truth they were probably on Stetian land but the village had tilled them for many a year now. When the centaurs came burning, they picked the night. The risen dead watchers had just watched. Food crops were of no interest to them and they feared the flames. Their orders were to guard the forest and that they had done. In truth they and the traps did the job well but some better defence was needed for the fields. He would speak to the Mark when he returned. It was his duty to protect their food supply as much as to annoy the enemy.

"Hark!" He heard shouting at the gate!

"Go to sleep," murmured his wife, woken by his restless turning. But he leapt out and got dressed; something was afoot. He went to the village gate, where the watchman had just admitted Hath and Cherd. They should have been on duty at the third-watch hut this night. They were panting, exhausted and had to sit down.

"What has happened?" demanded Vechad. "Tarkgh raiders in't forest! T'others r'all dead! Only usses got away!" gasped Hath. The commotion had woken other villagers who were gathering around.

"I knew it! I knew it!" screeched a woman. "The fool, going to be a hero dying for *Hagoth.* Much *Hagoth* will thank him for it! Never a thought for me and the children!"

"Be silent!" ordered Vechad. "The village will care for you and the others if necessary. Are you sure the others are all dead, Cherd?"

"Well it were like this. Wese were sleeping like, in't hut when usses heard t'groan. Larrel, he orders usses out sose we went on't track. Ah couldna see much but the Tarkghs killed our first three and I got a glimpse of a giant purple woman glowing in the dark. Fearsome she was and waving a great white sword. Leved in front o me says run or we're done! So we runs but Larrel stayed to fight the woman with his axe. When I dared look back he was down and the woman was running after us. Then she stopped and pointed and I just concentrated on running. I das'nt look back again for many a myle. When I did there was no sight of the woman or Leved."

"Aye. That's the way it were," corroborated Hath. "Dagon knows what's happened to the night-watchers."

"Apart from the purple woman, how many Tarkghs were there?" asked Vechad.

"Dunno. I glimpsed at least one behind her," answered Cherd looking at Hath.

"Aye but I heard horses too. From behind 'em. If we'd stayed to fight usses ud not be here."

"Right. You two can go to bed. We will have to go out to investigate. I hope it was Tarkghs you was fighting and not some of our own side. Some funny peoples on our side. From furrin parts as you know. The purple woman sounds like a Belmainian Dame[9]. Tarkgh women don't fight like that, if at all. This will have to be reported to the Mark. We will have to find out if the otherworld's horsemen know what has happened. It gives me the chills to speak to them but it must be done. I want you ten men armed, ready to come with me. And bring shovels."

"My Sedith had all us money ins pouch. Can I come too?" said a woman.

"Me too!" screeched Leved's wife, Raldah.

"Right. The wives of the squad can come if they want to but keep at the back of the men."

The third-watch hut was a fair distance from the village. The Tarkghs, if Tarkghs they were, would be far away by

---

9 Belmainian Dames are the brawny female equivalents of knights, following apprenticeships as debutantes.

now, thought Vechad. Really this was the job of Lindeskel the Mark but he was away raiding with some of his rivermen.

They marched off into the darkness, taking some shielded lanterns. Half an hour later, Vechad in the lead spotted Leved on the path ahead. "Leved," he called relieved that he at least was still alive but Leved gave a howl and fled into the underbrush. "Leved!" called Vechad again but got no response.

"Cursed with madness like as not," said Vechad. Raldah plunged into the undergrowth to search for her husband but the rest followed the spokesman. They came on Larrel's body, with his head cloven to the neck. Beside him, the watch hut was empty. The bodies of the other three lay a little further up the path. Sedith, the furthest, had his head smashed into his chest.

"That were no sword or even axe that done that!" wailed his wife. "Those Tarkghs, those filthy Tarkghs! They've taken allus money!" She burst into tears.

Vechad took six of the men up to the perimeter track. A little way to the left lay a piece of old rib bone and some scatterings of grey dust. There were the scuffmarks of a struggle near one of the exit paths. Up the path were large hoof marks and the traps had been unset. At the boundary marker, the pit was open and Trashik the risen dead skeleton, was a heap of inert bones at the bottom.

Mewersceld, at the next marker, reported seeing a score of Tarkgh knights coming up to Trashik's path. Trashik had sounded his trumpet so the patrol should have dealt with them. Vechad strongly suspected that the Tarkghs had dealt with the patrol but he did not tell Mewersceld that. He went back to the perimeter track and checked in the mounted-patrols daytime lair. As he suspected, it was empty!

For Morgana's party the problem of where to rest was where to find the space. Whilst it was a luxury to have fourteen steeds, there was no getting away from the fact that they took up a lot of space. Marching as they were in single file, the column was twenty-four hets long! At least with the leaves sprouting on the trees, the steeds had something to eat. Cherry had reported that they had three days' rations left. First they needed to find a clearing off the main path. That is, if it was the main path! Shortly they came to an obviously well used path branching off to the right. Morgana sent Tonaldo up to reconnoitre. Tonaldo crept forward on foot. This job was not to his taste. It was cold and there were a few spots of rain beginning to fall. He decided to climb a tree to get a view around him. Though it was a tall tree, its own foliage made seeing out difficult. When he had climbed as high as he dared, all he could see was more black leafage. He descended and crept further down the track. Ahead was a palisade tower and gateway, a Narchadian village! He halted a moment, wondering if he should approach to negotiate with the villagers but decided the leaders should make the decision.

When he returned Don Incio said, "Trust the hospitality of the Narchadians? Never! They are the enemy, remember."

They carried on along the main path, in the now steady rain, until meeting a little-used junction to the left. This time Morgana herself did the scouting. A dozen hets in, the path opened onto a large paved hardstanding, with a large rock crag on its left-hand side. All she could hear was the hissing and splashing of the rain. Back on the main path the others had found a marker board. On it was depicted a black bowl with some red liquid in it. "The symbol of *Khali, Magha* of the Risen Dead!" Morgana was now discovering a similar marker on a door in the rock face of the crag. To the left was a water trough and to the right an empty crate, on its side. Impatient and desperate to rest, the others filed in behind her.

"Best tether the steeds to the fence beside the paving," said Morgana. Minut tried the door, which did not have a lock, but found it was bolted from the other side. Morgana told Tonaldo to find some stones or heavy timber so they could block the door with the crate.

The others had just set up the two pavilions when a woman's voice was heard from inside the door. In heavily accented Kharsh she said, "Who is it being there? Thees temple iss clowsed. Leaf any offereengs een the box that iss waiting by thee side."

Sir Richard who was close enough to hear replied (in equally bad Kharsh), "We are weary travellers wishing to camp here for the night?"

"Thee temple of *Khali* iss not being a guest howse!" They heard movement behind the door. Morgana hastily put the crate back into its former position. More female voices were heard, speaking a tongue none could recognise (Undo). Soon figures could be seen on the crag above them, peering down. Sir Richard called up, "What offerings does *Khali* accept, the blood of people or animals?"

"Thee blood of peoples iss being thee much better but we are also accepting offerings of food."

"We will make an offering of food for now and put it in the box."

"Very well then." The figures watched suspiciously. In

consultation with Cherry and Lady Abigail, Morgana decided to put a third of their remaining food in the box. The door of the crag opened and a dark-skinned priestess, wearing very little, came out and looked at the food. She shouted something to the others above, who replied. Then two more priestesses came out of the crag to carry the box inside. Then the first one followed them and bolted the door behind her. The figures on the crag disappeared and the party at last went to bed. Except Don Incio and Minut who had to remain on guard. Tonaldo suggested he could play a lullaby to help them to sleep and was sharply told to keep quiet. Around the third hour of the eighth, Lady Abigail and Sergeant Hrolf came on watch. The rain had stopped but it was still chilly. The forest was quieter now and time went slowly as they waited for the first glimmers of the dawn. Then they heard surreptitious movement on the crag above them. The priestesses were massing up there!

"Awake! To arms!" shouted Sergeant Hrolf, fearing an attack. Excited foreign shouting came from above and a chakram (edged circular throwing weapon) glanced off Hrolf's mail. They were being attacked! Abigail dodged behind a pavilion whilst Hrolf ran to shelter against the foot of the crag. Minut borrowed Bergand's crossbow to loose a bolt at the Amazon priestesses above. Two more chakrams were thrown, whilst Abigail blew two enemy off their feet with her *Ventus Impetus* spell. Dropping the crossbow Minut ran across towards the crag door, followed by Morgana and Sir Richard. Don Incio went to the left, up against the crag whilst Hrolf started to climb its face. Morgana cast *Affarre Vertigo* at the head priestess but with no effect. A magic bolt in return left Sir Richard clinging to the cliff, disorientated. Minut pounded the door with his hammer as the priestesses threw large stones down at

The Temple of Khali: hearing the Amazons massing on top of its crag at dawn, some of the party got up to oppose them.

them. Don Incio tried in several places to climb up but the rock was too wet and slippery. Several times he slipped and fell back. Hrolf, however, did manage to scramble to the top despite a sword-wielding Amazon who he was obliged to kill. Bergand crawled out and reloaded his crossbow. Morgana tried another *Affarre Vertigo* and a priestess toppled off the crag to her death. She then moved to her right where she found some rough steps cut into the rock face. Don Incio had just slipped back from another attempt to scale the cliff when Minut finally smashed open the door.

Inside it was dark and gloomy, lit only by clumps of luminous fungus on the walls and a flickering fireplace to the left of the door. To its right was the box of food they had offered. The stony chamber had a large portrait of four armed *Khali* at the north end. In front of it was a black bowl full of blood, then a het further into the chamber, a bronze sacrificial slab with a dead man on it. At the far end were steps leading both up to a trapdoor at the top of the crag and to down below. Minut followed by Don Incio, headed for the steps. A strange smell met them from below.

"I think the smell is a cooking sauce from the Undo lands," said Minut.

Sir Richard picked up the fallen priestess and brought her inside. There he laid her on the altar. Though brought up in the Church of *Eru*, from experience he believed it unwise to be disrespectful to any *Maghi.* Morgana, her gown shimmering, ascended the cliff steps. The head priestess cast a spell at her, which failed. Morgana cut down one woman and then fought with the head priestess herself. Minut emerged from the trap door on top of the crag, to fight a sword-armed priestess and received a sore cut to his wrist. These priestesses better merited the title Amazons[10]. Like Morgana, they had spent long years practising weapon skills. Three of them, armed with spears, now attacked the isolated Hrolf. Despite all his skill, one got a thrust clean through his hauberk and he sank down finished.

The sight inflamed the others. Morgana bisected the head priestess and cut down a spear Amazon. Minut smashed his tough opponent to pulp. The remaining three priestesses lost their nerve and fled.

"Saxum Mutatio!" shouted Morgana at one, Revulsion of Rock. She would not be coming back to the crag for a while. Don Incio picked up one of their missile stones but they were out of range before he could throw it. He was white with rage, frustrated at having achieved nothing himself. Minut examined Hrolf but he was dead. Morgana searched the head priestess. She had a skull-topped staff, a dagger and a bunch of keys. There was a spring leading over a waterfall to a pond at the back of the crag. Morgana was so angry at the loss of Hrolf, she kicked the two halves of the head priestess over into it. Minut was worried that his wrist wound was *Nehruth*-infected, so Lady Abigail treated it with holey water. They could almost see it start to heal close.

All falling silent, they went to explore the odorous downstairs.

"Curry!" said Lady Abigail. "It is a mixture of Undo spices used for cooking. We had some at Relajar when I was young. The cook used too much and we could not taste *anything* for hours afterwards."

At the bottom of the stair, was a dimly lit chamber with

---

10 They were Durgids from the Chaotic Amazon State of Durgan.

ten pallets and some clothes. A corridor led to a first main chamber, a kitchen. There, Lady Abigail was glad to be able to loot a sack of rice, a tub of apples and some assorted roots. Some strips of dried meat and a jar of curry powder she left behind. Next was a locked purple-painted door. Minut picked the lock and entered. There was a bed covered with red silk, a carpet, some hanging clothes and a chest. The chest had three locks of unfamiliar design, presenting a fine challenge to the dwarf. Meanwhile Sir Richard pulled the bolts on the next door and went in. There was a short, unlit corridor leading to a pitch-black chamber. Peeping in, he glimpsed a crowd of upright skeleton forms. Hastily he rushed back and re-bolted the door. Putting an ear to it, he could hear nothing. Then he proceeded to the fourth and last door. It too was bolted on the outside and he cautiously opened it. A foul smell hit him, so foul that he felt nauseous and dizzy. He re-bolted it and rested before returning. Minut finally succeeded in opening his chest, just as Morgana arrived with the keys. Inside were three bottles of an unknown liquid, two books in an unknown alphabet (Sinsrit), a large bag of money and a bronze wand with more of the strange letters on it.

Sir Richard told the rest about the skeletons he had seen.

"These will be Risen Dead skeletons in their inert state I expect," said Don Incio. "These priestesses are from Durgan, where the worship of *Khali* is the main religion. Unlike the Undead of *Heghate* the risen dead have to draw their energy from living creatures. By drinking blood whilst they are unrotted and by touch, 'ghouls' grip' as it is termed. I expect the watcher skeletons come from here."

Morgana remembered it must be about dawn outside so she went to use her mirror. In the tents she found that both Cherry and Tonaldo had remained asleep through the whole morning's action! She put them on guard duty! Making successful contact, she found Begus holding out parchments in the mirror.

Make Contact at Green Monolith of Migh

and

Contact Alyson the drudge at Flora Makbuta's Hospital, in mid-morning.

She wondered where this hospital was but Begus disappeared after showing the message. They were indeed heading for Migh but really they were not too sure of their own location. She put the mirror away and looked at the mysterious bronze wand. Thinking about what Don Incio had said about the risen dead, she took it to the skeletons' chamber, accompanied by Sir Richard. She was thinking the wand might control the skeletons. First she waved it in the air saying, "*Obeodi!*" but nothing happened. Then she touched one and it moved its skull to look at her! "Follow me," she said but it stayed put. Then it spread its bony fingers wide to indicate it did not understand.

"Folghani!" said Sir Richard and the skeleton followed him. "It speaks Kharsh, which is what you might expect."

"I will take four as servants." She touched three more. As they went out, each skeleton collected a scythe each from a pile in the corner. Lady Abigail was horrified that Morgana wanted to make use of them. She took her unicorn horn and went down into the chamber. There she thrust through each of the eleven remaining skeletons, who became just heaps of dust. "These at least shall go to whatever rest they have earned," she declared.

Morgana like most of the rest of the party was still tired from the previous days so they decided to rest where they were. Cherry, Tonaldo and Bergand would remain on guard, whilst the rest sampled the priestesses beds. Morgana chose the red silk one of the head priestess. She soon fell asleep. Bergand still had a headache and a large purple bruise but was otherwise fit. He watched the path whilst Cherry and Tonaldo packed up their two pavilions. In the late morning they saw two dark-skinned Amazons approaching. These were surprised to see them and all the steeds and demanded, in Kharsh, why they were there. Cherry replied, "There has been fighting in and around this temple. We were ordered to help drive off the raiders. There have been losses inside and perhaps your sisters will be glad to have you rejoin them."

The Amazons muttered together and started to head for the temple door. At that moment Tonaldo, from the far end of the clearing began strumming his mandolin. "Tarkghs!" cried one of the Amazons and they both brandished their spears. Cherry threw her knife at one and Bergand loosed his crossbow at the other. Both fell, cursing something in Kharsh, but soon bled to death. Tonaldo and Bergand dragged them inside to add to the altar. Cherry then started to cook lunch, whilst Bergand went back on guard with Tonaldo. After lunch the party collected the other priestesses' bodies to heap around the altar. Then they buried Hrolf in the depths of the forest. Lady Abigail first pushed her unicorn horn firmly into the spear wound that killed him. She was determined the priestesses would not be able to call him back from the dead. They concealed the grave as best they could and sadly returned to the temple. After fighting so many successful actions, his death was a severe shock.

Morgana felt it bitterly. Hrolf was her oldest retainer. It had been he who taught her and Arthur to fence, all those years ago. Now he, like Arthur, like her father and also cousin Ines was gone forever. How was she going to tell Margery, Megan and Hlidric, when she returned? If she ever returned! No she must try and be positive. Her party depended on her and she must think for the future. At that moment the sun came out. From its angle to that of the main track they estimated that they had been travelling in roughly the right direction. They made ready to depart. The four skeletons were terrified of the sun and would not come out into it. Sir Richard eventually wrapped them up in Amazon blankets and tied them onto the captured horses. They seemed happy enough to stay as inert bundles of bones that way. Morgana put the head priestess' red silk coverlet onto the spare horse as a souvenir. Then they rode off.

Morgana spoke. "We need to find a guide if we can. This is a dangerous place to be blundering about lost."

They rode when they could, but in many places the branches were too low and they had to dismount. Occasionally they glimpsed a figure or creature ahead, plunging off the track to hide from them. Then they met a man and three women who had spades and bags of roots that they had been collecting.

"Is this the way to Migh?" asked Sir Richard in Kharsh.

"Yus, peoples wannin ta go Migh allus goes thataway. Never bin that way meself o'course. Not nor none of us. Wesall cum frum Chigwell, eh girls?"

"Would anyone at Chigwell know the way to Migh? We seek a guide."

"Well oi supposes wur priest or t'spokesman moight."

"There are no regular guides then?"

"Well there were Elbracht but he went away aguiding and never cum back."

Sir Richard discussed this with Morgana and Don Incio. Sir Richard thought there might be someone in Chigwell who could help but Morgana felt time was getting short and refused to go backwards. So they carried on. Morgana regretted her inability to speak Kharsh. Lady Abigail said her own knowledge of the language was poor. Don Incio offered to teach it to her and did indeed give her a few lessons on the move. Morgana resolved also to be instructed by Cherry who had learnt the Narchadian dialect, Kharsh.

Half an hour later they encountered a file of people carrying large baskets and sacks of food supplies. A warrior heading the column strode up to them in a confident manner. "Make way in the name of the commissary general!"

"But we have many horses, you should make way for us," said Don Incio scowling.

"I am Sergeant Bascend, escorting important SAVEWAY supplies for Dame Arisha. You impede us at your peril!" the sergeant replied, waving his shield at them. It was of lozenge shape, white with green and beige vertical stripes on it.

"I am a knight and we too have important business and we have many horses on the track!" snarled Don Incio, fingering his sword.

The sergeant then realised the strength of the party, which he felt was more than he could deal with. "Very well then. Everyone, pull into the side to let these people pass."

They carried on.

A myle further they met a green-clad man walking with a stick. "Good day to you, sir. Who may you be?" asked Sir Richard in Kharsh.

"Good day, sir. They call me Foglio the herbalist."

"Do you know your way around this forest?"

"Indeed I do, I know where all the rarer herbs grow."

"He is a healer," said Sir Richard aside to Morgana.

"Not one with more medicines out of a book?" she answered.

"No. That would be difficult, I just make medicines from plants as is normal," the green-clad man said in Simnith.

Morgana smiled. "Could you guide us to Migh from here, as we are lost? We would pay you a fair rate for your trouble."

After some brisk haggling, a "fair rate" of ten gilden pezzi was agreed. He led them off just as some chill rain began to fall.

Eventually Foglio asked, "Do you intend camping for the night? Darkness will fall in half an hour or so."

Morgana could think of no real reason to carry on marching into the night. In the darkness, perhaps even a guide that knew the way could get lost. The rain was not making the journey any pleasanter either. "Yes, but we need a sizeable clearing to have enough space for the steeds? Do you know any such near here?"

Foglio thought a while. "I do know a place that could suffice. It is a SAVEWAY storage depot. It certainly has the space but whether the operators will permit you to use it, I do not know."

"We will find out. Lead us there."

Foglio soon turned down a narrower side path. The wind had dropped completely but the rain came down at a steady rate. Just to touch the never-ending bushes that lined the track was to receive a cold douche of icy water. The gloom had begun to deepen when they reached a path branching right. It was marked with a post bearing the same striped lozenge device that Sergeant Bascend had borne on his shield. Sir Richard took over the lead with the others following tightly behind. They were all eager to find somewhere to shelter out of the rain. Sir Richard had just glimpsed a large wooden shed in a clearing, when a huge ogre stepped in front of him.

"Halt! State what doing!" it growled. It held an immense mace with a head the size of a man's.

"We are travellers looking for somewhere to camp for the night?" smiled Sir Richard.

"Not here. This is SAVEWAY depot!"

"Please ask whoever is in charge in *Hagoth*'s name."

The ogre thought a moment; the name *Hagoth* had impressed him. "I ask Mistress Ulrika."

He went away to the side of the hut and as he did so another ogre came out of a ruin at the side of the clearing. He was just as wet as the one standing in the rain and had a mace just as big. There was some muttering at the hut and the first ogre returned. "Mistress Ulrika, she say no! Dame Arisha not like it."

"But we would pay good money," wheedled Sir Richard.

"You go tell Mistress Ulrika! I not ask again or she get angry."

Sir Richard went to the shuttered window of the hut. "Mistress Ulrika, we are travellers badly needing somewhere to camp the night. We have thirteen steeds and our own tents. We are prepared to pay twenty gilden pezzi to stay the night."

The shutter opened a little and a woman poked her head out. She peered round at the party standing beside the ogres. "Make it thirty and you can stay. Provided you go within an hour after dawn. Paid in advance of course!"

"Very well, madam." Sir Richard counted out the money and Mistress Ulrika fastened the shutter to again. They set up the two pavilions and tried to start a fire. On this night, the rain defeated their efforts–there just was no dry kindling to get one started. They looked on enviously as Mistress Ulrika brought out two steaming buckets of mush to feed the ogres. The party had a cold dinner inside the tents. This night they let the ogres guard them. Don Incio asked Foglio if he had heard of a knight Sucio Fulminar in his travels but he had not. Lady Abigail tried to study Vejiga's grimoire with the light of a candle. Alas, her mind kept wandering, reverting to Hrolf's death and her distaste at having to push the horn into his wound. She blew out the candle. I must try to think of something else, she thought; I wonder when Lady Buija will return. Alas, she and most of her friends had been unjustly killed. Just like Arthur. What a lot of injustice there was in the world. With these gloomy thoughts she at last fell into an uneasy sleep.

At dawn, within her pavilion, Morgana, tried to contact Begus without success. Outside the rain had stopped but the sky was still threatening. Cherry had got up early to produce her own magic with a very welcome cooked breakfast. With Mistress Ulrika standing with an hourglass in her hand, they left the clearing with minutes to spare. Foglio took them on through the maze of paths. They passed several pale and ragged Narchadians on the way. Most of these gave curious stares at the two blue unicorns. Foglio admitted he had never seen one before though he had heard of them. "Beasts from the Arbor Deowyn I have been told."

"Yes I believe that was their original home. They were a gift to me," explained Morgana, not wishing to say too much. Foglio did not ask any questions; he had found this the safest policy in Narchad. In Narchad, "a gift to me" usually meant extorted by force, anyway. The paths were muddy from all the rain but they steadily covered myle after myle. There were occasional large clearings with crops planted in them and they stopped at one of these to cook some lunch.

In mid-afternoon they came to a Y-junction with a rune marked boulder. "We are now nigh to Migh," said Foglio, pointing at the boulder. "Down the left is a pond and the monolith of Migh. The palisaded settlement is half a myle further on but they may be reluctant to receive so many beasts. I do not know your intent but it may be better to camp in the clearing beside the Monolith."

"Indeed, it is good advice. Your task for us has been well done and we thank you. Mistress Cherry will give you some victuals and you are free to go where you will."

Cherry gave him a small bag of flour, a bag of prunes and a bag of the Amazon's apples. He returned the way they had come, smiling.

"I do not trust that fellow," said Don Incio morosely.

"If those runes do indeed read Migh, he has served us true," said Morgana. "I did not want him to see who we meet at the monolith. Come, let us go on." Sure enough, they came into a clearing with the stone and a large pond behind it. She had thought the green in the message related to the clearing but in fact the monolith itself was of a shiny green rock she had never seen before. As Morgana led them forward, a man stepped from behind the stone, so she motioned Sir Richard forward.

"Good afternoon to you," he said in Kharsh.

"Good afternoon," the man replied in Simnith.

"Do you know how far it is to Migh?" asked Sir Richard, following suit.

"Half a myle further beyond the *pine* woods, sir."

"Ah. They will likely be full of *pine martens*, like as not," responded Sir Richard, remembering the password.

The man held up his arm and a young woman clad in a green curtfrock (a short dress reaching only to above the knees) dropped down from a tree beside the path. She whistled and a monster the size of a horse, covered in pale green scales, emerged from the bushes to join her. It had a large beak and its tail ended in a spiked ball. The horses all jibbed at its presence and even the unicorns gave it a hard stare.

"I am Lady Robyn, sent to meet you. Our scouts reported your approach, so we came early. You are rather noticeable, you have nine people and fourteen steeds, two of which are blue unicorns."

"We are impressed by your scouting," said Sir Richard. Dismayed might be a more accurate word, thought Morgana.

"There is a clearing up the track behind you, which would be less conspicuous for camping overnight," Lady Robyn continued. "My servant Latchere here will show you it, if two or three of you will come with me to see my mother?"

"Yes, we will do as you suggest," replied Morgana, looking at her party.

Lady Abigail was glowering, scandalised at Lady Robyn's short dress.

"Abigail will you please get the rest to set up camp? The two knights and I will accompany the Lady here."

"Very well but be careful."

The two knights were only too pleased to follow this attractive nymph.

"Your mother is Dame Arisha?" guessed Sir Richard.

Lady Robyn laughed. "No, my mother is Bronwyn, Dowager Countess of Narchos. She rules this mark of the forest as Markess of Migh."

They walked on down the tree-lined path with the green

monster padding along behind. "What is he?" asked Morgana.

"He is a balgryphon from the great mountains to the west. I call him Baal."

The creature's head perked up on hearing its name. In time they came to another clearing with a crag beyond it. Skylined on the crag against the gloom was a house with lights showing in its windows. Nearing it, they could see a palisade fence jutting out beyond the crag, protecting the Migh settlement. Against the crag was a hardstanding, with a portcullised gateway, leading into the rock. Prominently displayed was a SAVEWAY lozenge.

"I will have to put blindfolds on you before we go inside– a standing rule to keep our defences secret," said Lady Robyn.

"Surely you know we are honourable people?" exclaimed Don Incio affronted.

"An understandable precaution," said Sir Richard.

"If you are afraid you may stay outside," said Morgana.

Lady Robyn blindfolded them and then had to re-adjust Don Incio's, as he had tried to lift it up a bit. "Martin!" she called and they heard the portcullis rise and the squeak of hinges. They were shepherded into a stone-flagged chamber and then up a newel staircase. Other hands came to guide them as the newel changed to a straight flight of stairs. At the top of this they were pushed into a warm chamber.

"You may remove the blindfolds," said a deep contralto voice in Simnith. "Who sends you on this mission? I know only that you have some task at Narchburz." A lady of ample proportions stood before them in a shimmering purple dress.

"*Shimmer*!" Morgana immediately gave her own gown

The Manor of Migh: before them stood an imposing woman whose purple gown was shimmering. "Shimmer!" commanded Morgana.

a matching glow. To one side stood a knight clad in bronze plate armour and a younger woman in a tawny curtfrock. "I am Bronwyn, Dowager Duchess of Narchos and Markess of Migh. These are my daughters Ladies Pandora and Robyn and this is Sir Pastym, Pandora's husband. I follow truly *Hagoth's* creed, that the mighty shall rule, for I strive always to be mighty."

"I am Lady Morgana Lefey and these are Sir Richard Nogent and Don Incio Fulminar. My Uncle Quixano, Peron of Stetia has sent us on this mission."

The countess curtsied and replied, "I do not know your mission but if it results in the death of Count Duffric and perhaps Punyer the Sekterar, I shall rejoice. Probably it is nothing so grandiose but I will assist you, so that you can assist me. My scouts tell me you have nine people and fourteen mounts. I cannot imagine why you should want so many horses in the forest but that is your affair. As you will have found, riding along the woodland paths is almost impossible. However, I have a large amount of food to be transported to Barak 1 under the terms of a SAVEWAY deal. Your steeds could carry it and give you cover for your movements. Under the commissary general's orders, anyone who interferes with any of the SAVEWAY food supply network gets fertilised. That is, cut up in small pieces and spread on the fields. The route to Barak 1 will take you past Narchburz. What do you think?"

Morgana looked at the two knights and they both nodded. "This seems a splendid idea, we will do as you say."

"Well let us drink on it!"

Morgana did not wholly trust the countess and brought out the Vinkalik. "I have an inexhaustible supply of my own. It will save wasting your supplies in these hard times. Currently it supplies Stetian sweet white."

"Well at least you can dine with us. We have fresh venison killed by Sir Pastym."

"Yes indeed, we thank you."

They now had time to study the chamber. On the floor was a large pentacle painted with the fiery volcano of *Hagoth*. Against one wall was a rack of shelves, laden with books and bottles of potions. In one corner stood an immense sphere of dark red glass.

"A crystal ball?" enquired Morgana.

"Yes it is supposed to be," replied the countess. "I bought it from some dwarves but have never managed to get anything out of it."

"Let me try," said Morgana. "I have a little magic myself."

"Be my guest."

Sir Richard, watching them muttering spells together, thought how much the countess looked like an older version of Morgana. They both had matching gowns and, whereas Morgana bore a sword, Bronwyn wore a broad dagger. Instead of Morgana's immense hennin, she wore her hair piled up in a beehive style almost as large. Eventually they gave up.

"I do not think it has any magic," said Morgana.

"Nor do I. The *Maghi* have mercy on those dwarves if I ever catch them. But I like you. You have good dress sense. In fact I will give you a pair of items you may find useful. They are called Lapidae of Opita Dam. They cannot be used by we Chaotics but one could save your life."

She went out and came back with two large baked clay tablets the size of small rolls. "You hold these against even a fatal wound and call out *Opita Dam*! The wound should heal rapidly though there may be side effects."

As Morgana took them, her gown shimmered even more brightly for a moment. "Thank you very much, your ladyship. Perhaps we had better return to our party now?"

"Never think of it. The paths are dangerous at night. You can sleep in this room–I will get you bedding. As you can see there is a bolt on the door and I can lock it from the outside so you cannot attack me?"

It was warm in the room and Morgana fancied a peep into some of the countess's books. "Thank you, we will." Bedding was provided and they snuggled down for the night, taking care not to lie on the pentacle of *Hagoth.*

Meanwhile the servant Latchere had led the rest of the party back to the Y-junction, where they had parted from Foglio. Turning left, they came to a small and muddy clearing. They tethered the steeds, pitched tents and cooked dinner. Then they set watches and went to bed. All remained peaceful until halfway through the middle watch, held by Cherry and Tonaldo. A crackling and rustling in the wood got louder and closer. Cherry started to wake the others. Soon a monster three hets high was seen snuffling through the bushes towards them. A dinosaur of some sort! Whilst the others were wondering how to tackle such a monster, Tonaldo began to play one of his mandolin tunes. The dinosaur stopped to listen. Then it growled and fled back into the forest. They heard it crashing about, further and further away.

"A Mondosaur," said Latchere. "They come scrounging around for scraps. They only turn violent if you attack them, but they can be a nuisance if they keep following you. That discordant noise your mandolin player made was a good idea. Milady Robyn uses her clap of thunder spell to drive them off."

Fortunately he said this in Kharsh, which Tonaldo could not understand. They then went back to bed.

Serving the SAVEWAY Organisation

At dawn another servant arrived, saying they should come on to the Migh Mansion, as soon as they were ready. They breakfasted and travelled on to Migh. There the hardstanding beside the crag was heaped with piles of food sacks. Morgana and the two knights were already there, supervising servants, who were ready to load these onto their steeds.

"We walk the rest of the way," she said. She had already breakfasted. She had tried to use the red crystal to contact Begus, as her mirror was still on Harold. But the dwarves' sphere really was a dud. In the daylight, they could see the settlement of Migh behind the crag.

Don Incio noticed a skeleton hanging from a tree nearby. "What had yon fellow done?" he asked the countess.

"He was caught stealing a turnip. We have to maintain the law and see that justice is done."

“Yes food is valuable at present,” said Morgana. “I do not suppose you have any surplus we could use?”
“There is a famine on here,” replied the countess. “Also, we are being *very* generous in assisting you in a mission that might, by the uncharitable, be construed as a tiny bit treasonable. However, I will offer you a deal. My servants tell me that you have four risen dead skeletons carried on your mounts. I will give you enough rations for two days for your party in exchange for them. I have a use for them.”

“Surely a day for each skeleton?” interjected Don Incio, seeing Morgana about to accept.

“Three days food for all four and that is my final offer,” said the countess.

“Agreed!” said Morgana and the exchange was made. The countess’s two daughters appeared, both bearing SAVEWAY lozenge shields. They were armed with large broad daggers similar to the countess’s. Lady Pandora went to the head of the column with her husband Sir Pastym. Lady Robyn went to the rear with her pet Baal and they all set off towards Pirote.

The path became a broader better-paved track. Typical! thought Morgana–for two days my hennin caught on every branch if I was mounted. Now there is clear headroom and I have to walk! After two myles the Dire Marshes appeared on the right. With the recent rains and the melt of snows in the mountains, the water level had risen. Soon they reached a place where a sheet of water covered the track. Standing knee deep in it were a herd of five beaked dinosaurs.

“Protoceratops!” exclaimed Lady Pandora. “These are dangerous and obstinate creatures. On the good side they do keep the crocodile population down.”

Morgana edged close to them and pointed at one:

"Homines mutatio!" (Revulsion of people) and it lumbered away to the other side of the water. Bergand fired a quarrel into the next but it failed to notice it sticking in its carapace. Morgana, Don Incio and Sir Richard cast the supplies from their steeds and mounted, ready to fight. Noticing them, the dinosaurs closed up together. Morgana tried her revulsion spell but it backfired and her intended victim lumbered towards her. "*Shimmer*!" She charged into the water followed by the two knights. The beasts were slow movers and they killed one each, striking behind the carapaces. The survivor fled after the one Morgana had cursed. Sir Richard's steed Melonda had received a severe nip from a protoceratop's beak. Cherry bandaged it but it still limped and had to be excused load-carrying duties.

The water across the road went fairly deep, so Sir Richard tried to find an alternate route through the woods to the left. However he had to give up. The way was always blocked either by dense bushes or patches of flooded marsh. They had to go via the road, ferrying stores and riders in stages. Riders of the larger steeds had no problem but Minut on his small pony Akrattithond were out of their depth. They had to swim, towed by Bergand. The others dragged out one of the dead dinosaurs and cut joints of meat off it. These were sliced up thin and roasted when they next halted for lunch. This took place in an open grassland area where the trees were fewer and shorter, mostly birches and sallows.

Beyond the track again they entered a forest of thickets intermingled with alders and sycamores. They were now leading the mounts two abreast down the track. Suddenly, from around the bend ahead, a huge grey beast ran towards them. "What sort of a dinosaur is that?" Sir Richard asked the Narchadians but they stood staring, rooted to the spot.

It had big ears and a long nose with a sharp horn either side. “I know not!” said Pandora, leaping aside into the bushes. The others nearest the front followed her, except for Tonaldo. He struck a couple of loud chords and then began to play a tune on his mandolin. The creature came to a halt and then started to edge closer. Don Incio had recognised the beast from a book of mythical beasts he had seen long ago. It was called an elephant and people from the jungle lands used them to ride and fight on. “Keep playing, Tonaldo. I will see if I can tame it.”

His fame and prestige would rocket if he could ride an elephant! It would be one up on Morgana’s unicorns. He crept close enough actually to touch a massive leg. The problem was how to mount such a massive beast. He stroked its large ear a while. Then he stuck his sword in the ground, intending to use the hilt as a step but the elephant had had enough. With a snort it turned and raced back down the track leaving the Don cursing. “Are there many elephants in Narchad?” he asked Sir Pastym.

“I have never seen or heard of such a beast before,” Morgana said. “I have read that such animals live in Oblivia, Nwan, Fresh and other countries in the west. They are used for towing logs, perhaps this one is a captive that has escaped. By the way, am I right in assuming that you and the two ladies are of Chaotic scelta?”[11]

“Yes I swore the oath but I believe my wife and her sister were born Chaotic. It seems to me but simple sense that the will of the mighty should prevail. The Lawic idea, to let others do as they please, in the hope that they will

---

11 Scelta is the Simnith word for alignment. Lawic and Chaotic alignments can be inherited, or assumed by swearing an oath of allegiance to Valarian or Hagoth respectively.

leave you alone, seems weak and cowardly. Countess Bronwyn said you were all of neutral scelta but I have a doubt. When your gown shimmered back there at the water, both Pandora and I felt a shock. Are you of Lawic scelta?"

Realising this could be serious, Morgana thought fast. "I am and have always been of neutral scelta. I think perhaps the Lawic Lapida of *Opita Dam*, which the countess gave me, may have influenced the magic in my gown."

In fact her mind flickered over her killings of Chaotics– the demon Testronitz, the wizard in Zarkanis, and the undead at the forest edge, perhaps the *Maghi* might take an interest in her.

"You slew that dinosaur with ease," said Lady Pandora with admiration. "You are a skilled warrior. I must explain why we are helping you. Mother was the only recognised daughter of Count Borgherid of Narchos. She married our father Panric, who was a knight from Belmain, serving in our army. As you may know our army is almost entirely composed of foreigners. When Borgherid was killed by the Thentians, our father was appointed to take his place by the Narch. Our father was a great warrior who relied on Mother for wisdom and statecraft. Last year he was killed in the Narch hall whilst trying to come between the Counts of Dorchad and Chaos Deeps. Count Draconia of Dorchad had abducted Queen Gimawl, fifth consort of Belmain and wished to keep her. Halflofe of Chaos Deeps wanted her handed back because his fortress was under threat from the immense Belmainian army. Draconia was destroyed, as we say, because he was already in the undead state and the Queen was handed back. The five survivors of the Narch appointed replacements for the two deceased counts: Manatan, the then Marshal of the army to Dorchad, and

Count Branamog's favourite, Duffric, to take our father's place. When Mother heard about it she was as mad as fire. Especially when her 'friend' Irene, a gherrin (concubine) of Count Oswild's told her that she had not even been mentioned when they debated the matter. She believes, with good reason she should be Countess Regnant of Narchos, following in her father's footsteps. She believes the Sektarar wants only counts with brawn but no brains, so he can rule Narchad as he thinks best. Duffric is a dunce whose folly had resulted in the present famine. Greater Kaosium is in a state of Bellagh at present. The Lawics say that this is the time we try to subvert them but it is also a time for the reorganisation of our forces. It is a time when we find out, for our own greater effectiveness, who the mightiest of us are. Thus, it is our hope that we are assisting you cut out some of our dead wood. Do not doubt that we may fight just as hard against you, in times to come. As it is, Mother has decreed we shall help you in your mission and that we shall do."

"We shall tell you more about the mission when we get close to Narchad. First we search for Flora Makbuta's Hospital."

Morgana was very interested in what Pandora had said. It seemed heiresses had an even poorer time of it in Narchad than did those in Bara. Her ears had pricked up even further at the mention of Count Branamog. It was he who had carried off her mother! If she were still alive, Morgana would like to rescue her and do any harm she could to Branamog. "Which county does Branamog rule? I have heard his name before."

"He rules Wearse. He has been around as long as I can remember but count for about six years."

Since she was being so talkative, Don Incio asked her,

"Do you know of a knight Sucio Fulminar who fights for Narchad, by any chance?"

"I believe I have heard of him. He took part in a raid several years ago but I know nothing else."

The weather was overcast but dry. A chill wind above was muted under the trees. They took their long pack train on and on, past the hamlet of Pirote. In the evening they camped in a field, between a pond and the forest edge. They unloaded the beasts and pitched the pavilions for the night. Lady Abigail struggled again with the grimoire without success. The wind above dropped and a mist began to rise. Lady Pandora told them that long ago there had been a mighty battle nearby. In it the Narchadii had sided with the Chaotics to defeat the remnants of the Belmainian elves. She said that elf ghosts were still sometimes seen.

"Keep a lookout for spectres frightening the horses," said Sir Richard. On the first watch were Bergand and Cherry. Following such talk of ghosts they stayed close to the fire where after about an hour they were startled by the most horrible screaming. Robyn's pet monster, Baal, was killing a man beyond the supply sacks. Bergand went to investigate whilst Cherry went to wake up the rest. The screaming had done it for her! Bergand glimpsed half a dozen figures dashing away in the gloom and loosed his crossbow at them. One sent a sling stone whizzing back, just missing his face. Dropping his bow, Bergand drew his sword and caught the culprit. His opponent, having only a knife to defend himself, was easily run through. Don Incio, Sir Richard and Minut mounted for a pursuit. They found the road empty and to go into the trees would have been a fool's errand. They decided against searching on foot, the thieves would be far away. Three sacks had been taken from the pile of forty.

"Probably taken by starving villagers from Pirote," conjectured Sir Pastym. "I will report the matter to Barak 1 when we get there."

At dawn Morgana contacted Begus. His messages read:

> **Juanta has written strong protests to**
> **Grand Duke of Bara**
> **Regarding the murder of Donna Ines &**
> **raid on Lozana.**

Her reply was:

> Contact with imposing person made
> Continuing task as planned.

They set off again after breakfast. Someone had to try and meet Alyson the drudge at Flora Makbuta's Hospital but they did not want to involve the three Narchadians. Apparently the hospital was down a sidetrack from the road. Morgana selected Bergand and Tonaldo to go there with her, when the time came. Nearing the hospital turning, they caught up with two peasants heading the same way. One was leading the other, who had a green cloth tied under his chin and knotted on the top of his head.

"Broken jaw?" enquired Cherry whose husband had once suffered such an injury.

"No, mistress, he can't stop talking. My brother Zhentrim here's a sick man. He keeps having dreams and won't stop talking about them. He says there's sixteen different planes! Now our sister Tanary, she who were taught proper by Mother Dukagsh, she says there's only seven planes and that includes *platanus pseudopilis* which ain't really a plane at all! Zhentrim here, he says its not that sort of plane he's talking about and hasn't anyone been listening? He says there's other places, planes like, where everything is different. Even the *Maghi* is different. Tanary then says if Father Zax*Eru*s hears him speaking heresy like that, he'll be gone to a different place sooner than he thinks. So I says as she's right. Look I says, you've studied all these years to be a swineherd, don't throw it all away now. But he kept going on about these dreams. He says as how in these planes of his, there isn't normal people and animals, like here in Morval Earth but creatures and such with silly names. I had to stop him. He were upsetting the pigs. Pigs is sensitive and intelligent animals and I could see they were aworrying. Besides pigs know there's nothing to eat grows on a plane tree. Not like oaks and beeches."

"Mmmmh mmmh mmmh!" said Brother Zhentrim. "All right, all right, different sorts of planes. I only hope the 'ospital'll knock some sense into you when we gets there."

Meanwhile at the head of the column, Sir Richard had reached the hospital turning. It was marked with a large blue board covered with a pattern of regular crossing yellow stripes. A separate arrow pointing up the track said

Hospital

in Kharsh runes. Morgana, Bergand and Tonaldo duly turned up that way. Soon they sighted a cluster of buildings with some people standing around outside. First came a guard hut with a pikeman lounging in the way. He was wearing a cloak and short gown of blue, with the criss-crossing yellow stripes that they had seen on the board.

"A Makgh warrior!" whispered Tonaldo. "A backward people are the Makgh. They rate the bagpipe superior to the mandolin!"

As he spoke, "Psst! Psst!" came from the bushes just beyond them. A woman in hiding there spoke to them in Kharsh. Morgana wondered what had possessed her to pick her companions, as none of them spoke more than a word or two in Kharsh. Worse, the pikeman had noticed them stop suddenly at the bush and was walking towards them to investigate. To allay his suspicions, Morgana advanced towards him and Tonaldo went behind to assist an aged crone who, bent double with pain, was shuffling towards the hospital. She welcomed his support and Tonaldo travelled to the hospital slowly, but unquestioned by the guards. Morgana found the pikeman could understand some Edin. She had overheard some of the conversation about the over-talkative swineherd. She claimed she was an apprentice sage, wishing to study the dreams of the mentally disturbed.

This was beyond the pikeman's Edin and he called for his sergeant. The sergeant said, "I doubt the dame will allow interrogating patients. You had best go elsewhere."

"I had also intended to make a donation of twenty-five gilden pezzi to aid the hospital."

"Very well. Give me the money and I will escort you to the main building." They went up the track past a row of graves and what the sergeant called the "Fresh Air Ward". This was a roofed building open on all four sides. It was divided by a hurdle fence, against which the patients huddled, the lucky ones having a blanket. A nurse in a red frock stood guard, glaring as they passed.

"Sister Swarphega," grunted the sergeant. The main building was of stone, covered with green lichen. Its door was opened by a woman dressed in a Makgh tartan gown and with a sheepskin smock and headband. She understood Edin but listened dubiously to Morgana's tale of wanting to listen to maniacs' dreams. The sergeant said something to her in Nors and handed her *some* of the money Morgana had given him.

"I will call Dame Flora," she said.

Dame Flora, a wizened crone leaning on a stick, glared at Morgana. "I would not dream of letting you risk damaging a patient's resignation to his fate! Thank you for the small donation."

Morgana hastily dug out another ten gilden pezzi. "Take this also for the splendid work you are doing here. I am sorry I had not realised I would be a risk to your patients. May the *Maghi* aid you." The refusal was a blessing in disguise, as her expected subject, Zhentrim, had not actually entered the main hospital as yet.

Tonaldo, having handed over the crone to Sister Swarphega's mercilessly efficient care, decided to entertain the patients. Despite the fact that few could understand him, he tried to organise a singsong. Sister Swarphega grabbed him and marched him back out of the ward. "Raus! Raus!" she shouted, pointing down the track. He guessed this might be a Kharsh hint to leave. So wishing everyone, "Good health," he left.

Meanwhile behind the bush, Bergand had exchanged passwords with the woman hiding in it. She spoke Simnith and was indeed Alyson the Drudge. She had a piece of parchment with some writing and a simple plan of the Narch Hall and the nearby Sektarar's Tower. Of course Bergand could not read, so he led her back towards the main track, so she could talk to Morgana when she returned. They hid in a spinney, as Bergand knew Morgana did not want their contact seen by the Narchadians. When Morgana arrived, Alyson said that it was her job to clean the Narch Hall. She had a large iron key to open its door and a bronze plaque that was needed to get past the guards. Morgana studied the parchment. The Narch Hall was surrounded by a palisade and gate, with the Sektarar's Tower around a dozen hets away.

> Suggest placing of device covered by apparent attempt on the Sektarar's life. Narch Hall enclosure guarded by 4 Theta. Around 12 more Theta in the Sektarar's Tower, plus him and his staff. Glue device to roof beams over table. 3 hets beam from floor. Theta are fanatical Jedonese goblins.

"Perhaps if you lent us the key and plaque we could do what we need and give them back to you later."

"No, I have a spare key but the plaque I could not replace. If you were captured with it, I would be executed."

"Well, would you come with some of us, to do some extra high cleaning?"

"It would be dangerous for me, why should I do it?"

"Here are fifteen gilden pezzi. We will pay another fifteen once we are in the hall."

"All right but there must not be more than two with me. The Theta are ordered to raise the alarm if four or more arrive at the enclosure. The hall and tower were moved from the city to reduce riots and threats of intimidation. Such has happened often in times past. There is little arguing with the Theta, most speak only Jedonese."

"What do you know about the Sektarar's Tower?"

"Little, I have never been in it. It has two stories and probably cellars. The Theta live there with the Sektarar and his staff. The Sektarar is an undead wizard who came from Jedon originally."

"Thank you. We had better catch up with the pack train now. We have some Narchadians with us who must think our intention is to raid the tower. The visit to the hall will be just an extra search."

Having caught up with the rest, they took their places and marched on. As they came closer to the capital of Narchad they encountered many travellers all of whom drew aside at the sight of the SAVEWAY device. They showed little curiosity. As long as they had lived, Narchad had attracted troublemakers from all the diverse races of Morval Earth. Even the unicorns rated barely a quick glance. To such persons as appeared intelligent, Don Incio constantly asked for information about Sucio Fulminar. No one admitted to any knowledge of him. A myle past the city of Narchburz, they all turned into a clearing in the woods. This was in the early afternoon. Morgana spoke privately with Lady Abigail and the two knights to inform them of what she was planning.

"We will need some glue to stick the ochyo to the beam."

"You can make glue by boiling bones I believe," said Don Incio.

"Yes but it has to be hot to use and it smells revolting anyway," demurred Lady Abigail. If I can find some pines, I could use resin for a good glue. It sets with Hallowherb, of which I have a sachet."

She was sent off with Minut to find pine resin. The operation was planned to take place after dark around the twentieth hour.

That night they split into three parties. Leaving first, half an hour before the rest, would be the "reconnaissance and search" party comprising Lady Abigail, Alyson the Drudge and Minut. The "main assault" party comprising Morgana, Sir Richard, Don Incio, Bergand, Lady Pandora and Sir

Pastym, were to attack the tower. Cherry, Tonaldo Lady Robyn and her pet Baal were to remain and guard the SAVEWAY supplies. It was a clear night with the waxing moon giving a fair amount of light. As they neared the "Government Place", marked by standing stones, a bell in nearby Narchburz rang twenty strokes. Abigail led her party onwards whilst the others, who had caught up sufficiently to be in sight now, waited a while. With a sinking heart, Abigail suddenly realised that she, as carrier of the glue, had volunteered herself for climbing up to position the ochyo!

They went to the gate of the compound to be challenged by a Theta officer. At least he spoke Kharsh and accepted Alyson's tale of high dusting without quibble. He shut the gate behind them as they unlocked and entered the stone hall. Alyson lit some lanterns and held out her hand. Abigail put the promised fifteen gilden pezzi in it. The hall had a wooden floor and ceiling and whitewashed walls. High up, a shelf ran all the way around. On it were many skulls with a name written under each. In the centre of the hall was a huge table, with a map carved and painted on the top. There were no seats. Alyson said that this was deliberate, to try and speed up the meetings of the Narch. High, *very* high up, thought Abigail, were ornately carved and painted roof beams. She climbed onto the table with the grapnel rope and threw it over the central beam. Even on the table it looked a long way up.

"You turn your back and guard the door," she told Minut. Alyson climbed onto the table to assist her. They tied knots in the ropes as far up as they could reach and Abigail began to climb. She had never climbed a rope before. It was not part of the training of Stetian ladies. A little light pruning of fruit trees from a short ladder was her closest experience to any such activity. She found it very sore on the hands and was very glad of the knots and Alyson's arms to support her feet. With a supreme effort, she struggled up the rope above the knots and clambered onto the beam. There she brought out the ochyo and glued it to a niche in the carving where it would not be too conspicuous. Then she climbed down, slipping and burning her hands on the rope as she did so. Now they needed to retrieve the rope but the knots had pulled tight as a result of her weight on them.

"We must cut it down," said Alyson.

"No!" said Minut. "Rope may not be easy to replace here, in such a hostile land. It is too valuable to waste." So they took it in turns to work the knots loose. Eventually they were all free and they could put out the lanterns and leave. Alyson locked the door and they waited whilst the Theta officer unbarred the gate. Going out, they saw fighting taking place outside the Sektarar's Tower. The Theta officer also noticed it and called his compound squad to come out to assist. Lady Abigail's party walked back up the track towards the main road. Minut wished to assist in the fighting but Abigail made him stay with them until they were out of sight. Then she let him return, to circle back using a cross-country route.

Once they were sure Lady Abigail was in the Narch Hall, Morgana's squad started across the grass towards the tower. There was a shout from its top in Jedonese. Bergand loosed a bolt at a head showing between two merlons. There was another shout and an arrow came back at him. He reloaded as the other five closed the walls. Another Theta archer appeared and Bergand began a protracted missile duel. Their rate of fire was rapid but his quilted jack kept out their light arrows. Morgana, Lady Pandora and Sir Pastym pounded on the large skull-surmounted door. They noticed a peephole in it. Don Incio and Sir Richard went to the north wall and tried to lodge a grapnel on the battlements high above. Don Incio made attempt after attempt but when he did get it over it was thrown back before he could pull it taut.

The three at the door realised that they had no adequate means of breaching the tower. Don Incio's and Hrolf's axes had been left with the mounts and Minut with his great hammer was in the Narch Hall party! Some planning! Heads appeared above and two hand-stones thudded down. "*Ibi Nebula*," commanded Morgana and a ball of mist formed above them, masking them from the stone-throwers. "Sir Pastym, why do you not hack through the door with your two-handed sword?"

"My sword cost fifty gilden pezzi. I have no intention of ruining it on such an impossible task. It would take all day, even if I did not collapse with fatigue at the attempt."

There was another clang as Don Incio's grapnel fell to the ground yet again. The mist cleared and two more hand-stones came hurtling down. They could hear laughing through the door.

Lady Pandora said to her husband, "If this is the standard of Stetian raiding skills, it is no wonder we have held them at bay so long. What a disorganised shambles!"

"*Shimmer*!" Morgana made her gown glow and the two Narchadians had to shield their eyes. The heads above disappeared with a scream. Don Incio at last gained lodgement with his grapnel and began to climb the rope. He reached the top and engaged a Theta archer while hanging on to the rope with one hand. A thrust through the head and the Theta fell back, the same moment as a Bergand bolt killed the other.

Clambering over onto the tower roof, the Don saw two Jedonese warrior women, one of whom had fallen and was holding her eyes, which had been dazzled by Morgana's shimmering gown. As he registered the threat, some more Theta started coming out from a trapdoor. He engaged two of them as Sir Richard started to climb the rope behind him. "We have a rope up!" he shouted.

The Don crippled one opponent and broke the sword of another, who was an officer goblin. Sir Richard came over the wall and Morgana began to climb up behind him. As Abigail had realised, climbing ropes was not a ladylike activity but Morgana was young, fit and could rest her feet on the rough stonework. As a precaution she had her "*Cling*" spell ready in mind but she did not need it. Even so, she was glad not to be weighed down by armour like the knights. Sir Richard slew an archer and then one of the women warriors. The officer disarmed by Don Incio had found another weapon and faced Morgana. Don Incio was fighting an elusive Theta armed with a naginata. This was a weapon from the Khanish lands. It comprised a pole with a curved sword like blade, a het and a half long on the top. Down below, Sir Pastym and Lady Pandora decided to move from the door round the side and follow them. Once they had, some Theta inside the tower decided to sortie out. Bergand loosed at them but missed. Hearing them, Lady Pandora turned and cast a spell on them: "*Caecare Fulgar*" (Dazzling Flash). Then before they could recover she and her husband slew three Theta and a Jedonese knight.

On top of the tower Don Incio killed the last remaining opponent, the second female warrior, so Morgana could check on the action below. Her gown's glow had faded so she commanded it to shimmer once more. It attracted the attention of an archer who fired up at her. The arrow was coming straight for her face and her life flashed before her eyes in an instant! There was a thwack and it stuck in her hennin. She stepped back to pull it out. Don Incio was finishing off two badly wounded goblins.

"Surely it is dishonourable to kill wounded opponents?" exclaimed Morgana.

"They would do the same to us. They are only goblins anyway."

Sir Richard had gone down through the trapdoor. He cut down two more Theta who were trying to fight their way up, and found himself in a hallway beside a purple painted door. It was bolted against him. Don Incio came down and tried to cut his way through the wooden wall beside the door but his sword broke! Morgana fetched a sword belonging to one of the female warriors to replace it. "Leave the door for later! We need to get down below to open the main door."

In fact, when they came down into the hall below it was empty and the door was open. The two Narchadians had dealt with three more goblins only just in time to face the four from the Narch enclosure. Another Dazzling Flash spell rendered them also easy kills. Minut, hurrying across the sward, was just too late to take a hand. He entered the tower to join Morgana and the knights. Sir Pastym and Lady Pandora killed some fallen but still breathing Theta and remained outside on guard with Bergand. The hall inside was lined with bunks and had a kitchen area. Minut found a locked trapdoor in the floor of the kitchen and started trying to pick it. There were two locked chests, one large and one small green one in the main chamber. Don Incio used a discarded naginata to force open the larger one. It was mostly filled with Theta clothes but he found fifty-seven gilden pezzi in the pockets. There was a stout door reinforced with metal strips in one wall, which Morgana could not open.

"Minut! Come here, we need to open this door."

As the dwarf came to help, there was an enormous **BONG!** similar to the noise of a very large gong. Minut dropped his hammer and they all found their ears ringing. Minut picked up his hammer and swung it against the door. **BONG!** went the gong again.

"What are you doing? That noise will wake the city!" screeched Lady Pandora entering with her husband.

BONG! Went the gong. Bang went Minut's hammer on the door. And so it went on for several minutes until the door gave way. Morgana pushed it open. "*Shimmer*!" and she went inside followed by the Don. Not only her gown but also a square of blue cloth hanging on the wall opposite the door shimmered! In front of it and behind a desk, wearing an apparatus with pieces of dark glass in front of his eyes, stood the undead Sektarar. "*Forma Alqm Vapor!*" he chanted and a cloud of gas filled the doorway choking Don Incio who reeled and fell to the floor. Morgana was past it and thrust Taglier through the Sektarar's chest. She drew it out ready for another blow but he fell down, dropping a dark, bladed dagger with a dragon-carved ivory hilt. He was clad in a pale blue gown heavily embroidered with white arabesques. His skin was grey and pulled taut over his bones. The cloud of gas was drifting upstairs. Sir Richard laid Don Incio on a bunk and found he was still breathing.

In the Sektarar's office Morgana looked around. On the desk were some state papers, quills, pots of black, red and purple ink, a short white stone cylinder and a small bronze box. She turned to a large chest, then, on finding it locked, moved on to a bookcase. Apart from the books, there was a skull and a casket on the top. Inside the casket were many locks of black hair, each with a tag with strange symbols written on it. A quick look at the books revealed that they were mostly written in runes, which she could not read. Some of them had columns of figures in them. A few books contained the same strange symbols as on the hair tags. She guessed it must be a Jedonese script. In the hall Don Incio had recovered his senses but needed to sit still for a while. Sir Richard and Minut went upstairs to force the purple door on the landing. Sir Pastym and Lady Pandora came into the office and thoroughly dismembered the fallen Sektarar in the hope of ensuring he could not return. They also took his signet ring of office and a bag of money, knowing Morgana would not notice whilst she was examining the books. Don Incio staggered in too and tried on the Sektarar's eye apparatus. All he could see through the glass were the shimmering silks of Morgana's gown and the square on the wall. He pocketed it as well as four keys he found on the floor. Morgana took down the piece of blue silk and a map of all the Marks of Narchad that hung beside it. She also took a few books, the bottles of ink and the quills. Sir Pastym opened the bronze box. **BONG!** So that was the source of the noise!

Upstairs, one blow of Minut's hammer burst open the purple door and he and Sir Richard found themselves in a well carpeted room. Towels and rice-paper paintings hung on the walls and there was a scallop-shell-shaped bath and two couch beds. An opening led to an inner chamber, which Sir Richard entered. There he was faced by three women in strange garments, each holding a dagger. "Surrender and I will do you no harm," he said in Kharsh.

To his dismay they all stabbed themselves in their stomachs, turning the blades to enlarge the wounds and chanting in a strange tongue. Two died almost immediately but the third, clothed in light blue, was so obviously consumed by terminal suffering that he finished her off with his sword. He had seen the results of such wounds before. Minut set himself to pick the lock of an ornate black lacquered chest.

"On guard! Enemies coming!" shouted Bergand, running inside the tower. "Hordes of them, all around us!" He slammed the great door and bolted it.

Sir Pastym stood ready beside him but Morgana and Pandora ran upstairs to the roof. They peered down through the embrasures. Morgana's heart missed a beat. There were perhaps a hundred armed people down there, some with torches. More were coming every minute, from the direction of the city of Narchburz. "Here it is, the last stand of the Lefeys!" sighed Morgana. She reached down for one of the hand-stones, ready piled in heaps round the battlements.

Narchburz: Morgana looked out to see at least a hundred armed people below! "Here it is, the last stand of the Lefeys," she sighed.

Trouble at Narchburz

Whilst the rest were away on the raid, Lady Robyn, Cherry and Tonaldo cared for the animals. These had been unloaded and watered before the others left. They sat by a fire beside a rock outcrop. It was only three days to the full moon, so with few clouds in the sky it was fairly light. They had not pitched the pavilions because they thought they might have to leave in a hurry when the others returned. *If* they ever returned! Even Tonaldo realised how hazardous the raid was. He sang some ballads to the enjoyment of Cherry and Lady Robyn but to the disgust of Baal. The balgryphon stalked off into the night. Then Cherry asked Lady Robyn what she knew about this undead Sektarar.

"He is Punyer Finimori and, as Sektarar, runs Narchad when the Narch is not sitting. As to his history, there is a long lay I heard a troubadour sing about the Finimori Clan. I have not the memory or talent to sing or recite it but I will tell it as best I can–if you are interested, as it is rather long?"

"Yes!" replied Cherry and Tonaldo together. Anything to take their minds off worrying about their comrades.

"It started in the Khanish lands to the West of Morval Earth. Back in the mists of time, a clan of people and a clan of goblins shared Shawatuni, an area in the foothills of the Miruku Mountains. The people called themselves Shawatuni after their area and the goblins they called Oshaburi. (The goblins just called themselves *us* but nobody was interested in what they called anything.) Both clans learnt how to cultivate crops from the more advanced tribes on the plains below. When food was short, the two clans fought but it was a fertile area, so this did not happen very often. The people established seventeen villages and the market town of Wanichiba. The Oshaburi kept to the hills and lived in caves. They had learnt to light fires and cook food like people. They it was who discovered the use of tea as a waking-up beverage. This they kept secret at that time. The Shawatuni were getting prosperous and contemptuous of the goblins. They had learnt to produce the rice wine saki. They had even begun to export some, when Khan Sun, a lord of the plains, decided to add them to his empire! When the clan elders objected, Sun sent his army to take control by force.

The Shawatuni people allied with two other hill clans and fortified a pass at Mingeihin. Khan Sun was advised by his astrologers to wait two moons before he struck. The hill peoples army grew short of food. Many deserted or became ill. The Oshaburi seized their chance. They stormed the town of Wanichiba, taking the women and all the loot they could carry, back to their caves. When Sun attacked at Mingeihin, the Clans were heavily defeated. Khan Sun set Primo Mori to be Governor of Shawatuni, making the people pay taxes–some tax money for the Khan and some for himself. Primo Mori soon realised that trade with the plains went via the river gap of Mingeihin, so he built a customs fort there. The widow and daughter of the headman of Wanichiba had been captured in the battle, so Primo married both of them. He also took as his concubines the prettiest girl from each of the seventeen villages. He had to enlarge the customs fort into a castle to house them all. This was the foundation of the Mori clan of Daimyos (Lords).

"A score of years later, peaceful relations were established with the Oshaburi goblins. The captured townswomen now had many half-goblin children who became the Theta. It was they who introduced tea-drinking to the women of Shawatuni. Previously they had mostly had to make do with water, whilst the men drank saki. Thenceforth the goblins started to sell tea to the humans in ever-growing quantities.

"Decades later, Mendacious Mori introduced tea to the Khan's court and it came to be exported all over Khanan as the empire was now called. Mendacious was a younger son who became a counsellor of the Khan and First Sage of Khanan. By this time the empire had reached its natural boundaries and the Khan's problem was to keep its many warlike tribes from rebelling. Mendacious advised the introduction of courtly cultural activities and entertainments to soften and civilise the youth of the aristocracy. One of these was the tea ceremony, dedicated to *Ono San* the *Magha* of Courtesy and Dignity. It sold a lot of tea for his home province! When a later Khan decreed the extermination of all goblins within the empire, there was consternation in Shawatuni. The goblins produced all their tea! However, the Daimyo, Katayude Mori, issued certificates, making all the Theta and Oshaburi honorary humans. They appreciated this and swore eternal allegiance to the Mori clan. Mendacious was famous for his wisdom. One of his sayings was: 'If a Lord tax too high, very soon he will die!' As he expected, his Khan asked him what was a fair rate of tax. He replied a third of the produce of the land. Since at the time this was more than the Khan was taking, he took it as a compliment to his financial control. He also felt justified in raising additional taxes for certain projects dear to Mendacious's heart. In later reigns when money came to be spent on frivolous things, such as roads, bridges, hospitals and poor relief, taxes often exceeded the third. When this happened, the Mori clan would automatically rebel. In fact the ideograph for Mori came to be used as rebel as well in the Khanish script.

"The castle at Mingeihin was now so strong it was never captured by assault. The Mori often led great revolts in other provinces and the Khans longed to weaken their power. Eventually Paipu Khan succeeded. One of Mendacious's sayings had been: 'If have problem bringing low, try to share it with a foe.' Khanan had been trading across the sea to the Undo lands of Morval Earth. A bloody civil war among the Undos found a Khanan adventurer Jedon Meron married to the heiress of Zidcut, one of the Undo states. Paipu Khan sent an army across to back him up. This ruthlessly carried all before it, leaving a swathe of the Occidoran plain depopulated. The Khan offered bribes to his most troublesome subjects to emigrate to Morval Earth. The Daimyo Kujo Mori was only too happy to oblige. He sent his twin brother Fini, with a large number of the Shawatuni and Theta people to settle over there. His province was becoming overpopulated and there was a rumour that Fini was actually the older twin. The Khanan influx led to the existence of the states of Jedon and Zythay in Morval Earth. The Mori, now called the Finimori in Jedon, became just as troublesome to the Khan of Jedon as they had back in the old country.

In 699ATN the Chaotic High Command told the Khan Han Som that, unless he sent strong forces to the war fronts of Greater Kaosium, he would be deposed! He therefore raised taxes to pay for a mercenary army. As tradition demanded, the Finimori rose in revolt. However, their main castle at Ehigaki was not as strong as Mingeihin. Worse, their Theta allies lived in caves far distant, where Han Som cut them off. He besieged Ehigaki and stormed it. All inside were killed or committed suicide, or so it was thought. In fact, Punyer Finimori, brother of the dead Daimyo Suedo, in committing suicide had really become undead. He had studied magic at Swarzberg in Azyra. There he had obtained and improved a Nehruth dagger, designed to change the living to undead. He had encouraged the revolt but had not expected to be trapped in the castle himself, so he used the dagger to preserve his existence.

"That night he escaped to the Theta caves where the heiress of the Finimori was staying with a few retainers. This was Fugin (Lady) Ultima Finimori, the eighteen-year-old daughter of Suedo. She, with Punyer's mistress Maikuru Sensu, had been attending the Theta Ono San tea festival. Now that he was undead, Maikuru and he felt their relationship cool, though he did give her his Nehruth dagger as a token of his devotion. Han Som took his army up to the Theta caves but was reluctant to attack as his opponents were so strong. He was also disgusted to find Punyer was still around. He demanded that in all honour he should make his suicide genuine but Punyer said there was no precedent for doing so in the Khanish code. The Theta chief Nobiki said that they would loyally follow the new

Daimyo, Fugin Ultima, to the death if necessary. Han Som realised that he had to negotiate or fight. He offered to pardon the Finimori if they agreed to a ten-year banishment. They must assist the frontline armies of Greater Kaosium with two hundred warriors; otherwise he would starve them out! Fugin Ultima agreed to these terms, which is how she and the Theta came to be in Narchad now. When they arrived, their lack of allegiance to any faction made them ideal as guards for the Sektarar's Tower. In the early days, Punyer was much needed as an interpreter for the old Sektarar Ghyrro and his new guards. With his undead ability to work night and day, he was used to control the spy network. When Ghyrro retired in 702ATN, he recommended Punyer for promotion. With the support of the also undead Count Draconia, he was appointed Sektarar."

At that moment, the three at the camp heard "Bong!" in the distance. Lady Robyn stopped and they listened. "Bong!" again.

"It sounds like an alarm gong," said Tonaldo.

"Bong!" The row of steeds closest to the road became restless and started to whinny. The three stood up, and, looking around them, spotted a large pack of rats, which was moving rapidly towards them from the road. In their rear was a much larger rat and Cherry, taking this to be their leader, threw a knife at it.

"Baal! Baal!" called Robyn drawing her dagger.

Then the rats were on them in numbers. Cherry went down, a mass of blood and the other two received nasty nips. Then Baal arrived and turned the tide. He drove the rats from Cherry and she shouted, "Deer!" to the unicorns. These joined in and Harold slew the big leader rat. The rest ran away but as Tonaldo started to clean Cherry's mass of wounds, they saw a man advancing on the pile of food sacks with five more giant rats. "Deer!" shouted Cherry again, with which Lady Robyn, Baal and the unicorns charged this new threat. The man made a gesture of casting a spell but nothing happened. Four of the rats were killed and the last one fled with the man. Harold chased after them and soon came back with the aggressor impaled on his horn. By a lead medallion on the body, Lady Robyn identified him as Schatzen, a priest of *Shikald, Magha*, of waste recycling. Cherry thought the correct term was pollution but she was too polite to say so.

"There is a temple to *Shikald* at the Narchburz rubbish tip. It is responsible for processing the rubbish into fertiliser," said Robyn. The gong had fallen silent and they had begun to throw the rats' bodies into a thicket, when Lady Abigail arrived.

"What happened?" asked Lady Robyn, worried about her sister.

"We searched the hall but there was nothing much there. The others were fighting at the tower when I left. Alyson has gone home. What has happened here?"

"We were attacked by rats. Poor Cherry here has a lot of bites around her throat."

"Let me see, bring the lantern."

She redressed Cherry's wounds and treated them with holey water. Now only one phial of it remained unused.

In Narchburz, Master Draper Sekunde finished the last of his goblet of Stetian wine. In the midst of the famine it had been a good dinner. Pigeon pie, roast pork and chestnuts with a fig blancmange for desert. Though not as rich as he would like, he could still afford the best food available–and to hire the muscle needed to maintain his position as Burz Councillor. His accounts were done for the day. Business was slack. With the famine, people were spending more on food than cloth. He was wondering how to spend the rest of the evening, when he heard the bong of a gong. A gong? That was most unusual. The time in Narchburz was tolled by the bell of the Dwarfclock. He was trying to remember how he knew it was a gong's sound when it bonged again!

The Narch Hall! That was it, they sounded a gong at the opening and closing of sessions of the Narch. But that was in daytime and the Narch was not yet in session anyway. The gong had been an innovation of Sektarar Punyer. Bong! It sounded again. Strange, perhaps, perhaps it was a distress signal? Perhaps the Narch Hall was being attacked! He rose and reached for his dagger belt and hat. As a Burz Councillor it was his duty to find out what was going on. He called for two of his men servants to follow and went down into the street. He lived close to the West Gate and found it was open wide, despite it being long after dusk. A knot of commoners was waiting to go out in order to investigate the alarm. He hurried to join them. Behind him, more people were flocking into the streets carrying weapons. He stepped alongside a knight of the Burzguard, Sir Sorbett. Sir Sorbett, was one of the relatively few young knights employed by the Burz Council. His duties were concerned mostly with thief-taking rather than defence of the Burz. Unfortunately he did not have a patrol with him. The gate guards would stay behind, as it was their duty so to do. There were growing numbers of people available, yet Sekunde was distrustful of mob power. But some led off and he and Sir Sorbett had to follow or be left behind. Over a hundred people were soon streaming up to the Sektarar's Tower.

The gong had ceased and the mob split and went either side of the edifice. There was the slam of a door and the squeal of bolts thrust home. In company with the knight, Sekunde followed the right-hand flow, discovering some dead bodies on the ground. The Sektarar's Theta guards! He had supplied the coarse linen from which their clothes were made and it still had not been paid for! It probably was not going to be now! A larger body, a Jedonese warrior, another of the guard. Some of the mob was already starting to search and strip the bodies. There were more of these in front of the door of the tower and he could see the gate of the Narch enclosure standing open.

"What's to be done?" asked Sir Sorbett.

"It will be a sore job as we have to force that door. What think you has happened?"

"These are the Sektarar's guards and whoever slew them will be hard to best. We had best find out who is friend and who is foe."

A woman waving a SAVEWAY lozenge shield stood up on the battlements above. "I am Lady Pandora, daughter of the old Count Panric!"

The crowd hushed to hear what she had to say.

"Good people of Narchburz, we, true patriots of Narchad have just sent the treacherous Sektarar spectre to his rest!"

A babble of talk erupted. This was news indeed. People allowed that Punyer had been competent but nobody really liked an undead foreigner. Who would take his place? Would this be good or bad for the cloth trade, wondered Sekunde?

"I am Pandora, *Narchadian* daughter of the old Count Panric. Were you ever hungry when my father was count?

We believe Narchad should be ruled by Narchadians and its Sektarar should be a Narchadian!" declared the woman.

Sekunde remembered seeing her before. Then she had been in the company of Countess Bronwyn.

"In this tower is food, illegally diverted from the SAVEWAY organisation and stored to make Punyer a profit. This food should have been delivered to the people of Narchburz! It is food of the finest quality. In justice you people should have it. On behalf of Count Panric's Narchadian wife, Countess Bronwyn, I am willing to open the food cellar ready for you. Countess Bronwyn discovered Punyer's plot to profiteer at your expense and sent us to expose his guilt. Countess Bronwyn has years of experience helping Panric rule Narchos. I believe she should be made Sektarar in the spectre traitor's place. *If Bronwyn were Sektarar, we would know where we are!* What say you, people of Narchburz?"

"What should we do?" asked Sir Sorbett. Food! "We want food" seemed to be the consensus of the crowd.

"*If Bronwyn were Sektarar, we would know where we are!* What say you, good people of Narchburz?"

The crowd took the hint. *"If Bronwyn were Sektarar, we would know where we are!"*

"Well said, fine people. I will open the cellar and then my party will come out, so as not to be in your way. Then you can help yourselves to the food and what you will."

"I think we had best let them out and take charge once we are inside," whispered Sekunde to Sir Sorbett. "Countess Bronwyn was the power behind Panric and I do not fancy falling foul of her now. If the Narch thinks she has done wrong, let them fight the battle. These people are only interested in food anyway. Stand back! Stand back! Let Lady

Pandora and her patriots out! No hurry, the food will be shared out for all."

Lady Pandora appeared at the door and came out, followed by three knights, an arbalister, a dwarf and a lady in a silk gown. Not the Countess Bronwyn, but he had sold her four ells of just such a purple silk. Magic silk that shimmered on command. She had haggled his price down to only double what he had paid for it but she had paid cash! He well respected Countess Bronwyn. What use were deals for higher prices when the money was never actually paid? They were now inside the tower and the commoners were pouring down into the cellar. Sir Sorbett was stemming the rush with some soldiers. He found himself looking into what was obviously the Sektarar's office, through its shattered door.

He grabbed his servants. "We had best make the office secure, you two guard the door."

He went inside noticing a strange smell as he did so. Punyer lay dismembered into several pieces but not a drop of blood was to be seen. Several books lay on the floor but others remained in the bookcase. Papers, a bronze box and a white rod lay on the desk and the great chest was untouched. The raiders were obviously not common thieves. Returning outside, he found that the commoners had been formed into a chain and were passing out a stream of sacks and barrels from below.

"Sir Hale and Sir Gherringer are laying it out outside. There is a small green chest here which I think we had best take care of ourselves."

"Indeed we will," said Sekunde, dragging it into the Sektarar's office. Then he went upstairs to find three commoners looting the chambers there.

"Out, out you thieves!" he cried and they hurried down

clutching their booty. He looked around. The tapestries on the walls, though of a foreign style, were finer than anything he had ever seen. Two musical instruments lay on a table and fine silk clothes were strewn across the floor. A wardrobe, dressing table and two couch chests had been rifled. Then he saw the three women lying dead with daggers sticking in them. He winced to see the priceless craftsmanship of their gowns, ruined! Shaking his head he hurried back down. Godwhist the Burzmaster had arrived. "We must secure everything until the Narch takes control. I have sent messages to all its members. I will personally assume authority for the Sektarar's office."

As Morgana was about to throw the hand stone, Lady Pandora stopped her. "No, I have a plan to win them over."

She stood in a crenell and began: "I am Lady Pandora, daughter of the old Count Panric!..." Since she was speaking in Kharsh, Morgana could only understand the odd word but Don Incio caught the drift and went down to try and unlock the cellar with the keys he had found. Of course, the right one was the last one he tried. A quick glance told him that there *were* many sacks and barrels, which probably contained food. Minut grabbed some maps and money out of the chest he had opened and they all headed for the main door. A knight and a merchant kept the way open for them to get out before the mob rushed in. They all made their way to the main road and halted.

Lady Pandora said, "I must report what we have done to my mother immediately. If you carry on with the SAVEWAY supplies, Pastym and I will leave a false trail leading south. Then if our patriot ploy fails, they will think we have fled to Oblivia. The border is only five myles from here. Then we will return to Mother. By the way can I have those keys, Don Incio, you will not be needing them?"

Don Incio handed them over, he was not intending ever to return to the tower.

"We thank you for your help," said Morgana. "Without it we would have failed and had an early death. May the *Maghi*, unspecified, be with you."

"Thank you for the adventure. Disposing of Punyer makes it all worthwhile. May you return to your own lands safely."

She and her husband headed back southwards. Morgana and the other four walked back to the camp. There they reloaded all the food onto the steeds and travelled onwards for two hours. Cherry had to be tied to a horse for she had lost a lot of blood. On the way they exchanged stories of what had happened that night.

"I wish I had been there," sighed Lady Robyn.

"If you had been there, Cherry and I would be dead now," said Tonaldo. "It has turned out for the best."

"Yes, who knows what will happen, now Punyer is dead. The sooner we get this food delivered the better, so I can return to Mother."

Morgana kept quiet but she was thinking about the future. Quixano's mission was accomplished so they could now escape as best they could. If there were a pursuit, the Narchadians would expect them to head for the Oblivian or Stetian borders. She thought they should therefore head north, the last direction anyone would expect. Up that way, lay the County of Wearse, where her mother was held. She dreamed of rescuing her, if she could only find her whereabouts. Lady Robyn had told her that Crogh was the capital of Wearse, so that would be her next destination.

They stopped to sleep in the open, amongst some open woodland, the night still being dry. At dawn Morgana tried to contact Begus but failed again. The skies were now dull and a strong breeze had risen from the east. They breakfasted and headed off to the north-west. There was a trickle of travellers and a mounted messenger, coming from behind shouted, "The Narch is being called!" as he passed.

"As long as it is not, 'Arrest the foreign raiders,' it will suit us," thought Morgana.

The next people encountered were a knight and two soldiers coming towards them. They stood still to let the pack train pass until the rearguard appeared.

"Why it's you, Fulminar! You thief! Eight years you have owed me one hundred gilden pezzi! Remember! To bribe the servant at Girrin you said. I'll pay you within the moon you said!"

"But I don't know you?" blurted out the bemused Don, whose mind had been on other things.

"Sucio you old liar, of course you know me, Svent Pelzrok, well enough. It's the debt you are forgetting."

"I think you mean my brother, sir, I am not Sucio."

"Don't you try that with me, Sucio. Your brother fights for the enemy. Pay one hundred gilden pezzi, now or else!" He shook his mace in Incio's face.

"Do you have a problem paying this money you owe?" asked Minut pointedly.

"No, I will get it out." He pretended to go to his pouch but in fact drew his Jedonese sword. He had it through the knight's heart in a flash. One soldier pulled an arrow from his quiver whilst the other swung a two-handed horse hammer at the Don. Incio dodged it and nearly severed the man's leg, with a slash to the thigh. Panicking, the bowman loosed a hasty arrow at him, which missed. Then before Minut could help, Don Incio stabbed him through the hip and he curled up moaning.

"Sucio, am I?" snarled the Don, his temper taking over. Sheathing his sword and picking up the horse hammer, he beat all their heads to pulp.

Cherry, riding on the last mount, looked back horrified. "Surely it is wrong to kill helpless wounded men."

"They are Narchadians! They killed my father! That knight lent the money that betrayed my castle! They deserved a grimmer death. Come, Minut, we had better hide them in the bushes."

Cherry rode on, shaking her head, whilst the other two hid the evidence of the struggle.

An hour later, the leaders of the party sighted the large drum tower that housed the SAVEWAY supply depot for the Barak 1 army camp. As they advanced, Bergand spotted a man watching them from the bushes to the right. Sir Richard went to investigate, calling out, "Good morrow to you, my man."

The man trained an arrow on him. "Good morrow, sir. What business have you with me?"

"First, why are you threatening me with your bow?"

"It is the standard salute around here. It helps one keep healthy. I am Semet the hunter but have only a fox this day."

"Why not come and eat with us?" offered Sir Richard, thinking they would need a guide soon.

"What! One fox will not go far amongst your great company."

"No, I mean come and join us in friendship."

"You can keep your friendship, foreigner," snarled the

hunter and fled into the forest. The column had now turned off the road down the track to the tower. In front was a small office hut, with a knight and two women standing waiting to receive them. Behind them were several work-squads of Schwaz aughed, moving piles of sacks and barrels–some through the door and some being craned up into the top of the tower. Ignathik's 1,473 Polk was earning its rations.

Lady Robyn said, "Greetings, This is Lady Morgana, whose people have been guarding these supplies. Morgana, this is Clerkess Andromeda. I bring thirty-seven sacks of supplies from my mother the countess. Three were stolen near Pirote. I have a written report here of the occurrence."

"Good morrow. Let me check what you have." Andromeda moved forward to peer into each sack in turn, writing down the contents into a ledger. Then the aughed carried the sacks to a designated pile. The column of beasts moved forward slowly.

The second woman approached Don Incio. "Why, it's Sucio! I did not know they were letting the handsome men out early, this year."

The knight beside her grimaced. "I think you mistake me for my brother, madam," replied the Don.

"Oh surely there are not two such dashing gentlemen in the world?" tittered the woman.

The knight beside her gripped his sword and glared at Incio. "No, I am not Sucio, who is my brother. In fact I seek him, as I have not seen him for years."

"Sucio is Mark of Nettar now. That lies halfway between here and Crogh, as the goose flies."

"I thank you, madam." He backed away.

"Oh pray tarry a while. Tell us the latest news," implored the woman.

His eye on the fuming knight, the Don grabbed the

nearest horse. "I must get the beasts ordered, ready for our journey, madam." He escaped back towards the main road.

Clerkess Andromeda, noticing some of this exchange, turned to the knight. "Sir Ingst, prithee fetch the woodsmen from the tower. Lady Robyn, your mother has sent four men to escort you and the money back to Migh."

Morgana, idling in the background, noticed that the office hut had some bundles of quarrels and torches. She remembered Bergand had expended all his quarrels at the Sektarar's Tower. They were short of other supplies, such as wound dressings and bandages. Once all the animals were unloaded and Lady Robyn had left with her escort, she asked if the depot would sell them any equipment.

"Lady Arisha allows us to sell equipment for a profit but not food at any price. Food is only issued or sold by her written command. What do you want?"

They bought quarrels, medical supplies, lamp oil, torches, climbing spikes and two grapnels. For himself, Don Incio purchased a brown leather target, similar to the one he had had smashed at Lozana. He implored Morgana to let them travel by way of Nettar. "We are so close, I must try to revenge myself on Sucio and my wife, Lealtad. I may never get another chance..."

"Very well, but if it means too much danger for the rest of the party, we must leave it. I hope too to find and rescue my mother, who I think may be at Crogh. So that is the way we shall go. Our main mission is complete."

The first member of the Narch to reach Narchburz was Count Oswild of Halbrad. He arrived on the 13th of the Third Moon. He took over from the Burzmaster in the Sektarar's Tower and authorised the burying of the dead bodies. The next day he was visited by Lady Robyn, daughter of the late Count Panric. She gave him the Sektarar's Ring of Office, keys and a sealed letter to the Narch from Countess Bronwyn. She explained that the countess said that this would explain the events leading to the late Punyer's demise. Oswild read it and re-sealed it.

"Where is your mother now?"

"In her home at Migh, in her Mark."

"I think you had better remain here at Narchburz in my retinue. The Narch will need to reply to the countess's letter."

Two days later the Marshal and the Counts of Narchos, Chaos Deeps and Wearse arrived. They questioned such witnesses as could be found, regarding the raid on the tower. A full formal meeting could not be held until Count Manatan of Dorchad had arrived, on the morning of the 18th. Then, Swazine the Marshal took the chair. He opened the bronze box. **"Bong!"**

"I declare this special session of the Narch open. First item, to summarise for the record, the circumstances leading to the death of Punyer Finimori, our late Sektarar. The second item will be to elect a replacement. First, from our investigations, it appears that on the night of the 11th, just seven persons slew all the Sektarar's twenty-one guards. And the Sektarar himself, Fugin Ultima Finimori, Ishida Shinju and Maikuru Sensu are also deceased, though the last one's body has disappeared. Access was obtained by the use of grapnel ropes onto the top of the tower. One grapnel was discovered still in position. Of the guards, eight bodies were found on the roof, two by the stairs and eleven outside. All their wounds were to the front, so they fought as best they could. The main door was undamaged, so some trick must have been played to lure the guards outside. The Sektarar's office door was forced and we know he sounded the box gong, in order to summon aid which came too late. He was dismembered and his signet ring, keys, two volumes of Narch Minutes and the map of the Marks were taken. I believe it was the raiders who took these rather than the commoners of Narchburz. Some other items were pilfered, more likely by the mob. The missing Narch Minutes cover the years 682 to 687 and 687 to 693ATN. We cannot think of any important significance attaching to these particular years. Of the seven raiders, the identities of only two are known with certainty. Sir Pastym and Lady Pandora, daughter of Count Panric. The Lady claimed to have carried out the raid on the orders of her mother, the Dowager Countess Bronwyn. The countess has sent a letter giving her reasons:

> **To the honourable members of the Narch,**
>
> **I Bronwyn, Dowager Countess of Narchos, Markess of Migh, gave the order to destroy Punyer, the Undead Jedonese Sektarar. This in return for his Treason against our State and for his attempts to achieve my death. For some time I have been aware that there are Stetian spies**

in our midst. One of my agents has informed me that Quixano, the newest Peron of Stetia, controls them. One of these spies was suspected to be Lindeskel, Mark of Stechen and I reported as such to Punyer. Lindeskel failed to protect the fields burnt by the Stetians and he, like Punyer had accumulated extra food stocks, making the famine worse. I believe that they hoped to gain financially with the rise in prices. Anyway, Punyer ordered me to track Lindeskel, so as to catch him making contact with Stetian agents. My information was that his contact was a certain Don Cuerpo, who patrolled the Stetian border. I was to take only three soldiers, so as to remain inconspicuous but would be enough to capture the pair of them. I was issued with passwords to re-enter the Arbor in the area Punyer specified. Later I received a note from Punyer (enclosed) saying Lindeskel would be meeting Don Cuerpo, in the ruins of Zarkanis, on the 7/03/706. I duly went to that area on the

6th. Fortunately I had with me Baal, my daughter's balgryphon, as well as my son-in-law Sir Pastym and two warriors. We arrived just before Lindeskel. When I showed myself he immediately ordered his dozen men to attack. Fortunately my ambush, aided by a little magic from myself, allowed us to overcome them. Lindeskel and all his men were killed, but I lost Nieno, one of my warriors. We had barely hidden all the bodies when Don Cuerpo arrived with six soldiers. Again my ambush prevailed and we killed them all. On Don Cuerpo I found an incriminating letter from Punyer, telling him to ambush me (enclosed). I then returned to the Arbor by the way advised. At the forest edge we were challenged by skeleton Trashik. My warrior Hargine gave the password we had been supplied with, but the skeleton killed him. Sir Pastym destroyed Trashik and the remaining two of us advanced, carrying Hargine's body. On the perimeter track, we were attacked by Narrthing and his mounted patrol. We drew back, calling out our identity but they obviously had orders to kill without question. I had to destroy them with a lightening strike. This also burnt up poor Hargine's body. Further on we met a day watch patrol, led by squad leader Larrel. Again we were attacked and had to fight our way through. I am glad to say a few of them escaped and I bear them no malice. Then I met with my daughters and a few servants. On the way home we sheltered at the Chigwell Temple of Khali. At dawn, the priestesses, who had been friendly when we arrived, attacked us. We fought them off and my enraged servants killed perhaps more than was necessary. I discovered a letter from Punyer, to Magdah the Head priestess (enclosed), ordering her to kill me should I come that way. Having survived all this, I was not ready to take any more risks. Thus I ordered my daughter and my servants to deal with Punyer before he heard of my survival. I believe that under the circumstances, these actions were entirely in accordance with Mightiest Hagoth's creed.

Bronwyn
Dowager Countess of Narchos
Markess of Migh

"Well, do we believe all this?" asked Swazine the Marshal. "Was Punyer likely to betray us? It was certainly true a lot of food was stored in the tower cellar. Even so, how much larceny and profiteering is needed actually to constitute treason against the state? I have had reports that a Stechen squad was attacked by a woman wearing a glowing purple gown. Just such as what the countess wears. The same reports both Narrthing and Lindeskel have disappeared with assorted followers. Magdah the High Priestess of *Khali* was killed with most of her Durgid Amazons. The survivors say Magdah ordered them to attack and that it was a woman in a glowing purple gown that killed her. These letters she sends bear the Sektarar's seal, but Bronwyn has had that seal. What do you think?"

Manatan Count of Dorchad spoke. "Punyer claimed he had agents in Goujon but they never gave me any useful information. Have we found any of his records of agents' reports?"

"No, but we have had little time to search. They will have been written in Jedonese anyway. Since the raid, we have had no interpreters to hand."

Halflofe, Count of Chaos Deeps, spoke. "I never trust

the undead, they are different. Remember Draconia! I am glad Punyer is gone, right or wrong."

Duffric Count of Narchos spoke. "I have no trust in that witch Bronwyn. She has made it plain enough she thinks she should be count rather than myself. She has intrigued ceaselessly, to turn the people against me. I believe she has murdered Lindeskel and Magdah and forged all these letters. I think we should execute *her* for treason."

Oswild Count of Halbrad spoke. "Such a course could be dangerous. She has certainly won the support of the people around here. They were restive enough with the famine anyway. If we drove her into revolt, she could muster many followers."

Count Branamog of Wearse spoke. "I agree. It seems to me that we must also think of item two on the agenda. Who do we pick to fill Punyer's shoes? Bronwyn is a very cunning and dangerous woman. Good qualities in a Sektarar! Who else do we honestly have that could do the job as well? It matters not whether her tale be true or just plausibly fabricated. She is a power to be reckoned with."

There was silence whilst they thought this over. Then Swazine the Marshal summed up. "We agree that the choice is to kill or promote Markess Bronwyn of Migh? Remember the campaigning season is almost upon us when the Sektarar's power is less important." He looked round at the others and they all nodded.

"I vote she is secretly declared traitor and killed!" growled Duffric. "Who will vote with me?"

No one else raised a hand.

"Who votes for Bronwyn to become Sektarar?" asked the Marshal.

The four remaining counts raised their hands. "I declare Bronwyn, Count Borgherid's daughter, widow of Count

Panric and Markess of Migh, Sektarar of Narchad!"

Far away Begus had watched these proceedings in the Or mirror. For him the significant thing was that at no time had anyone pointed to the table map. Thanks to Morgana, he knew Stetia was safe from attack for another moon at least!

Glossary

Words in Italics pertain to Morval Earth, the rest are Medieval English.

Abigail	Lady's handmaid
Aishagh	Open war phase
Alpen	Lawless Chaotic State
Arragh	Western name for ***Eru***
Amelia	Lawless Neutral State
Amnaesia	Oblivian fortress city
Arbalist	Crossbow
Aquetate	Magic negating rock
Argent	Heraldic silver or white
Aughed	Dark skinned goblins
Azelad	Lawic State
Azure	Heraldic Blue
Azyra	Chaotic Western State
Banneret	Senior knight
Baphomet	Leading Neutral *Magho* of Magic
Bara	Grand Duchy

Barii	Original people from Bara
Bellagh	Corrupting phase
Belmain	Powerful Chaotic Kingdom
Caltrop	Foot spike obstacle
Chanelsanq	Oblivian scent
Chaotics	Followers of **Hagoth**
Chiarites	Order of Eruvian nuns
Cobret	Lady Abigail's crystal ball
Consigliore	Councillor
Cyng's primer	Simnith Language textbook
Dagon	Expletive from a demon
Daimyo	Lord
Danrin	Chaotic Kingdom
Delvon	Lawic State of the Dimini
Destrier	Knight's expensive warhorse
Dorith	Lawless Chaotic State
Doucer	*Magho* of just rewards
Dowry	Woman's portable estate
Durgid	From the state of Durgan
Dwelf	Dwarf/Elf half-breeds
Edin	East immigrant Language
Edini	East Sea borne Immigrants
Ekthalon	Capital of the kingdom of Thentis
Elysia	Edini Chaotic State
Eru	Overall Neutral Deity
Fara	Lawic Grand Duchy
Flache	Place of existence
Fleury	Scattered with flowers
Florin	Silver coin
Foix	Former Kingdom
Gashad	**Hagoth's** Chaotic base State
Gelu	Lawless Chaotic State
Gherrin	*Concubine*

Gilden pezzo	Gold piece coin
Grimoire	Book of spells
Gules	Heraldic red
Hack	Cheap riding horse
Hagoth	Head Chaotic *Magho*
Halvings	Dimini midget people
Hamora	Lawless Chaotic State
Heghate	Chaotic *Magha* of the undead
Heriot	Inheritance tax
Het	Man high unit of length
Hildalgo	Lord
Hobilar	Mounted spearman
Holey Water	Enchanted healing water
Horg	Chaotic State
Hunara	Lawless Chaotic State
Imlinead	Lawic Elf Kingdom
Jedon	Chaotic Western Empire
Juanta	Stetian Governing body
Kaosium	Whole Chaotic area
Khali	*Magha* of the risen dead
Kharsh	Chaotic Language
Lapida	Magic baked clay tablet
Lawic	Law scelta/alignment
Lerumint	Old elvish alphabet
Limura	Lawic grassland state
Lucrecians	Order of Eruvian nuns
Madre Vera	Bishopess Barbara's heretical book
Magha	Demi-goddess
Maghi	Demi-gods plural
Magho	Demi-god
Mark(ess)	Minor lord or lady
Menie	Group of followers
Monseigneur	Head of the church of *Eru*

Morval Earth	Continent
Myles	*Six bowshot distance*
Naginata	Long curved bladed polearm
Narchad	Chaotic State
Narchburz	Capital city of Narchad
Nehruth	Undead cursed weapons
Nemeke	*Magha* of just retribution
Neradh	Forest Dwarf Kingdom
Nizandor	Oblivian head of state
Nor	Pine forested Chaotic State
Nors	Language from Nor
Oblivia	Lawic Jungle State
Ombardi	Scattered banking people
Occidoran	Pertaining to the far West
Ochyo	*Palantyte spying device*
Odki	Pine spirit liquor
Omgano	Chaotic home of the Ombardi
Ogrimor	Chaotic Ogre state
Opita Dam	Lawic Motherhood *Magha*
Or	Heraldic gold
Palantyte	Magical obsidian type rock
Palfrey	Lady's docile steed
Perigord	Grand Duchy
Pentacle	Magical circle
Peron	Member of Stetian Juanta
Pezzo	Piece (gold piece coin)
Podesta	City magistrate, usually a foreigner
Polymorphia	*Magha* of monsters
Pozum	Force, Magic Power
Prudella	*Magha* of Marriage
Purpure	Heraldic purple
Quarrel	Short, sharp crossbow missile
Quenith	Lawic elvish language

Rouncey	Common soldiers horse
Runes	Dwarfish alphabet
Saurus	*Magho* of Dinosaurs
Scelta	Creed alignment
Schmerite	Glowing magical rock
Sektarar	Chief Official of Narchad
Shikald	*Magha* of Pollution
Shoon	Shoes
Simnith	East Morval Earth language
Snagass	*Magho* of reptiles
Springald	Two man crossbow
Taglier	Morgana's magic sword
Tarkgh	Chaotic name for enemies
Telepin	*Magho* of Agriculture
Tempania	Chaotic State
Tengthin	Alphabet of Edini origin
Tennorito	Lawic *Magho* of Duty
Thalia	Lawic Amazon State
Valarian	Head Lawic *magho*
Valles	Capital of Perigord, and formerly Foix
Varadh	Mountain Dwarf Kingdom
V*enditara*	Lawic State
Vinkalik	Morgana's magic chalice
Villeins	Privileged half-free serfs
Wergild	Crime compensation money
Zabajhka	*Magho* of physical cruelty
Zythay	Far western state

Lefey Family Tree

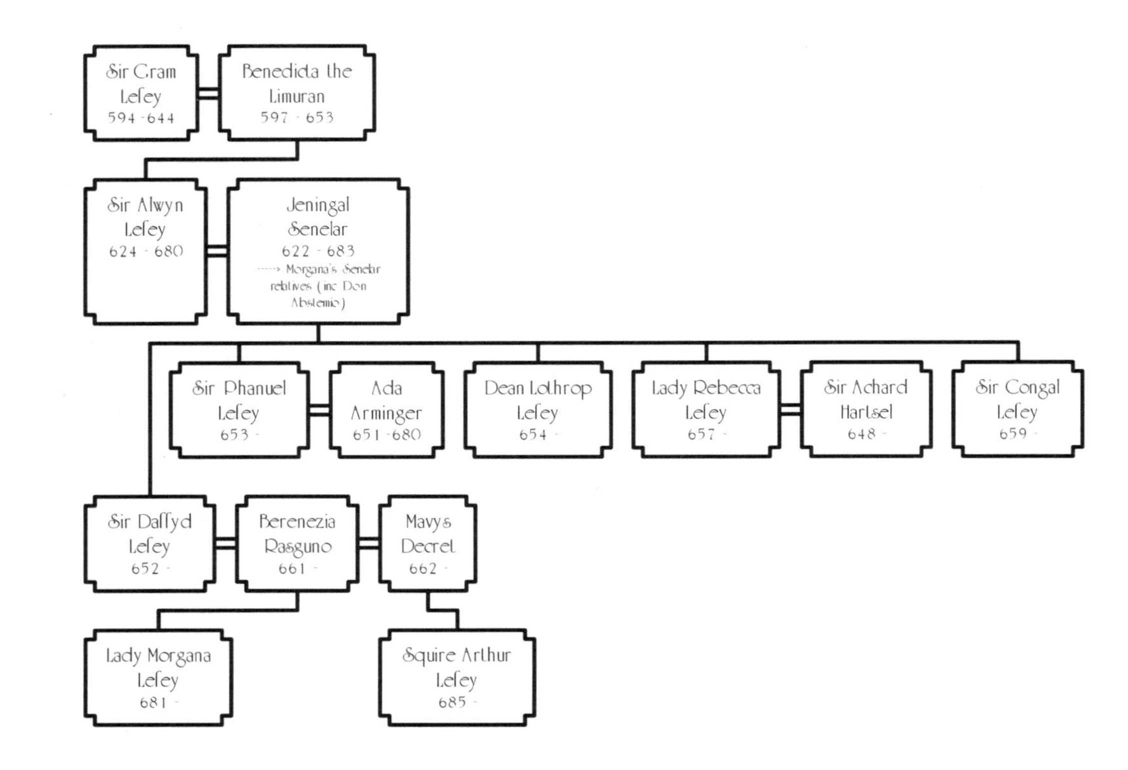

Rasguno Family Tree

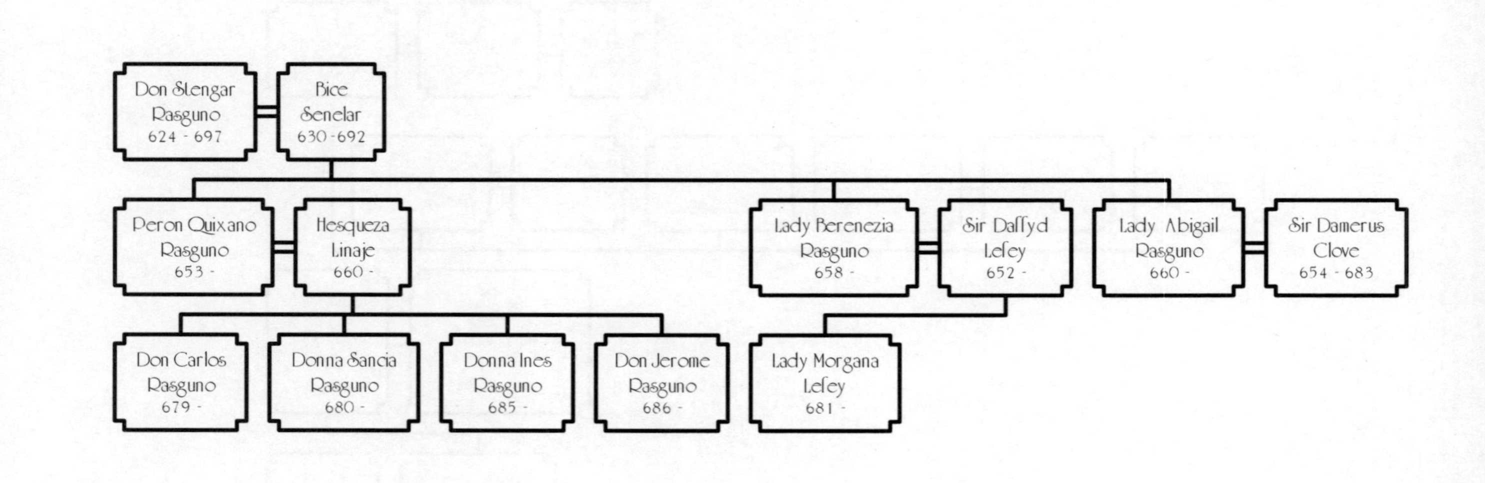

Chateaumont Family Tree

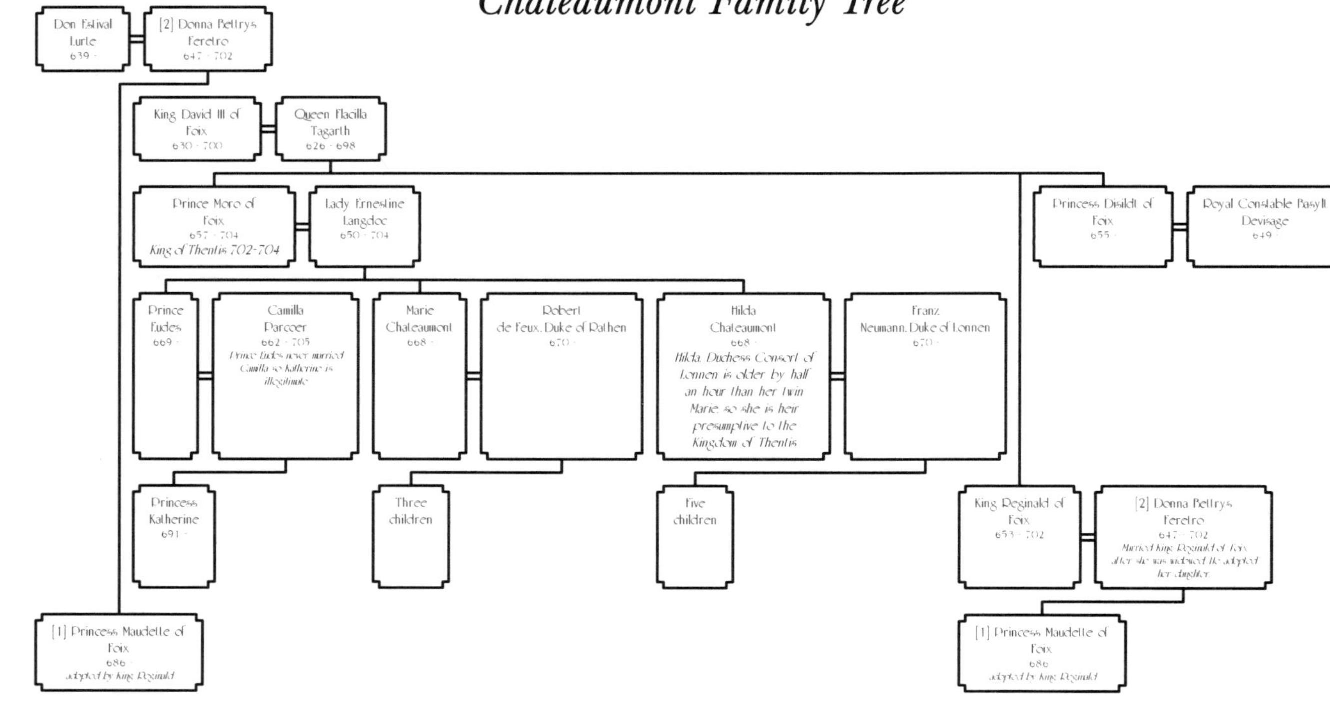